P9-CFB-846

EVERY
REASONABLE
DOUBT

EVERY REASONABLE DOUBT

PAMELA SAMUELS-YOUNG

sepia™

EVERY REASONABLE DOUBT

A Sepia Novel

ISBN 1-58314-669-5

www.kimanipress.com

Printed in U.S.A.

To my mother, Pearl,
who taught me the power of prayer.
And my father, John,
who taught me that hard work always pays off.

Acknowledgments

Publishing a first novel is not something that happens overnight. This journey began with an idea and took off down a path paved with roadblocks. I managed to stay the course, but I never would have arrived at my destination without the encouragement and support of many wonderful people.

First, I'd like to thank fellow lawyers Cheryl Mason, Ellen Farrell, Fesia Davenport and Terrye Cheathem. Every writer needs a circle of smart, supportive friends who have the guts to tell you what works and what doesn't. I was fortunate enough to have the four of you.

To my agent, Sha-Shana Crichton, my editor, Glenda Howard, and my publisher, Linda Gill—thanks for pulling *Every Reasonable Doubt* from the pile of manuscripts that crossed your desks and selecting it as a novel worthy of publication. To writing coach extraordinaire, Michael Levin, thanks for sharing your incredible talent for teaching writers how to plot and pace a story, and for your ever-present words of encouragement. To Carol Mackey, editor of Black Expressions Book Club, thanks for recognizing my work at a time when I needed confirmation that *Every Reasonable Doubt* was a novel others might enjoy reading as much as I enjoyed writing it. Ditto for the SEAK Legal Fiction Writing Competition; your "Honorable Mention" provided a much-needed boost every wannabe novelist needs. To Nubian Queens Literary Club of Los Angeles, thanks for welcoming me into your sister circle and making me feel like a bestselling author.

Thanks also to the host of family and friends who read my drafts and gave me valuable feedback, often under deadline pressure: Debora Diffendal, Karey Keenan, Cynthia Hebron, Halima Horton, Bobbie Copeland, Brittany Carter, Ginger Heyman, Kristin Byrdsong, Pat Rowles, Jennifer Rowles, Donna Ziegler, Gail Herring, Marsha Silady, April Quillen, and my brother and niece, Jerry and Jeanette Samuels.

To my incredible inner circle of sister-friends Olivia Smith, Sara Finney-Johnson, Renee Cunningham, Donna Lowry, Monique Brandon, Russana Rowles, Felicia Henderson, Alisa Covington, Karen Copeland, Syna Dennis, Laurie Robinson, Sharlene Moore, Stephanie Winlock, Colleen Carraway-Higgs, Tonya Jenerette, Mary Flowers Boyce, Janet Swerdlow, Linda Tolbert, Val Clark, Bettie Lewis, and Antoinette Tutt, and, of course, my homeboys, Greg Sawyer, DeWitt Tolbert, Ed Robinson, Leroy Farley, Colin Bowen, Eric Sawyer, Kelvin Tolbert, and Anthony George, thanks for always supporting me, no matter what the venture. I am indeed blessed that this list was so long.

And finally, to my husband, Rick, who never doubted that I would eventually become a published author. Thanks for propping me back up every time a new rejection letter arrived in the mail and for being secure enough with who you are to allow my dream to become our dream.

PROLOGUE

If Max Montgomery ever had to commit to monogamy to save his wife's life, she would just have to come back and haunt him from the afterlife.

Max rested his forearm on the registration desk as his eyes anxiously crisscrossed the lobby of the Beverly Hills Ritz-Carlton. He watched as people milled about, dressed in tuxedos and evening gowns. He made eye contact with a short, brown-skinned cutie who sashayed by in a dress so tight he could see the faint outline of her thong. Max smiled. She smiled back. Too bad he was already about to get laid. Otherwise, he definitely would've taken the time to follow up on that.

"Here's your key, Mr. Montgomery," said a cherub-faced girl with a shrill voice. "You'll be in room 502. One of our most elegant suites."

When he reached for the key, his fingertips accidentally brushed her hand and she nervously looked away. She wants me, Max thought. But she was way too young for his taste.

He thanked her and headed for the bank of elevators in the rear of the lobby. Max tapped the elevator button and the car to his left instantly glided open. Some of the tension eased from his body once he was safely inside. He had waited nearly a week for this night and his wait was almost over.

The anonymous invitation to a "private evening of intimacy" had intrigued him and he had immediately decided to accept. No questions asked. A man like Max didn't make hasty decisions very often.

On the rare occasion that he did, it was only because he was banking on a huge payoff.

Max stepped off the elevator, studied the sign directly in front of him, then turned left down a long hallway. He walked with a distinctive, self-assured stride, like a male model taking a slow stroll down the catwalk. He stopped in front of a door near the end of the hallway and fished the plastic card key from his breast pocket.

A huge smile of anticipation spread across his face as he entered the lavish suite. The place was a classy ensemble of muted colors, luxurious fabrics, and calming scents. From the flowing silk curtains to the massive mahogany sleigh bed to the sleek suede comforter, everything in the room spelled class with a capital C. And that pleased him.

Max made his way over to a nightstand near the window, his feet sinking into the plush, caramel-colored carpet with every step. He examined a champagne bottle sitting near an antique lamp. Dom Pérignon, vintage 1995. Definitely his style. He only hoped his host was familiar with some of his more erotic personal preferences.

The sight of a red teddy hanging from the corner of the headboard triggered a twinge of arousal that warmed him inside. He rubbed the soft fabric between his fingers, smiled again, then tossed it onto the bed. On the floor near the nightstand was a large wicker basket with three packages of rose petals, twelve scented candles, two champagne glasses, and a book of matches. He set the basket on the bed and read the fancy gold card inside. It provided additional instructions for the evening.

Max glanced at his watch. He didn't have much time. He scooped up the basket with one hand, began undoing his tie with the other, and proceeded into the bathroom. It was just as dazzling as the rest of the suite. The marble floor, the shiny granite countertop, the extravagant gold fixtures were all symbols of an affluent lifestyle Max knew well.

As the card commanded, Max filled the oversized Jacuzzi tub with water, sprinkled it with the rose petals, and positioned the candles strategically about the room. He lit each one, then turned off the lights to admire his handiwork. *Yes, yes, yes.* He was about to have himself one big ball.

Max ripped up both the invitation and the card and flushed them down the toilet. A married man could never be too careful. Just as he was about to head back into the bedroom, the enormous mirror on the wall directly across from the tub stopped him in his tracks. Max grinned. He would get to watch.

Marching into the bedroom, he stripped off his Hugo Boss suit and draped it over the back of an armchair near the bed, making sure his pants were carefully folded along the crease line. After removing the rest of his clothes, he grabbed the champagne bottle and strutted naked into the bathroom, where he eased into the steaming hot water and waited.

All day long he had tried to figure out who his freaky little hostess might be. He had instantly ruled out Janice. A single parent with three kids didn't have the time, not to mention the energy, to plan something this elaborate. She could barely escape from her solo law practice for their once-a-week lunchtime romps. That left Paula, a stewardess who had served him on a flight to New York three months earlier, and Natasha, the big-breasted Swede who was temping as a receptionist at his firm's Newport Beach office. She had straight out boned him with her eyes when he walked up to the reception desk to find out her name. Yeah, both Paula and Natasha were kinky enough to plan something like this.

Max poured himself a glass of champagne and took a slow, satisfying sip. The air jets pelting his back with spurts of water felt great. He closed his eyes and slowly twisted his head to the left as far as it would go, then repeated the move on the opposite side. The muscles along the base of his neck felt like dense, knotted fists. Maybe she would give him a massage afterward.

At the sound of the hotel room door opening, Max bolted forward, causing rose petals to splash onto the floor. He could feel his pulse racing as he waited for his mystery date to appear, and when she did not, he settled back into the tub and tried to calm himself down. She was probably just slipping into that sexy little teddy. He was so hard now he had to fight the urge to jack himself off.

Max reached for the champagne bottle to refill his glass just as a sharp, searing pain attacked his left temple. He hoped it wasn't another migraine. There was a time when he could almost will them away if he concentrated hard enough. But that wasn't working anymore. He set the bottle back down. He would wait and share the rest with her.

Max leaned back, sucked in a long, deep breath, and closed his eyes for several seconds. When he reopened them, he could not focus. A thick curtain of haze had suddenly filled the room. He tried to sit up, but his head felt heavier than a bowling ball and fell backward, slamming hard against the tiled wall. He was now blind, dizzy, and in excruciating pain.

By the time the bathroom door opened, Max could feel the presence of someone else in the room. He could even hear a voice. A voice he was too dazed to place, speaking words he could not quite make out. Max had never had a migraine like this one before. He tried to speak, but his lips spewed nothing but gibberish. *Had the champagne been spiked?*

Without warning, a powerful jolt of pain pierced the right side of Max's chest at the same time that his head seemed to explode.

His visitor, hovering over him now, plunged a knife deep into Max's chest, then repeated the motion. A second time, a third time, a fourth time. The stabbing continued until the rose petals disappeared into a pool of deep, dark red.

CHAPTER 1

The brain is a funny thing. Sometimes it'll just go numb for no apparent reason. Like when you're in the middle of a conversation and whatever you were about to say just tumbles out of your head. That's exactly what happened when I heard the jury's verdict. My brain went totally numb.

"Congratulations, counselor," beamed David Winslow, my ever-arrogant second chair and a fellow associate at O'Reilly & Finney. He was smiling just like Howdy Doody. "Think this verdict'll get us a multimillion dollar book deal?" he whispered.

I took exception to his use of the word "us" since he'd been nothing but a pain during the entire trial, and shook his extended hand anyway. I could smell the stale scent of the three double lattes he consumed each morning before eight.

Turning away, I gripped the edge of the plaintiff's table and tried to steady myself. I'd just won the biggest verdict of my career and I felt faint. The entire courtroom was one big, beige blur. The judge was speaking now, but I didn't hear a word he was saying. I was buzzed from a strong blast of adrenaline, but trying hard to play it cool. As if juries handed me five-million-dollar verdicts every day.

I suddenly remembered my client, Roland Hayes, standing next to me. He was gasping for air like an elderly asthmatic. The verdict obviously meant a whole lot more to him than it did to me. He'd be set for life. I pulled out his chair and motioned for him to sit.

When I saw the jury rise, I assumed we were done. I sloppily stuffed papers into my Coach briefcase, hugged Roland for the second time, and watched as he ran off into the arms of his ecstatic wife. David, meantime, was flashing our despondent opposing counsel a gloating smile.

As we headed out of the courtroom, a gang of reporters rushed toward us, nearly knocking us back inside.

"Vernetta Henderson," somebody shouted, "the jury's five-million-dollar verdict is a pretty hefty award in a single-plaintiff race discrimination case. How do you feel?" I looked to my left and saw that the question came from the skinny blonde with the bad split ends from Channel 7.

Before I could answer, another reporter hurled a question my way. "Ms. Henderson, why do you think the jury went so heavy on the punitives?"

Because my client worked for a bunch of racist yahoos.

I squeezed through the crowd, chin forward, shoulders erect, ignoring them. Just like they did on *Law & Order*. I looked over at David. His thin lips were tightly pursed. No one had bothered to stick a microphone in his face and he was pissed.

When we reached the elevators, we found the buttons blocked by a fortress of reporters. The hot, gleaming lights from a small TV camera nearly blinded me and somebody's microphone kept nudging me in the back of the head.

"Ms. Henderson, were you surprised at the verdict?" yelled a voice from the rear.

I brushed passed the inquisitive mob, determined to ignore them. "No questions for now," I said finally, as David and I escaped toward the stairwell. "We'll talk to the media later this afternoon."

CHAPTER 2

By the time we made it back to the offices of O'Reilly & Finney, word of the verdict had already raced through the firm. I barely had time to touch up my lipstick and shove my purse underneath my desk before I was whisked off to the twentieth floor to continue bathing in the glory of my mind-blowing victory.

A handful of my colleagues pounced on me the second I stepped into the conference room, corralling me in a small circle of professional envy. Lawyers are a lot like ten-year-olds. They smile and pretend to be happy when someone else wins the big case, but on the inside they're pouting.

Al McAndrews, a tax partner, was the first to congratulate me. "Incredible work, counselor," he said, giving me a benign pat on the back. McAndrews routinely ignored me during our morning elevator rides. I hoped this didn't mean I would have to make small talk the next time we were stuck in an elevator together.

For the next twenty minutes, I graciously accepted praise heaped on top of praise even though I knew most folks were there for the jumbo shrimp. I spotted David across the room entertaining his own flock of worshippers. I could hear snatches of his conversation. He was explaining how well we had worked together. All lies.

The post-trial victory celebration was an O'Reilly & Finney tradition. It was a first for me, having been at the firm for only nine months. I scanned the room, looking for Jim O'Reilly, the firm's managing partner, but he was nowhere in sight. When I saw Neddy McClain walk in, my body stiffened.

For a reason I had yet to figure out, the woman acted as if she despised me. The fact that we didn't get along was especially tragic since we were the firm's only African-American attorneys. Black folks are like crabs in a barrel, my grandmother used to say. As soon as one climbs up, another one pulls 'em back down.

As usual, Neddy's lips were ziplocked into an obnoxious frown, broadcasting the perpetual state of discontent that she wore like an old sweater. Thank God we had different practice areas and never had to work together.

I took a sip of a Diet Coke somebody handed to me and checked my watch. If I didn't leave soon, there was no way I was going to make it across town for dinner with my husband. I had promised Jefferson that as soon as the trial ended, I was all his. I had also agreed to give some serious consideration to starting a family. The first pledge I planned to keep. I was still searching for a loophole big enough to get me out of the second one.

All the bodies hemming me in were beginning to make me feel claustrophobic. Just as I was about to make a break for it, an attorney I barely recognized shoved his way through the huddle. "Way to go, Henderson!" he yelled, giving me a high five.

All I could do was grin. The rays of praise beaming down on me felt so good I almost wanted to squeal. Truth be told, I had actually fantasized about this day in law school. This was what it was all about.

While the praise-fest continued, I watched out of the corner of my eye as Neddy studied the colorful display of hors d'oeuvres. She did not appear anxious to make her way toward me, but decorum dictated that she must. I wondered just how long it was going to take her to march across the room and give me my props.

O'Reilly finally towered in, giving her a temporary reprieve. He grabbed an empty wineglass from the tray of a passing waiter and gently clinked it with a knife.

"May I have your attention?" He didn't actually need to ask for the floor. When O'Reilly walked into a room, all heads automatically turned his way. An oversized, gregarious Irishman with curly, reddish-brown hair, he had an easygoing, Clintonesque style about him. He was just as comfortable addressing a room full of wealthy bankers as a congregation of black Baptists.

"I want to give an official O'Reilly & Finney congratulations to Vernetta and David on the Hayes verdict and a jury award so big even I couldn't believe it." O'Reilly looked extremely pleased. Probably because forty percent of that five-million-dollar award would go straight into the coffers of the eighty-attorney litigation boutique founded by his grandfather.

"It just shows you what good, solid legal work can produce. Keep on kicking butt, guys!" He raised his glass and everyone applauded. Except Neddy. Her hands were conveniently occupied. She took a sip of wine and dipped a broccoli spear into a bowl of ranch dip.

A few minutes later, O'Reilly headed my way and pulled me off to the side. "You won't believe it," he whispered excitedly. "You heard about Max Montgomery's murder Saturday night, right?"

Who hadn't? Max Montgomery was a local icon. Rich, attractive, politically connected, and undeniably brilliant. His investment banking firm owned most of the city's prime real estate. The murder made the front page of the *L.A. Times* and every news station in town was milking the story like it was a cow with fifty udders.

"Well, guess who's a suspect, and guess who wants our firm to defend her?"

I had absolutely no idea who "her" could be.

"His wife!" There was sheer joy in O'Reilly's voice. "And you, lucky lady, are going to be sitting at the defense table." He turned his back to me and began scanning the room.

He was right. I couldn't believe it. This was the kind of case that turned lawyers into celebrities. Although I was wiped out from the round-the-clock hours demanded by the Hayes trial, the prospect of handling a sensational murder case filled my weary body with a tingle of excitement. Then I remembered my promise to Jefferson. He would freak when he found out I'd taken on another, even more demanding case. I downed the last of my Diet Coke and momentarily wiped that worry from my mind. I'd deal with Jefferson later. I was about to be catapulted into super-lawyerdom.

Then I heard O'Reilly call Neddy over and my heart did a flip-flop.

"This is going to be a helluva case," he said, turning back to face me as Neddy walked up. "You ladies can thank me later."

"Thank you for what?" Neddy asked.

"For teaming you up on L.A.'s next high-profile murder case."

Neddy and I locked eyes, but we both chose to exercise our right to remain silent.

O'Reilly, still all smiles, threw his burly left arm across my shoulder and pulled Neddy to him with his right. We were the perfect *Jet* Picture of the Week.

"Yep," he said, looking first at Neddy, then shining his gaze on me. "I'd say you two ladies are about to become very, very famous."

CHAPTER 3

I tried to ignore the knots forming in my stomach as I followed O'Reilly and Neddy out of the conference room and into O'Reilly's spacious corner office. As soon as he closed the door, his face took on a childlike elation.

"L.A.'s long overdue for another big, juicy murder trial and this is it." He sat down in his cowhide chair and propped his feet up on the desk. He was smiling so hard his cheeks looked like they had been stuffed with grapefruits.

Neddy and I took seats in the matching Queen Anne chairs in front of his desk. We had yet to acknowledge one another.

"The police tried to question Montgomery's wife last night, but she refused to talk without representation." He turned to face Neddy. "She called us because she remembered that acquittal you got in the Langley murder case last year. But it was my idea to pair you up with Vernetta."

O'Reilly was definitely satisfied with himself. I almost expected him to stand up and pat himself on the back.

This kind of case was right up Neddy's alley. She'd spent fifteen years at the Public Defender's office before O'Reilly & Finney recruited her four years ago to strengthen the firm's criminal defense practice. Since joining the firm, she had successfully defended a string of high-profile criminal cases, including two wealthy murder suspects and a string of accountants and bankers accused of securities fraud. My practice area, however, was strictly employment law.

I was the first to speak. "O'Reilly, have you forgotten that I'm not a criminal attorney?" I couldn't exactly tell him I didn't want to team up with Neddy just because she walked around acting like the Wicked Bitch of the West.

"Wait a minute," O'Reilly protested, "didn't you tell me you'd be open to learning other practice areas when I hired you? Well, now's your chance."

I hated having my own words thrown back at me. "You'd actually want me to cut my teeth on a case this big?"

"Why not? You're an incredible litigator, Vernetta. You just won one of the biggest verdicts this firm has ever had. And without a doubt, Neddy's sharper than ninety-nine percent of the prosecutors down at the D.A.'s office. You two have 'Dream Team' written all over you."

Neddy's left eye began to twitch.

"And anyway," he continued, "Tina Montgomery was elated when I mentioned your name. She's been following the Hayes trial on TV."

O'Reilly was leaning forward now, his elbows planted on his desk like a pair of inverted turkey legs. "Think about it? Two smart, attractive, African-American women defending a prominent, African-American socialite accused of murdering her wealthy husband. Hell, the defense team'll get more publicity than the trial."

So that was it. We would no doubt be the first all-black, female defense team to handle such a high-profile case. That would mean coverage in the mainstream media, the legal press, and the black community. And O'Reilly was banking on all that publicity bringing more clients through the door. But teaming up with Neddy would relegate me to second-class citizenship. That definitely wouldn't work. I had to find an escape clause, and fast.

"So let's be clear here," I said, feigning indignation. "Are you assigning us to this case because we're black or because we're women...or both?"

"Aw, don't give me that politically correct bull, Henderson." O'Reilly swatted away my question with one of his mammoth hands. "You two know me better than that. I'm all about getting whatever mileage I can out of any case that comes through this door. Do you know how many attorneys would kill for a case like this?"

"But I'm not a criminal attorney, O'Reilly." Of course, that hadn't been a concern for me when he first mentioned the case. I slowly inhaled and hoped I didn't sound too whiny.

"Yeah, but Neddy is. And she can teach you all the procedural stuff you need to know inside of two weeks. The real job in trying a case like this is analyzing the evidence. It's all about how you present the good facts and how you spin the bad ones. You're a whiz when it comes to the nuts and bolts of a case. And don't quote me, but after the Hayes verdict, with this case on your resumé, when your name comes up for partnership next year . . ." He arched his eyebrows and smiled.

Finish the sentence, O'Reilly. But he wasn't stupid enough to make that kind of binding oral promise with a witness present. I knew he was right. After the Hayes victory and an attention-grabbing murder case like this, win or lose, my fate as far as partnership was concerned would be happily sealed. I'd become the firm's first African-American partner.

I wondered why Neddy was playing mute. I doubted she wanted to work with me either. But O'Reilly couldn't dangle the partnership carrot in front of her face. She had negotiated a deal for a permanent of-counsel position and seemed satisfied with that arrangement.

While I was still pondering my predicament, Neddy finally opened her mouth. "Hold on a minute," she said. I couldn't tell from her tone exactly how she felt about O'Reilly's proposed arrangement. "You only said the police wanted to question Montgomery's wife. Who says she's even a suspect?"

O'Reilly smiled. "C'mon Neddy, don't bullshit me. We both know innocent people don't go calling lawyers just because the cops want to talk to them."

"That's not necessarily true," Neddy challenged. "Anybody with any sense knows you don't talk to the police without a lawyer present. Thank God she was savvy enough to demand one. It doesn't mean she killed the man. If you ask me, it just means she's smart."

O'Reilly frowned. I could tell he was alarmed that his visions of a media feeding frenzy might be vanishing before his eyes.

"I agree," I said hurriedly. "Maybe she's just being cautious.

There's no reason for us to assume the police plan to charge her with murder."

O'Reilly leaned back in his chair and stroked his chin. "Well," he said with a sly grin, "I don't know about you two, but I'm sure hoping like hell they do."

CHAPTER 4

It was close to eight and I was twenty minutes late for a romantic dinner at G. Garvin's on Third Street with my handsome husband of fourteen months and two days. Not that I was counting my blessings, that is. I would have called to let Jefferson know I was running late, but he routinely turned off his cell phone after seven o'clock. He was an electrician who, unlike me, refused to allow distractions of any kind to interfere with his personal time.

When I approached the table, Jefferson did not give me the look I expected. The one that silently chastised me for devoting more time to my job than to him. Instead, he jumped up and locked me in his arms.

"Sorry, I'm late," I said, out of breath. "Please don't be mad."

"How can I be mad?" he said, pecking me on the lips and pulling out my chair. I was 5'8" and in heels I had almost an inch on him, something that had taken a little time for me to adjust to, but had never been a big deal for Jefferson. "A brother don't mind waiting for the finest, smartest, baddest attorney in L.A."

This time I leaned over and kissed him.

"I heard them talking about the trial on KNX on the way over here," he beamed. "Congratulations, baby."

"Thank you, sweetheart," I said.

Jefferson had a thick, muscular, Mike Tyson-like build, and a genuine self-confidence that I found attractive from the first moment we made eye contact while standing in adjacent lines at the Albertson's supermarket, a block from my old apartment. Tonight he was wearing black linen slacks and a black Lycra shirt. The one he knew I liked because of the way it showed off his pecs.

"I'm just glad that damn trial is finally over." He smiled seductively. "Now I finally get to spend some time with my woman." We kissed again, this time for much longer.

"Did you already order for me?" I asked.

"Nope, I was beginning to think you might've forgotten. You've been so wrapped up in that trial. But some appetizers should be here in a minute." He handed me a menu. "So," he said smiling, "how much of that five mil are we getting?"

"None of it," I laughed. I wiggled out of my jacket to reveal a soft gray chiffon blouse underneath my navy blue, good-luck Tahari skirt suit. After tossing my car keys to the valet outside, I'd unbuttoned an extra button on my blouse to reveal what little cleavage I had. Just because I was a successful, assertive lawyer by day didn't mean I couldn't be a sexy vixen by night.

Jefferson shook his head. "I'll never figure out how this law firm shit works. It would seem to me that the person who did all the work should at least get part of the damn jury award."

"Sorry, babe, it don't work like that. I'll get the same bonus everybody else gets at the end of the year." I turned to inspect a delicious-looking spinach salad a waiter was delivering to an adjacent table. "But when I make partner next year, I'll get a piece of the pie. A pretty nice piece. So, what were they saying about my case on the radio?"

"That the verdict was pretty surprising and that it should be a wake-up call to other companies," Jefferson said, with real pride in his voice, as if it were his victory, too. "I bet you don't regret leaving Brandon & Bass now, do you? When they hear about that verdict, they'll know what a mistake they made not making you a partner."

The mention of my prior law firm still caused a miserable lump to settle in my throat. I'd worked my butt off at Brandon & Bass, assuming I was on track for partnership. Unfortunately the joke was on me. I left after six years to join O'Reilly & Finney and, so far, hadn't regretted it one bit. Jefferson was right. Their loss.

A waitress approached our table. "Your appetizers will be right out," she said to Jefferson. "And here's your Diet Coke, easy ice, Mrs. Jones."

I liked it when Jefferson ordered for me, but I was not pleased when people automatically assumed that I'd taken his last name. This time I let it pass.

Jefferson smiled as the waitress walked off. "Mrs. Jones," he said, holding his chin between his thumb and forefinger as he mulled over the words. "I like the sound of that. You know, it's not too late to go the more traditional route."

"Nah," I said, taking a sip of my drink. "Vernetta Jones just doesn't have the right ring to it. Besides, you just want to keep me barefoot and pregnant."

"Now that's a segue if I ever heard one." Jefferson reached underneath the table and retrieved a package that was about half the width of a videotape, but four times the height. It was wrapped in gold foil, and tied with a long red ribbon. The uneven corners and the lopsided bow told me Jefferson had wrapped it himself.

"You bought me a present?"

"Yep," he grinned.

When I extended my hand to take it, he playfully pulled it out of my reach.

"Hold on, hold on. You have to hear my speech first."

Jefferson cleared his throat and sat up straight in his chair. He placed the box off to the side and grabbed both of my hands. He had long, thick fingers that could have belonged to a man twice his size. As our palms met and our fingers entwined, I could feel calluses that publicized what he did for a living. Still, his touch was gentle.

"I was going to start by telling you how much I love you, but then I said, 'nah, she already knows that.' So I had to come up with something else." He paused. "Now, I didn't practice this, so don't be too hard on me."

I loved it when Jefferson tried to be romantic. It was not something that came naturally for him. But what he lacked in finesse he made up for in raw sincerity.

"Being married to you has been pretty cool. Cooler than I ever thought it would be. When I was listening to that radio show on the way over here, I kept saying to myself, 'that's *my* woman they're talkin' 'bout.' Before I met you I didn't believe in all that soul mate stuff. But now I can definitely say you're my soul mate. And I love you to death."

He squeezed my hand and we kissed again.

Before I could ask for my gift, the waitress set a plate of miniature crab cakes on the table, my favorite.

Jefferson stuffed one into his mouth, quickly chewed it, and continued his presentation. "And if the rest of our marriage continues to be half as cool as it's been so far, then I know we're going to live happily ever after. Okay, now you can have your present."

He handed the box to me and I slowly untied the ribbon. I had no idea what was inside. It was too large for jewelry and not big enough for a pair of shoes. Not that I needed more of either.

"Is this a victory present?" I was bubbling with excitement as I tore off the beautiful wrapping paper.

"Nope." Jefferson was leaning back in his chair, his arms folded across his chest, looking quite pleased with himself.

"Then what's the occasion?"

He grinned big. "Let's just say it's time."

I had the box completely unwrapped, but still couldn't tell what it was. I picked up the tiny table candle and angled it so I could read the writing on the side of the box. When I finally made out the words, my throat constricted.

Clear Blue Easy Ovulation Prediction Test Kit.

Jefferson mistook the shocked look on my face as confusion.

"C'mon, girl, how many degrees do you have? You don't know what that is? It's an ovulation kit," he said proudly. "And we might as well get started tonight."

There was a long silence as I sat there, trying to remember how to breathe.

CHAPTER 5

The day after my husband set his sights on putting my womb to work, I left the office at one o'clock for a meeting with my new client, Tina Montgomery. And if getting there was supposed to be a test, I was about to flunk it.

My frustration level grew as I circled the winding streets of Brentwood, the L.A. suburb best known as the place where O.J. allegedly murdered Nicole. If I didn't find the house in the next thirteen minutes, I was going to be late. That would be unacceptable.

I had dreadfully mixed emotions about my new case. There was no question that it would be great for my career. What it would mean for my marriage was another story. Jefferson would be furious when he found out I would be tied up on another, even bigger case. Then there was the Neddy issue. Luckily, I had not asked God for any really big favors lately, so I still held out hope that He was going to answer my prayers and make the case disappear.

The pleasant voice coming from the navigation system of my new Toyota Land Cruiser had just informed me that my destination was ahead on the right. The damn thing must have been broken because for the life of me I couldn't find the house number I was searching for. Then I had a disturbing thought. Maybe Neddy had given me the wrong address. As evil as she was, I would not put it past her.

"How could anybody locate an address in this neighborhood?" I mumbled to myself. The streets curved and twisted in eight different directions and you needed binoculars to read the house numbers from the street. This was broad daylight. Finding an address in the dark must be next to impossible.

I continued to peer out of the window, straining my neck as I tried to read the numbers painted along the curb. Neddy and I had talked briefly about our meeting just before lunch. We agreed that there was no strategy to plot until we heard what our new client had to say. Neddy had abruptly rejected my suggestion that we drive together. Said she had an errand to run afterward. A definite lie.

Just as I was about to pick up my cell phone to make a distress call, I spotted my destination, as well as a convenient place to park. The Montgomery house, or I should say mansion, was hidden behind huge steel gates and thick shrubbery. It stretched the length of what would have been about three houses in my neighborhood. The modern, brownish beige monstrosity could have been lifted right off the pages of *Architectural Digest*. I made my way up a long, stone walkway bordered on both sides by a lawn so green and plush that just looking at it made me want to lie down and take a nap.

A petite woman, dressed in a snowy white sarong that fit her like a tent, answered the door seconds after my first press of the doorbell. She had a subdued, exotic look about her. Her toffee-colored skin was only a shade lighter than mine and she spoke in a soft East Indian accent. I followed her into a sizeable entryway, where she instructed me to wait.

The view from the street advertised a world that was quite different from my own, but the home's foyer shrieked it. Large enough to be a bedroom, the marble floor, the natural lighting, and the Oriental vase full of fresh tulips reeked of a life of privilege. One where the cost of a particular item played no role whatsoever in the purchasing decision.

When I was finally escorted into the living room, I could sense that Tina Montgomery had already bonded with the more experienced half of her defense team. A nervous churning deep in my gut also told me that Neddy had probably arrived early to accomplish precisely that goal. The muscles in my neck began to contract as a flashback of one of my clashes with David during the Hayes trial replayed in my head. I was not looking forward to another case where I had to engage in a daily battle of one-upmanship with my co-counsel.

What I saw in the living room concerned me. Tina and Neddy were both sipping red wine, Neddy from a crystal wineglass and

Tina from a gaudy silver goblet. A fancy gold-plated serving tray held an array of tiny edibles that looked as if they had been whipped up by Wolfgang Puck. This was a business meeting, not the cocktail hour. We needed to be all business.

I quickly scanned the rest of the room. A wall of French doors framed an expansive yard with landscaping Martha Stewart would have envied. The living room, color-coordinated in varying shades of grays and purples, was too big to be comfy. The furniture, mostly oversized pieces, slanted toward the contemporary. Every piece had a one-of-a-kind museum feel, designed for guests to take an admiring look and move on.

Neddy was relaxing in a cushy lavender armchair. Tina sat across from her on a dark purple couch that looked more like a work of art than a place to rest one's tush.

The partial smile on Neddy's face was the happiest I could remember seeing her. Ever.

"Nice to meet you Mrs. Montgomery. I'm Vernetta Henderson." I extended my hand, then pulled a business card from my purse.

"Yes, I recognize you from the news stories about your recent trial." She reached for my business card and placed it on the coffee table in front of her without looking at it. Her eyes looked everywhere, except at me. "And, please, call me Tina."

Her handshake was reasonably firm, but her baby-soft skin told me that manicures and paraffin treatments were part of her weekly regimen. She reminded me of what Halle Berry would probably look like in twenty years. Her short, curly hair was sprinkled with just a hint of gray and her makeup had a clean, polished look to it. At fifty plus, she was a beautiful woman. Twenty years earlier, she had probably been a knockout.

I wiggled out of my jacket, laid it across the arm of a chair next to the one Neddy occupied, and sat down. The small woman in white appeared from nowhere and retrieved it.

"We were just chatting until you arrived. Let's get started." Neddy set her wineglass on the coffee table. Her voice was soothing and sympathetic. This was obviously an act she saved for clients. "Mrs. Montgomery—excuse me—Tina, why don't you tell us why you called our firm."

Tina curled up on the couch and placed her hands in her lap. It was a seductive, feminine move that might have been useful had any testosterone been in the vicinity. During the Hayes trial, our jury consultant had taught us how to study body language. If Tina had been in our jury pool, I would have pegged her as a woman who enjoyed enticing men.

"I'm probably just being paranoid." Tina reached for her wine goblet and cupped it with both hands. She glanced at me, then turned to Neddy. "I guess I just got scared when the police said they wanted to talk to me and look through Max's home office. When I refused, they got pretty pushy."

"What happened?" Neddy asked.

"They went from empathetic to confrontational. One of the officers threatened to get a search warrant." Her eyes indeed bore the pain of a woman who had just lost her husband, and I could tell she was struggling to hold it together. Though she had tried to camouflage the puffiness around her eyes by applying extra foundation, the grief still seeped through.

Tina's refusal to talk to the police left me unsettled. If someone had killed Jefferson, I could not imagine telling the police that I needed to call a lawyer before I would talk to them, and I *was* a lawyer. When someone you love is killed, you don't think about yourself. If you're innocent, that is. So if Tina had nothing to hide, what was she so concerned about? Didn't she want the police to find her husband's killer?

"Why'd you refuse to talk to the police?" I asked.

"I don't know. I guess I wasn't thinking straight." I noticed her body shudder. I thought she was about to start crying, but she held it in. "He wasn't killed here," she continued. "I didn't want them barging in and destroying my home. We've all heard about the L.A.P.D. engaging in some pretty outrageous conduct. I just didn't trust them."

"Well, as far as I'm concerned, you did the right thing," Neddy said.

I wasn't so sure. "Has anyone told you you're a suspect in your husband's death?" I continued.

I noticed Neddy shift in her seat.

Tina's eyes nervously darted about. "No, of course not."

I opened my mouth to ask another question, but Neddy cut me off.

"Well, we're glad you called us. Even though the police are likely to get more suspicious if you insist on having a lawyer present during your questioning, it's really in your best interest to do so." Neddy had real empathy in her voice. Her new softer side was making my head hurt.

Tina smiled. She seemed happy whenever Neddy offered words of approval. The room fell uncomfortably silent, which apparently bothered Tina because she proceeded to fill the void.

"There's no reason for anybody to think that I killed my husband." A single tear rolled down her cheek and she reached for a Kleenex from a box on the coffee table and dabbed at her cheek. "I just know how the police can turn things around."

Something still didn't sit right with me. Her run-for-cover attitude just didn't make sense. "Have you had any prior run-ins with the police?"

Tina's face told me that she was offended by the question and I immediately regretted asking it.

She stared down into the goblet. "No. But I read the newspapers. They can make you a suspect and destroy your reputation without ever arresting you. In that JonBenet Ramsey case, the police leaked enough evidence to convict the parents without a trial. Same thing with that security guard who saved those people during the Olympics in Atlanta a while back. I'm just being cautious." The woman in white appeared from nowhere and refilled Tina's wine goblet.

"We'd like to ask you some questions about your husband," Neddy said. "Some of the same questions the police will likely ask."

Neddy spent the next few minutes covering various innocuous details of Tina and Max Montgomery's life together. How long they had been married, where they had met, and what Tina knew about his business affairs.

I was a little perturbed that Neddy seemed to be beating around the bush about the very reason we were there. I also wished someone would offer me something to drink other than wine. Maybe the woman in white could bring me a Diet Coke.

I decided to interject and get to some of the important stuff. "Do you have any idea who may've wanted to kill your husband?"

I wasn't looking over at Neddy, but I could feel her staring me down.

I couldn't tell whether Tina noticed the tension between us. She'd had three glasses of wine since I'd arrived. Probably not.

Tina took a moment to mull over my question. "Frankly, I have no idea who could've killed Max." I heard sadness in her voice. "But I don't think it had anything to do with his business."

"Why not?" I asked.

"My husband was extremely ethical when it came to his professional life. He never cheated anybody." She stopped to take another sip of wine. "He saved that for me."

"What do you mean?"

She raised her head slightly and her words came out much softer than the ones before. "Let's just say honoring his marriage vows wasn't exactly high on my husband's list of priorities."

She seemed embarrassed to be discussing such a personal subject with us. Her husband's riches had allowed her to distance herself from ordinary life and mundane people. Her days were filled with formal dinner parties, trips to tropical islands, and extravagant shopping sprees. But the state of her marriage would definitely be pertinent to the police, so I forged ahead.

"You didn't have a happy marriage?" I asked.

"I didn't say that." She seemed close to breaking down now. "It was as good as any marriage of twenty-seven years. We treated each other civilly, made our obligatory public appearances, and kept our disagreements to ourselves. Max may've been seeing other women, but I still believed he loved me. And, of course, I loved him very much."

"Were you and your husband still intimate?"

This time I felt Neddy hurling invisible daggers my way. I had no idea why. I had asked a legitimate question. We needed to know the real deal about the Montgomerys' relationship.

"Of course we were intimate. He was my husband." Her suddenly snippy tone conveyed that my question was ridiculous. "But Max had a sexual addiction. There was no way one woman could satisfy him."

A heavy silence hung in the air. This time I broke it. "Were you okay with him...uh . . ." I wasn't quite sure of the appropriate verb to use, "seeing other women?"

"No, of course not." She paused to take another sip of wine, then looked away, in the direction of the French doors and into her beautiful garden. "Max did his best to keep his affairs from me."

I decided it might be best to back off, so I turned to Neddy.

"He was a good provider and a good husband," Tina continued, as if she regretted painting such a bad picture of her dearly departed. "As long as you didn't include monogamy in the definition of marriage."

I crossed and uncrossed my legs, feeling as uncomfortable as Tina apparently did. I wanted to get this interview over with. "Tina, I hate to ask you this next question, but the police are certainly going to ask it, so it makes sense for us to get it out of the way now. Did you kill your husband?"

She did not flinch or blink, but turned to face Neddy, not me. "Of course not, I loved my husband more than I loved myself."

I wasn't sure I believed her. There was nothing about her body language that told me she was lying, but my gut just wasn't willing to commit to her innocence yet.

"Where were you the night your husband was killed?"

She briefly closed her eyes. "That's the problem," she said, sitting her wine goblet on the coffee table and wringing her hands. "I was attending a Crystal Stairs fundraising dinner at the Ritz-Carlton in Beverly Hills. I was chairperson of the committee that organized the dinner."

I leaned forward in my chair. "You were at the same hotel where your husband was murdered?"

Tina nodded.

I tried to will the astonishment from my face. "Did you two go to the dinner together?"

"No."

Neddy also sat at attention. I paused to give her time to ask the next question. When she didn't, I continued.

"Did your husband know your fundraiser was being held at the Ritz-Carlton?"

"No," she said shaking her head. "He'd planned to escort me, but the day before, he told me he had to leave town on business. At least, that's the lie he gave me. I never got a chance to tell him where the dinner was. The events I organized were usually at the Century Plaza or the Biltmore."

Neddy and I looked at each other without meaning to.

"It gets worse," Tina said softly. "During the middle of the event, I wasn't feeling well, so I went back to my room to lie down."

"Wait," Neddy said, "you had a room there that night?"

"Yes. I'd checked in the prior evening. I had to be there throughout the day to make sure all the proper arrangements were made for the dinner."

"Don't tell me," I said. "Your husband was killed during the time you went back to your room to lie down?"

Tina's eyes finally met mine. "Exactly."

CHAPTER 6

The woman in white showed us to the front door and Neddy and I trudged down the long walkway toward the front gate in silence. When I opened the gate, Neddy reached in front of me and slammed it shut.

"I don't know how you conduct client interviews in employment cases, but what you just did in there won't work in a criminal case," she snapped. She sounded like a high school coach berating a player for fumbling the game-winning play.

It took me a few seconds to gather my thoughts. First, because I had a habit of momentarily retreating when under attack and second, because I had no idea what Neddy was so mad about. I did know, however, that if we were going to be equals on this case, I needed to start laying the groundwork now.

"I don't like the tone of your voice," I said, my attitude just as ugly as hers. "Since we've been assigned to handle this case *together,* you need to show me the basic courtesy of talking to me like an adult." My right hand was confidently planted on my hip. My left gripped the handle of my briefcase so tightly a shot of pain went halfway up my arm. "Anyway, I have no idea what you're upset about."

Neddy seemed surprised that her words had not caused me to cower. Most associates at the firm never stood up to her, but Neddy's seniority and extensive trial experience didn't intimidate me one bit.

Her lips twisted into a frigid frown. "Interviewing clients is a skill you apparently haven't mastered yet. In a criminal case, it's not your job to question your client like you're some prosecutor or a damn rookie cop. Particularly not during the first interview. Our first priority is to gain the client's trust. Most of your questions, particularly your little 'Did you kill your husband?' inquiry, were way out of line."

I didn't know what to say next. I was certain I'd seen Eugene on *The Practice* ask his clients if they did it, but I wasn't about to admit that TV was the source of what little I knew about criminal law. Okay, so I screwed up. Like a skilled politician, I sidestepped the real issue.

"What's up with you? Why're you always so angry? We need to be working as a team. Okay, so I'm not a criminal lawyer. O'Reilly knew that when he assigned me to this case. But I'm a good litigator and I learn fast. If you'd take that mountain-size chip off your shoulder, maybe we'd be able to focus on defending our client rather than battling it out with each other."

Neddy sighed loudly. "I'm not looking for a fight. Lord knows I'm already fighting enough battles in my life right now. Just don't go asking any more stupid-ass questions, okay?"

"Fine," I fired back. "I'll be more careful with my questions if you agree to work on your bitchy attitude. We're supposed to be trying this case together. So the first thing you need to do is stop acting like you're my mama. If that's the kind of relationship you want, then go home and make a baby."

Neddy looked as if I'd just slapped her across the face. Her eyes moistened and she seemed momentarily stunned. I quickly replayed my words in my head, trying to understand why they seemed to hit so hard. I was mad as hell, but I still liked to play fair.

"And anyway," I said, "I don't understand what was so wrong with my question. Are you telling me criminal lawyers don't ask their clients if they're guilty?"

"No! Not lawyers who know what they're doing." Neddy acted like she wanted to put up her dukes. "Our investigation will lead us to Tina's guilt or innocence. And besides, if she'd admitted killing her husband, it wouldn't have changed anything. We're still going to defend her. You've defended supervisors accused of discrimination. You can't possibly tell me the first thing you do is ask your client if he's a racist?"

"Not in those words. But I certainly want to know if the allegations of racism are true. When I know early on that my client screwed up, it affects my approach to the case. I have to decide if it's a case I'm willing to try or whether the information is so damaging, I'm better off trying to settle."

"Well, it doesn't work that way in a criminal case," she snapped. "In my world, a settlement still means prison time. And that's not usually a viable option for most clients. You think Johnnie Cochran asked O.J. if he did it? I don't think so. It's irrelevant. Guilty or innocent, our job is to defend."

I still wasn't willing to concede this point to her. "I just don't see the harm in asking. Anyway, our conversation is attorney–client privileged. If we know whether she did it or not, then we'll know how hard to fight."

"Are you kidding me?" Neddy had an incredulous look on her face. "First off, the harm is the client's perception. No matter what, we want her to trust us. And second—and this is a very big point so you'd better commit it to memory—guilty or innocent, you always defend your client with everything you got. If you can't do that, then you need to get off this damn case. Now!"

Wow, coach was making some good points. I resorted to my safety net—sarcasm. "You definitely sound like a public defender. You work this hard for child molesters, too?"

Her eyes narrowed into thin slits. "My allegiance is to whoever's paying the bills."

"Fine. But based on what we just heard in there, my gut tells me Tina may've actually killed her husband."

Neddy set her briefcase on the grass and threw up her hands. "Are you hard of hearing? I just told you it doesn't matter. Not yet anyway. And your gut isn't trying this case. During my first few years of practice, my gut was wrong a helluva lot more than it was right. So I learned to rely only on the facts. We don't have any facts that conclusively tell us that Tina killed her husband. And until we do, the assumption is, she's innocent. You have heard the phrase 'innocent until proven guilty,' haven't you?"

I hated her patronizing attitude and there was no way I was going to continue to put up with it. "I really don't like the way you talk to me," I said. "How in the hell are we going to handle this case with this kind of working relationship? I don't have an issue with you and I don't understand why you have one with me."

She locked her arms across her chest. "I don't have an issue with you."

"Judging from that scowl pasted on your face every damn day of the week, I would think you had an issue with the entire world."

Neddy looked like she wanted to hit me. My body stiffened and my chest protruded in a way that said "go ahead." I was wearing the most expensive Anne Klein suit I owned and I'd just gotten a touch-up and a cinnamon rinse, but if we had to roll around in the grass to set things straight, sometimes a sister's gotta do what a sister's gotta do.

When I saw Neddy's right arm extend toward me, I tried to duck, but she managed to reach behind me, throw her arm across my shoulder, and pull me close to her. I tried to pull away, but she had me snagged in a vicelike grip. So now she was trying to hug me? She must be schizophrenic.

When I heard a voice from the rear, I understood.

"Is everything okay out there?" Tina called out to us. She was poking her head out of a set of double doors that had to be two stories high. We must've looked like a pair of unhappy Siamese twins.

"We're just fine," Neddy said smiling, her fingers clamped around my shoulder. "We were just out here strategizing. Sorry if we made too much noise."

"No, not at all," Tina said. "I just walked by the window and saw you two standing there. It's good to know I have such hardworking attorneys on my team."

"We're a team all right," I said, looking over at Neddy, my body as stiff as a two-by-four. I wrapped my free hand around her waist and mimicked the fake smile pasted across her lips.

"Well, we better get going," I said, untangling myself from my new archenemy. "We've got a lot of work to do."

CHAPTER 7

I was seated in my favorite booth at my regular neighborhood hang-out, the T.G.I. Friday's restaurant owned by Magic Johnson in the Ladera Center, waiting for my best friend to arrive. After my verbal sparring match with Neddy three hours earlier, I desperately needed some bonding time with my homegirl.

The restaurant was usually packed on Friday nights and tonight was no exception. I waved when I saw Special walk in. She flashed me a big smile and pranced over.

Exactly two seconds after giving me a quick hug and sliding into the booth, she let me have it. "Okay, girlfriend, I know you're my homegirl and everything, but I have to tell you the truth. The next time you're going to be in the media spotlight, you have to make sure your gear is tight."

"What're you talking about?" I said.

"This!" She slapped three newspaper articles about the Hayes trial on the table. "That suit is not happening. You've got at least a dozen suits in your closet that look a whole lot better than that. Were the lights out when you pulled that bland thing out of your closet?"

I reached across the table and picked up one of the articles. The photo showed David and me outside the courtroom right after the verdict. "I know you're not bagging on my favorite suit," I said. "I look fabulous. Don't hate."

"Please!" Special said, screwing up her face like she had just sucked on a lemon. "I don't see nothing about that suit that should make it your favorite. You need to take a good two inches off the hem. My mama wears skirts shorter than that." She took the article from me and replaced it with another one. "Now, in this one, your hair looks good, but I still have to convince you to try some highlights."

All I could do was laugh. Special always made me laugh. There were three things Special was one hundred percent serious about: fashion, men in general, and men with money. She had a model-thin frame with healthy curves in all the right places and flawless, cream-colored skin. Today, she donned a purple chiffon blouse and a pair of black leather pants so tight it looked as if they had been painted onto her legs. Her hair was pulled back into a long, fake cherry-blond ponytail. No telling what color it would be next week. At 5'9", she was an inch taller than me.

A woman walked by, stopped, then glanced back as if she recognized me but couldn't place my face.

"Girl, you're famous!" Special squealed. "That woman probably saw you on the six o'clock news. You were damn near on every channel. You're 'bout to blow up. Oooooh, and what if you get a TV show like Star Jones?"

I had absolutely no desire to host a TV show and Special knew that. When I first left Brandon & Bass, I had only wanted a break from the demanding pace of corporate litigation. I felt the much smaller O'Reilly & Finney would offer me that, as well as a realistic shot at partnership. But with the Hayes trial under my belt, I had to admit that the thrill of victory left me itching to get back into the ring for another big win, despite the toll it would take on my body and my marriage. It was just too bad my new case had me teamed up with Neddy.

I wanted to tell Special about my new client, but she could only keep a secret if you locked her in a closet until you were ready to reveal it. So instead, I shared my other news.

"Jefferson bought me a present," I said.

"I have to call that boy and tell him he's spoiling you so much you're not going to be good for any other man," she said with feigned envy.

"That's a good thing."

"Yeah. Too bad I'm not the one being spoiled." She took a sip from her water glass. "So what lavish gift did Mr. Ideal Husband give you this time? A trip to the Bahamas, a diamond necklace?"

"Nope," I said. "An ovulation kit."

Special tilted her head to the side. "That brother trying to tell you it's time to make some babies?"

"Yep."

"You feeling him?"

I picked up the menu even though I already knew I wanted the Jack Daniel's shrimp. "Nope."

"So, what did you say?"

"Nothing. He was so excited and proud of himself, there was no way I could tell him I wasn't quite ready for motherhood."

She grabbed the menu out of my hands. "What're you looking at that for? You order the same damn thing every time we come here. So what are you going to do?"

"Hell if I know. I bet the minute I go off birth control, little Jefferson will be pounding on the door of my womb trying to get out."

She looked confused. "But I thought you wanted children."

"I do, but not nine months from now. I at least want to wait until I make partner."

"Ah shoot, here we go." Special folded her arms. "Let's not start that mess all over again. You nearly lost Jefferson slaving away at your last firm trying to make partner. I thought you had your priorities in order. Your eggs aren't getting any younger, you know."

"O'Reilly & Finney is nothing like Brandon & Bass. Except for when I'm in trial, I don't work nearly as hard. And the managing partner thinks I'm God's gift to the law. I'm going to make it this time."

Her eyes scolded me. "Girl, you need to keep your eyes on the prize and the prize is your sexy-ass husband, not partnership. Besides, it's about time for me to be a God-mommy."

I could always count on Special to give it to me straight. Since our freshman year at USC, we had been joined at the hip, drawn together by the many similarities in our lives. Both first-generation college students and only children, no matter where we went, we were usually the tallest women in the room.

Unlike me, however, Special's stint at USC did not survive freshman year. A direct consequence of her intense preoccupation with the opposite sex—primarily athletes—rather than any particular course of study. Special dropped out and went to work for Telecredit, where she eventually became a supervisor. Somehow, the separation strengthened our friendship. She was always on hand to help me type a paper, make a late-night library run, or ply me with coffee and NoDoz during finals.

I fumbled with my napkin and pondered my predicament. "Like I said, I do want kids. I just need to work out the timing. But if I tell Jefferson I want to wait a while, I know he's going to go off."

"Well, let me give you some advice." She twisted her lips and cocked her head to the side. Special handed out advice so often she could have rented a couch and charged for it. "Just don't tell that brother partnership is the reason you're stalling. That would be déjà vu for him. He loves your ass, but if I were him, I wouldn't play second fiddle to your career twice and I don't think he will. Getting pregnant might be a good thing. Anyway, you don't want to be showing up for the first day of kindergarten with gray hair and crow's-feet."

I chuckled sadly. "That's Jefferson's argument."

When the waitress arrived, Special ordered a Long Island iced tea, a cup of clam chowder, the Cajun fried chicken salad, and the strawberry cheesecake. Special always ordered her dessert up front. She ate like a linebacker and didn't have an ounce of fat to show for it.

"Anyway, I might have another big case, and it would be stupid for me to get pregnant until it's resolved."

Special's eyes lit up. She loved hearing about my cases. "I'm so happy you represent the good guys every now and then. Who's the racist, sexist corporation you're going after this time?"

"It's not an employment case and I can't talk about it right now. But it could be extremely high profile."

"Really?" Special leaned her head in closer to mine and lowered her voice. "C'mon, tell me. I won't tell anybody."

"Yeah, right. I've heard you tell that lie before. You'll have to read about it in the newspapers just like everybody else."

"Aw, c'mon," Special said, pretending to pout, "pretty please."

"Nope," I said firmly. "So stop begging and let's just change the subject. What's up with you? Have you gone out with that guy you met at La Lousanne? What's his name? Derek?"

She huffed loudly. "Girl, that brother's history."

"Special, you just met the guy a week ago. What happened?"

"I must have drank too much that night 'cause when I got a look at him in daylight he was tore up from the floor up," she said, dramatically rolling her eyes. "And on top of that he had no class, no money and now, no mo' dates with my ass."

I couldn't help but laugh. Special had more dates than any woman I knew. Unfortunately, no man was ever good enough for her. "So you're manless again?"

"Girl, please. You know me better than that. It's a poor rat that ain't got but one hole to go to. I've always got some backup." She picked up a chip of ice from her water glass and began crunching on it. "Anyway, I think I've figured out what I've been doing wrong when it comes to men."

"Oh, that's an interesting admission," I said. "I never knew you felt you were doing anything wrong. So let's hear it."

The waitress set my Diet Coke and Special's Long Island iced tea on the table. Special stirred her drink with a spoon then took a sip.

"I've been dating guys with the wrong name," she said.

"What?"

She looked me dead in the eyes. "I'm not dating any more brothers whose names begin with D."

"What're you talking about?" Special has said some bizarre stuff before, but this topped the list.

"It just came to me last night. Eight of the last ten guys I've dated have names that begin with D. That's too many to be just a coincidence. Think about it. Even your cousin Donald, with his fine-ass self, fell into that category. And then there was Daniel, David, Donnell, Damarco, Deke, and that fool I just went out with, Derek."

"That's only seven."

"Well, Ronald, that Carson sheriff's deputy, technically counts because everybody calls him Dap."

I still didn't get it. "Excuse me for being dense, but I don't understand why the letter D is a problem."

Special rolled her eyes. "You can think up more negative words that begin with the letter D than any other letter in the alphabet."

I picked up her drink and looked inside. "Somebody must've spiked this thing with something besides alcohol because what you just said is nuts."

"I'm serious," she said, taking her drink back. "Think about it. Death, divorce, danger, disaster. They all begin with the letter D."

"Special, a lot of negative words begin with other letters, too. Not just D."

"Yeah, but not as many begin with D. We would be here for days if we tried to list them all. Discipline, darkness, damnation, devil, dying, disgusted. I fell asleep last night trying to count them. And when I got up this morning and looked in the dictionary, it only confirmed my theory."

I still refused to believe she was serious. "That's why you think your relationships haven't worked out?" I said, laughing. "You really believe what you're saying?"

"Laugh if you want to, but I'm as serious as a heart attack." She pulled a pen from her purse and started jotting down more words on her napkin. "Diarrhea, disease, depression, disability."

I laughed even harder.

"It ain't funny. My theory makes complete sense."

She continued to scribble down every negative D word she could think up. "Defective, dysfunctional, diabetic, diaper rash, drug dealer, donuts."

"Donuts?"

"Yeah, donuts. Do you know how many fat grams there are in one of them little tiny-ass Krispy Kreme donuts? About a zillion. That's a helluva negative."

I just stared at her, shaking my head. "Special, please don't repeat this to anybody else."

"Laugh if you want to, but I'm not going out with another brother whose name begins with D. I might even extend it to men with the letter D anywhere in their damn name."

I looked around the restaurant. "Okay," I said, spotting an attractive catch sitting at the bar, "if that cutie-pie over there in the beige T-shirt with the huge biceps wanted to get with you and his name happened to be Dean, you're telling me you'd refuse to go out with him?"

Special glanced at the man and turned up her nose. "Please! You know I ain't feeling that brother. He's hella blight. I need me a big chocolate buck."

Blight was Special's nickname for black men with light skin. Even though the guy we were looking at was a good two shades darker than she was, he wasn't even close to the hue she preferred.

"Forgive me," I said. "How could I forget how color-struck you are?" I scanned the rest of the bar area. "Okay, what about that charcoal-colored stud over there in those black jeans?"

"Well . . ." Special squirmed in her seat as she checked him out.

"Well, what?" I said, demanding an answer.

"I might have to make an exception for really, really fine-ass men."

We both cracked up.

The waitress showed up with our food and we took a break to enjoy it.

"So," Special said between bites, "what're you going to do about your little motherhood dilemma?"

I shrugged. "For right now, I'm just hoping that case I told you about disappears. If it doesn't, there's no way I can get pregnant right away."

"Have you told Jefferson about the case yet?"

"Do I look crazy?" I said.

Special raised an eyebrow. "Nah, you don't look crazy. But, if you ask me, if you choose that damn law firm over your man, you might as well be."

CHAPTER 8

My conversation with Special weighed heavily on my mind all weekend. She was right. I could not afford to keep putting my career before my marriage. Especially not over a case that was bound to be a miserable experience for me anyway. Just after noon on Monday, without allowing time for reconsideration, I marched straight into O'Reilly's office to do what I had to do, regardless of the impact it would have on my career.

O'Reilly was sitting at a small, circular table across from his desk reading the *Wall Street Journal* and munching on one of two footlong Subway sandwiches spread out before him. The room smelled of onions and pickles. His suit jacket hung over the arm of an adjacent chair and his tie was thrown backward over his shoulder. He had one shoe off and I could see that his sock was badly worn at the heel. O'Reilly's wacky socks were his trademark. The ones he was wearing at the moment were black with bright orange squares.

I walked in, closed the door behind me, and took a seat directly across from him. "Lunch at your desk again?" I teased. "You're working too hard."

He smiled. "Have to set the right example for the troops."

I liked the fact that I felt comfortable talking to O'Reilly about almost anything. He was raised in a predominantly black, working-class neighborhood in Detroit not much different from where I had grown up in Compton. That upbringing had given him a comfort level with a whole mix of folks. He may've had his own racial biases, but I hadn't picked up on any.

I sat up straight in my chair and proceeded with my mission. "I want off the Montgomery case."

His face showed no reaction. "Why?" he asked, taking a big bite of his sandwich.

"Personal reasons."

"I'm listening," he said, his eyes glued to his sandwich.

"O'Reilly, I'm not a criminal attorney." My voice came out in a childish whine and I wanted to kick myself. The girly emotional stuff didn't work with O'Reilly. I needed to be firm, not wimpy.

"That's a good thing in a case like this," he said. He was making an annoying smacking sound between sentences. "It means you'll be apt to think outside the box. Anyway, like you told me the other day, who says there's a case yet? It hasn't even been a week since Mrs. Montgomery retained you. She may never even be charged."

"I know, but something tells me she's guilty as hell and I'm not sure I have what it takes to defend a murderer. At least not on an emotional level."

O'Reilly stopped chewing and stared at me. "Since you work here, I gather that you did graduate from law school, so I know you're familiar with the concept that everyone is entitled to a strong defense." He took another sloppy bite from his sandwich and continued talking with stuffed cheeks. "Since when does guilt or innocence have a bearing on what we do?"

Since my husband wants me to have a baby and since you assigned me to work with the Antichrist. I didn't respond, at least not with words.

"Everybody—innocent or guilty—deserves the best defense that money can buy," he continued. "And that's exactly what we provide. This could be one of the most watched cases this city has seen in years. Do you know how many people had ties to Max Montgomery? I bet every dignitary in L.A. and several politicians from Sacramento and D.C. will show up at his funeral."

"I just don't know if I want to be consumed by another long case. The Hayes trial took a lot out of me."

"Criminal cases move much faster than civil. You don't have all those bullshit motions and discovery battles to deal with."

My appeal for release wasn't quite working out the way I had expected it to. I needed to tell him the real deal. "To be honest, Neddy and I don't seem to click," I said.

That excuse didn't move him either. "Give it some time."

Time would only make matters worse, I thought. We would probably be throwing blows in a week. I wanted to be straight with O'Reilly, but I also didn't want to come off like I was trashing Neddy. No matter how much I disliked her, we were still the only two black attorneys in the firm. Our not getting along wouldn't just reflect badly on us. White folks had a way of attributing negative behavior by one black person to the entire race. If word got out that we despised each other, every other black attorney who stepped foot in the firm would be tainted by it. So I had to tread carefully, even with O'Reilly. I tried another tactic.

"David's a former D.A.," I said. "Wouldn't he be a better fit for this case?"

"Nope."

"I disagree," I said defiantly.

O'Reilly chuckled. "You're overruled." He unwrapped his second sub and went to work devouring it. "Besides, the client wants you."

"She doesn't want me," I said. "She wants Neddy."

"No, she wants both of you," he insisted. "I didn't have to work hard at all to sell you two as a team. Your stock is up right now after all the press coverage from the Hayes trial. You did a fantastic job and got an incredible verdict. You need to jump on that wave and ride it out. I know you think I assigned you and Neddy to this case primarily for publicity reasons. I'll admit that was a factor, but I also felt you two would do a good job. You think this firm wants a malpractice lawsuit?"

O'Reilly was doing an excellent job of stroking my ego, but with Jefferson pressuring me about starting a family and Neddy acting like we were marching off to war, it made sense for me to pass on this case. There would always be others.

O'Reilly popped three pickle wedges into his mouth. "I can't believe you, Vernetta," he said, crunching loudly on his pickles. "Lawyers pray for cases like this."

"So you're telling me I should be looking at this case for what I can get out of it?"

He grunted. "Aw, don't go getting all weird on me. This is business. In a high-profile case like this, win or lose, you win. If you get her off, other clients'll be lining up at your door expecting you to perform the same miracle on their behalf. If you lose, people won't blame you because a guilty verdict means she did it and deserves to be punished. In the interim, you get a chance to show the world what a helluva lawyer you are. In a year you'll be asking me for a leave of absence to write a book or quitting to take a job as a legal consultant for some TV station. It's a win–win for you."

I slumped down in my seat. "Wow, I guess I should be happy a man was killed."

"Stop it with the self-righteousness, Vernetta. You know exactly what I mean. You can't possibly be that naïve."

"If you're so hot on all the publicity this case'll attract," I said, "why don't *you* try it with Neddy?"

I knew that was out of the question. O'Reilly hadn't tried a case in over ten years. He was more of an administrator/PR man than a lawyer. A job he relished.

"No go," he said with his mouth full. "The beauty of this case is the all-black, female cast."

"O'Reilly, it's not appropriate to assign cases based on race or gender."

He stopped chewing. "That's crap. I assign cases based on what-ever factor I think'll give us an edge. We just got a case before Judge Vanderbuilt. The man's close to seventy and thinks women should be nurses and kindergarten teachers. You think I'm sending a woman into his courtroom to argue a motion before him? Hell no. If I did, the client would suffer because of it. That's not sexism, that's reality. Judge Mansfield thinks any lawyer who graduated from Stanford Law School, his alma mater, is God's gift to the legal profession. And when we get a case before him, you're damn straight I'm giving first shot at it to one of our lawyers from Stanford. And I'm definitely as-signing a Jewish lawyer to Judge Levin's cases."

"You act like a lawyer can win a case simply by playing to the judge's biases. There *are* some judges out there, you know, who actu-ally focus on the evidence, not the lawyer who's presenting it."

"I never professed to be describing all judges." He took a sip of his Pepsi. "But if I know a judge has a particular bias, I'm definitely playing to it. The same rule applies to the jury. If Tina Montgomery is charged with murder and it gives her an edge with the jury to have two black female attorneys flanking her in the courtroom, that's a good thing."

"It could also backfire," I said. "We might look like three scorned women. Having a guy on the case would add some balance."

O'Reilly shook his head. "Not buying it."

I shrugged. "I'm not sure jurors care about race or sex. What matters most is whether the attorney trying the case walks into that courtroom with an air of confidence, as opposed to arrogance. That he or she knows the facts, doesn't talk down to the jury, and treats them with enough respect that they actually begin to have as much faith in the attorney as they do in the evidence that the attorney is presenting. That's what wins cases."

"Yeah, yeah, yeah, I know all that," O'Reilly said. "But if you have that and some extra edge, you need to use it. I still think people in general identify with people who look like them and who share their same experiences. This is a criminal case. All you need is one juror to go your way to win. If you happen to connect with some black juror, it may mean the difference between a guilty verdict and a hung jury."

"That's crap, O'Reilly. You act like every black juror is going to ignore the evidence and vote not guilty because they like me."

"I'm not saying it's that black and white," he said, holding his sandwich with both hands. "If there's a shred of reasonable doubt, a shred of uncertainty about Mrs. Montgomery's guilt *and* they like you and think you're credible, I do think they're more likely to go your way."

I didn't want to admit it, but there was a sliver of truth to what he had just said. I wasn't sure where to go from here, so I decided not to push the issue any further. For now. I got up to leave. Just as I reached for the doorknob, O'Reilly's words stopped me.

"She needs you."

"What?" I said, turning back to face him.

"I said she needs you," he repeated.

"Who needs me?"

"Neddy."

I laughed. "Could've fooled me."

He folded up the remains of his sandwich and waved me over. "Close the door and sit back down."

O'Reilly wiped his mouth with the back of his hand. As I rejoined him at the table, I noticed a big grease stain on his shirt, right below the collar. I decided to let somebody else give him the bad news.

"I knew Neddy when she worked at the P.D.'s office. Back then she was a friendly, outgoing, free spirit who was everybody's pal." His onion breath was pretty strong. I hoped he didn't have any afternoon meetings.

"That seems hard to believe," I said.

He ignored my skepticism. "I don't know how much you know about her personal life, but she's had it pretty rough lately. She's in the middle of a very heated divorce. Her husband is a complete jackass. I hear he's trying to get alimony. You think Max Montgomery had a reputation for getting around? Neddy's husband could've given him a run for his money. On top of that, she lost a young son about a year ago. After that, she just closed up like a clam, to everybody. I think this divorce is about to push her over the edge."

I considered everything he was telling me without responding.

"I had more than one reason for putting the two of you together on this case," he continued. He was no longer lecturing me. He was talking to me like an ally. "She needs a friend—badly. When you work together day and night on a murder case, the day-to-day pressures of litigation force you to bond. She's hurting and I think you can help her."

"She doesn't seem to want any help."

"That's only because she's not used to asking for it. She's pushed everybody away who's tried to help her, including me. And all her family's back in Chicago. You're a lot like her. You're both smart, strong women. You'll be able to penetrate the walls she's put up to protect herself."

Of course, there was no way I could bail out after that sappy appeal. I got up to leave.

"Hey," he said, as I opened the door, "keep this stuff to yourself. I wouldn't want anybody else to know I actually have a heart."

CHAPTER 9

O'Reilly's revelations about Neddy forced me to look at her in a far more sympathetic light. I understood now why my remark about making a baby when we were going at it outside Tina Montgomery's house the other day had stopped her in her tracks. And I felt pretty bad about it.

My guilt did nothing, however, to help me deal with my own little mama drama. I would just have to pray that the cops found a suspect other than Tina Montgomery and that my eggs could outrun my hubby's sperm in the interim.

I could still smell O'Reilly's sandwich and it made me hungry. I pulled ten bucks from my purse and headed for the Subway shop in the lobby of our building. Before I reached the elevator, I had a kind thought. I did an about-face and made my way past my office, down the hall to Neddy's.

Since it looked like I was going to be stuck on this case, Neddy and I had to mend our working relationship. If O'Reilly was right and there was a decent human being hiding under her mean-spirited exterior, her alter ego had to make an appearance sooner or later. I was still pissed at the way she had attacked me outside Tina's house, but I decided to suck it up for the sake of the case. Somebody had to extend the olive branch and that somebody was going to be me. Maybe we could start this whole bonding thing over lunch.

When I reached her doorway, I saw Neddy standing near the window. She was on the telephone, her back facing me.

"I don't give a damn about that spousal support order!" she hissed into the telephone. Her voice was low and controlled but at the same time filled with rage. "I'll kill you before I give you a dime." She turned and slammed down the phone just as I took a step backward, out of her line of vision.

My timing sucked. I wanted to flee, but I wasn't sure whether she had seen me. I counted to five, then knocked on her open door.

Her palms were planted flat on her desk and her head hung low. When she saw me standing in the doorway, she composed herself.

"Do you have lunch plans?" I asked hurriedly. "I was going to run downstairs and pick up a sandwich. Want to join me?"

Neddy stared at me, but not in an annoyed way. There was a contemplative look on her face. She was probably trying to figure out how much of her conversation I had overhead. I assumed she was talking to her no-account husband.

"I usually skip lunch, but thanks." Her lips attempted to turn upward into a smile, then suddenly stayed the course.

"Can I bring you back a soda or something?" I asked.

"No. But thanks for asking." She pulled out her leather chair and sat down.

Her face looked grim, no doubt enhanced by the fact that she wore no makeup, not even lipstick. Her short hair was unstyled and needed a trim. I was certain I saw her hands tremble.

Just as I was about to leave, she actually said something nice.

"Hold on a minute. I never got a chance to congratulate you on the Hayes verdict. So congratulations."

"Thanks."

I didn't know what else to say and I guess she didn't either. "Heard anything more from Tina Montgomery?" I asked.

"Nope," she said. "No news is good news, I guess. I just hope Tina had nothing to do with her husband's murder. I really can't handle another big case right now."

We had finally found something we could agree on. "You're reading my mind," I said.

CHAPTER 10

I left work around four o'clock so I could spend some quality time with my husband while I still had some time left to share with him.

We were sitting at the kitchen table finishing up some *lard na* noodles with chicken, *pad prik* green beans, and vegetable spring rolls delivered by our favorite Thai restaurant. The house was quiet, except for the soothing vibes from an old Maxwell CD.

"I always thought married life would mean I'd get a home-cooked meal every night and wild sex 24/7," Jefferson joked, stuffing half of a spring roll into his mouth.

I leaned across the table and kissed him on the forehead. "Well, somebody lied to you big time, baby. Because we ain't Ozzie and Harriet and it ain't 1955."

"That's cold. Y'all rope a brother in with regular home-cooked meals and nonstop sex, then you pull a bait 'n switch. You used to cook for me all the time when we were dating."

"What can I say? Next time I guess you better get it in writing."

He grinned. "So how's work?" I could tell Jefferson had something on his mind. He was just trying to find the right moment to strike.

"Fine," I said.

He put down his fork and pushed his chair back from the table. "I see you haven't started using that ovulation kit yet."

Damn. Back to the baby stuff.

I took my time chewing my green beans. They were extra spicy tonight. "Jefferson, I can't get pregnant just like that," I said, snapping my fingers. "I have to go off birth control first."

"So when's that going to happen?" His arms were tightly folded across his chest, which made his biceps more pronounced. I remember from my freshman psych class that this posture communicated defensiveness.

"As soon as I make an appointment with my gynecologist," I said.

"And when's that going to happen?"

"As soon as I get some time."

"And when do you plan to make some—"

I held up my hand. "Jefferson, don't do this. You know I want kids, too, but you can't expect it to happen overnight."

"Why not?" He had purposely lowered his deep baritone.

Hell if I know. "Because I have a job that requires me to plan something like this."

He stared at me without blinking. "Have you told them we're thinking about having a baby?"

"Of course not. And when I do tell them, it'll be after I'm already pregnant." I stuck a fork full of *lard na* noodles into my mouth so I'd have a reason not to talk.

We continued to eat in painful silence.

Jefferson stood up and walked over to the sink and began rinsing his plate. "You know, I've been waiting for you to just tell me the truth," he said.

"What are you talking about?"

"Just go ahead and admit that you don't want to get pregnant instead of stalling and beating around the bush like you're doing now."

Unfortunately, Jefferson knew me like a book. "I do want children...I'm just not sure I want any right now."

He didn't say anything at first. Then he tucked his bottom lip between his teeth, something he did only when he was pissed. "Okay," he said slowly. "If you don't want kids now, when do you want them?"

"I don't know," I snapped. If I gave him a time frame, he would hold me to it.

I looked down at my food, but I could feel his frustration without even seeing his face. "This is starting all over again," he said, trying to temper his anger. "I thought you had your priorities in order after leaving Brandon & Bass. But it looks like our marriage is being pushed off to the side again."

"That's not true." I didn't want to look at him, so I picked up one of the Styrofoam containers and dumped more green beans onto my plate even though I had lost my appetite. I wanted to run from the room, or maybe even the house.

"Sure seems like it to me." He marched back over to the table and sat down again.

"I don't want to argue, Jefferson."

"We're not arguing. This is a discussion."

I inhaled. "Having a baby is a big decision. It's my body that's going to blow up like an elephant for nine months. It's my life that's going to change."

"You know I'll be there helping you every step of the way."

"Yeah, like when I'm having morning sickness and I have a brief to write, a deposition to take, and a client to interview. I'm sure you'll be right there feeling all my pain."

"So it *is* all about the job," he said accusingly.

"No, it isn't. But you act like I can just walk away from what I do. We need two paychecks to pay the mortgage on this house."

My statement was not intended to say he wasn't an adequate provider, but the quick flinch of his left eye told me he had interpreted it that way.

"So you're saying you'd quit your job if I could handle paying all the bills? Because if that's what it takes, I can make it happen. The rental income from the duplex in Gardena my grandmother left me could easily cover your half of the mortgage."

"I'm not quitting my job, Jefferson," I said. "I didn't go to law school so I could stay home and bake cookies."

"Nobody's asking you to stay home and bake cookies. Anyway, you told me your firm gives you four months of paid maternity leave. So, it's not about the money then, is it?"

When the hell did I tell you that? And why did I tell you that? "Jefferson, I can't make a life-changing decision like this overnight. Just give me some time."

"I'm not asking you to make a decision overnight." The way his nostrils flared told me he was getting even more upset. "We've been talking about this for months, except every time I bring it up, you want to put it off. Well, we ain't putting it off any longer."

I wasn't sure I'd ever seen him this mad. I didn't like where this conversation was going. It would be a mistake for either one of us to put an ultimatum on the table. "Jefferson, I just need some time," I pleaded.

"Okay, you want time, how much time do you need? We don't have a lot of time to play with. You're 32, I'm 36. I want to be able to enjoy my kids while I'm still young."

I pushed my plate away. The pungent odor of the food was suddenly making me nauseous. "I know lots of women who have babies in their forties," I said.

His body tensed. "I'm not waiting eight years to be a father." His statement sounded like a threat.

"I'm not asking you to wait that long. I just—"

"Just forget it." He got up from the table and headed for the den. "Take all the time you need."

I followed after him and joined him on the couch. I tried to find the words to make him understand my point of view, but before I could speak, the telephone rang. It was Special.

"Girl, can you believe it? That woman murdered her fine-ass husband!"

"What are you talking about?"

"The wife of that rich, fine-ass Max Montgomery. They just showed her on TV. They brought her in for questioning in her husband's death. And I just know she did it. That boy was a big time ho. He even tried to hit on me once. I was at this pool party up in Bel Air and I was wearing these shocking pink hot pants and he—"

"Wait," I said, running into the bedroom to turn on the TV. I hoped Jefferson didn't follow me. This was not the way I wanted him to find out about the Montgomery case.

It seemed to take forever for a picture to appear on the television screen. "You saw Tina Montgomery on the news?" I asked, as I paced in front of the TV.

"Yep. Standing right out in front of Parker Center."

I held the phone between my ear and shoulder and frantically pressed the remote, switching from channel to channel. "What station is it on?"

"Eleven. And her attorney is that chick from your firm. The one you don't like with the country-ass name who always looks like she wants to bite somebody."

My blood began to boil. "Neddy?"

"Yep. A reporter was interviewing her. Girl, you need to help that sister with some makeup tips. She didn't even have any lipstick on. And it looked like Stevie Wonder did her hair. Give that girl Shawnta's number so she can hook her up with some extensions. She can't be going around looking like that. Don't she know she's representing her people?"

I could hardly think. "What did she say?"

"The typical lawyer nonsense y'all are always spouting. 'My client's innocent. Justice will prevail.' Yada, yada yada."

"I can't find it," I said.

"Girl, the story's over now. Your girl claimed her client was only brought in for questioning. But that's a straight-up lie. They could've questioned her ass at home. Homegirl's about to go down."

I was so mad I was seeing red, black, and purple. I kept channel surfing in the hope that another station was running the story, but no luck. "This is that case I was telling you about the other day at Friday's," I said.

"No shit! Then why weren't you out there talking to the media with your client?"

"I don't know," I said, still stunned. "But I'm damn sure going to find out."

CHAPTER 11

The first thing I did when I arrived at the office the next morning was check my voice mail. I'd checked it right after I got off the telephone with Special and again during my drive into the office, but I wanted to check it one more time just to make sure Neddy hadn't tried to call me. I suffered through three lengthy new messages to find out that she had not.

I glanced at my watch. It was 8:15. Neddy was usually in by 7:30. I'd already stopped by her office twice. She was probably avoiding me. And it was a good thing she was. I still needed more time to calm myself down before confronting her. No need for me to be facing a murder charge, too. Before I could decide whether to visit her office a third time, Neddy walked into mine.

I didn't give her a chance to speak. "Is there a reason you didn't let me know *our* client was being brought in for questioning last night?" I asked with mucho attitude in my voice.

As usual, Neddy was grim-faced and distant. "Everything happened really fast last night. When I got the call from Tina she was already on her way to the police station so I had to just rush down there."

I stood up, but remained standing behind my desk. "You could've called me."

She closed the door and walked over near my desk. Maybe things were about to get ugly.

"I knew you had already left the office and I didn't have your home number," she said, her look as unpleasant as the tone of her voice.

"You could've left me a voice mail message," I replied.

She raised her eyes to the ceiling, like I was annoying her.

I just glared back at her. I was so hot I was scared I might do something crazy, like reach over and start choking her.

"Look," she said finally, "I don't have time for this territorial bullshit. If you want to be on TV, I'll make sure the next interview is yours. I didn't even want to talk to them but they ambushed us."

"It's not about being on TV, it's about being included." I couldn't believe Neddy was trying to act like excluding me was no big deal. I had to let her know that I would not stand for her blowing me off. "If we're going to be working together, then that's exactly what we should do. Work together. I don't know what kinda stuff you're going through but—"

"Who says I'm going through anything?" The worried look on her face mirrored the panic in her voice. I smiled inside. It was nice to finally find a pressure point. The woman did not like having her business in the street.

I paused, careful not to disclose anything O'Reilly had shared with me. "You must be going through something because you're always walking around here like somebody's got a foot up your ass."

Her body language told me she was willing to take that shot only because she could see I was too hot to be played with. "Nothing's going on. I'm fine."

"I'd appreciate it if you'd include me in anything else dealing with this case from now on."

"No problem."

She made a move toward the door, then stopped. "I forgot to mention it," she said, trying to sound matter-of-fact, "but I hired an investigator the day after we met with Tina to gather some background information on her husband. Can you stop by my place tonight to go over what he's come up with so far? I really need to get out of the office."

Forgot to mention it!

My lips were perfectly poised to spew some hateful words that I probably would've regretted later when O'Reilly barged through the closed door of my office.

"Didn't I tell you!" he said, throwing a copy of the *L.A. Times* in the middle of my desk. "You two are about to become household names. When you get the first book deal, just make sure you thank me in the foreword."

I picked up the newspaper as Neddy walked over to get a closer look. The headline on page one of the California section read UNIQUE DREAM TEAM IN MONTGOMERY MURDER CASE. The article went on to explain that Tina Montgomery had retained two of L.A.'s finest African-American, female litigators to represent her even though she had yet to be charged in her husband's murder. It tracked our legal careers, including my big win in the Hayes case and a series of victories Neddy had at the P.D.'s office and more recently at O'Reilly & Finney. The article even noted that I attended Compton High School and that Neddy was raised on the south side of Chicago. The picture of Neddy looked pretty decent. The one they had of me made my face look bloated.

The article was even more complimentary of my legal talent than the ones following the Hayes verdict. If this case proceeded to trial, we really could end up being celebrity lawyers.

"How did they get this story?" Neddy asked. She eyed O'Reilly suspiciously, as if she were the boss, not the other way around.

He responded with a broad, telling smile.

"You actually leaked this stuff to the *Times*?" she asked in disbelief.

"I wouldn't exactly call it a leak," he grinned. "I just happened to mention it to a friend whose wife is on the paper's editorial staff."

"O'Reilly, c'mon!" Neddy scolded. "We need to be thinking about the best interests of our client. Tina hasn't even been charged with anything yet."

"And that's exactly what the story says," O'Reilly said defensively.

Neddy looked down at the article again, then back up at O'Reilly. "This story pumps us up like we're some magical saviors. Everybody's going to think Tina's guilty because she hired us. You're already poisoning our potential jury pool."

"There's nothing about this article that causes any harm to Tina Montgomery's defense. You two should be ecstatic about it." His face was lit up like a Christmas tree. "Do you know what kind of advance Marcia Clark got for her book deal after the O.J. trial? Millions. I bet she's still pulling down ten or twenty grand a pop for speaking engagements. And I don't even have to tell you how that case made Johnnie Cochran a household name."

"The firm pays us quite well, thank you," Neddy quipped, but there was nothing but cynicism in her voice.

"Lighten up, Neddy. Your life's about to change—dramatically. You two are about to become members of the legal elite."

I tossed the newspaper on the desk. I agreed with Neddy regarding O'Reilly's big mouth, but just the same, I felt a tingle of excitement about the attention. "I hope we don't get too famous," I joked. "I can't have any paparazzi stalking me in the grocery store."

"Well, I can't promise you that." O'Reilly grabbed the newspaper. "I have to go talk to the folks in marketing to see how much mileage we can get from this." Few firms our size had three full-time people dedicated solely to marketing and publicity.

"Do you know how many clients are going to be calling us because of this article?" O'Reilly winked as he left the room. "Just get ready."

Neither Neddy nor I said a word for the first few seconds after O'Reilly's departure.

"So where were we?" she said finally. "Can you stop by my place tonight?"

O'Reilly's interruption had allowed my anger to dissipate some, but seeing Neddy standing there looking like an irate schoolmarm recharged my engines.

"Yeah, I can make it, but we have some things we need to get straight first."

Her hands flew defensively to her hips. "You don't need to keep harping on this. Let's just focus on representing our client."

I couldn't believe her gall. She was trying to screw me and expected me to act like I enjoyed it. "I'd be perfectly willing to do that if you'd remember that Tina is *our* client, not just yours," I said.

"How long do we have to keep rehashing this?" Her voice was louder and sharper than before. "I already apologized for not calling you."

"Excuse me? I don't remember you apologizing."

She threw up her hands. "You're really blowing this thing all out of proportion."

I took a step closer to her. Our faces were only inches apart and I saw a troubling weariness in her eyes. "I'm not blowing anything out of proportion," I said. "First you run off to the police station without telling me. And then you tell me you've hired a private investigator? When were you planning to let me in on that little detail?"

Neddy's face tensed for a second, then her entire body seemed to wilt. She plopped down in one of the chairs in front of my desk and stared down at her hands. "I—just—I have a lot going on right now, okay? I'm not myself. You're right, I'm really going through some things. I'm sorry you've been taking the brunt of it. I promise it won't happen again."

She finally looked up at me. "Anyway, I need to debrief you about Tina's interview with the police," she continued. "I really would appreciate it if you could meet me at my place around seven." This time her words seemed sincere.

I couldn't believe I was actually seeing her in a moment of weakness.

"Fine," I said. Her show of vulnerability had softened my rage.

"And you might as well prepare yourself for a long, taxing trial." She stood up. "Based on the grilling Tina took from the police last night, she's definitely their prime suspect."

CHAPTER 12

Just after five o'clock I rushed home to change clothes before heading over to Neddy's condo in Redondo Beach.

I stuck my key in the front door and was about to turn the knob when Jefferson snatched the door open. I could see veins the size of pencils protruding from his neck. His bottom lip was tucked between his teeth.

"Why'd I have to read the newspaper to find out you're handling some big-shot murder case?" he asked. The level of his voice was half a decibel shy of shouting.

Because if I'd told you about it, you'd go off just like you're doing right now. I could've kicked myself for not using the drive home to come up with an acceptable explanation to appease Jefferson until I could figure out if there would even be a case.

"Uh...I...uh, I wanted to tell you, but I couldn't talk about it," I said. I stepped around him and headed for the kitchen. "The client hasn't been charged yet. So there may not even be a case."

I dropped my purse on the kitchen table, grabbed a bottle of Evian water from the refrigerator, and headed into the bedroom.

"That's bullshit," he said, close on my heels. "You always tell me stuff you're not supposed to tell me."

I unbuttoned my blouse, tossed it on the bed, and began looking through my closet for a pair of jeans. "This case is different. I've never handled a criminal case before. I didn't tell anybody about it. Not even Special."

He gave me a patronizing look that called me a liar. He was right. I'd told him enough confidential stuff about some of my cases to get me disbarred.

"I'm sorry." I brushed his lips with a kiss and scurried past him into the bathroom. "I've just had a lot on my plate lately," I said.

Jefferson was unwilling to be appeased with a peck on the lips. He followed me into the bathroom and stood in the doorway, taking up the whole frame. "Your working on this case means I'll be lucky to see you five minutes a week. You just got done with a trial. You're not the only attorney at that damn firm."

I reached for a washcloth from the towel rack and began scrubbing my face with Oil of Olay soap. "Jefferson, I'm a lawyer. This is what I do. I swear I tried to get off the case, but O'Reilly wouldn't let me."

"Did you tell him why you wanted off the case?"

"What do you mean?" I said, even though I knew exactly what he meant.

"Did you tell him you wanted off the case because we're trying to have a baby?"

You must be insane! "Nope."

He tilted his head sideways and stared harder at me. "Why not?"

"Because that's not the way I want to do it."

I could see muscles bulging beneath his white T-shirt. Either he'd been hitting the gym a lot harder or he was so pissed every muscle in his body was flexed in frustration. "So how *do* you want to do it?"

"I haven't figured that out yet."

His chest heaved up, then slowly back down. "I'll say it one more time. This whole thing would be much easier if you would just come clean. You've never been any good at lying anyway. Just be honest and tell me you don't want to have kids."

"I do want to have kids," I insisted. "Just not this instant." I made a move to leave the bathroom, but he didn't budge so I had to squeeze past him. I walked over to the dresser and pulled a sleeveless cotton shirt from the top drawer.

"I guess with this new case you've got, it'll be at least another year before we can even start thinking about having a baby."

"Jefferson, I might not even have a case. Tina Montgomery was just brought in for questioning. She hasn't even been charged with anything."

He was sitting on the edge of the bed now, looking up at me. "Okay, I'm willing to compromise with you," he said, his tone much more conciliatory. "If she isn't charged and the case goes away, promise me we can start working on having a baby right away."

Whoooaaa. With my luck, they would find another suspect tomorrow. I took way too long to respond.

Jefferson started chewing on his lower lip. "I thought the reason you left Brandon & Bass was so you could have a life. We don't see each other any more now than we did when you were working there." Disappointment had replaced his anger. "You just finished one trial and now you're about to be back working every second of the day on another one."

I didn't want to deal with this right now. "Jefferson, I don't need you jumping all over me about my job, okay? We had time for each other during the Hayes trial and if there's another trial, I'll have time for you again. Damn, sometimes you need more attention than a five-year-old."

Hurt blanketed his face and I wished I could have snatched my words back.

Jefferson opened his mouth to speak, then apparently changed his mind and stormed into the den.

I had not figured out what excuse I planned to use for not being able to hang around for dinner. All I knew was that it wouldn't involve the Montgomery case.

I slipped into my new Apple Bottom jeans, put on my lipstick, and strapped on a pair of sandals. I walked into the kitchen and slung my purse over my shoulder.

"Where're you going? Back to the office, your real home?" he sniped.

I was not going to let him bait me into an argument. "Nope," I said, stopping to browse through the mail, my voice still pleasant. "I have a few errands to run."

Jefferson joined me in the kitchen. I refused to look at him though I could feel him staring me down. I didn't need to see his eyes to know he knew I was lying.

"I'll try not to be too late," I said. "Don't worry about waiting up for me."

CHAPTER 13

When I got to Neddy's place forty minutes later, I walked into a living room that was wall-to-wall paper.

"How many investigators did it take to dig up all this stuff?" I asked, as she cleared a place for me to join her on the floor.

"Just one," she said. "Detective Danny Smith. And they don't come any better. He was an L.A.P.D. detective for several years, then headed up the team of investigators at the P.D.'s office. He opened up his own private firm, Smith Investigations, two years ago."

"What's all this stuff?" I crouched down on the floor next to her.

"Most of these documents are from Max Montgomery's home office. I was hoping I'd run across something significant. But so far, no luck."

The comfy feel of her condo surprised me. It was small, but homey. Lots of floral prints, light curtains, and soft beige walls. A balcony off the living room provided a view of the ocean as well as a cool breeze. I looked around for a photograph of her son, but didn't see one.

She handed me one of Detective Smith's reports.

"Looks like our girl stands to get quite a bit of cash when her husband's estate is finally settled. His investment banking firm will get even more."

I scanned the document. "Dang! She's getting eight million dollars?"

"And everything he owned. Keep reading," Neddy said.

I skipped ahead to the next page. "And the firm's getting thirty-five million? Isn't that a bit much?"

"No, not really. He was the mastermind behind two very successful companies. But your reaction would be the same as the typical juror's. They'll assume both the firm and Tina had a reason to want him dead."

I was sitting Indian style, resting my back against the couch. I was glad I wore jeans. "But money couldn't have been the motive," I said. "Tina was already rich. She had everything she could've wanted."

"Except a faithful husband. Check out this report." Neddy handed me a thick document. "Mr. Max really liked to spread himself around."

I quickly read the first few pages. According to the report, Max had been sharing himself with six different women. Two in L.A., one in New York, two in D.C., and one in Paris. He apparently had no particular racial preference. Based on the photographs of the women attached to the back of the report, the only trait they seemed to share were unusually large bazoongas.

"My God, how did the man have time to conduct any business?"

"You tell me," Neddy said, wide-eyed. "That report only covers the last six months. Detective Smith is still researching his affairs prior to that time."

"He was fifty-two years old," I said. "What the hell was he like in his twenties? I swear he must've had a Duracell strapped to his pecker."

Neddy laughed. "A DieHard is more like it. According to Detective Smith, he wasn't even taking Viagra. When Tina said her husband had a sexual addiction, I figured she was just making up an excuse for his infidelity. But this boy had it bad. He could have been on the *Jerry Springer Show* I was watching last night."

My eyebrows kneaded together in surprise. "So you watch Springer? That's some interesting information to have in my little back pocket."

She laughed again.

I couldn't believe we were actually having a civil conversation. I watched as Neddy organized the stacks of paper in front of her. She seemed relaxed, happy even. Dressed in gray sweatpants and a powder-blue tank top, she looked like a different person. With a little makeup, she'd be a fairly nice-looking woman. Maybe we should have all of our meetings at her house. I began to feel optimistic that things might finally gel between us.

"Here's where we begin." She handed me a folder. "Our client says she didn't do it, so we operate on the assumption that she didn't. Which means we have to poke holes in any evidence that points to her guilt. And assuming we can, we need to find somebody else to point the finger at."

"What about his business partners? Maybe somebody wanted to get their hands on that thirty-five mil," I surmised.

"Detective Smith's already checked that out. Max's firm was doing great financially. It's also not unusual to have that much insurance on a top executive. As far as his business dealings, Max was on the up-and-up. Very ethical, just as Tina told us."

I scanned the documents in the folder she handed me. It contained a copy of Max's personal calendar for the last two years. "So, we're starting with his mistresses?" I asked.

"Yep. Detective Smith knows an investigator in the DA's office who has some pretty loose lips. Based on the crime scene investigator's report, they believe the killer was most likely a woman, who was no taller than 5'5". The investigator reached that conclusion based on the size-six footprints in the hotel room and the angle and force of the wounds to Max's chest. So it makes sense for us to start with the women in Mr. Max's harem. We can eliminate those with airtight alibis and big feet."

"What do you consider an airtight alibi?" I set the folder aside and went back to reading the report listing Max's mistresses.

"Anyone who has an unbiased witness who can attest to her whereabouts on the night he was killed drops off the list. For example, the woman he was seeing in New York was running a marathon in Hawaii on that day and has the photographs, the registration form, and the stub from her airplane boarding pass to prove it."

"This is really different from what we have to do in a discrimination case," I said, definitely intrigued. "We rarely have to do much digging outside of reviewing a personnel file and interviewing a few employees."

"This is the part I like most." Neddy looked over at me and actually smiled. "It's like piecing a puzzle together. Just call me Angela Lansbury."

"So what happened down at the police station last night?" I asked.

"They were definitely on a fishing expedition. I think they were just trying to scare her, but she held up pretty well. They don't have anything on her yet, but they're looking for it. Hard."

I was still itching to know what Neddy really thought about Tina's guilt. After that tongue-lashing the other day outside Tina's house, I was hesitant about broaching the subject again. Since she seemed to be in such a good mood, my curiosity forced me to test the waters.

"I know you told me you don't rely much on your gut," I said cautiously, "but I have to know. Do you think Tina killed him?"

This time Neddy didn't get upset. She paused a long time before responding to my question. "No," she said succinctly.

"Really?" I said. "What makes you think she's innocent?"

"First, she was madly in love with the man. You can see that in her eyes. He cheated on her for years and she never left. It wasn't because of the money. She stayed because her heart wouldn't let her leave."

"But wait a minute. A lot of women who profess to love their husbands end up killing them."

Neddy unfolded her legs and stretched out her arms. "But not women like Tina. Her whole life was about appearances. Joining the right clubs, helping the right charities, hosting the perfect dinner parties. I just don't believe a woman who spends her whole life pretending, suddenly snaps like that and kills her husband. Tina could've continued her charade for another fifty years."

"Well, I think she did snap," I said. "And right now, she's just going along with the act, pretending it never happened. Her being at that hotel is no coincidence."

"A coincidence isn't evidence of murder," Neddy said.

"But there're too many of them," I insisted. "That article in the *Times* claimed a hotel waiter supposedly saw a woman of Tina's height and complexion going into Max's room around the time he was killed," I pointed out. "The woman was wearing a black dress and so was Tina. A woman reserved the hotel room and gave Max's personal credit card number. Tina would have had access to it. And then there's the size-six footprints, which just happen to match Tina's shoe size."

Neddy rubbed her forehead. "The stuff about that waiter concerns me, but I learned a long time ago you can't always believe everything you read in the newspapers. And there's no telling how many women in black dresses and size six shoes were in that hotel that night."

"Okay, but you have to admit that Max's affairs definitely supply the motive."

"Yeah, but he'd been screwing around for years." She grabbed a stack of papers and flipped through them. "Tina had accepted her husband's behavior as a way of life, like a lot of women do. His affairs aren't enough to convince me. I need to see something more concrete to link her to his murder."

She was the criminal defense attorney, so I guess I had to defer to her judgment. I stood up to stretch. "Any idea who'll be prosecuting this case if Tina's charged?"

"The word is Julie Killabrew wants it bad."

"You know anything about her?"

She took a deep breath. "Regrettably, yes. She's affectionately referred to as J-Killer by her closest friends and she's the most ambitious, conniving, self-centered excuse for a human being I've ever had the displeasure of knowing."

"Sounds like you two have quite a history."

"Yeah, we do. But don't worry, in a matter of weeks you'll be hating her as much as I do. Every case for Julie is personal. A loss is unacceptable." Neddy repositioned herself on the floor. "Fortunately or unfortunately for me, I'm 4-0 against her. And she hates our firm."

"The firm? Why?"

"She used to date O'Reilly. I think it might've had something to do with him dumping her for a cute, mild-mannered Barbie-type."

Most of the women I've seen O'Reilly with were straight-up bimbettes. I couldn't imagine him with a woman like the one Neddy was describing. "How'd he end up with her?"

"Beats me," Neddy said nonchalantly. "But that's obviously why it didn't last. Julie's supersmart and has quite an imposing presence. She's almost as tall as he is. They made a very striking couple when they entered a room together."

"But why take her hatred for him out on the firm?"

"A victory against our firm is a victory over O'Reilly. And I told you, every loss for Julie is personal. She'd probably like to see the firm fold. As my Daddy used to say, she's a real piece of work. So just get ready."

Neddy got up and walked into the kitchen and peered into the refrigerator. "I wish I could offer you something to eat," she said apologetically, "but going to the grocery store is not something I tend to do on a regular basis."

I rose and took a seat at the small counter that divided Neddy's kitchen and living room. "Do you think whoever murdered him set up the tryst and intentionally lured him to the hotel room to kill him?" I asked.

"I have no idea," she said. "The champagne, the rose petals, and the teddy definitely suggest that he was waiting for someone. The police believe someone else set up the room. But we don't know for sure that Max didn't make all those arrangements himself. According to some of the women Detective Smith interviewed, he was quite romantic when he wanted to be. And with as many women as he was seeing, the odds are there had to be at least one fatal attraction in the bunch."

"Maybe he was rendezvousing with one woman and got busted by another?"

"That's certainly a possibility."

"Can't the hotel tell us when someone entered his room? I thought those plastic room keys were linked to a computer that tracks every time a door is opened."

"They are. But as luck would have it, the hotel's computer system had been on the blink for two days. The Ritz-Carlton has no record of when anyone entered or left the room. All they know is Max checked into the hotel just after six."

I was really enjoying this exchange. O'Reilly was apparently right. There was a real person hiding underneath Neddy's thick skin.

"Oh yeah," she continued, "the steak knife that killed Max, which had been wiped clean of fingerprints, was traced back to the hotel kitchen. The main course at the Crystal Stairs fundraiser was chicken, so there was no need for any steak knives. And Tina never had a reason to go into the kitchen."

"But she'd stayed there the night before," I reminded her. "She could've ordered steak and got the knife then."

"Good point." Neddy reached for a legal pad and scribbled down some quick notes. "I better have Detective Smith see if he can get a copy of her hotel bill and find out what she ordered for dinner. Let's pray she didn't have steak."

I was mulling over everything we had just discussed. "If she's charged, do you think we can get her off?" I felt like a first-year law student. This criminal stuff was a whole different ball game.

"Of course," Neddy said, not even taking time to consider my question.

"You sound awfully confident."

"They call it reasonable doubt. All we need is some police screwup, some key witness who lacks credibility, or an empty chair to point the finger at. We only have to get one 'not guilty' vote," she said, raising her right index finger. "I'd love an acquittal, but a hung jury will suit me—and I'm sure Tina, too—just fine."

Her confidence was contagious. "You seem really psyched about this case," I said.

"I guess I am. I haven't had a case this juicy in a while and I really need something to take my mind off my personal troubles." She paused as if embarrassed to have admitted that she had any problems.

I glanced down and pretended to be reading one of the reports. "You don't feel weird knowing that it's possible we could be helping a murderer go free?"

She paused, but not long. "I learned a long time ago that it's not my place to judge my clients. God'll do that. My job is to make sure Tina Montgomery has the best legal defense possible. And as far as I'm concerned, she does."

CHAPTER 14

Two days later, I was reluctantly sitting in the waiting room of my OB/GYN's office holding, but not actually reading, a copy of *Modern Motherhood*, doing what I had to do. My husband, seated next to me, had been smiling like one of those bright yellow happy faces since we left the house. The last time I remembered seeing him this excited was right after we had sex for the first time.

My own lie had landed me here. Jefferson had been pretty hot when I'd returned home at close to eleven o'clock from my meeting at Neddy's place. After two days of his foul mood, telling him I was going to make an appointment with my gynecologist to discuss getting off the pill was the only thing I could think of to make him smile again.

As soon as the words were out of my mouth, however, Jefferson offered to make the appointment for me, then proudly announced that he planned to tag along. To my dismay, Dr. Bell, my longtime gynecologist, was able to squeeze me in that afternoon.

A nurse showed us into a small office with bright pink and blue walls and told us that Dr. Bell would be with us shortly. A huge poster board behind her desk caught my attention. It contained a collage of pictures of dozens of infants, presumably ones Dr. Bell had delivered. The tiny smattering of faces, most just a few minutes old, stirred something inside me.

Jefferson reached for my hand.

"We're going to have my son's picture up there pretty soon," he said proudly, pointing at the poster board.

"Who said we're having a boy?"

"I did," he declared.

"And what if we have a girl?"

"I'll love little Jefferina to death, but we'll just have to keep on trying till Jefferson, Jr. gets here."

"Jefferina? There's no way in hell I'm sticking my daughter with a name like that," I laughed. "And what's this big power trip men have about naming their offspring after them? Isn't it enough that the child gets your last name?"

"Nah, I want me a little junior. It's a man thing. You wouldn't understand."

Before I could protest further, Dr. Bell walked in.

"Congratulations," she said, as she took a seat behind her desk. "Parenthood is an exciting venture. I like to spend some time talking to my prospective parents about the process of conceiving. It's nice to finally meet you, Jefferson. I love it when fathers really get involved."

"That's me," Jefferson beamed. "I'm one hundred percent involved and two hundred percent ready to be a daddy."

Dr. Bell winked at me. "Vernetta, I definitely think you lucked up with this man."

Jefferson smiled big, then slid his arm around my shoulders and gave me a sloppy kiss on the cheek. As conflicted as I was about being here, it felt good to see my husband so happy.

Dr. Bell picked up a folder from her desk. "First, I don't want you to be disappointed if you don't get pregnant right away." She thumbed through what I assumed was my medical file. "Since you've been using birth control pills for several years, Vernetta, it'll take a while for your body to adjust."

"How long?" Jefferson asked pointedly, before Dr. Bell had even gotten her words out.

"It differs from person to person. But I'd like to see you off the pill for at least a month, preferably three, before trying to get pregnant. During that time, you should use a condom."

Jefferson looked up and started counting off the months on his fingers. "Okay, if we get pregnant in one month...June, July,

August…December, January, February. That means my son'll be an Aquarius, just like his daddy!"

One month! Whoooaaa, cowboy. I could feel perspiration drip from my armpits.

"Aren't you the excited one," Dr. Bell said. "But again, there's no guarantee that Vernetta's going to get pregnant as soon as you two start trying. In fact, few couples do."

Jefferson smiled. "That's most people, Doc. I don't want to sound arrogant or anything, but I hail from a long line of sexually potent men. My great granddaddy had thirteen children, my granddaddy had ten and my daddy had eight."

I wanted to reach over and give Jefferson a good sock. He might as well have stood up and grabbed his nuts.

"I can't argue with a lineage like that," Dr. Bell grinned. "Since you two are so gung ho, I'd like to take some routine fertility tests just to make sure everything's in proper working order. Jefferson, you included."

He leaned back and loosened his grip around my shoulders. "That won't be necessary, Doc. I can assure you my shit is working just fine."

"Jefferson!" I screamed as Dr. Bell chuckled.

Jefferson held both of his hands in the air in a surrender position. "Please excuse my language, Doc. I meant no disrespect. If that's what we need to do, I'll take all the tests you want me to take."

Dr. Bell picked up a pad and began scribbling on it. "First, we'll need a sperm sample. We can do that here in the office today or you can collect the sample at home and bring it in."

"Let's just get it done while we're here," Jefferson said. "The sooner we get started, the better."

"And I'll also need some blood samples."

Jefferson's eyes widened.

"What's the matter, Jefferson," Dr. Bell teased. "Giving a little blood shouldn't be a problem for someone as virile as you, right?"

Jefferson was slow to respond. "Uh, so do you have to draw the blood with a needle?"

"Yep, I'm afraid that's still the way we do it," she laughed.

I reached over and grabbed Jefferson's knee. "Dr. Bell, I'm afraid my big, macho husband has a little phobia about needles. But I'm sure if I can endure the pain of childbirth, he can handle giving a little blood."

Jefferson's cheeks filled with air. "Uh, you don't have to get the sperm samples with a needle, do you, Doc?" he asked timidly.

"No," Dr. Bell said laughing. "That process isn't painful at all. I can show you to a private room for that."

"Now that's what I'm talking about," Jefferson said, perking up. "Y'all got any porno videos back there, Doc?"

"Jefferson!" This time I did sock him. "I'm sorry Dr. Bell. He's just joking around."

"No problem," she said smiling. "No, we don't have any videos, Jefferson. But we may have a magazine or two that might be of assistance."

Jefferson smiled at me gloatingly.

Dr. Bell picked up my medical file. "Vernetta, your tests are a little more involved, can you come in tomorrow?"

"She'll be here," Jefferson said, before I could even get my Palm Pilot out of my purse. "Just name the time, I'll have her here."

Fortunately, or maybe not, my schedule was clear.

Dr. Bell continued looking through my file. "Vernetta, I see you had an IUD several years ago. Did you have any problems with it?"

"No, not really," I said. "At least not that I remember. But that was a long time ago. I had the IUD removed after about a year because of all the negative news reports about them. But I didn't personally have any problems with it."

"You're very fortunate. A lot of women weren't so lucky."

Jefferson inhaled. Having a son was so important to him. *What if I couldn't?*

When my face flushed, Dr. Bell sensed that her words had frightened me and she quickly backtracked.

"I'm sorry. I don't mean to alarm you. Let's just get some testing done so we know where we stand. Even if there is a problem, you'd be amazed at what technology can do today."

"We won't be needing any technological help, Doc," Jefferson said.

He reached over and patted me on the stomach. "I'm sure this womb is ready, willing, and able to help extend the Jones family lineage. We believe in going forth and multiplying."

Both Dr. Bell and I asked the same question at exactly the same moment. "Just how much multiplying do you plan on doing?"

CHAPTER 15

One of the most immediate benefits of putting our pregnancy plans into motion was Jefferson's willingness to do almost anything I asked. The day after our visit to Dr. Bell's office, he agreed to escort me to one of O'Reilly's Friday night dinner parties. Normally, it took a good week of whining and moping around before he would consent.

"You know you owe me for this, right?" Jefferson said, as he sat on the corner of the bed, slipping on his Bruno Maglis. I was standing in front of the dresser, fussing with my hair.

"Yeah, yeah, I know," I said. "How about if I promise you twins?"

"You got it, baby." He smiled as if he expected me to actually deliver on my promise.

"Yeah, you wish. Anyway, the people I work with aren't that bad."

"That's bull," he said. "Your coworkers are insufferable."

My mouth fell open and I turned and stared at him. "Insufferable? Where'd you learn that word?"

"What? I can't use big words? What're you trying to say about the extent of my vocabulary?"

"No, nothing," I said laughing. "It's just not a word I've ever heard you use before."

"I haven't had to. I don't know any other insufferable people."

I walked over and thumped him on back of the head. "Stop being a baby. They're not that bad. And you better behave tonight." I wagged my finger in his face. "And, Jefferson, please try not to cuss."

He grabbed his keys from the nightstand and looked at me as if my words had gone in one ear and out the other. "Like I said, you owe me."

The small gathering at O'Reilly's home in Newport Beach was in full swing by the time we arrived. We were one of seven couples, not counting O'Reilly and his latest flavor of the month. This one was a tall brunette with hair that hung down to her butt. It had to be a major hassle to wrestle with that much hair every morning, I thought. She was very different from the last woman I'd seen with O'Reilly. Every woman he dated was certainly attractive. This one had a pert nose and piercing hazel eyes. But two months ago he was with a gorgeous blonde with boobs big enough to use as flotation devices. Carrie, as she later introduced herself, was barely an A cup. She was dressed in slacks and a tight-fitting sweater that showed off a firm, curvaceous body. The one thing she did have in common with the others, however, was her height. She had to be at least six feet and she was wearing flats. He definitely liked them tall. Even Julie Killabrew fit that bill.

We ordered drinks from a passing waiter and joined a small group standing around an unlit fireplace. I recognized all but two of the couples from the firm. I spotted David, accompanied by a frumpy-looking wisp of a woman, in the far corner of the room. I kept my distance to avoid having to make small talk with him.

I didn't expect to see Neddy. She never attended O'Reilly's dinner parties. Since our meeting at her house, she had been cordial, but nothing like the open, friendly person she had been that night. I knew she was under a lot of pressure because of her marital situation, so I decided not to fret about her Dr. Jekyl–Ms. Hyde personality. I just hoped she'd make up her mind to either be an angel or a devil so at least I'd know who I was dealing with.

"So, Jefferson," O'Reilly said, walking up to us and enthusiastically pumping his hand, "how's business these days?"

"I can't complain," Jefferson said.

O'Reilly lowered his voice and leaned in close to him. "I don't mean to take advantage here, but I've got a light in my downstairs study that flickers for the first few minutes after you turn it on. Maybe we could set up an appointment for you to take a look at it?"

"No problem. I might even be able to check it out before we leave tonight."

He gave Jefferson a thumbs-up. "Great. I'll definitely take you up on that offer."

When O'Reilly walked away, Jefferson whispered in my ear. "I bet Mr. Boss Man is going to try to get me to do the work for free. I'm telling you now, I'm charging his rich ass double. And can't he afford a damn stereo? Every time we come to one of these boring-ass parties, they don't ever have any music. All they do is stand around sipping wine, nibbling on chunks of fancy cheeses with names I can't pronounce, talking about work. This ain't no party, it's a fuckin' wake."

"Jefferson!" I whispered through clenched teeth. "You better behave."

"I haven't done a thing," he said, playfully backing away from me. But a minute later, he was back at it. "Look at the women in here," he said with disgust in his voice. "Ain't a single one of them got a behind. The asses up in here are flatter than the flapjacks at IHOP. That shit is not attractive."

I elbowed him in the side. Hard. "Stop it, Jefferson!" I said, trying not to laugh since I knew that would only encourage him. "Somebody might hear you. And you promised not to cuss."

"No, I didn't," he said, massaging his rib cage. "You know I'm telling the truth. That's why your ass is laughing."

A young Asian woman dressed in a black and white maid's uniform gently rang a chime, summoning everyone to the dinner table. I grabbed Jefferson by the hand and squeezed it tight. "I'm not playing, Jefferson. You better act right during dinner."

He pursed his lips and pretended to pout.

We joined the other couples at one end of a shiny, mahogany dinner table long enough to seat twenty comfortably. Black plates with tiny gold squares, gold utensils, and crystal water glasses trimmed along the rim in gold sat in front of each chair. The enormous table reminded me of the one they showed in all the news shots of the president and his cabinet. O'Reilly assumed his usual position at one end of the table, presiding over the group like the Godfather. Away from the office, he wore a thick gold chain and a pinky ring, which almost made him look like he belonged on *The Sopranos*, except he didn't have dark hair. Two male waiters scurried around the table

dishing out healthy portions of blackened salmon, sautéed aspara-
gus, and garlic mashed potatoes.

The dinner conversation, as usual, was pretty boring. A few minutes about the upcoming election for governor, a polite debate about
the next nominee for the U.S. Supreme Court, followed by a benign
joke or two from O'Reilly. Then David told a couple of highly exag-
gerated war stories about the Hayes trial.

I felt Jefferson's knee bump up against mine. I looked over at him
and he nodded in the direction of the grandfather clock in the corner
of the room. I understood his message, but there was no way we
were leaving before dessert. One, it would be rude, and two, O'Reilly
had a personal chef whose desserts rivaled Emeril's. I gave Jefferson
a look that told him to cool it.

After another few minutes, I excused myself and headed for the
bathroom, taking in O'Reilly's extensive art collection as I mean-
dered down a long, colorful hallway. The subtle lighting along the
hallway gave a comforting, seductive feeling. O'Reilly's home was an
architect's wet dream. I walked past the bathroom and peered into
his spacious playroom. It was nearly fifteen hundred square feet and
equipped with every convenience that a man who hadn't quite grown
up yet could want. The room held a fully stocked bar, a pool table, a
plasma TV, and a home theater with twenty-four plush, red velvet
seats. Like every other room in the six-thousand-square-foot house,
the ceilings ran a full two-stories high. Was this what making partnership at O'Reilly & Finney would buy? If Jefferson had a playroom like this he would never go to work.

I finished up in the bathroom and fought the urge to nose around
the rest of the house. As I made my way back toward the dining
room, I picked up the sound of Jefferson's voice at a slightly elevated
level.

"Nah, man, you got it all wrong. It ain't about that."

"That's exactly what it's about," I heard David say, equally ani-
mated.

"It's a respect thing, a pride thing," Jefferson insisted. "Ain't nobody trying to disrespect the Indians."

I rushed back into the room and slid into my seat next to
Jefferson. *Indians? What the hell were they arguing about?*

"In this day and age, it's just not politically correct for any team—
high school, college, or the pros—to have an Indian as a mascot,"

David argued. "The Washington Redskins, the Atlanta Braves, the Cincinnati Reds, and anybody else should be ashamed of themselves. Team mascots are usually animals. So what's that say about the Indians? It's just plain racist."

David regularly bragged about the fact that he had won four national debating titles during his senior year at Stanford, and he loved verbally sparring with anyone who unwittingly wandered into his web. But when in the hell did he become so politically correct? And why was Jefferson taking him on? I needed to find the proper entry point to cut the conversation short.

"Man, you're way off base!" Jefferson was talking as loud as he did when he was playing dominoes and talking trash with his boys. "I went to Gardena High. We were the Mohicans and we were proud of that. We weren't disrespecting the Indians. The image of an Indian is a warrior, somebody powerful. We were giving the Indians their props."

I nervously placed my arm around Jefferson's shoulder. "I see you've roped my husband into your little debating fetish," I said, glaring at David.

Jefferson ignored me and continued. "And you need to double-check your facts, my man. Not all teams have animals for mascots."

"Name some?" David challenged, clearly trying to put Jefferson on the spot.

Jefferson didn't miss a beat. "The Dallas Cowboys, the Tennessee Titans, the Oakland Raiders. Is that enough? You want some more?" Jefferson taunted, scooting his chair up closer to the table.

David waved his hand dismissively. "That's different."

"How?" Jefferson demanded.

"The mascots you named aren't races of people."

"Really?" Jefferson replied with a belittling laugh. "What about the Vikings? They're Scandinavian, aren't they? You don't hear no Scandinavian people demanding that Minnesota change the name of its football team."

David stuttered for a second, then recovered. "They haven't been annihilated like the Indians."

Jefferson leaned across the table and got right in David's face. "Oh, so *now* you're changing the rules," he said with a taunting smile. "It's okay as long as they haven't been mistreated?"

"You're missing my point, I—"

"Aw, man, you don't have a point," Jefferson said. "Your argument is weak, man. And anyway, there ain't enough Indians left for it to even matter."

The room went silent and everybody at the table stared at Jefferson.

I opened my mouth to speak but my brain wasn't quick enough to come up with some snappy one-liner to ease the tension bearing down on everybody in the room except Jefferson. O'Reilly finally came to my rescue.

"Okay, time out," he said, holding his hands in a T formation. "David, it looks like you may have to brush up on your debating skills. I think Jefferson just scored a few points on you."

David scratched the back of his neck and laughed uncomfortably along with everybody else while Jefferson glowed with satisfaction.

CHAPTER 16

Total silence filled the car during the first fifteen minutes of our ride home. Jefferson hated it when I gave him the silent treatment. I knew there was no way he'd be able to make the entire trip home without saying something.

"Okay," he said finally, "you want to tell me why you're trippin'? Are you mad because I showed up that white boy tonight?" He glanced over at me sitting in the passenger seat of his Chrysler 300. He was one of those drivers who needed to make eye contact with his passenger when he talked. I wanted to tell him to pay attention to the road before we crashed.

Instead, I continued staring out of the window, ignoring his question. We were headed north on the San Diego Freeway. Even though it was almost ten o'clock on a Friday night, the traffic was still fairly heavy.

"If you're pissed off, at least tell me why," Jefferson prodded.

Even when Jefferson was upset, he was usually willing to talk things out. I, on the other hand, closed up like a clam. If we had a serious argument, it could take a good week before I had cooled off enough to say a civil word to him. The last time we had a big blowout, he told me I needed to take some anger management classes. That had pissed me off even more.

But this time, I wanted him to know why I was so mad, and as hard as it was to do, I forced myself to speak. "I just wish you hadn't gotten into that stupid debate with David," I said finally, my gaze still fixed on the traffic.

"I was just expressing my opinion," he said apologetically. "At least I didn't cuss."

I turned to look at him. "Yeah, but your opinion wasn't exactly appropriate." My words were unintentionally condescending.

He sucked his teeth. "Appropriate? Appropriate for who? You telling me I can't say what I think?"

"That's not what I'm saying. You need to think about the setting you're in and how you might be perceived before you go sounding off like that."

"How I might be perceived?" he said, practically shouting. "I don't give a fuck what they think about me."

I let out a long sigh. "Never mind. You don't get it."

Jefferson started gnawing on his lower lip and I could feel the car pick up speed. "If you're telling me I can't be who I am, then I guess I don't get it. What? You're scared they're not going to make you a partner or something just because I said I think it's okay for Indians to be mascots?"

"That's not what I'm talking about, Jefferson. You need to look at the big picture."

"The big picture?" Now he *was* shouting. "I have no idea what in the hell you're talking about."

"Yeah, I know," I said sarcastically.

I could feel him seething. "You're acting just as uppity as them stuck-up people we just left," he said. "It was just a conversation, Vernetta. A debate. You expect me to back down on my opinion?"

"No, I just wanted you to keep it to yourself."

"Why?"

I closed my eyes. I wasn't sure how to explain what I meant. "Because some of the people I work with are jerks," I finally said. "And they don't understand how other people view the world."

"So I'm supposed to act like one of them? This is some bullshit!" He made an unnecessary lane change, cutting off another driver and giving me a momentary scare. "If I can't say what I think, then don't be taking me around them weak-ass people. You spend too much time worrying about what other people think of you. You don't need their validation. They're going to make you a partner because you're a good attorney. Not because you're kissing somebody's ass."

"Just forget it, Jefferson." I didn't want to talk anymore. But I knew it was too late for that. A lot of women complain about men who won't communicate. Jefferson loves to talk and when he gets mad, he won't shut up until he's said everything he has to say and then some.

"I'll tell you something else," he said, looking over at me for far too long before turning back to the highway. "I bet I feel better about myself than everybody at that fuckin' table. I don't need six figures or a house that's too big to even live in or a two-hundred-thousand-dollar Benz to make me feel like a man. When I look at myself in the mirror, I know who the fuck I am. And I don't have to adjust my opinion to fit anybody else's bullshit."

"Do you have to cuss so much?"

"Yep." This time he smiled. "It helps me reinforce my point. If that dude O'Reilly had taken my side, that punk-ass David wouldn't have said shit because he ain't got a damn backbone. That little boy gets up in the morning, licks his finger and holds it out the window to see which way the wind's blowing and off he goes. You see how red he got? He was embarrassed because somebody with less education was going toe-to-toe with him."

Jefferson was quiet for just a moment, then started up again. "I like me just the way I am and I ain't changing what I think to try to impress nobody."

We rode the rest of the way home in silence.

Jefferson pulled into the driveway and shut off the engine. He threw open his door and had one foot on the ground before he realized I hadn't made a move.

"So you sleeping in the car tonight?" he asked.

I was still too mad to even respond. Neither one of us said anything for a few seconds, then Jefferson got back inside and shut his door.

"Look baby, we shouldn't be arguing over this. We had a cool evening. Let's just forget about it."

I kept my arms folded across my chest and my head turned away from him.

"C'mon, baby, don't be mad at me. I can't help it 'cause I like Indians."

I felt a smile coming on and tried hard to suppress it. I hated the way Jefferson could piss me off one second and make me laugh the next.

He reached over and tickled my earlobe, which he knew annoyed me. "C'mon, baby, don't be mad. It ain't my fault you work with a bunch of tight-ass white people."

"Stop it, Jefferson!" I slapped his hand away, and failed to stifle a laugh.

"See, I made you laugh." He tickled my earlobe again. "You know you like Indians, too."

"Stop it, boy!" My laughter was now unrestrained. "This isn't funny, Jefferson." I was more angry at myself for laughing than with him for making me laugh.

"Okay, how about this? What if I apologize to the Indians?" Jefferson waited for me to respond, and when I didn't, he rolled down the window, gripped the roof of the car, and hoisted half of his body through the opening. He looked up to the sky and started shouting. "Oh, Great Geronimo, please understand. I meant no disrespect to your people. Y'all get big props from me. I think y'all was some bad dudes. Y'all just fucked up when you trusted the white man and let him take all your shit."

I was howling with laughter now and so was Jefferson.

"You're crazy," I said, as he pulled himself back inside.

"Yep. Crazy about your little prissy ass."

Jefferson took me into his arms and kissed me. I eagerly kissed him back.

"If you don't stop being mad at me," he said, "I'm not giving you any tonight."

"Who said I wanted some?"

"You did."

"I don't recall saying that."

"You didn't say it out loud," he said with a smirk, "but you're definitely thinking it. I could tell by the way you just kissed me."

"I hate you, you know that?" I said smiling.

"Yep," Jefferson said, as he pulled me closer to him and kissed me again. "C'mon inside so you can show me how much."

CHAPTER 17

The following Tuesday morning, I got to work to find a voice mail message from Neddy asking me to meet her at Tina Montgomery's house at two o'clock. I picked up on the alarm in her voice after her first few words. One of her contacts at the D.A.'s office had given her an unofficial heads-up that Tina would be charged with Max Montgomery's murder any day now. According to her source, Julie Killabrew would be trying the case and the politicos she reported to had given her the nod to make it a media spectacle. Neddy had a meeting out of the office, but promised to give me all the details when we met at Tina's house.

I spent most of the morning finishing up some outstanding matters on my other cases. I dictated a couple of letters, returned some telephone calls, and edited a brief while gulping down a Big Mac, Diet Coke, and fries. I left the office for Tina's place around one and was surprised to find that Neddy hadn't arrived by the time I got there ten minutes late.

The tiny woman in white met me at the door but didn't make me wait in the foyer. This time she led me into what looked like a second living room. It was just as large as the other one, but was a tad less formal. No purple here. There was a definite green theme going on. Pea green curtains, apple green chairs, a forest green couch. All of the furniture was an ultra-contemporary mix of lacquer, glass, and chrome. If the furniture hadn't been so expensive, the room would have made a perfect cover photo for an IKEA catalogue.

Tina was already seated, her silver wine goblet in hand. The woman apparently found a great deal of solace in a wine bottle.

"Would you like something to drink?" she asked.

"A Diet Coke would be nice," I said. She called for the woman in white, and used her name, Kinga, for the first time.

As we waited for Kinga to return with my drink, there was a deafening silence in the room. After our last meeting, I was afraid to open my mouth for fear of saying the wrong thing. *Where the hell was Neddy?* But I couldn't just sit there and say nothing.

"This is certainly a fabulous house," I said looking around. "Did you decorate it yourself?"

"Most of it. It was really a lot of fun. I was almost sorry when I'd finished."

I didn't know where to go from there. The thought suddenly came to me that I was alone in a room with a woman who had probably brutally stabbed a man to death, a man she supposedly loved. What if she were emotionally unstable? She might snap and plunge a knife into my chest, too. I tried to force myself to think about something else.

"Well, how're you holding up?" The question sounded insincere, even to me.

"As well as can be expected, I guess."

She was wearing a blue jogging suit, and her face was fully made-up, her lipstick, blush, and eyeliner expertly applied. But like before, the foundation that covered her face failed to camouflage the puffiness around her eyes. I could picture her in the mirror, applying layer after layer after layer of foundation. The thought that she had probably been crying made me feel guilty about what I had been thinking about her. Maybe she wasn't a murderer after all.

"So what happens next?" she asked.

I don't know! I'm not a criminal attorney. Didn't you know that when you hired me?

"Well, uh, once, I should say, if, they charge you, you'll have to go down to the police station to get booked, which basically means getting photographed and fingerprinted." I knew that much from *Law & Order.* "Then there'll be an arraignment." *I think.*

"What exactly is an arraignment?" she asked.

My brain time-traveled back to Boalt Hall and my first-year criminal law class but came up blank. The procedural fundamentals of employment law and criminal law were as different as peanut butter and jelly. Asking an employment lawyer to explain the criminal arraignment process was like asking a podiatrist to demonstrate the insertion of a heart valve. But I considered myself a good lawyer. And all good lawyers knew how to wing it.

"An arraignment is when you formally enter a plea of guilty or not guilty and when the court determines whether there's enough evidence to charge you." *Damn*. Did I just describe a preliminary hearing or an arraignment or a combination of both?

Kinga arrived with my Diet Coke before Tina could ask me another question. I took as long as I could to remove the plastic twist-off cap and pour the brown liquid into a tall crystal glass filled with ice. I wasn't sure I'd ever drank Diet Coke from a glass this fancy before. I hoped I didn't drop it. I took a long swallow. Anything to keep from having to answer another one of Tina's questions.

"We can go over this stuff in more detail when Neddy gets here," I said, sitting my glass on a coaster that looked like it was made of fourteen-carat gold and probably was.

"I can't believe they actually think I killed my husband." I heard emotion in her voice and prayed that she didn't start crying. "I'll get out on bail, right?" Her eyes were pleading with me to tell her exactly what she wanted to hear.

Hell if I know. Neddy, where are you?

Once again, when in doubt—hedge. "That's our hope, but you can never know what a particular judge will do. We wanted to meet with you tonight to talk about our defense strategy. The prosecution's case is almost completely circumstantial. That's a plus. And in some people's minds, your husband won't be all that sympathetic a victim because of his extramarital activities."

"But that could also hurt me," Tina correctly pointed out. "They'll assume I had a reason to kill him. Not to mention the eight million dollars in insurance money."

Did you kill him?

"You're right," I said. *Neddy, please get your ass here!*

As if on cue, I heard the doorbell ring.

When Kinga escorted Neddy into the room, she looked a mess. Her hair was wild and uncombed, as if she had just taken off a hat. Her clothes were disheveled and her skin was ashen and gray. She gave Tina a brief hug, then sat down.

"Okay, let's get started." She fumbled around in her briefcase and pulled out several folders.

Neddy started to speak when Tina leaned across the coffee table and placed a hand on her knee. "Are you okay?"

Neddy smiled weakly. "Shouldn't I be asking you that?"

"I'm serious," Tina said. "You don't look so good."

"Let's just call it the stress of divorce. The most ugly, angry, awful divorce you could ever imagine." Neddy sat back in the chair. "I just had a face-to-face with my husband and his attorney and it didn't go too well."

Neither Tina nor I knew what to say.

Neddy closed her briefcase and set it on the floor. "Your husband may've had affairs, but at least he kept it out of your face and paid the damn bills. My lazy excuse for a spouse screwed around, refused to work, and now expects me to pay him close to four thousand dollars a month in alimony for the next four years."

Tina eyed me as if it were my place to offer the appropriate words of comfort. But I had no idea what to say.

"I'm sorry," Neddy said, closing her eyes. "I really shouldn't be boring you two with my troubles. But I need to be up front with you. I'm seriously thinking about asking the firm for a leave of absence."

At first I couldn't tell what emotion had attacked my body. Then I realized it was relief, followed closely by a twinge of disappointment. There was no way I could handle this case by myself. If Neddy was out, that meant I was, too.

"There's another lawyer in our office, David Winslow, who's a former D.A.," Neddy continued. "And since you haven't been charged yet, it would be pretty simple for him to jump in and take my place. If I were ever in trouble, he'd be the person I'd call. David and Vernetta just finished a big trial together, so they're used to working as a team."

What the hell was this? I'd rather have somebody stab me in the eyeballs with a pitchfork than try another case with David. If Neddy was bailing, so was I. Besides, I had to get to work on making some babies. I couldn't believe Neddy didn't have the courtesy to discuss her decision with me before raising it with our client. That was more than disrespectful and I was definitely going to tell her that.

I reached for my Diet Coke and took a sip. I guess I was too busy dealing with my own mixed emotions to notice that Tina had gone into cardiac arrest.

"You can't take a leave! My life depends on you!" There was so much desperation in her voice it scared me. "You got that guy off who was accused of killing his wife. Everybody thought he was guilty. But you proved he wasn't."

Does that mean you're guilty? I could tell from the way Neddy looked at Tina that her thoughts were similar to mine. Besides, Neddy didn't prove that the man was innocent, only that the state failed to prove that he was guilty.

Neddy moved over to where Tina was sitting and placed her hand on Tina's forearm. "Mrs. Montgomery—"

"Call me Tina."

"I'm sorry. Tina, from what you've told me so far, I think you have a very solid defense if you do end up being charged. But just because my client went free in that case, doesn't mean I'll have a victory in your case."

Tina reached for her goblet, cupping it with both hands. She did not like Neddy's answer.

"I'm not expecting miracles. But I need you in my corner," she begged. "I didn't kill my husband and I know you can prove it." Tina's hands shook as she raised the goblet to her lips. "Maybe you just need a long, relaxing weekend. Why don't we call off this meeting and do something fun. We can go to Odyssey in the Marina. A massage and a facial is exactly what you need. It'll be my treat."

"That sounds wonderful," Neddy said, clasping her hands in her lap, "but I'm afraid our little outing wouldn't make a nice headline on the front page of the *L.A. Times* tomorrow morning. I can see it now: MURDER SUSPECT AND HER ATTORNEYS LOUNGE AT DAY SPA. Besides, the only thing that'll relax me is getting word that my soon-to-be ex has disappeared from the face of the earth."

Tina looked over at me, then back at Neddy. "You say that now, but there's something about loving a man, really loving a man, that prevents you from ever really letting him go."

Tina had a distant look in her eyes. It was obvious that she was thinking about Max.

"Even when I knew Max was spreading himself around, I kept hoping and praying he would simply grow tired of it. But even in his fifties, he still ran the streets like a teenager. And while I cried myself to sleep far too many nights, I still wanted him in my life. I still wanted this life," she said, sweeping her hand around the room. She patted Neddy's hand. "Just focus on the things that made you fall in love with your husband. You can't punish the man for being who he is. It's probably not even his fault. There're a lot of factors beyond our control that make us the people we are."

Neddy's face had an exasperated expression. She wasn't buying Tina's it-ain't-his-fault line.

"You really believe that?" she said, astonished. "That a man who cheats on his wife isn't to blame for his actions?"

I was surprised at her tone. Neddy might as well have told the woman that she was stupid for hanging onto such a cheat.

"It's not that simple, but yes, I do," Tina said. "My husband had a lot of issues that date back to his childhood. Max's mother was rarely around. And when she was, she was running men through the house like a grocery store checkstand. As my therapist explained it, Max spent most of his adult life searching for the love he never got from his mother. And he found it in sex. Even though he couldn't keep it in his pants, he was basically good to me," she said.

Neddy returned to her chair, as if she needed to distance herself from Tina. She closed her eyes for just a second and an uncomfortable silence filled the room.

"Well, Lawton Joseph Brown was never really good to me," she said. "Don't ask me how I fell in love with a man who humiliated me for most of the time I was with him." Her hands gripped both arms of the chair and her voice fell to a sad monotone. "I'd be too embarrassed to even describe the way he treated me sometimes. Losing my son was the worst of all."

A look of concern glazed Tina's face and I assumed she wanted to ask Neddy how her son had died. So did I. But we didn't. We both somehow knew that Neddy just needed to talk. So we listened.

"Lawton is the classic womanizer," Neddy continued, seemingly more for her own benefit than ours. "For him, lying is as easy as breathing. He feels no guilt saying exactly what he thinks you want to hear. I can still remember the precise moment that I knew I had to leave, no matter how much I thought I loved him. We'd had a really ugly fight. Tears were streaming down my face. I reminded him that we supposedly loved each other. You know what he said to me?" She looked as if she were still shocked by his words. "I'll never forget his words as long as I'm black. He said, and this is a quote: 'I know I said I love you, but those are just words and words don't mean nothing to me.' "

The pain on Neddy's face was real enough to touch. My heart went out to both her and Tina.

"The difference between your husband and mine," Neddy went on, "is that Lawton doesn't mind lying and hurting people. Every woman he was with thought she was the one and only. They had no idea he was married. He can't blame who he is on his mother. He had two wonderful parents."

Tina looked away.

All this emotion was dragging me down. I felt lucky as hell. All my husband wanted was a son. I needed to run home to Jefferson and tell him how much I appreciated him.

Kinga popped in to refill Tina's empty wine goblet. I wondered how she knew exactly when to show up. *Was she listening in?* Her arrival allowed our conversation to finally turn to the case. Neddy reviewed the various pretrial stages and then discussed our preliminary defense strategy. She told Tina that we'd have a better idea of our precise strategy once we saw the prosecution's witness list and evidence. Neddy was hoping to arrange a voluntary surrender if Tina was charged. She reminded Tina for the second time that it was important not to withhold any information from us, good or bad. Doing that, she said, could cause us to be blindsided in court. Neddy then called Kinga back into the room and instructed both of them to call us immediately if the police or anyone else contacted them about the case.

Tina showed us to the door and we walked somberly down the walkway together. The minute we got outside the gate, Neddy headed off in the direction of her car without even saying good-bye to me.

"Hey, wait a minute," I said, taking giant steps to catch up with her. "Are you really serious about asking for a leave of absence?"

"Yeah, I'm pretty sure I will." She seemed anxious to leave.

"Well, there's no way I'm going to handle this case with David."

"That's not my problem," she said coldly.

I couldn't believe her attitude. The old Neddy was definitely back. I tried to remember that she was probably just stressed out from everything her husband was putting her through. "Well, it would've been nice if you had discussed your plans with me before raising it with the client."

"I don't report to you," she snapped.

I couldn't take it anymore. I didn't care what she was going through. It didn't give her the right to be rude to me. "I have no idea why you find it so easy to be such a bitch," I said, my hands on my hips. "There's no reason our relationship has to be like this. I know you're going through a difficult time right now, but I—"

"I don't need your sympathy."

"And I don't plan on giving it to you," I spat, "because you don't deserve it. You make your own situation worse by being so damn hateful."

She glared at me for a long time, then totally shocked me by crumbling into tears right before my eyes. She let her briefcase and purse fall to the ground and dumped her head into her hands. Her sobs were so loud I had to look around to make sure we weren't drawing any attention. We were standing on a public sidewalk and Neddy was bawling like a five-year-old. I had no idea what to do.

Damn! Part of me wanted to reach over and hug her, but I didn't know if the snake in her would rear up and bite me. So I just stood there hoping she wasn't having a nervous breakdown.

"I'm sorry," she said finally, wiping her eyes with the back of her hand. "You're right. I've been a total bitch. It's just that I—that everything is so crazy right now. I just—"

She started sobbing again.

I watched her for a few more seconds, then took a step closer to her. When she didn't move away, I took another step.

"You don't have to apologize," I said finally. I reached over and pulled her into my arms. And to my surprise, she let me.

CHAPTER 18

Thirty minutes later, Neddy and I were sitting outside the Starbucks on San Vicente Boulevard near the UCLA campus, sipping iced lattes and watching the traffic whiz by. We didn't talk much. Just enjoyed the warm, early evening air, lost in our own individual thoughts.

After a long while, I blurted out words that surprised even me. "I have to get pregnant."

"You *have* to get pregnant? Says who?"

"Says my husband."

"Whoooaaa. I have to warn you," Neddy said, turning to face me, "it's kinda hard for me to talk about the male species in an objective light these days. But I'll say this, it must be nice to have a man who actually wants to be a father. Lawton wanted me to have an abortion."

I didn't know how to respond to that statement, so my lips remained sealed.

Neddy shifted in her chair and stared straight ahead. "Colin would've been four years old today." Her voice was just a whisper, as if she were speaking only to herself.

That explained her outburst outside Tina's house earlier. My heart went out to her. I couldn't imagine what it was like to lose a child.

"Thanks," she said after a few minutes.

"For what?"

"For not saying something useless, like 'I'm sorry for your loss.' I can only imagine the rumors that circulated through the firm. For the first six months after Colin died, they watched me like I was a pressure cooker ready to blow any second, and I guess I was. I know I've been really awful to deal with lately, but I just can't seem to get it together."

"What happened to your son?" I finally asked.

She paused and then continued as if she were reading directly from a police report. "Lawton left the front door open and Colin marched right out of it into the path of a 2002 Ford Explorer driving 45 in a 25-mile-an-hour zone. California license plate number XZ57145. My worthless excuse for a husband, who happened to be between jobs at the time, was busy smoking a joint and talking to his bookie on the phone." She fidgeted with her empty Starbucks cup. "I have no idea why I can still remember that license plate number."

Tears began to well up in her eyes and she turned away. "Why don't you want kids?" she asked.

"I do, but the timing's a little off."

"Your husband's not willing to wait?"

I began cracking my knuckles, a nervous habit of mine I was trying to break. "I think he's just concerned about how long he'll have to wait."

"And how long will he?"

"Okay, now you sound just like Jefferson," I chuckled. "Frankly, I'd like to make partner first."

"Motherhood is an incredible gift," she said. "Don't take it for granted. I can't imagine a deeper love." For just a moment, she had a blissful look in her eyes. "When Colin was born, he was so tiny and helpless, I was scared to death I was going to do something wrong and maim him for life. When I looked at him, I would have these incredibly intense feelings. I found it so amazing that we had actually produced another human being. Anybody who says miracles don't happen never witnessed the birth of a child. I thank God for the few years I had him."

"You're not angry with God for taking him from you?"

"Nope. Never was. I guess that's what faith is all about."

The traffic on the street in front of us was finally beginning to thin out. We refocused on the cars zooming by.

"Just make sure your husband is who he says he is," Neddy advised gently.

I grabbed a chair from another table and propped up my feet. "You can never be sure of that," I said.

She nodded. "That's certainly no lie. I'm a good lawyer. I'm smart, I'm perceptive, and I've made my living for quite awhile defending murderers and rapists. Not everybody has the *chutzpah* to do that type of work," she said. "But I definitely fell for the okey-doke when it came to Lawton. He showed up at a time when my life was all work and no play. And frankly, there hadn't been that many guys before him. He promised to love me for life and I never stopped to look at who he was. Everything about him flashed warning signals."

"Like what?"

"First, he couldn't keep a job for more than a couple of months. Then, he insisted on getting married right away. I met him at a hotel in Atlanta, where I was attending a conference. It should've rung a bell when he proposed after only five months of long-distance dating and agreed to pick up and move to L.A. Supposedly because he couldn't stand being away from me. While he was looking for work out here, he ran through money, my money, like it was water."

She lowered her head for a moment. "But I'd never had a man who made me feel like he could stop the earth from turning for me. When we were dating, he pampered me to death. Trips, gifts, foot massages, you name it. But then we got married and I needed a husband, not a spoiled little boy. But he couldn't be somebody he wasn't. And, of course, I wasn't the only woman in his life. Never was."

"Sometimes it's hard to see the bad side of a person when all he's showing you is the good," I said.

"I saw the signs," Neddy said, not content to put it all on Lawton. "But I ignored them. After the third time an angry woman approached our dinner table or called the house at two in the morning when I was visiting him in Atlanta, I shouldn't have accepted his excuse about her being an unstable ex-girlfriend. I think I knew, but I told myself I was special. He'd never been married before and he chose to marry me, not one of them. Of course, in retrospect, I realize now that my financial status obviously played a big role in that decision. Lawton definitely could've given Mr. Max Montgomery a run for his money. Except he didn't have the cash to bed-hop around the world." She laughed.

"You'll fall in love again," I said.

"Not if I can help it." She tossed her cup into a nearby trash can. "Sorry about tonight. You're right, I should've talked to you before telling Tina about my plans to take a leave of absence. I was also out of line by not trying harder to reach you that night Tina was called in for questioning."

"No problem," I said.

"No problem? Girl, you were ready to kick my ass."

I nodded playfully. "Yeah, I thought I was going to have to eventually. You know I'm from Compton, right? Don't let this suit fool you."

She grinned. "I'd whip you like Laila Ali."

"I don't think so. I got youth on my side."

"Aw, now that was cold!"

I laughed and enjoyed hearing her do the same. Finally, I was seeing the real Neddy, the one O'Reilly had described, and I liked what I saw.

"Don't leave the case," I said, changing our light mood. "I don't really want to work with David again."

"Wow, you despise the guy so much you'd rather work with me?"

"Any day," I said. "You've got your mood swings and all, but I hear you're an incredible trial attorney. I could probably learn a lot from you."

"Hey, buttering me up might actually work."

Our attention drifted back to the dissipating traffic on San Vicente Boulevard. After a few minutes Neddy stood up. "You want a refill?"

"No, thanks."

She returned a few minutes later with another iced latte and quietly sipped it.

"How long did it take you to get to the point where you could defend somebody you knew might be guilty and feel okay about it?" I asked.

She shrugged. "Not that long, really. It's kind of an ego trip to see if you can get them off. For every guilty person I help go free, there're a dozen innocent brothers rotting in some prison cell. So it all balances out in my mind."

"I have a good friend who's a public defender. That's his rationale, too," I said.

Neddy set her drink on the table and stretched her arms over her head. "Don't give me that," she said, yawning. "You've defended people accused of discrimination."

"That's different."

"Not really."

"My clients never killed anybody," I insisted.

"Yeah, but I'm sure you've thought some of them were actually guilty of discrimination," Neddy said. "Are you telling me you've never forced a mediocre settlement down the throat of some poor black man when you knew if the case went to trial and all the facts came out, a jury would award him ten times what the case settled for?"

I couldn't exactly say that I hadn't.

"So in my mind, what you do is not much different from what I do when I defend a murder suspect," she continued. "We both protect the bad guys. In your cases, the victim's alive, but his life's been destroyed by your client's actions just the same."

I had never looked at it quite that way. "I guess you may have a point," I said.

Neddy began tracing the rim of her cup with her finger. "To be honest, I've had some issues with some of the people I've defended over the years, but I don't have any issues with Tina Montgomery. In fact, I think I empathize with her. You do everything you can to love a man and he refuses to love you back. It would drive anybody to murder."

"Wait a minute," I said, sitting up. "Not anybody. I don't think I could kill."

"Then you're fooling yourself. Everybody has the potential."

"If my life were in danger or if I were trying to protect somebody I loved, yeah, I probably could," I said. "But I'm just not the kind of person who flies off into a rage. If I went home tonight and found Jefferson in bed with another woman, I'd be devastated but I wouldn't run to the kitchen, grab a butcher knife, and start stabbing him to death."

"Well, maybe you're different, but I'd be lying if I said I didn't have dreams about seeing Lawton laid out on the floor with a chalk line around his body."

"Nobody deserves to die the way Max Montgomery died," I replied.

"Lawton does," she said quietly.

I looked at her in disbelief. "You don't really mean that."

"Like hell I don't. Every time I think about the fact that I'm going to have to pay that asshole alimony, that's exactly how I feel."

"Well, we asked for equal rights didn't we?"

Neddy twisted her lips. "I don't know what's so damn equal about it. Lawson didn't work for almost the last six months before I moved out because he was too busy getting high. Just tell me how in the hell he's entitled to nearly a fourth of my monthly income for the next four years and half the value of the house I bought. He never paid a dime of the mortgage."

"Hey, you happen to live in a no-fault divorce state. It's the law."

"Law, my ass. I should've gotten a prenup. Then he wouldn't be getting jack."

I laughed. Neddy was beginning to remind me of Special.

She shook her head. "If I had asked for a prenup, he probably would've tried to talk me out of it. And I was so in love with him I would've let him. But there's no way I could've endured what Tina Montgomery did."

"Well, I just hope the police don't end up charging her," I said. "There's a good chance my marriage might not survive it."

"If Tina is charged, you can handle the arraignment," Neddy offered.

"So you're not leaving the case?"

"I don't know," she said, her face a ball of confusion. "One minute I want to stay, the next, I want to leave. Unlike a lot of lawyers, I really love this stuff. It could be a pretty challenging trial. It's probably just what I need to keep my mind off the divorce."

"I know my motives might be a bit suspect," I said smiling, "but I agree wholeheartedly. A nice juicy, attention-grabbing trial is exactly what an experienced trial attorney like you needs to get your engines all revved up again. And thanks, but no thanks, regarding the arraignment. I've never done one before. I'd like to watch you work for a while."

"It's easy," she said encouragingly. "It probably won't even last five minutes."

"I'd still prefer to defer to you," I said. "Anyway, Tina likes you better."

Neddy made a face. "No she doesn't."

"Yes, she does," I insisted. "I was dying before you got there tonight, trying to think up something to say to the woman. She definitely has a better rapport with you."

"If that's true," Neddy said dryly, "it's only because we share something in common—the pain of betrayal."

CHAPTER 19

Within a couple of days, Neddy was dropping by my office and chatting me up like a long-lost sorority sister. We'd even had lunch together and were planning to do it again. O'Reilly was right. She was actually a pretty cool person. I just prayed that this new kinder, gentler Neddy would stick around for a while.

We continued to hear rumors that Tina's indictment was imminent, but so far, no word. Neddy and I had both put contingency plans in place to transition our existing cases to other attorneys in the firm in the event the Montgomery case went into full swing.

I was trying to finish editing an opposition brief I had to file the next day in a sexual harassment case when my cell phone rang. I could see from the caller-ID display that it was Jefferson calling me from home. I glanced at my watch. It was 7:43 P.M. I picked up, knowing he was about to berate me for working so late again.

"Hey sweetie," I said, hoping to soften him up. "Why're you calling me on my cell? You know I'm at the office."

"Because," he grunted.

"Because what?"

"Because I'm jealous of that place for seeing you more than I do and it kills me to even dial the damn number."

"Aw, baby, I'll make it up to you," I said, in a mock baby voice I'd heard Special use with one of her men. "I promise."

"Yeah, yeah, yeah, promises, promises. So how's it going?" he said, a hint of anticipation in his voice.

"Slow but sure. So what's up?" I knew he had a specific purpose for calling, but for some reason he was beating around the bush.

"Can't I just call to say hello to my woman?"

"You could, but you rarely do. So what's on your mind?"

"I was just thinking," he said, actually sounding nervous, "maybe we could get started making my son tonight."

I tried to speak, but I couldn't. It had only been a week since our visit to Dr. Bell's office. "Jefferson, the doctor told us I needed to be off the pill for at least a month, preferably three."

"Aw, that's only a safety precaution. I was just talking to my sister. She got pregnant with Quentin a week after she went off the pill and he was perfectly healthy."

Jefferson's excitement about fatherhood amazed me. Three days earlier, I'd caught him checking the package of birth control pills I kept in the medicine cabinet. I pretended not to notice when he shoved the container back on the shelf and picked up a bottle of Advil instead. At first I was angry because I figured he was counting them to make sure I had actually stopped taking them. Then I realized he was right not to trust me. Every time I opened the medicine cabinet, I was overcome with doubt about our decision to start a family.

"Now get your ass home," Jefferson said. "I got something big and juicy waiting for you."

"I bet you do," I laughed nervously. Dr. Bell said it was unlikely that I'd get pregnant right away, but she didn't know my luck. The minute one of Jefferson's little spermazoids got loose, my eggs would be cooked.

"We haven't even gotten our fertility tests back yet. Shouldn't we wait?"

"Stop worrying. I'm sure everything's fine. Come on home so I can prove it to you." There was a sexy playfulness in his voice. "Besides, Jefferson, Jr. is anxious to get here and make his mark on the world."

"You know, I still haven't decided to hang my son with that name."

"Ain't nothing wrong with my name," he said, offended. "It's got presidential heritage written all over it."

"Yeah, right. Wasn't President Jefferson the one making all them babies with his slave, Sally Hemings?"

"See, it's no coincidence that I'm named after a white boy who was out getting his freak on way back in the day."

I laughed. "Boy, you're nuts."

"Just hurry up and get home so we can make some babies," he ordered.

As I began packing up, I realized that Jefferson's excitement about having a son was slowly growing on me. In my line of work, there was no perfect time to plan for anything, much less a child. There would always be another big case, another deposition to take, and another brief to write. There was really no reason to put off starting a family.

When I walked through the door, Jefferson greeted me wearing only a towel wrapped around his waist. His body was all oiled up and he was wearing his favorite cologne, Jordan by Michael, which also happened to be my favorite. He took my purse and briefcase and set them on the dining room table.

I opened my mouth to speak, but he shushed me. "I'm running things tonight."

Jefferson undressed me right there in the darkened living room, then helped me slip into a red silk robe. He took my hand and led me into the den where several layers of blankets were laid out on the floor and our gas fireplace was burning low. There had to be at least twenty candles positioned all over the room. An oil burner gave off a pleasant, sensual aroma and Luther Vandross was crooning *If Only for One Night,* real low.

Though I was much too paranoid not to follow the doctor's advice about waiting a month before trying to conceive, I found myself silently praying that God would bless us with the son Jefferson so badly wanted. I spotted a plate of tiny tuna sandwiches, cranberry juice and Doritos laid out on the coffee table.

"Is this dinner?" I laughed, pointing at the display.

"Nah, just a snack. I didn't want you getting too full since we've got some important business to take care of tonight. I knew if I gave you some wine, your ass would be asleep in five minutes."

We crouched down on the floor and Jefferson positioned his body over mine and opened my loosely tied robe. "Your body's beautiful," he said, and ran his hands up and down my thighs. "Promise me you'll look like this when you're sixty-five."

"I promise."

"You lawyers lie about everything, you know that," he said grinning. "I love you, girl."

As I stared at my happy husband, I thought about the men Tina and Neddy had fallen for and an overwhelming feeling of gratitude, affection, and desire took hold of me. I drew Jefferson to me. We held each other, then kissed for a long, long time, our bodies pressed hard against each other. He rolled over and pulled me on top of him and I could feel his heart beating hard against my chest. The stubble along his chin grazed my breasts as he kissed his way up to my neck and back down again. We drank from each other, with a hurried, ravenous thirstiness, both of us deliriously in love and anxious to make a life.

Hours later, I heard the faint ringing of the telephone. I glanced at the clock. It was 7:15 A.M. Whenever my phone rang before eight o'clock it was usually Special. I fumbled around until I finally found the telephone sitting on a nearby end table. As I reached for the receiver, I felt a shot of pain streak down the middle of my back. We definitely wouldn't be sleeping on the floor again anytime soon.

I answered without waiting to hear what Special had to say. "I'm a married woman now," I said groggily. "You can't be calling me at all hours of the day and night just to brag about your sexual conquests."

"What? It's me. Neddy."

"Oh, I'm sorry." I sat up. Neddy had never called me at home. Not to mention this early in the morning. It had to be important. "Are you okay?"

"I'm fine," she said. "But I can't say the same for our client. You need to meet me at Tina's house right away. The police just showed up with a search warrant."

CHAPTER 20

I showered and dressed in a flash and less than an hour later, I arrived at the Montgomery mansion to find the place crawling with L.A.'s finest. Judging from the hoards of black and whites parked haphazardly in front of the house, there could only be a handful of officers left to protect the rest of the city. I was surprised to see a respectable number of female cops milling about doing whatever it is police do at a scene like this.

As I approached the steel gates leading to the walkway, I came face-to-face with a short, balding man wearing a navy T-shirt with LAPD tattooed across his chest in bright yellow letters. He raised his hand, palm forward like a crossing guard, motioning for me to freeze.

"I'm sorry, miss, there's a police investigation underway here at the moment. You're gonna have to come back a little later." His words were drenched in machismo. His job was obviously his life.

"I'm Vernetta Henderson," I said, distracted by all the activity going on around us. "I'm Mrs. Montgomery's attorney."

A skeptical look spread across his face and he shifted his body weight from one foot to the other. "Her attorney's already inside," he grimaced. "You wouldn't be a reporter looking for a story, now, would you?"

I pulled out my State Bar card and driver's license and flashed them at him. "She has two attorneys."

"From what I hear, she's gonna need 'em," he said snidely, then stepped aside. "Go right ahead."

As I plodded up the walkway, I saw police officers everywhere, combing the place like roaches. A thickly built woman with short auburn hair searched the shrubbery in front of the house. Two men carrying large plastic bags headed off in the direction of the backyard. A handful of officers stood in a semicircle in the northwest corner of the yard.

When I got close to the front door, a commanding female presence at the center of another small gathering of men in blue caught my attention. I'd never met her before, but I immediately knew the blond Amazon had to be Julie Killabrew. *Imposing* was not an adequate description of her. Six feet tall and reed thin, she was dressed in a black pants suit with a long jacket that came almost to her knees, which had the effect of making her seem even taller. Thick, bleached-blond hair fanned across her shoulders and she wore no makeup except for a shocking red lip gloss. As she spoke to a team of officers, her index finger pierced the air with the speed of a guppy darting around a fish bowl.

She spotted me and abruptly marched over, boldly blocking my path before I could reach the front door. "May I help you?" she asked, acting like the top cop that she wasn't.

"I'm Vernetta Henderson, Mrs. Montgomery's attorney. I understand Neddy's already here. Can you tell me where I can find them?" I was purposely pleasant.

Julie didn't answer right away. She looked me up and down and wasn't the least bit discreet about it. Her gaze unnerved me, but that wasn't something I wanted her to know. So I just gawked right back at her.

"I'll be prosecuting this case," she volunteered without my asking. "I'm Julie Killabrew." She extended her hand and I cautiously shook it. "You'll find your client and your colleague in the backyard." She pointed through the picture window.

"Thanks," I said. Before I reached the door, she called after me.

"Nice work on the Hayes trial," she said.

When I looked back, she had already walked off.

"Thank you," I said to no one in particular.

It felt strange opening Tina's front door and not having Kinga there to show me in. I made my way through the living room, which was in complete shambles. The police had turned over tables, pulled the stuffing from seat cushions, and removed pictures from the wall in an apparent attempt to displace every single item in the place. I saw Tina's cherished silver wine goblet on the floor near an end table. I guess she had been right not to let them into her home the first time they had come calling.

One officer glanced my way as he jogged up the stairs, started to say something, but apparently changed his mind.

I peered through the French doors and spotted Tina and Neddy in the backyard. Even though they were a good thirty feet away, I could see distress on both of their faces.

"Just tell me I won't have to spend the night in jail," I heard Tina say in a panic as I approached.

"That's not an issue right now," Neddy said, placing a hand on Tina's shoulders. "They're just here to conduct a search. Nobody's said anything to me about arresting you."

That was good news. If they took Tina off to jail now, on a Saturday morning, she wouldn't be arraigned before Monday. She'd have to spend at least two nights in the clinker before a judge would even consider whether she was entitled to bail.

But it were as if Tina hadn't heard a word Neddy said. "I don't belong in jail," she cried, her voice full of fear. "I didn't kill my husband. This is crazy."

Neddy put an arm around Tina's shoulder and ushered her to a nearby bench. We all sat down.

"Look, Tina, I want to be straight with you," Neddy said. "I'll do everything in my power to keep you out of jail, but I won't make you any false promises. The D.A.'s office thinks they have enough evidence to charge you and bail is very hard to get in murder cases. When the time comes, I'll try to get the Deputy D.A. to agree to some reasonable bail amount, but I don't know if she will."

Tears were streaming down Tina's face now. "So it's up to her?" she whimpered.

"No, it's up to the judge. But if the prosecutor agrees, the judge will likely agree."

Tina covered her face with her hands and started to sob.

Neddy hugged her, but spoke in a firm, controlled voice. "Look, Tina, now is not the time to have a meltdown."

"I can't handle going to jail," she cried out.

"I'll tell you what," Neddy said, "I'll go speak to the Deputy D.A.

right now." She looked over at me, then stood up. "Don't leave her alone."

Just as Neddy turned to leave, Julie marched into the backyard.

"May I speak with you for a second?" Neddy said, meeting her halfway. They walked a few feet to the left of us, but were still within earshot.

"I'd like a heads-up if and when you decide to arrest my client."

Julie eyed Neddy the same way she had stared me down. The woman definitely had some issues. Before Julie could respond, two female officers, one of them dangling handcuffs, rushed up to Tina and ordered her to stand.

Neddy charged back in our direction and blocked the officers' access to Tina. "Hey wait a minute! There's no need for this."

"Oh sorry," Julie said smiling, "I was just about to tell you the reason I came back here. We're ready to take your client down to the station for booking."

"You're arresting her? I haven't seen an arrest warrant," Neddy said.

Julie pulled a folded piece of paper from the pocket of her jacket. "You can have my copy. You'll get the original from one of the officers."

Neddy snatched it from her hand and quickly read it. "We'll bring her down voluntarily," she shouted.

"What? You want special treatment for your client because she's rich?" Julie asked.

I looked at Tina, who seemed to be in shock.

Neddy tried to keep her voice professional and humble, but the Chicago Southside in her was ready to rise up. "C'mon, Julie. I was hoping you'd be agreeable to a reasonable bail."

Julie tilted her head to the side and pressed her finger to her cheek. "Bail? What bail?"

"So you're opposing bail?" Neddy exclaimed.

"Of course. I always oppose bail when the defendant is a murderer or a flight risk. Here we have both."

Neddy inhaled and exhaled in a single breath. "There's no need for us to argue the facts of this case out here, Julie. But I can assure you Tina Montgomery isn't going anywhere."

I wondered how Neddy could give that assurance. A murder suspect as rich as Tina was an inherent flight risk.

"And just how can you assure me of that?" Julie asked

"By giving you my word."

She grinned wickedly. "With all due respect, counselor, your word isn't good enough. Your client's loaded. If she decided to leave the country, her dead husband's millions, not to mention the eight mil in insurance she's about to collect, are enough to set her up for life. If she gets out on bail, it won't be because I agree to it."

The two women scowled at each other. Neddy impatiently tapped her foot on the pavement. She was dying to get funky with Julie. I was ready to back her up if I had to, but with all the cops around, all three of us would end up in the slammer.

"Are we starting fresh here, Julie, or are you still having flash-backs from our last trial?"

Julie laughed. "I never hold on to my losses," she said confidently. "I hope it's the same for you."

"If I remember correctly, I don't think I've ever lost a case against you."

Julie smirked. "And if I remember correctly, I don't think you've ever gotten an acquittal either. Hung juries don't mean your clients weren't guilty."

"Yeah, but they do mean you didn't prove your case," Neddy shot back at her. "If you did a better job of gathering your facts be-fore running off and charging people, you could save the taxpayers a lot of money."

The old Neddy was back and this time I was glad to see her.

"Whatever," Julie said. She had the upper hand and was about to use it. "Now we can do this the easy way or the hard way. I'm ask-ing you nicely to step aside so the police can do their job."

When Neddy didn't move, one of the female officers gently shoved her aside, and the other one pulled Tina's hands behind her back and clasped the handcuffs around her tiny wrists.

Tears, this time unaccompanied by sound, rolled down Tina's cheeks and her whole body trembled violently. We all followed as one of the officers marched her through her now-wrecked house, to-ward the front yard. As soon as the door opened, blinding lights hit us in the face. There had to be at least a dozen TV cameramen and photographers crowding the doorway.

"Clear out! Make some room!" the officer holding Tina com-manded. The officer stuck out her chest and stood as erect as a Marine in uniform. She no doubt wanted to look her best when her family and friends saw her on the news carting her rich, attractive suspect off to jail.

"This is private property," Neddy yelled. "These reporters have no right to be here!"

Julie motioned toward one of the officers. "Get rid of the media," she said. "Tell them to wait by the front gate. I'll be down to make a statement in five minutes."

CHAPTER 21

Bright and early on Monday morning I accompanied Neddy on my first visit to Division 30 of the Los Angeles County Criminal Courts building. Our client, now an accused criminal, was being arraigned today with a bunch of other accused criminals.

The minute we walked into the arraignments courtroom, I felt like I'd just been hurled off a merry-go-round. The entire room vibrated with activity. The judge, peering down from his perch, was listening to a spiel from an attorney standing behind the prosecutor's table while a host of different conversations was going on all around them. I counted a couple of bailiffs, a court reporter, three court clerks, and at least six attorneys standing inside the well of the courtroom, the sacred ground where all the action took place. Sloppy stacks of papers were piled everywhere. My first thought was that somebody needed to hire a housekeeper.

The entire courtroom had a gloomy, depressing aura about it, due in part to the dark teak wood paneling that ran from floor to ceiling. Ancient, low-watt lighting painted the air with an ugly yellow film. I wasn't even facing any charges and I felt doomed. Along the west side of the wall, a glass-encased area held two long benches with rows of men and women, mostly black and brown, in bright orange jumpsuits. Except for the smoking lounge at LAX, I'd never seen human beings caged like animals before.

Farther down, along the same wall, five or six bored-looking people sat behind huge metal desks, reading newspapers and magazines.

The sign on the wall above their heads identified them as interpreters. Directly in front of them were several rows of graffiti-scarred
wooden benches that seated an array of courtroom spectators. Most
of the worn-looking occupants sitting in this section had their eyes
glued on the cage, straining their necks in all directions, trying to get
a glimpse of a loved one. A young woman in the front row balancing
a toddler on each hip was trying to read the lips of a battered-looking
black man trapped inside the cage, ignoring the sign in English and
Spanish that read: "Communicating with prisoners is forbidden by
law."

A handful of TV cameramen sat slumped on the back row of the
spectators' section. I assumed they were waiting for Tina's arraignment since I wasn't aware of any other major case in the news recently.

"This is wild," I whispered to Neddy. "I can't believe how much
is going on in here. How can anybody concentrate? In a civil courtroom, you can hear a pin drop."

"I guess that's why they call what you do civil and what I do criminal." She smiled.

I stayed put as Neddy entered the well, another distinct difference
from most civil courtrooms, where entering the courtroom's inner
sanctum while court was in session without the clerk's permission
was a definite no-no.

Neddy gave the bailiff a big hug, then waved me over.

I followed her, feeling like a scared teenager who'd mistakenly
ventured onto gang turf. I was definitely out of my element. I longed
for the civilized calm of a federal district courtroom.

"This is making me woozy," I said. "It sounds like everybody's
talking in code. How can anybody keep up with everything going on
in here?"

Neddy smiled again. "You just do. It all seems kind of normal
after a while." Neddy whispered to the bailiff. "How many arraignments today, Bobby?"

He picked up a clipboard. "We've got almost two hundred and
we just got started. Who's your client?"

"Tina Montgomery."

Bailiff Bobby scanned his clipboard again. "You might be up before midnight," he joked.

"I need a favor," Neddy said. "We're on our way to meet with our client. When her case is called, can you bring her out without seating her in the cage?"

"You got it," he said.

We walked over to a door near the cage. From there, a guard led us down a long, white corridor and into a room barely bigger than a bathroom. About ten minutes later a guard brought Tina into the room. Her hands were cuffed in front of her and she was wearing a dingy orange two-piece outfit that resembled a surgeon's garb.

"Could you remove the handcuffs, please?" Neddy said to the guard, who complied without responding and stayed planted near the door.

"How're you making out?" Neddy asked, as Tina sat down across from us.

"I can't stay here another night," she cried. It was the first time I'd seen utter defeat in her eyes. "I can't do this. I don't belong here. You have to get me out of here."

"The guard's going to bring you out for arraignment shortly," Neddy said, occasionally eyeing the deputy, who pretended to be ignoring us. "It'll be a very short proceeding. The judge is going to ask you the questions we already went over with you. Do you remember what we discussed and how you should answer?"

Tina nodded.

"We're going to push for bail, but—"

"But nothing!" Tina snapped. "I don't care how you do it, just get me out of here. I cannot—I will not—spend another night in here!"

Both Neddy and I were rocked by the hostility in Tina's voice. She still hadn't come to terms with the seriousness of the situation she was facing. The rich bitch's syndrome, I thought. There was no way her husband's money was going to buy her out of this mess.

"We'll do what we can," Neddy said, undaunted by Tina's angry outburst. "The D.A.'s opposing bail, but this judge is pretty lenient. Still, I can't make you any promises."

Tina gave Neddy a look so hateful it summoned up my doubts about her innocence, not to mention her emotional stability.

When we returned to the courtroom, we saw Julie standing near the interpreters' desks. Neddy marched off in her direction and I followed.

"Hello," Neddy said, making an effort to be cordial. "How are you?"

"Just fine."

"Should I assume that your position on bail hasn't changed?"

Julie chuckled arrogantly, as if she couldn't believe the insanity of Neddy's question. "That would be an accurate assumption. You should also know I'm thinking about amending the indictment and filing this as a death penalty case."

"What!?" Neddy said, her voice far too loud for the setting. Several people looked in our direction, including the judge. "You have to be kidding!"

"Well, I'm not," Julie said and stalked off.

"This is Julie's typical grandstanding, overkill bullshit," Neddy hissed, as we watched Julie walk out of the courtroom. "Which is exactly the reason she has such a poor win–loss record."

It was another ninety minutes before Tina was trotted out for her arraignment. The cameramen jumped to attention, focusing their lenses on Tina as the sheriff's deputy positioned her in front of the cage. She looked even smaller and weaker than she had just minutes ago. I sat in the spectator's section while Neddy stepped forward to represent Tina.

"People versus Montgomery," the judge said, perking up, obviously realizing he was going to be on the six o'clock news tonight. He solemnly read the charge. "Murder in the first degree. How do you plead?"

"Not guilty," Tina squeaked.

Neddy straightened her shoulders. "Defendant requests to be released on her own recognizance, Your Honor."

The judge looked as if he wanted to laugh. He turned to the prosecutor. "Ms. Killabrew?"

"The People request that the defendant be denied bail. She's a very wealthy woman accused of an extremely heinous crime and we believe she's a flight risk. Furthermore, we're considering filing this as a capital case."

"There's no evidence of any aggravating circumstances here," Neddy said quickly.

"There's plenty, Your Honor, and it will all be introduced at the appropriate time."

Neddy remained composed. "Your Honor, my client is innocent until proven guilty. There's no reason to keep her confined in jail. She's a longtime member of this community with no prior criminal record. The prosecution's case is totally circumstantial. There's no reason she shouldn't qualify for the electronic surveillance program. She will also surrender her passport to the court."

Neddy hadn't discussed the electronic surveillance program with Tina or with me.

Julie didn't relent. "The People object, Your Honor, and we reiterate our request that the court deny bail. We don't want to send the wrong message that wealthy defendants get special treatment."

The look on the judge's face said he resented Julie's attempt to publicly shame him into keeping Tina behind bars. With all the media attention following Max Montgomery's death, the judge knew his every move would be dissected on the evening news.

He began fumbling with some papers on his desk. "After careful consideration of the argument on both sides," he said sternly, "the court sets bail in the amount of one million dollars. The defendant must also surrender her passport to the court and will be subject to the electronic surveillance program while out on bail."

"Mrs. Montgomery, you have the right to a preliminary hearing in ten court days. Do you wish to waive time?"

Tina hesitated for far too long. My heart skipped a good three beats. Neddy had given her clear instructions to respond in the affirmative when she was asked this question. What was she doing?

"Mrs. Montgomery, do you understand my question?"

"Yes, Your Honor," Tina said tentatively. "I want my hearing in ten days."

Even the court clerks stopped what they were doing to take note. Defendants never rushed to prelim. And there certainly was no reason to rush now since Tina was being allowed to post bail.

I thought Neddy's head was going to explode. Tina refused to look at her.

"Counselor, have you discussed this matter with your client?"

"Yes, I have, Your Honor," Neddy said through clenched teeth. It was not good for the world to see that she did not have client control.

"And does your client have a clear understanding of the consequences of proceeding with her preliminary hearing in ten days."

"Well, Your Honor, I'd like to talk to my client again to—"

Tina interrupted her. "We don't need to talk again, you've already explained it to me. I don't want to waive my rights. I'm innocent and

I want this thing over with. I want my preliminary hearing held as soon as possible."

Even Julie looked a little panic-stricken. The prosecution probably needed more time to prepare for the prelim than we did.

"Okay then, counselor," the judge said. "I'm setting the prelim for one week from Wednesday in Division 5, before Judge McKee."

CHAPTER 22

The bailiff took Tina back into lockup to process her out. I traipsed after Neddy as she stormed into the hallway outside the courtroom.

"Can you believe that crap Tina just pulled!?" Neddy was trembling with anger. She glanced up and down the corridor to make sure none of the TV news cameras was within earshot. But they had all taken off after Julie. "We're not ready to defend that prelim in a week. We haven't even seen the prosecution's evidence. She's sabotaging her own damn case."

"How long before they release her?" I asked.

"At least a couple of hours."

"Are you going to confront Tina about this?"

Neddy looked at me like I was nuts. "You're damn straight. If we're handling this case, then these are the kind of decisions *we* should make. If not, she can find herself some new lawyers."

Neddy took a seat on a wooden bench and I joined her.

"Do we pick Tina up downstairs?"

"We shouldn't pick her ass up at all," she said, still steaming. Her stiff shoulders suddenly sagged. "We have to meet her over at the Twin Towers on Bauchet Street. I can't believe she screwed us like that," Neddy said again. "I've never had a client do that to me."

It wasn't quite lunchtime yet, but we decided to head for the cafeteria anyway.

"What now?" I asked when we were alone on the elevator.

"Assuming Tina doesn't fire us after I read her the riot act, we need to get to work on our cross-examination outlines. Julie will probably call the crime scene investigator and the coroner. We can start there until she discloses the rest of her witnesses."

Neddy was staring off into space, apparently still reeling from Tina's deliberate act of defiance. "Can you make it over to my place tonight?" she asked.

"No problem," I said, although I knew another late night would be a very big problem for Jefferson.

When we stepped off the elevator, the huge tinted windows that lined the exterior of the Criminal Courts building provided a perfect view of Julie standing on the front steps surrounded by a half-circle of reporters and cameramen.

Neddy groaned and took off in the opposite direction.

"Wait," I said, grabbing her by the sleeve and pulling her toward the window. "Don't you want to hear what the competition has to say?"

"No, not really. I'll catch the 30-second version on the eleven o'clock news tonight. If those reporters see us standing here, they'll be on us like bees on honey. I don't exactly need that right now. Let's get out of here."

"C'mon," I said, inching toward the double doors, still tugging on her sleeve. "We'll stand right here where they can't see us." We remained inside the building, close enough to the doors to hear Julie's words but safely out of view of the TV cameras.

"Max Montgomery contributed tremendously to the growth and success of this city," Julie announced sanctimoniously, occasionally taking a single wisp of blond hair from her forehead and daintily sweeping it behind her ear. "And we owe it to him to see that his killer is brought to justice. Once this trial is underway, the evidence will show that Tina Montgomery is the person responsible for brutally stabbing Max Montgomery to death. While I'm puzzled over the judge's decision to grant her bail request, I have to abide by the court's ruling."

"Oh, I like that one," Neddy whispered. "Piss off the judge."

Julie paused for just a second and the reporters all shouted questions at her at once.

Neddy abruptly walked away. "Let's go."

"I think we should stay and listen," I groaned, as I squeezed through the crowd to catch up with her. "She might say something that could help us with our defense."

Neddy stopped and looked back at me. "Julie's a bitch and a media hound, but she's not stupid. This case could put her on the map. She's not throwing us any freebies."

"Well, it can't hurt to hear what else she has to say," I complained, as I scurried after her into the ladies' room.

"And just what're you going to say if one of those reporters sticks a mike in your face?" She pushed on the doors of each of the four stalls to make sure we were alone, then spun around and stuck an imaginary microphone inches from my lips. "Ms. Henderson, the D.A. feels she has very strong circumstantial evidence against your client. How do you expect to win this case?"

The question came at me much too fast to form an intelligent response.

"Ms. Henderson," Neddy said, tapping her foot and pushing her balled-up fist closer to my lips, "the cameras are rolling. Do you have a response?"

"Well," I said, a bit more composed now and ready to play the game, "we're equally confident that justice will prevail at trial and that the jury will acquit our client."

"Trial? What about the preliminary hearing, Ms. Henderson? Are you conceding the fact that the prosecution has enough evidence to prevail at the preliminary hearing next week?"

I instantly realized my misstep. "Okay, I see your point. Stay away from reporters."

"Exactly," Neddy said, satisfied with her little communications lesson.

We left the restroom, walked into the cafeteria, and grabbed trays and silverware.

"So you don't plan to do *any* interviews during this trial?" I said, lowering my voice in case someone was listening. "Do you know how easy it is for a lawyer to become a celebrity after a case like this?"

"Watch it," Neddy said, this time with a smile, "you're starting to sound a lot like O'Reilly."

"Oh, that's a low blow," I laughed. "All I'm saying is there could be some benefits to defending this case. Let's not be too high and mighty about this TV stuff."

"I'll talk to the media when it's in Tina's best interest for me to do so," she said. "Right now, we need to lay low and put all of our energies into defending our client. When the time is right, we'll go on the attack. We don't need to get into a catfight with Julie now. That's exactly what she wants us to do."

Neddy proceeded down the cafeteria line and stopped to grab a turkey sandwich wrapped in Saran Wrap. "Besides, I guarantee you, whether we talk to the press or not, we'll reap all the glory we can handle when Tina gets acquitted."

CHAPTER 23

We'd been sitting in the release area of the Twin Towers for more than three hours. Every time we asked when Tina would be released, we were told "shortly" by a grumpy, balding officer who had his nose buried in the latest edition of *Gun World*.

Neddy finally made a call to Bailiff Bill and found out that the deputies holding Tina had been given instructions to take their time releasing her. We both knew who was behind that order. Neddy was still hot from the stunt Tina had pulled. Now she was boiling.

When I spotted Julie Killabrew entering the room from an interior side door, I briefly said a silent prayer for peace because I knew once Neddy spotted her, there would be fireworks. Julie either didn't see us sitting in the waiting area or was purposely ignoring us. She'd almost made it through the double glass doors leading to the street when Neddy looked up and tore out after her.

"Can I speak to you for a minute?" she said.

Julie held up her wrist to check her watch. "All I have is a minute."

"Can you tell me why it's taking so long for my client to be released?"

"That's a question you should address to the desk sergeant. Not me." She turned to leave.

Neddy boldly jumped in front of her. "Don't walk away from me. I'm not done yet."

A pompous smile formed on Julie's lips. She pulled the strap of her purse higher on her shoulder and looked at her watch for a second time. "You're in my way."

"I know for a fact that you've instructed the police to take their time processing Tina Montgomery out of lockup. I know you like to play dirty, but I'd appreciate it if you would make whatever calls you need to make so my client can go home."

"You shouldn't make unsupported accusations like that, counselor. You could end up facing a defamation lawsuit."

"So sue me," she challenged. "Truth is a complete defense, isn't it?"

They stood there in the entryway of the building staring each other down. Julie had a good six inches on Neddy, but the D.A.'s height didn't seem to intimidate her. I noticed that they were beginning to draw the attention of officers inside the lobby as well as people walking in and out of the building.

I tugged at Neddy's forearm. "Let's just go back inside," I said.

"You need to do something with her," Julie spat before stomping off.

"I hate her ass," Neddy mumbled under her breath as we walked back inside. "I hate her ass, I hate her ass, I hate her ass!"

"Calm down," I whispered

"You have no idea how much I wanted to give that giant twig a good slap."

"Good thing you didn't. We're in a jailhouse, remember? You want to take Tina's place inside?"

She slumped down into one of the hard, rickety chairs. "A few nights in jail would be worth the pleasure."

It was another forty-five minutes before a deputy escorted Tina into the lobby. She was dressed in the same burgundy, two-piece Capri set she had been wearing when the police snapped handcuffs on her wrists and carted her off two days earlier. Except now it was dirty and wrinkled.

The three of us walked in silence to Neddy's three-year-old, silver-blue BMW, which was parked in a public lot a block away. Tina slid into the backseat and I took the front. As soon as we were all strapped into our seat belts, Neddy let loose.

"What happened in that courtroom today can't happen again," she said sternly, twisting her body around to face Tina in the backseat. "I explained to you that we wanted to waive time so we'd have a chance to better prepare for the preliminary hearing. But then you go and tell the judge you don't want to waive time. That was just fuckin' crazy."

Tina seemed surprised by Neddy's anger. But Tina was fuming, too. "Prepare for what?" she fired back. "You told me they're going to find probable cause and that the prelim is just a formality. I don't see why we need to wait. I just want to get this over with."

Neddy inhaled and narrowed her eyes. "Even if we don't get the case dismissed, what we learn at the prelim will be extremely important for us at trial," she said slowly, struggling to control her rage. "You hired us to represent you, so let us."

"You're not the one who had to spend two nights in jail, I—"

Neddy held up her hand cutting Tina off. "And you're not the one who has the legal expertise to keep your ass out of jail for the rest of your life. When we give you advice regarding procedural matters, you need to take it. If you can't do that, then you need to hire somebody else."

I turned back around and stared out of the window. I was certain that we were about to be fired. But instead of pointing out that we worked for her and not the other way around, Tina started to cry. "I'm sorry," she wailed, "I just want this thing over with."

Neddy wasn't falling for the sympathy play and continued her lecture. "Well, it may go away faster now, but not the way you want it to go. What you did in there was screw yourself!"

She stuck the key in the ignition and started up the car, still harping about how stupid Tina had been. I began to feel sorry for Tina and I definitely thought Neddy was overdoing it. Tina had already been beaten up enough from her jail stint.

As we headed up Grand Street, I turned to face Tina in the backseat. "There's a reason behind everything we do, every decision we make," I said gently. "The only reason you're sitting in this car wearing that lovely ankle bracelet is because of Neddy. We're going to do everything we can to fight these charges, but you have to trust us."

"Okay, okay," she said, wiping her tears. "I just thought—"

Neddy cut her off again. "The next time you have a thought you want the judge to hear, do yourself a favor. Share it with us first."

CHAPTER 24

Neddy dropped me off at the office to pick up my car, then left to deposit a sufficiently berated Tina back at home. After running upstairs to grab some files from my desk and picking up a Subway sandwich, I drove to Neddy's house where we spent a long evening strategizing about the prelim.

I worked on drafting the cross-examination outline for the coroner while Neddy worked on one for the crime scene investigator. We tried to think up every possible question Julie might ask, as well as how each witness was likely to respond. Then we explored ways to poke holes in every answer that pointed toward Tina's guilt.

It was close to midnight by the time I made it home. I hoped Jefferson was already asleep. I was not in the mood to be scolded about my late hours. Once I'd discarded my purse and kicked off my shoes, I found him in the den, sitting in front of our Sony plasma watching *The Tonight Show*. When I spotted the pint of Ben & Jerry's Coffee Heath Bar Crunch ice cream in his hands I happily exhaled. There was something about Ben & Jerry's that always mellowed Jefferson out.

I eased down on the couch next to him, resting my head on his shoulder.

"I'm exhausted," I yawned.

He pulled an empty tablespoon from his mouth, licked it clean, then dug out another huge scoop of ice cream. "You've been working late almost every night since that other trial ended. Can't you take a few days off to chill?" he asked, stuffing the spoon back into his mouth, crunching loudly on the toffee.

"I wish," I said. "Tina Montgomery's preliminary hearing is next week, which means I'll be eating and breathing this case until then."

"So what else is new?"

I decided it was best to let that statement ride. We sat quietly for a while, occasionally laughing out loud at Jay Leno's antics. The "Jay Walking" segment, where Leno stood on a street corner asking people simple questions and getting outrageously stupid answers, was Jefferson's favorite part of the show.

"I don't understand why people that dumb would even get in front of the camera," Jefferson said, howling with laughter.

When Leno went to a commercial break, he put his arm around me and pulled me close. "So just how tired are you?" he said suggestively.

"Definitely too tired for what you've got in mind, young man." I gave him a peck on the lips and hoped he wasn't serious about having sex because I was dead tired.

"So what do I have to do, make an appointment?" There was levity in his voice, but it had a serious undertone to it.

"Of course not, sweetheart." I kissed him again. "Just give me a little while longer to get familiar with this case. Now that Tina's been arraigned, things are really going to pick up speed."

Jefferson eyed me skeptically, then turned back to the TV.

"I know you hate my working so hard all the time," I said, "but I'm going to get my life under control. Soon."

He didn't say anything for a while and neither did I. I snuggled up closer to him, but I felt his body stiffen.

Jefferson stuck his spoon in the center of the ice cream container and set it on the coffee table. "How are we going to have kids when we never have time to work on making 'em?" There was no anger in his voice, just concern.

"It's going to get better, I swear." I pressed my head against his chest. "I just need your support through this trial. I swear I'll make it up to you as soon as it's over."

"So how do you plan to do that?"

I reached down to scratch my left foot even though it didn't itch. I was just stalling for time to come up with a suitable response to my husband's question. "How about if I promise to make you a home-cooked meal every day for three weeks straight and give you a back massage every night for a week?"

"We've got a deal," he laughed. "Except my back ain't exactly what I need massaged."

"Get your mind out of the gutter, boy." We kissed in a slow, loving way that almost made me forget how tired I was.

"By the way," Jefferson said, coming up for air, "have you heard anything about those fertility tests? Shouldn't the Doc have called us by now?"

"Don't forget she told us she was going on vacation," I said. "That's probably the only reason we haven't heard anything. If there was a problem, I'm sure somebody from her office would've let us know."

I had not shared my concerns with Jefferson, but I was actually pretty nervous about the test results. Even if Dr. Bell was away on vacation, one of her assistants could've easily called to tell us everything was fine. Or that it wasn't. In my mind, the fact that nobody had called meant that there was a major problem and they were waiting for Dr. Bell to come back and deliver the bad news.

While I had tried to convince myself that my fears were unwarranted, I knew that the possibility that the IUD had damaged my body in some way was very real. I'd read news reports claiming that the IUD was a dangerous, defective product that left hundreds of women sterile. But what were the odds? One in ten thousand? One in a hundred thousand? Whatever they were, at the time I'd selected it as my method of birth control, statistical possibilities had not been much of a concern for me. That certainly wasn't the case now.

Jefferson was so psyched about becoming a father. If I couldn't give him that, how would he handle it? How would I handle it?

"Why don't you go get out of your clothes and get to bed," Jefferson said, assuming my closed eyes meant I was falling asleep.

"Are you trying to get rid of me?" I mumbled into his chest.

"Never."

"I definitely feel whipped, but I like sitting here with you. We never get a chance to spend any quiet time together anymore."

"And whose fault is that?"

"Mine," I said quietly.

He kissed me on the nose, then scooped me up from the couch and carried me off to bed.

CHAPTER 25

The next morning, Neddy failed to show up for our ten o'clock meeting. Unlike me, she was like clockwork. We had planned to exchange our cross-examination outlines and give each other notes on any changes we thought needed to be made. By 10:30, she hadn't even touched base with her secretary. I knew something was wrong.

After repeatedly trying her cell phone, I called her home number for the second time. She picked up on the fourth ring.

The weakness of her "hello" sent my pulse racing. I flung the anxiety from my voice before proceeding. "Hey, you standing me up?"

It took her a long time to respond and when she did, her words were slow and measured, as if she had a massive headache that intensified every time her lips moved. "I'm sorry. I couldn't make it in this morning."

"You okay?"

"Uh, no—not exactly," she stuttered, offering no further explanation.

The raspiness in her voice told me that she had been crying.

"I had a visit from the police right after you left last night." She exhaled long and hard. "Lawton's dead."

I gasped unintentionally.

"I've been crying most of the night and I have no idea why." I heard her break into a quiet sob. "I'm really feeling pretty crazy right now."

"I'm on my way over," I said.

"No. You don't need to. I'm fine."

"Yes, I do." I hung up the phone before she could say another word.

When Neddy opened her front door, I was not prepared to see her in such bad shape. She was wearing a faded bathrobe over a wrinkled T-shirt and dingy white shorts. Her hair was matted to her head and her eyes were nearly swollen shut from what I assumed had been hours of crying. She poured both of us a cup of coffee and we sat down on her living room couch.

I wanted to ask how Lawton had died, but decided that for now, the fewer questions the better.

"Can you believe I'm crying over that fool?" she said, shaking her head. "The last time I talked to him was when we had that ugly shouting match at his lawyer's office. I should be thanking God he's finally out of my life—for good. This is silly. I have no idea what I'm crying for."

I hugged her, which seemed to make her cry even more. After a few minutes, she composed herself and reached for her coffee.

"I know you must think I'm nuts," she said, obviously embarrassed.

"I don't think you're nuts. You loved the man. You had his child. It's perfectly normal for you to be upset about his death."

"Yeah," she said sarcastically, "the same man who did nothing but betray me almost from the day I met him."

I thought another crying spell was about to start, but she seemed to will it away.

"This is so crazy." She stared into her coffee. "After all he put me through, I should be glad he's dead."

Her words sounded harsh and she looked at me as if she wanted to take them back.

"You're not crazy. Love is crazy. We can't always control our emotions. How did Lawton die?" I finally asked.

"I guess he met his match. He was murdered." An irony-filled smile touched her lips. "What's that saying? What goes around, comes around?"

"When did it happen?"

"The housekeeper found his body yesterday at our house in Leimert Park, but they haven't established the time of death yet." She stopped to sip her coffee. "They think he may've been lying there on the floor with five bullets in his chest for several days." She closed her eyes.

I didn't know what to say, so I waited for her lead.

"I just know some woman killed him. He was such an asshole. But he obviously toyed with the wrong person."

"What makes you think a woman killed him?"

"Had to be," she said. "You don't treat women the way Lawton did and not expect to pay for it sooner or later."

In watching Neddy, it struck me how different her grief was from Tina's. Both women had been cruelly deceived by men they loved. During our initial meeting, Tina seemed to work hard at hiding her grief, as if it were unacceptable to show her pain. Neddy appeared unable to control hers, which made her deep anguish seem as odd as Tina's lack of it.

She stood up and walked over to open her sliding-glass doors, allowing a strong surge of ocean air to freshen the room. "I have to get past this," she said, more to herself than to me. "The prelim's in a few days."

"Don't worry about that. I think we should request a continuance. And if the judge denies it, I can handle it by myself if I have to." *No I can't. Why in the hell did I say that?*

She got up and walked into the kitchen. "It's foolish for me to use the word love and Lawton in the same sentence, but I guess everything I'm feeling right now must mean I still loved him. Maybe that's why I fought so hard during the divorce. Paying him alimony wasn't going to break me financially. But emotionally, the whole ordeal was killing me."

"Like I said, love is crazy."

She refilled her coffee cup. Mine was still untouched. "It's weird, but I think Lawton's murder is going to help me do a better job of defending Tina."

"How so?"

She waited a long time before answering. "I'm not sure I can put it into words. I feel like I have an even better sense of what Tina's going though now. I always felt like I understood the betrayal part. After all, her story is basically my story. But now I know firsthand what it's like to have a man you love murdered. There's something different about someone dying at the hands of another. Even a man you despised."

"I know you still don't think Tina killed her husband, but I'm just not there yet."

Neddy stopped and took another sip of her coffee.

"I can't explain why, but I just don't think she did it. But like I told you, I've been wrong before."

"Do the police have any suspects in Lawton's murder?" I asked.

"I don't know. I didn't ask." She set her coffee cup down and retied her robe. "I only wish I could say I don't care that he's dead or whether they find his killer. But at the moment, I do."

CHAPTER 26

The chore of planning Lawton's funeral fell to Neddy despite their long, antagonistic estrangement. She decided to take a couple of days off, but only after O'Reilly basically banned her from the office. The court agreed to grant our motion to continue the preliminary hearing for a week.

Julie, surprisingly, didn't oppose our motion. She even provided us with a list of witnesses she planned to call at the prelim without us having to fight for it. She listed four names: the crime scene investigator and the coroner, whom we expected; Ernestine Frye, Max Montgomery's personal assistant; and Oscar Lopez, a room service waiter at the Ritz-Carlton.

While Neddy was busy making funeral arrangements, I asked Detective Smith, the investigator she had hired to do the background check on Max Montgomery, to accompany me to the Ritz-Carlton. I was hoping to interview Lopez. We found out that not only did he tell police that he saw a woman who resembled Tina outside Max's hotel room the night of the murder, but that the woman supposedly had a knife in her hand. That was some pretty damaging evidence, and I wanted to hear it from the horse's mouth.

Detective Smith was a tall, well-built African American who had a cop's walk, full of bravado, and a therapist's demeanor. Perceptive and supportive. A black Dr. Phil.

"Excuse my fashion critique," he said with a full smile upon greeting me in the hotel lobby. "But I'm not sure you're really dressed the part."

We had met a couple of times at the office and I'd taken an immediate liking to him.

"So just how am I supposed to be dressed?" I pretended to be put out by his comment. "This is one of my nicest suits."

"You're dressed like a lawyer," he chuckled. "The kid's already going to be scared to death. He probably hates the thought of having to testify and no telling what the prosecutor has threatened him with if he doesn't. I doubt you're going to be able to get him to say a word dressed like that. You're decked out like you're ready to deliver closing arguments to a jury."

I surveyed Detective Smith's jeans and golf shirt. "No offense," I said, "but you haven't seen me work yet. I'm a pretty decent interrogator."

"You're the boss," he said with a friendly shrug.

We headed for the registration desk. "Can you tell me where I can find Oscar Lopez?" I asked. "He's a room service waiter here."

The desk clerk, a pretty sorority-girl type, sensed a problem. "You'll have to check with the catering supervisor. I'll call him."

A few minutes later, a young Filipino man approached. I extended my hand. "I'm Vernetta Henderson. I'm investigating the murder that took place here a few weeks ago. We'd like to speak with Oscar Lopez."

"He's on duty right now," the man said impatiently. "I'm afraid you'll have to talk to him before or after work. And I'll tell you now, I doubt he'll have anything to say."

"I was hoping to catch him during one of his breaks," I said, wishing I could whip out a prosecutor's badge and force the supervisor to drag Oscar out to talk to me now.

"Lunch was over an hour ago and we're pretty busy. We're gearing up for a big banquet tonight." He wasn't budging.

"What time is Mr. Lopez off duty?"

"Six. He works nine to six. It could be later if there's overtime."

I glanced at my watch. It was only two o'clock. We couldn't afford to hang around for another four hours.

"Thanks," I said. "We'll come back later."

As the supervisor walked off, I turned to Detective Smith. "Well, this was a wasted trip."

"Not yet it isn't," he said. "Let's go have a late lunch. You can watch me do *my* work. But you'll need to sit at a different table."

I was puzzled by his instruction, but complied anyway.

"Make sure you sit within earshot though," he said with a wink. "And take notes."

The hotel restaurant was nearly empty. I took a small table near the detective. I'd already eaten lunch. I looked for something on the menu I could take home to Jefferson. Detective Smith ordered coffee and a club sandwich. I ordered the spicy chicken pasta.

I was getting bored watching the detective slowly munch on his sandwich and loudly slurp his coffee. When he was nearly done eating, he signaled for the waitress. After reviewing the bill, complimenting the service, and placing a twenty-dollar tip on the table, he struck up a conversation with the waitress as she freshened up his coffee.

"Everybody around here must've been pretty shaken up about that murder, huh?" he said, trying to sound matter-of-fact about it. "Something like that doesn't happen at a classy place like this very often."

"You can say that again," she replied. She was a middle-aged white woman whose leathery skin, dull gray hair, and wrinkled hands advertised that she'd had a hard life. "The cops were all over the place. I still see 'em around every now and then."

"I heard one of the waiters saw the murderer," Detective Smith said.

The woman stopped and turned back to look over both of her shoulders. "You're talking about Oscar," she whispered, leaning in closer to the detective. "He's scared to death. The day after the murder he was walking around telling everybody he saw a woman on the fifth floor with a knife. But when the police picked him up for questioning, he got really scared."

"So Oscar really didn't see anybody?"

"Who knows?" she said. "Oscar is always mouthing off. He exaggerates quite a bit. Likes to be in the middle of things. I hear he's afraid that if he changes his story, the INS might come looking for him."

"He's not here legally?"

"He's legal, but his work visa expires in a few months. He thinks they might try to deport him."

Detective Smith rested his forearms on the table and leaned forward. "So his testimony might not be too reliable?"

"I wouldn't bet the rent on it," she said, looking over her shoulder again. "He swears he saw someone, but he can't remember much else. I think he made up the stuff about the knife. He wasn't even sure whether the woman was wearing a long dress or a short one. Oscar's eyes aren't too good."

When the waitress walked away, the detective waved me over.

"Well?" he said smugly.

I had to admit, I was pretty impressed. "Let's make a deal," I said, pulling out a chair and sitting down across from him. "From here on out, I'll handle the legal stuff and leave the investigating to you."

"Deal," he said.

After agreeing that Detective Smith would follow up with Lopez and also interview some of the other hotel workers, we walked to our respective cars. Just as I was about to climb into my SUV, Detective Smith stopped me.

"I have something I need to share with you, but you have to promise to keep it confidential."

"Can I tell Neddy?" I asked.

"Definitely not."

What could he possibly have to tell me that I couldn't share with Neddy? "Get in," I said, my mind already jumping to conclusions.

He walked around, climbed into the passenger side of my Land Cruiser, and closed the door. "This is only a rumor," he began, "but I think it's a pretty reliable one. The police have a suspect in the murder of Neddy's husband."

"They do? Who is it?"

Detective Smith took in a lungful of air. "It's Neddy," he said. "The police think Neddy murdered her husband."

CHAPTER 27

It took only a matter of hours for Detective Smith's rumor to transform itself into fact. Just after one o'clock the following day, O'Reilly walked into my office and tossed the *L.A. Times* on my desk.

"Did we make headlines again?" I asked, taking a sip from a can of Diet Coke. I had just finished eating lunch at my desk.

O'Reilly didn't respond. He simply towered over me and waited for my eyes to take in the headline.

When they did, the Diet Coke I'd just taken in squirted from my mouth, dousing the newspaper with brown dots. DEFENSE LAWYER IN MONTGOMERY MURDER CASE MAY BE MURDER SUSPECT HERSELF, the headline read.

I jumped to my feet. "What the hell is this? Have you talked to Neddy? Has she seen this crap?"

O'Reilly dabbed the newspaper with a napkin that had come with my Caesar salad. "This doesn't look good for the firm," he said sternly. He took a seat in front of my desk, then pointed his finger at my chair, directing me to sit down.

The firm? "I think we need to be thinking about Neddy right now," I said. "How can they print this stuff? This is defamatory. The *Times* doesn't usually run stories like this without checking out their facts first. What's going on?"

O'Reilly looked over his shoulder at the open door, then got up to close it. "It's not defamatory if Neddy's actually a suspect," he said in a low, measured voice. "I made some calls. There could be a pretty strong circumstantial case against her."

Even though Detective Smith had told me this was a possibility, it still upset me to see it in black and white. "Are you telling me you actually think Neddy killed her husband?" The question didn't even sound right coming from my lips.

His lips remained shut, but his eyes answered yes.

"O'Reilly, this is nuts. I'll bet Julie Killabrew planted this story. It's probably a ploy to get the upper hand in the Montgomery trial. I hear she plays dirty."

"I know Julie," he said. "She's ambitious and she doesn't always play by the rules, but I doubt she'd stoop this low."

"This is insane," was all I could say. "Neddy couldn't kill anybody."

"The first thing I learned during my days as a prosecutor is that anybody is capable of murder."

"So you believe Neddy killed her husband?" There. I'd said it again.

"I have no idea." O'Reilly dropped his head back over the edge of the chair and studied the ceiling. His face was heavy with worry.

"O'Reilly, I was with Neddy after she found out about her husband's murder. She was in too much grief to have killed him."

O'Reilly laughed softly. "You definitely aren't a criminal attorney, Vernetta. Since when does showing grief have anything to do with guilt or innocence? And just like Tina Montgomery, Neddy had motive. She was going nuts over having to pay her husband alimony."

"That's still not a reason to kill." The words I'd overhead Neddy scream at her husband suddenly rang in my ears. *I'll kill you before I give you a dime.* And that night outside Starbucks, she'd even said that he deserved to die. The same way Max Montgomery had died.

"There was more to Neddy's riff with her husband than money," O'Reilly continued. I could tell by the look on his face that he was really troubled. "I don't think she's ever gotten over the death of her son. And nobody but her husband was to blame for that." He stood up. "I'm taking her off the Montgomery case until this blows over."

"No way!" I said, bouncing out of my chair again. "Neddy's all prepared for it."

"It's just a prelim and everybody knows the judge is going to find probable cause and the case is going to trial. You can handle it. You know the facts as well as Neddy does. You'll do fine. Hopefully Neddy's situation will be resolved long before the case is set for trial."

I continued to protest. "You're reading too much into that newspaper article. It's just gossip. Nobody's charged Neddy with anything."

"That's true. But everybody interviewed by the police fingered her as the only one who wanted Lawton dead. I just hope she has a solid alibi."

"Have you talked to her yet?"

"No," he said, in a way that told me he dreaded even thinking about the task.

"Shouldn't you give her that courtesy before taking her off the case?"

"Of course I plan to talk to her." He sounded as if I were getting on his nerves. "But I have to do what's in the best interest of the client and the firm."

"Neddy being falsely accused of a crime might actually benefit Tina Montgomery. It would make her even more empathetic to Tina's plight."

"Neddy can empathize all she wants," he said. "But she can't defend Tina Montgomery if they're sharing the same jail cell."

He had a point, but only if Neddy actually ended up in jail. As far as I was concerned, she was innocent until proven guilty. "O'Reilly, I really think you're overreacting. And you're forgetting that I'm not a criminal attorney. I can't handle this case by myself."

"I haven't forgotten that." He averted his eyes. "David's joining you on the case until this thing with Neddy blows over."

Please God, no! "Isn't there anybody else?" I said, my voice registering panic. "Somebody with less of an ego."

"Nope." He knew I wasn't happy about this news, but he was holding firm. "David and Neddy are the best criminal attorneys we've got. This case could make national headlines. I need my best troops on the front line. You two did a fine job in the Hayes case."

"Yeah, because I tolerated him. What if Tina doesn't go for this?"

"She will. Just tell her that until Neddy's name is cleared, David's filling in. I still want Neddy calling the shots from behind the scenes. I'm sure Tina Montgomery'll agree that it won't look good to have a murder suspect heading up her defense team."

"So we're letting the *L.A. Times* dictate how we staff our cases now?"

"The *Times* isn't dictating anything. I am." O'Reilly grabbed the newspaper and walked toward the door. "I just dropped by to let you know what was going on, Vernetta. Not to get your permission."

He was pulling rank and there was nothing I could do about it.

CHAPTER 28

As soon as O'Reilly left, I dialed Neddy's office. No answer. When I called her home phone, she didn't pick up until she heard my voice on her answering machine.

"I need to warn you," I said.

"Too late. I've got the great *L.A. Times* right here in front of me and I'm reading all the news that ain't fit to print. Think I should sue 'em for defamation?" She actually sounded lighthearted.

"Speaking as your attorney, I'd advise against that for the time being. You, okay, girl?"

"Hell no. I've defended dozens of murder suspects. Didn't think I'd ever be one."

I could hear the running of water and the clinking and panging of dishes in the background. "You're not. This is just media hype. You think Julie had anything to do with planting that story?"

"God, I hope not. The *Times* is pretty good about verifying their sources. So I guess the police are going to come knocking on my door and drag me away any minute now."

"I can't believe you're taking this so calmly," I said.

"You should've called here an hour ago. Before I had a chance to calm down."

I moved on to the real purpose of my call. "I think O'Reilly's going to take you off the Montgomery case," I said.

She didn't make a sound. But I knew her well enough to know that she had closed her eyes and was probably shaking her head.

"You okay?"

"Yep," she replied. But I could tell she wasn't. "I guess he has to do what he has to do. I told you I was thinking about asking for a leave of absence anyway. Maybe this is God's way of forcing me to proceed with that plan. Can't have a murderer defending a murderer."

"Don't joke like that, Neddy," I scolded. "I don't know about Tina Montgomery, but you're not a murderer. And you can't leave the case."

"Thanks for the vote of confidence, but didn't you just tell me I'm getting booted off?"

"Only temporarily," I said. The background noise quieted down and I assumed she had left the kitchen. "Just until this thing with Lawton is resolved."

"Let's hope so," she said. "So who's O'Reilly teaming you up with?"

"David," I said sadly. "But he still wants you involved behind the scenes, making sure we don't screw things up."

"You two are turning out to be quite a twosome," she teased.

But this was no laughing matter for me. "I'm definitely not looking forward to working with David again. I guess we should tell Tina about this as soon as possible. I'll try to set up a meeting with her this evening."

"I know David's a little hard to take sometimes, but to be honest, I've never worked with anybody who was better at focusing in on the minute details of a case. He can comb through a box of documents and come up with the one piece of evidence to turn the case around. He did that in a couple of cases I've had with him."

"Yeah, whatever," I said. "I don't care who they assign me to work with. I'm still going to be relying on you for guidance."

CHAPTER 29

When David and I met with Tina Montgomery later that evening, she did not respond well to the news that Neddy would not be handling her preliminary hearing.

"Neddy's the main reason I hired your firm," she said, her eyes wide, her face wrinkled with worry.

David and I were seated in Tina's living room, the weird green one. Her court-ordered ankle bracelet was hidden by a pair of extra-long slacks. This was the first time I'd seen her without her silver wine goblet.

"Well," I began, "Neddy's facing a difficult time right now. The police think—"

"I don't know if you've been reading the *L.A. Times,*" David said, rudely interrupting, "but Neddy's husband was murdered and she's a suspect in his death."

Tina raised both hands to her mouth. "Oh my God!"

I didn't like the way David had characterized Neddy's predicament and I needed to correct it. "Well, she's not exactly a suspect," I clarified. "The news story hinted at that because, as you know, Neddy and Lawton were going through a bitter divorce. Frankly, I think the D.A.'s office may've planted the story as a way of hurting your case."

"I haven't been reading the newspapers or looking at TV because of all the ridiculous things they're saying about my case." Tina was shaking her head, as if she couldn't believe what we were telling her.

Then her eyes clouded. "Who's making the decisions down there at the D.A.'s office, a bunch of kids?" Her voice was full of anger.

Both David and I interpreted that as a rhetorical question and let it ride. As if on cue, Kinga appeared with Tina's wine goblet.

"So Neddy didn't ask to be taken off my case?" she said, reaching for the goblet and taking a sip. "Your firm took her off?"

David turned to face me as if I should respond to Tina's question. I just glared back at him. Since he'd jumped in and started running the show, he could take the heat from our disappointed client.

He swallowed, then looked over at Tina. "Well, with this kind of attention focused on Neddy, right now—"

"I hate it when people avoid answering my questions," Tina said abruptly. "Did the firm take her off my case or was it Neddy's decision to leave?"

"It was the firm's decision," David said, growing suddenly timid. "O'Reilly didn't think it would be good for her to be trying a murder case right now. Her situation would draw unnecessary attention to your case."

"There couldn't be any more attention placed on my case than there already is. She didn't kill that man any more than I killed Max and I still want her to defend me. She'll know firsthand what it's like to be falsely accused of murder."

"Well, if you want her back on the case, you should give O'Reilly a call," I eagerly suggested. Maybe Tina could help me ditch David. "We think this is only a temporary situation. Of course, Neddy will be working with us on strategy from behind the scenes. In the meantime, we need to prepare you for your preliminary hearing. It's only three days away. First—"

"Let me explain what's going to happen," David said, cutting me off again.

I couldn't believe this. O'Reilly had a long conversation with both of us and made it clear that I would be lead counsel on the case in Neddy's absence. But David was plodding along as if he was the kingfish.

"A preliminary hearing is like a mini-trial," he explained, "except there's no jury. All the evidence is presented to the judge and decided by the judge. The prosecutor has the burden of proving that there's enough evidence to proceed with a trial. Unlike at a trial, however, the prosecution doesn't have to prove guilt beyond a reasonable doubt, only that there is probable cause to believe that you murdered your husband."

"So if they don't prove that, then there's no trial and I go free?" she asked.

Neddy and I had already gone over this with Tina. She was obviously testing David.

"Yes," David said cautiously. "But the burden of proof at a prelim is very easy to establish. In a case like this, it would be very unusual for the judge to find that there wasn't sufficient evidence to proceed to trial."

"So then this is just a waste of my time?"

"Well—uh—you could look at it that way," he said, "but there is also an advantage for us. The prelim gives us a chance to hear the prosecution's theory of the case and to lock in the testimony of their witnesses."

"Will I have to testify?"

"No," David said quickly. "Not at the prelim and not at trial either."

Tina pressed her hands against her cheeks. "I still can't believe this is happening to me."

David didn't attempt to offer any words of comfort to his new client. "We'd like to go over the testimony we think the prosecution's going to present as well as the evidence we plan to introduce." David started combing through a folder stuffed with papers. After his search turned up empty, he pulled out his car keys.

"Vernetta, I think I left the folder with my witness outlines in my car. Could you run out and get it for me?" The keys were dangling inches from my nose.

I sucked in air and mentally counted to five before opening my mouth, realizing I might not be able to control the words that came out. Instead of giving him a piece of my mind, however, I calmly took David's keys and stood up.

Once I'd made it outside, I parked myself on Tina's front steps and tried to practice a new meditation technique I'd read about in *Shape* magazine. Anybody watching me would have thought I was hyperventilating. Surprisingly, it made me feel much, much better. I could almost visualize my body temperature declining.

I had a very important decision to make. I could go back inside, take David's neck in my hands and squeeze it until his eyes popped out. Or, I could go fetch the folder, make a serious effort to tolerate him, and spend all my free time praying to God that the police found out who really killed Neddy's husband before I was forced to murder David.

CHAPTER 30

A nurse from Dr. Bell's office called early the next morning to ask if Jefferson and I could make it to her office that afternoon to discuss the results of our fertility tests. Anxiety instantly seized my body. When the nurse refused to give me any specifics over the telephone, my anxiety turned to panic.

During the drive over, Jefferson tried valiantly to calm me down.

"Stop overreacting, baby. It's probably no big deal." He gripped the steering wheel with his left hand and used his right to hold both of mine.

"I know she's going to tell me I can't have kids," I said, close to tears. "I never should've gotten that IUD."

"Hey, c'mon, you have to calm down. Didn't Dr. Bell say that with the help of technology it was almost impossible not to have a baby these days? So what if we have to make my boy in a test tube?"

He smiled over at me, but I didn't smile back.

"I'm so sorry for stressing you out about starting a family. Now, I probably can't even have a baby." Tears rolled down my cheeks. "It'll kill me if I can't give you a son."

Jefferson didn't say anything. Instead he made a sharp right turn and pulled into the parking lot of a strip mall.

"What're you doing?"

After turning off the engine, he hopped out, walked around to the passenger side and gently pulled me out of the car.

"Jefferson, what's going on?"

"Come here," he said, taking me into his arms. "I love you. And no matter what the doctor tells us, I'll still love you. And if the news is bad, I'll handle it. We'll both handle it."

We stood there in broad daylight in front of 7-Eleven, holding each other.

"I don't deserve you," I said.

"Tell me something I don't know," he grinned.

This time, as we waited in Dr. Bell's office, all the baby pictures plastered behind her desk haunted me. I could not shake the feeling that we would never be able to paste one of our kid's pictures on that board. I closed my eyes and said a silent prayer.

When Dr. Bell walked into the room, there was no trace of a smile on her face and the aloof way her eyes avoided mine told me that whatever was wrong was not some minor, fixable matter. She took a seat behind her desk before greeting us.

Jefferson squeezed my hand. His eyes told me that no matter what the problem was, he would fix it.

"I've never been good at delivering bad news," Dr Bell said, glancing down at a single sheet of paper on her desk. "So I'll just spit it out. The fertility tests detected a problem."

I gripped Jefferson's knee.

He scooted his chair closer to mine and slid his arm around my shoulder. "C'mon baby, don't freak out. Calm down."

"According to the tests we took," Dr. Bell continued, "I'm afraid you're sterile...Jefferson."

The arm that had been holding me moments before, fell away. "Sterile?" Jefferson sat up straight. "You must've gotten somebody else's tests results mixed up with mine, Doc." Jefferson tried to smile.

Dr. Bell looked apologetic. "I'm sorry."

Jefferson responded with a resentful huff. I tried to take his hand in mine, but he shook off my touch like it was toxic. "What do you mean, sterile? Are you saying my sperm count was low or something?"

Dr. Bell kept her gaze on me, unable to hold up under Jefferson's angry gaze.

"No. The tests showed no sperm at all," she said gently. "This is typically what happens when there's damage to the groin area as a child. Jefferson, do you recall suffering a groin injury as a kid?"

"No, I don't." He was incensed at the question. "This is some bullshit. I'm—"

He stopped and turned his head in my direction, but was actually looking past me. He'd obviously remembered something that caused him to freeze.

"What is it?" I reached over and forced my hand into his.

"I had an accident on my bike when I was about ten. Ran into a fence and got banged up pretty bad. Particularly my nuts. I remember my mother always telling me she was worried I wouldn't be able to make any babies." He turned back to Dr. Bell. "Are you telling me that because of that accident, I can't have kids?"

Dr. Bell's lips formed a straight line. "That's probably it."

Jefferson closed his eyes and his chest heaved forward.

"Why don't I give you two a few minutes alone." Dr. Bell picked up a folder and headed for the door.

Once she had left, I searched my mind for words of comfort to shower him with. The thought of Jefferson having a fertility problem had never crossed my mind and apparently not his either. "Jefferson, it doesn't matter," I said.

He responded with a cold, sarcastic chuckle.

"We can adopt," I said. "There're so many kids who need good homes. We can—"

He held up his hand. "Please, just stop."

"Baby, I know this is devastating news, but we love each other. It doesn't matter."

"That's bullshit! Of course it matters."

His voice was razor sharp. I felt like he had just thrown ice water into my face. He got up and walked over to a window near the door. He kept his back to me, blocking me out.

"Wait a minute, Jefferson," I said. "Isn't that what you just said to me on the way over here, when we thought it might be *me* with the problem? You said we could handle this. Are you saying it's different because it's you?"

At first, he didn't answer and just continued to stare out of the window. "Hell, yeah, it's different," he said finally.

Now I was getting incensed. "Why? Why is it different?"

"Because I'm a fuckin' man," he said heatedly. "I bet you know fifty women who can't get pregnant for one reason or another. How many brothers you know with a zero sperm count?"

I tried not to take the anger in his voice personally, but his look was too intense for me not to. "Jefferson, the fact that you're sterile doesn't mean you're not a man."

His cheeks filled up with air and he let it slowly seep out. "Damn. The word even sounds fucked up. 'Sterile.' Ain't this a muthafucka." He gripped the window ledge.

I stood behind him and forced my arms around his waist, pressing my face into his back. He remained rigid at first, then turned around and took me in his arms. I could feel the heavy pounding of his heart. His eyes were closed and he was biting his bottom lip.

When he finally spoke, I realized that I had never heard fear in his voice before. "Baby," he said, his voice filled with resignation, "this is some shit I ain't too sure I know how to handle."

CHAPTER 31

David and I sat stoically facing each other in one of the firm's large conference rooms. Stacks of documents and boxes from the Montgomery case covered the long rectangular table. It had only been a couple of days since we got the news from Dr. Bell, and Jefferson was still walking around like a shell-shocked Vietnam vet. I felt guilty as hell about being at work instead of at home with him. But Tina's preliminary hearing was less than forty-eight hours away and we still had a lot of work to do. I decided to work late tonight, to avoid an all-nighter tomorrow. I promised Jefferson that I'd be home by nine and I planned to keep that promise.

"Okay, let's go over the cross-examination outline for Oscar Lopez one more time," I said. "Then we can get out of here."

"I still say you're making a mistake not using the stuff we found out about Lopez's propensity to stretch the truth." David's tone was critical.

"Look, Neddy's already made that call and I agree with her. Even if we used what that waitress told us to discredit Lopez's identification of Tina, there's still a very strong chance that the judge is going to find probable cause. Since there's going to be a trial anyway, we'll be better off surprising Lopez with that information on our cross in front of a jury."

David started doodling on the side of his Starbucks cup. "The fact that the guy may have being lying about seeing Tina with a knife is some pretty powerful evidence. I would take the risk and use it at the prelim, even if the odds of success are low."

"You made that argument when we discussed this with Neddy." I was tired and I didn't want to expend what little energy I had left arguing with David. "How many times do we have to rehash this? That was the problem during the Hayes trial, you could never support a decision that wasn't yours."

He shifted in his seat. "No, the problem during the Hayes trial was that *you* refused to consider any idea that you didn't come up with."

I smiled to keep from blowing my top. "That's not true," I said calmly. "I considered every single idea you proposed. I just rejected them because they weren't workable. And obviously, I made the right decisions, because we won."

David had no response to that. He sat up in his chair and tossed his empty cup toward the trash can, missing it by a mile. "There's something else we need to figure out then," he said.

I couldn't imagine what was on his mind now. There was nothing else to figure out. The same game of one-upmanship that drove me nuts during the Hayes trial was happening all over again. With the news about Jefferson, and then Neddy possibly facing a murder charge, I was under too much stress to deal with any bull from David, and I planned to make that clear right now.

"Exactly what do we have to figure out, David?" I said, turning to look him in the eye.

"I think we should rethink you taking the lead at the prelim."

I chuckled. "That's already been decided. I know the case."

He loosened his tie and began rolling up his shirtsleeves, still avoiding my gaze. "I know the case, too, and I also know criminal procedure. You don't."

"I know enough," I said. "The prelim's not going to be any different than presenting evidence at a civil trial. I can handle it. You're just filling in until Neddy's back on the case, remember?"

"She may not be back on the case," he said.

"Do you know something I don't know?"

David rested his arms on the table. "Look, I'm the criminal attorney. There are a lot of procedural rules that could come up that you may not be equipped to handle."

"When that happens, then you should feel free to step in. Anyway,

I doubt you'll have to. I've been brushing up on the rules of criminal procedure."

"I still think I should take the lead."

I forced myself to stay cool. My lips formed a fake smile. "Like I said, David, this is a simple probable cause hearing. I can do it and I'm going to do it."

His face had turned beet red.

I went back to reading the Lopez outline, hoping I hadn't missed any important areas. I was so focused on the document, I almost forgot David was sitting there sulking until he abruptly stood up and slammed his chair into the table.

"Okay, go ahead," he muttered. "Everybody knows the only reason you're on this case in the first place is because you're black."

An unknown voice from someplace on high quietly encouraged me to count to ten before opening my mouth. I decided to count to twenty. I put down the Lopez outline, but continued to stare down at the documents in front of me.

"You can believe I'm on this case for whatever reason suits you," I said, still visibly unruffled. I knew David wanted to get a rise out of me, but I refused to give him that satisfaction. White folks were always claiming that we played the race card, but they had a whole deck full of them that they pulled out whenever it suited them.

"Every time a whiny little white boy like you doesn't get his way, he has to find something or somebody to blame," I said, still outwardly calm. "But you and I both know that I'm good—very good—at what I do. Now if you can't handle that, so be it. But the fact remains, I'm taking the lead at the prelim and there's not a damn thing you can do about it."

"Fine," he said, snatching his papers from the table. "I guess there's nothing more you need from me tonight. I hope you break a leg."

CHAPTER 32

O'Reilly trudged into my office without knocking the following afternoon. I knew he'd be stopping by. He needed to satisfy himself that I had everything under control for the preliminary hearing scheduled to begin the following day. He'd done the same thing the day before the Hayes trial.

"I hate to do this to you," he said, puffing out his cheeks and shoving his hands in his pockets, "but I have a new client for you."

It was probably the pressure of everything I was dealing with, but I lost it. "Are you out of your friggin' mind! I'm up to my neck in this Montgomery case. I barely see my husband as it is. By the time this case is over he'll be serving me with divorce papers. I can't take on another case. I won't take on another case!"

O'Reilly didn't react to my outburst. He gave me a few seconds to quiet down before he continued. "I think you'll want to take on this client," he said, more gently than I'd ever heard him speak before.

I opened my mouth but he raised his hand to quiet me.

"It's Neddy. The police want her down at the station for questioning. David's already on his way. I think you should be there for moral support."

I could barely stay within the speed limit as I raced over to Parker Center. I finally realized why I had never pursued a criminal law practice. It took too much out of you. Working on Tina's case, and now Neddy's, was like riding a roller coaster of emotion I had never had to face in an employment lawsuit. Suing on behalf of a fired worker or even defending a company accused of discrimination hadn't left me with many sleepless nights. The worst that could happen was the plaintiff walked away with nothing or the defendant had to pay millions. Nobody's freedom or life was on the line.

I exited the Harbor Freeway on Fourth Street, made a left onto Olive and a right onto First. I felt emotionally drained. I wanted to pull over and have a good cry, but I knew I had to be strong for Neddy as well as Jefferson.

I got to Parker Center in record time. A female officer showed me into a small room where David and Neddy were already waiting. She hugged me in a way that let me know she was grateful I was there.

This was my first police interrogation. The room looked nothing like the ones on *Law & Order*. The lighting was elementary-school bright, not dark and ominous, and the furniture was in decent shape, though a bit dated. The only sign that criminals may have inhabited the place was a faint musty smell. Body odor masked by Pine-Sol.

I turned to examine all four walls. "So where's the two-way mirror," I asked, though I realized my question sounded as if I were trying to crack a joke.

"This isn't TV," David said, as if he were talking to a child.

Before I could think up something cruel to fire back at him, the door opened. Two men walked in with identical swaggers. Detective Mark Wilson was thin, white and probably in his mid-thirties. He looked like your average, nonthreatening high school history teacher. He was wearing a cheap tie and sports jacket, which he probably wore for months before dry cleaning. He definitely didn't own an iron. His partner, Detective Phillip Graham, was a chubby black man with bad razor bumps along his jaw line. He was older, probably by about ten years. A toothpick dangled loosely from the corner of his mouth. By the way he scowled at us, I figured Graham would be playing the bad cop.

"We just have a few questions," Detective Wilson began, "so this shouldn't take too long." He sat down across from Neddy, David, and me. Detective Graham leaned against the wall with his arms folded.

Before they could ask their first question, Julie pranced in.

"Why is she here?" Neddy said angrily.

"For moral support," Julie answered snottily.

"Girls, girls," Detective Graham injected. "Can't we all just get along?"

Neddy stared harshly at Julie as if her predicament were all Julie's fault. Julie sat down in a wobbly chair near the door and crossed her long legs.

"First, can you tell us where you were at the time your husband was murdered?" Detective Wilson asked.

"When was he murdered?" Neddy said with attitude.

"Don't you know?" Detective Wilson seemed prepared to spar. Maybe I was wrong and he was the bad cop.

Neddy folded her arms. "Should I?"

"Well, I figured you might've read it in the papers," Wilson said.

"I don't recall any of the articles I read listing the time of death," Neddy said, even more sarcastically than before.

I didn't think it was wise for Neddy to act like such a bitch. She knew the routine and she also knew that it was a mistake to antagonize the police.

Detective Wilson definitely didn't care for Neddy's attitude. "Based on the time he was last seen alive, the neighbors' reports of gunshots, and the autopsy report, we believe your husband was killed on the fourteenth, sometime between 10:15 and 10:30 P.M. So where were you?"

"I was home reading a book."

"What book?" Detective Wilson asked.

"James Patterson's *First to Die*."

I placed my hand on Neddy's forearm and whispered into her ear. "You're not going to gain anything by pissing them off. Just answer their questions so we can leave."

She stared back at me with a look that said she knew what she was doing.

It surprised me that Detective Wilson looked as if he was straining to hear what I had just said to Neddy.

"What time did you leave the office on the fourteenth?" he asked.

Neddy thought for a moment. "I don't know. Probably around nine or 9:15," she said. "You already asked me these questions when you came to my house the other night," Neddy sneered. "Why'd you drag me down here to go through this again?"

Julie huffed impatiently. "Because we—"

"This is our interrogation," Wilson said cutting her off. Julie slumped back into her chair. Having to sit on the sidelines was killing her.

Detective Graham, still leaning against the wall, decided to jump into the fray. "When we first spoke to you, we didn't know how much you hated your husband," he said, pulling up a chair and sitting down directly in front of Neddy. "Seems you were pretty upset about that spousal support order."

"Yes, I was upset about it. But not upset enough to kill him."

"Did you know he was killed with a gun that was registered to you?" Graham asked.

Neddy's eyes widened for just a few seconds, demonstrating an absolute lack of knowledge. "No—no, I didn't," she said, her first words spoken without hostility.

Graham smiled, as he closely studied her reaction. "So, when did you buy the gun?"

"You just said it was registered to me. Don't you know?"

"We know the date you registered it. We don't know when you bought it."

Neddy stopped to think again. "I'm not sure. I've had it a while. At least nine or ten years."

"Did you have a particular reason for buying it?"

"Protection."

"From what?"

"Criminals. I used to be a P.D. Sometimes my clients weren't happy about being convicted and they blamed me rather than their criminal activity."

Graham seemed dissatisfied with her answer. "Any client ever threaten you?"

Neddy smiled. "Sure."

"Ever file a police report?"

"No," she spat. "I don't like cops."

I heard Julie grunt from her corner of the room. I had almost forgotten she was there. Detective Graham was getting annoyed. He cracked his knuckles. "So when was the last time you saw the gun?"

Neddy looked down at her hands. "About ten months ago. I left it at the house when I moved out."

"When you lived there, where'd you keep the gun?" he asked.

"In the bedroom closet." She looked up at him. "Locked in a cabinet."

Wilson leaned across the table. "Did Lawton have a key to that cabinet?"

"No," Neddy said.

"So no one had access to that cabinet but you?"

"That's right," she said boldly.

What the hell was Neddy doing? She'd just admitted that she was the only one who had access to the weapon that killed her husband. She might as well stand up and confess to murdering him right now. I pushed my chair back from the table and got up. "I need a few minutes alone with my client," I declared.

"I told you, we don't need to talk," Neddy snapped.

I stayed put. "Yes, we do."

David stood up, too, but did nothing to help me get Neddy outside.

"Sit back down," Neddy said, grabbing my forearm and pulling me back into my seat. "I'm answering the questions posed to me and nothing more," she said. "Yes, I was the only one who had the key to that cabinet." She turned back to Detective Graham and continued. There was a condescending edge to her voice. "This expert interrogator here asked me where I kept the gun when I lived there and that's the question I answered. Before I moved out, that's where it was kept. Locked in a cabinet."

Detective Graham twisted his lips sideways and his toothpick seemed poised to fall, but somehow hung on. "Okay, then, what happened to the gun after you moved out?"

"I left it with Lawton."

"And why'd you do that?"

Her hands were balled into fists. "Because I was no longer a P.D. and he wanted it."

Graham could tell he was getting to her and he was enjoying it. "Did you give Lawton a key to the cabinet?"

"No. I took the cabinet. He kept the gun."

"Do you know where he kept it?"

"No, but I know he didn't keep it locked up." Neddy suddenly looked exhausted, as if the short Q & A had taken the wind out of her.

"And how do you know that?"

"Because we fought about it. He didn't think it made sense to keep it locked up because you couldn't get to it if you needed it in an emergency. And since we no longer—" She stopped and took in a breath. "Since we didn't have kids in the house, he said there was no reason to lock it up. I insisted on locking it up anyway and we had a big fight about it."

"It seems you two fought about a lot of things," Graham taunted.

Neddy's bottom lip began to tremble. "I'm here to answer questions, not to respond to your sarcastic comments."

Graham passed the baton back to Wilson. "Why did Lawton need a gun?" Wilson asked. "He hadn't freed any criminals who could turn on him."

Neddy let Wilson's remark roll off her back. "He grew up with guns. He liked the idea of having one around for protection."

"Protection from what?" Wilson asked.

"I have no idea."

The two detectives stared at Neddy for a good long while, and she stared right back. Julie, still uncharacteristically mute, obviously liked seeing Neddy in the hot seat. She took out a small note pad and wrote something down.

"Look, I don't have time for this nonsense," Neddy said finally. "There's no way you have any evidence that links me to my husband's murder because I didn't kill him. Let's just finish the rest of your questions so I can go home."

Detective Graham got up and sat on the edge of the table. His stomach rested in his lap in two overlapping folds of fat. His cotton shirt was stretched so tight around his belly that the buttons seemed poised to pop off at any minute and put somebody's eye out. I moved my seat to the right, out of the line of fire.

"When was the last time you talked to your husband?" Detective Graham asked, leaning in. He was coming dangerously close to invading her personal space. Mine, too.

Neddy opened her purse and pulled out her date book and began flipping pages. "The thirteenth."

"That's the day before he was killed," Graham said.

Neddy stared blankly back, challenging him with her eyes. "And your point is what?"

Graham didn't answer her question. "Where'd you talk to him?"

Neddy folded her arms, then unfolded them again. "At his attorney's office."

"What did you two talk about?"

"How much of an asshole he was."

Graham chuckled. "Your words or his?"

"Mine."

"So did you two always argue a lot?" Graham continued, his sidekick now relegated to an inferior role.

"You might say that. I don't think we've had a conversation that wasn't an argument since I moved out of the house."

"Your husband took five bullets in the chest, you know."

"And once again, your point is what?"

"My point is, whoever killed him wanted to make it personal. Whoever was holding that gun had a lot of hatred for the man."

"A lot of people hated him."

"So you say." Graham leaned against the wall. "Now when did you say you last saw the gun?"

Neddy clasped her hands together, her frustration obvious. "I told you that already. Before I moved out of the house ten months ago."

"The gun was wiped clean except for one partial print. You mind submitting to a fingerprint check?"

Neddy laughed. "Of course my prints are going to be on the gun. I owned it. You can take my prints when you arrest me. Not before."

David interrupted. "Neddy, are you sure you don't want to step outside to talk for a moment?"

She turned to him and rolled her eyes. "I'm quite sure."

I felt like I should be doing something, but I didn't know what. I agreed with David, though. We needed to get Neddy outside so we could tell her to cool it.

The detectives asked a few more questions to which they already knew the answers and then let us go. I was convinced that they had only ordered Neddy down to the station to make her sweat. While she had a motive to kill Lawton, there was nothing else that tied her to his murder except her gun. Since she owned it, it only made sense that it would have her fingerprints on it. They would need much more than that to arrest her for killing him.

Once we were safely outside, David was the first to berate her. "You didn't do yourself any favors by pissing off the cops like that. And you know that. I've heard you tell clients the same thing a thousand times." He was really mad.

"I know what I'm doing," Neddy said.

"I don't think you do. I would advise you to be a little less hostile the next time the police come calling."

Neddy knew David was right, but she was stuck on evil. "Like I said, I know what I'm doing."

David shrugged, then walked off toward his car.

Neddy and I began walking toward the opposite end of the parking lot. I had something to say along the same lines as David's comments, but decided to save my speech for another time—after Neddy had cooled off. We reached Neddy's car before we got to mine.

"He's dead and he's still fucking with me," she said, her voice quivering.

"It won't be that way forever."

"Easy for you to say. You have the perfect husband."

That comment hit me like a bowling ball in the gut. "Not exactly. There's a one hundred percent chance that when I walk through the door tonight my husband will be angry, drunk, or out someplace doing God knows what."

Neddy looked at me with concerned eyes. "What's going on?"

"You know how much Jefferson wanted a son?"

"Yeah."

"Well, we just found out that one of us is sterile and it's not me."

"Oh my God! I'm so sorry. How is he handling it?"

"He's not," I said, digging into my purse for my keys. "He's drinking so much now it's beginning to scare me."

"Are you going to be okay? Does he get violent when he drinks?"

"Thank God, no. If anything, he's even nicer when he's drunk."

She reached over and gave me a hug. "I had no idea," she said. "You must be under a lot of pressure right now. Tomorrow's prelim, Jefferson, and then I get thrown into the mix."

"Don't worry about me," I said. "It's you I'm worried about. I'm just glad I could be here for you." I hugged her back.

Maybe now was a good time to say what I had to say about her performance in that interrogation room. "I know you don't want to hear this," I said, "but David was right. The way you acted in there was a mistake. A big one."

She looked down at her hands. "I know, I know. But I couldn't help it. There's no reason for them to be subjecting me to this. And I don't think they would be if I weren't an ex-P.D. I destroyed a lot of cops on the witness stand during my heyday." She smiled wryly.

"Yeah, but they had the upper hand in there, not you. If Tina had acted that way with the police, you would've pulled her out of that room by her ear."

Neddy's face tensed. "You're right. It won't happen again." She pressed a button on her key, opening the door to her BMW.

"Wish me luck at the prelim in the morning," I said. "I'm going to need it."

"No you won't. You're going to do great, I know it. I'd love to watch you in action but I'd probably attract more TV cameras than Tina right now."

"I understand," I said. "I know you'll be there in spirit." I walked over to my Land Cruiser, only one car away, and unlocked the door. "Why do you think Julie was here tonight?"

"For intimidation purposes, of course," Neddy said. "That's one of the reasons I acted the way I did. I wasn't about to let her see me sweat."

"You think she's behind them bringing you down?"

"I wouldn't put it past her." She was about to climb inside, then stuck her head back out. "Julie can pull all the stunts she wants. The bottom line is I didn't kill my husband. I may have wanted to, but I didn't."

CHAPTER 33

By the time I made it home, Jefferson was already asleep.

I peered into the bedroom and saw him sprawled across our king-size bed. Jefferson knew I hated it when he slept on top of our five-hundred-dollar Calvin Klein comforter. I thought about waking him up to fuss about it, but headed into the den instead.

I gently opened the cabinet underneath the bar, being careful not to make any noise, and scanned the shelves. Yesterday there had been a full bottle of Hennessy sitting on the second shelf. Now it was gone. I walked into the kitchen and gingerly lifted the lid of the trash can. There were four empty beer cans, but no Hennessy bottle.

From the kitchen, I opened the door to the garage and switched on the light. The cold air sent a chill through my body. Inside one of the city-issued trash cans, buried at the bottom, were not one, but two empty Hennessy bottles, as well as half a dozen beer cans that weren't there three days ago.

I went back inside and sat down at the kitchen table. I'd never seen Jefferson consume this much alcohol. His deliberate efforts to hide his drinking from me meant it was even more of a problem than I'd thought it was. We'd had a big argument about his drinking the day before. If I brought it up again, it would be more of the same. He would accuse me of overreacting and storm out of the house. For now, all I could do was pray his binge drinking would pass.

I tiptoed into the bedroom and tried to undress without waking him.

"So tomorrow's your big day, huh?" he said groggily.

"Yep."

"You ready?"

"I guess so." I unbuttoned my blouse, tossed it onto the chaise in the corner and stepped out of my skirt.

"You don't sound too confident." He sat up and turned on the lamp on the nightstand. "Anything I can do to help?"

"Yeah, how about a big hug," I said, pulling back the comforter, forcing him to crawl underneath the sheet.

When I fell into his arms, I could smell alcohol on his breath. We lay together for a long while, neither one of us speaking. *How long could I ignore this problem and how bad was it going to get?*

"How're you feeling?" I asked.

"How do you think I'm feeling?" he said, without any hostility. "Pretty fucked up."

"Jefferson, I know you think I don't know what you're going through, but—"

"Don't," he said, putting a finger to my lips. "Just don't."

But I couldn't let him keep shutting me out. "Jefferson, I don't know how to help. I don't know what to say. I don't know what to do."

"There's nothing you can say and there's nothing you can do. Let's just talk about something else."

At some point, we would have to talk. But for now, I agreed to abide by his decision not to. I nuzzled in closer to him. "Okay," I said, "what do you want to talk about?"

"You think this chick you're defending is innocent?"

I didn't reply. I didn't want to talk about Tina Montgomery either, and I was too tired to tell him what was going on with Neddy.

He gently nudged my shoulder.

"You're not falling asleep on me, are you?"

"No, I'm still awake." I still didn't answer his question.

"Wait a minute," he said. "You think she did it."

"What I think is irrelevant."

"Oh that's a new one. I don't think I ever recall hearing you say your opinion about a case was irrelevant. So this criminal stuff is kinda messin' with your head, huh?"

Jefferson knew me well. Too well. "That's one way of putting it."

"I'll never understand how you do what you do."

Another whiff of Jefferson's pungent alcohol breath hit me in the face. "It's not that hard," I said. "You just focus on the facts."

"But what if the facts say your client's guilty?"

This conversation felt like déjà vu for me. His questions were the same ones I had asked Neddy during that first night at her house. "It's never that black and white," I said. "There'll always be some facts in your client's favor. So you concentrate on those." *Did I actually believe that or was I simply echoing Neddy's spiel?*

"Your client may've actually killed her husband. Do you realize you could be helping her go free?"

"The jury makes the decision. Not me. I'm just putting the facts on the table."

Jefferson wasn't buying that. "Yeah, you're putting the facts on the table, but not all of them. How could you? You think she's guilty."

"I never said that."

"Yeah, but you haven't said she's innocent either."

"You realize this conversation could get me disbarred, don't you?"

"Really," he said, feigning excitement. "Tell me who to call and I'll dial the number right now. That might be the only way for me to get some time with you."

"Aw, c'mon, Jefferson. It's not that bad. We spend time together."

"When's the last time we went out to dinner or to a movie?"

"I don't know. You never ask me out."

"That's because by the time you get home, everything's closed."

"You're exaggerating," I lied.

"Am I?"

"Yep."

The room fell silent. Jefferson reached up and turned off the lamp. "Baby, I don't want to stress you out the day before your first big criminal case, but we can't continue like this."

"It's not that bad."

"Maybe to you it isn't."

I exhaled and pulled the thin blanket up to my neck.

"I'm just asking you to find some balance in your life. You want to practice law, cool. Just pencil in some face time with your husband every once in a while."

"Okay, I will," I mumbled, drifting off. "But if I don't get to sleep right now so I can wake up in time for that prelim tomorrow, you're going to have me around 24/7 because I won't have a job."

CHAPTER 34

This was my first preliminary hearing and I wanted to throw up.

The courtroom was packed, mostly with reporters. David sat at the far end of the defense table with Tina sandwiched between us. She was dressed in a classy, purple linen suit that looked as if it had been tailor-made for her petite frame. How she dressed didn't matter so much before the judge, but it would be a different story with a jury present. I made a mental note to remind her to dress down for the trial. I wanted the jurors to view her as one of them, not some rich, snobbish socialite.

While I reread my witness outlines, which I'd already memorized, David doodled on a piece of paper. We hadn't said very much to each other since we exchanged words in the conference room. Although he was second-chairing the case, I knew he planned to offer me zero help.

Julie and her co-counsel, Sandy McIntyre, were seated at the prosecution table a good four feet to the right of us. Sandy was only three years out of Hastings Law School and looked like she belonged behind the front desk at the nearest public library. She had a mousy air about her and avoided making eye contact with anyone who looked her way. Her bland beige suit probably came from the sale rack at Target. Her more-experienced colleague overshadowed her in every conceivable way.

Julie was wearing a large-collared white blouse and a striking midnight blue, Bill Blass skirt suit. I knew the label because I had seen the same suit in a store window in Century City a month earlier. When I'd walked inside to check out the price, I gagged. I guess Julie spent a good chunk of her check on clothes. Tiny pearl earrings dangled from her earlobes and a matching necklace draped her neck. The look on her face told me that she'd drank blood with her scrambled eggs that morning. I tried to convince myself that she was just as nervous as I was. Too bad she didn't look it.

"All rise," the bailiff called out, "the courtroom of the Honorable Betty McKee is now in session."

We briefly stood as Judge McKee hobbled into the courtroom from a private entrance to the left of the bench. McKee was one of the city's first female judges, which meant she had endured a lot of crap. She was a short, squat woman in her mid-sixties who conducted her courtroom in a fast-paced, no-nonsense manner. She was considered smart and fair and was well liked by both prosecutors and defense attorneys. I heard that Julie had appeared before her several times and it was soon apparent that there was a strong mutual respect between them. Hence, Julie was already one-up on me and the hearing had barely started.

I looked around the courtroom and realized that I'd never had a case where women played all the key roles. A local tabloid had dubbed the case the "All-Chick Show."

Judge McKee flipped through a stack of documents on her desk and called out the case name and number, then reviewed some other administrative matters, which, frankly, I was too nervous to pay close attention to. The judge looked at Julie and ignored me.

"Are The People ready to proceed?"

"Yes, Your Honor, The People are ready."

Judge McKee turned an expectant glance in my direction, but didn't say anything. I took the cue.

"The defense is ready as well, Your Honor."

I glanced at Tina, who had a hopeful look on her face. She was keeping up the same front she had maintained so well during her marriage to Max. David might as well have been asleep.

Behind us, reporters and onlookers were squeezed into the eight rows of wooden benches like a box of matchsticks. Only one TV camera was allowed inside the courtroom. It fed video into the media room on the fifth floor, which was packed with even more reporters.

Though we had told Tina there was only a slim possibility that she wouldn't be held over for trial, in reality, there was no way in hell Judge McKee was going to dismiss this case at the prelim stage. Max Montgomery was too well-known and the case had attracted too much publicity. The judge had her career to think about, too. Hopefully, by the time the trial started, Neddy's name would be cleared and I'd be joining her at the defense table.

Julie's first witness was the coroner, Dr. Michael Winthrop. Julie breezed through the doctor's impressive educational and professional background and then covered a few boring minutes of medical jargon about the cause of death. After verifying that he had written the autopsy report, Dr. Winthrop established that Max Montgomery died from multiple stab wounds in the neck and chest.

My cross-examination of Dr. Winthrop lasted all of ten minutes. We had no evidence to indicate that anything other than the stab wounds caused Max's death, so it would have been a mistake to waste time trying to attack the doctor's testimony.

The prosecution's next witness was the crime scene investigator, Detective Richard Lowery. He was the person who had scoured the hotel room where Max was killed and come up with a sophisticated theory of what had likely happened in the suite that night.

Julie took Detective Lowery through several key points he'd uncovered during his investigation, facts she would undoubtedly use at trial to persuade the jury that Tina Montgomery was guilty of murder. The detective testified that a hotel worker spotted someone who resembled Tina outside Max's room carrying a steak knife, the same type of weapon used to kill Mr. Montgomery. He also pointed out that Tina was at the Ritz-Carlton on the night her husband was killed, that the footprints found in Max's hotel room belonged to someone who wore a woman's size six—Tina's shoe size—and that there was no sign of forced entry into Max's suite, which was apparently set up for a romantic tryst. Detective Lowery further claimed his investigation uncovered that Max had a penchant for extramarital affairs. Finally, he surmised that the killer wasn't very strong and was most likely a woman.

Julie paraded back and forth from the witness box to the prosecutor's table, reigning over the courtroom as if she owned it. "Detective Lowery, I'd like to direct your attention to page six of Exhibit 5, your crime scene report," she said. Julie handed the document to him and he quickly confirmed that he had prepared it. "Can you read the last sentence on that page?"

I hesitated a second, then sprang to my feet. "Objection, best evidence rule, the document speaks for itself."

Judge McKee shot me an annoyed glance. "Overruled."

I felt like an idiot. That was not a proper objection. I needed to relax.

Detective Lowery read from the report. "It's likely that the suspect was between five and five-feet-five inches tall." He looked up at Julie, then responded to a question that he hadn't been asked. "I think Mrs. Montgomery is 5'4"."

"Objection, nonresponsive," I said. "Your Honor, please instruct the witness to respond to the questions asked."

The judge groaned and peered over at the witness box. "Detective Lowery, this is not your first time testifying. You know how it works. You're instructed to respond only to the questions asked."

He nodded. "Sorry, Your Honor."

Julie did not appreciate my interruption. "Can you tell me how you reached your conclusion regarding the murderer's height?"

"My conclusion is based on my analysis of the size-six footprints, the angle of the stab wounds, as well as the force and depth of the wounds."

"What else can you tell us about the killer?"

"She was—"

"Objection!" I was out of my seat in an instant. "There's been no determination that the killer was a woman."

"Sustained."

I was focused like a radar, tracking Julie's every word. I was prepared to object the minute she headed down an improper path.

"In light of that objection," Julie said, "what can you tell us about the killer, besides his or her gender?"

"He or she was not very strong."

"And how did you reach that conclusion?"

Detective Lowery went into a long diatribe based partly on physics. Julie asked a few more questions, then walked back over to the prosecution table.

"I have no further questions at this time, Your Honor." Julie looked my way before taking her seat. In a prelim, it would have been a mistake for the prosecution to expose its entire hand. The only goal here was to produce enough evidence to convince the judge that there was probable cause to proceed. At trial, when impressionable jurors were present, I was certain Detective Lowery's direct testimony would last much longer.

When I stood to begin my cross-examination, my legs felt as wobbly as two strands of spaghetti. I remained close to the counsel table. If I fainted, I wanted something to break my fall.

"Detective Lowery, you testified that you believe Max Montgomery knew his killer because there was no indication that he tried to fight off the attacker."

"Yes, that was my testimony."

"Isn't it possible that the killer snuck in on him and surprised him in the tub before he could stand up and defend himself?"

He shrugged. "It's possible, but I don't think that was the case."

"And why is that?"

"The bathroom was a big, wide open room. No one could've snuck in on anybody. The minute someone appeared in the doorway, the person would've been spotted."

"Isn't it possible Mr. Montgomery might've been asleep in the tub?"

He chuckled. "Anything's possible, counselor."

I didn't like Detective Lowery's arrogance. "You were one of the investigators on the scene when Mrs. Montgomery's home was searched, weren't you?"

"Yes."

"And you didn't find a single pair of shoes that matched the footprints found in the hotel room?"

"That's correct," he said. "But we found dozens of size sixes in Mrs. Montgomery's closet."

He was going off on his own tangent again, but I decided not to complain to the judge. "And you found some other sizes as well, didn't you?"

"Yes."

"Exactly how many different sizes did you find?"

I knew he didn't want to answer my question. "I don't remember."

"Let me see if I can help you." I walked over to the defense table and opened a folder. "I direct the witness to Exhibit 10."

"Do you recognize this document?" I said, handing it to him.

"Yes."

"Can you tell the court what it is?"

He grudgingly browsed it. "Yes, it's a list of the items we took from the defendant's home."

"Is that your signature on the last page?"

"Looks like it."

"Does it look like it, or is it your signature?" I challenged.

"Yes, it's mine."

"Based on your own report, how many pairs of shoes did you take from Mrs. Montgomery's home?"

He looked down at the document. "Fifty-two."

"And none of those fifty-two pairs matched the shoe prints found at the scene, did they?"

He smiled. "No, but most killers dispose of their shoes and clothes."

I was livid. "Objection, Your Honor! Detective Lowery's statement was totally inappropriate!"

"All right, Mr. Lowery," the judge admonished. "Enough of the wisecracking. You know better. One more time and I'm holding you in contempt."

I heard David chuckle and that rattled me even more. He was sitting back, looking completely relaxed, his right ankle resting on the opposite knee.

I swallowed hard and continued.

"So, Detective Lowery, does Exhibit 10 refresh your memory as to the number of different shoe sizes you confiscated from Mrs. Montgomery's home?"

He frowned. "Yeah, a few sevens, several six and a halfs, but mostly sixes."

"And you found no hair, fibers, or any other evidence tying Mrs. Montgomery to the crime scene, isn't that correct?"

"Yes," he said. He was half slouched in the chair, his body leaning carelessly to the side.

"And you also didn't find any blood matching Mrs. Montgomery's blood type at the scene either, did you?"

"Nope." He answered more quickly this time.

"Considering the number of times that Mr. Montgomery was stabbed, don't you think it's odd that the killer didn't cut himself—or herself?"

"No, not at all. Not as long as the killer kept her—excuse me—his or her hands away from the blade of the knife."

"Detective Lowery, you've testified that the killer wasn't very strong."

"That's correct."

"Do you know any men who aren't very strong?"

He smiled. He knew exactly where I was trying to lead him. "Sure."

"And what about men who are between five feet and five-feet-five, ever met any of those?"

"A few." The confident way he pursed his lips told me he wasn't the least bit worried about my line of questioning.

"You can't point to any evidence that conclusively rules out the possibility that the killer was a man, can you?"

"Only DNA evidence is conclusive," he said. "But based on my investigation, the odds are greater that the killer was a woman."

I really had no place else to go. "But you wouldn't bet your career on that estimate would you?"

He paused. "I don't bet."

I asked a few more questions that didn't really gain me any ground. The judge called a recess and Tina, David, and I convened in a small meeting room across from the courtroom reserved for the defense.

Before we could even get seated, David went on the attack.

"You should've gone after Lowery a little harder," he said, chiding me.

David was really out of line criticizing my cross in front of the client and he knew it. "It wouldn't have done any good," I said. "He's an experienced detective and he testifies all the time. He's not the kind of witness you can shake."

"I'm not talking about shaking him," he said. "There's a lot of information in that crime scene report. I would've gone through each piece of evidence: the estimated time of death, the type of knife, where the body was found. We needed to pin him down on those elements so that if he changes his story at trial, then we have something we can use to impeach him."

All that sounded reasonable, it's just too bad David didn't raise any of it when we were prepping. I couldn't let Tina see how much

David's Monday morning quarterbacking was getting to me. Right now, she was waiting for my explanation.

"Let's just concentrate on our next witness," I said, ignoring his comments. "I'm purposefully saving our more aggressive tactics for Oscar Lopez. When he takes the stand tomorrow, he's the one I plan to go after."

CHAPTER 35

The prosecution began day two of the preliminary hearing by calling Oscar Lopez, the witness who posed the most significant threat to Tina Montgomery's freedom.

Lopez had smooth brown skin, a waiflike physique, and bad teeth. He was dressed in jeans and a faded cotton shirt. When he sat down in the witness box, he looked like a scared teenager. He had a nervous habit of running his fingers through his dark, greasy hair every few minutes and his eyes darted all over the courtroom, but never in the direction of the defense table.

Julie began her direct examination of Lopez from her seat. She looked unusually smug as she took him through his workday on the night Max Montgomery was murdered.

"Mr. Lopez, tell us what you saw that night after you stepped out of the elevator onto the fifth floor." Lopez spoke fairly decent English, but with a strong Spanish accent that made it difficult to catch his every word.

"I saw a lady, a black lady, walking down the hallway."

"What was the lady wearing?"

He paused. I assumed he was trying to remember the lines Julie had fed him. "A black dress."

"Please describe the dress."

"It was very shiny."

"Was it a long dress?"

I stood up. "Objection, leading." My objection was technically valid, but I knew I would be overruled. My only goal was to throw off Julie's flow.

Judge McKee grimaced. "Overruled," she said, giving me a hard look to let me know she knew exactly what game I was playing.

Lopez looked from Julie to me to the judge and then back to Julie again, uncertain of what was expected of him following the exchange of legal jargon.

"Mr. Lopez, was the woman wearing a long dress or a short dress?" Julie asked.

He seemed confused. "Long," he said wringing his hands. "I think."

Julie kept her cool, but Sandy winced. Tina's black cocktail dress wasn't long. It fell just below her knees. Score one for the defense.

"Did you get a good look at the woman?"

He nodded.

"Mr. Lopez, you need to answer audibly," Julie said.

The word "audibly" had apparently thrown him.

Judge McKee leaned over the side of the bench and peered down at the trembling witness. "Mr. Lopez, you have to answer 'yes' or 'no.' The court reporter cannot transcribe a nod of the head."

"Oh, okay," Lopez said, even more frightened now that he'd been admonished by the judge.

Julie took over again. "Is the lady you saw on the fifth floor that night in this courtroom today?" she asked.

Lopez kept his eyes on the floor of the jury box. "Yes."

"Can you identify her for us?"

Lopez lifted his head and looked over at Tina. "That's the lady," he said. He turned back to Julie, then looked as if he'd forgotten something. "Yes, that's the lady," he said again. This time he dramatically extended his arm and pointed a finger in Tina's direction. A classic prosecution-inspired move.

I felt Tina flinch, but the blank expression on her face did not change. We had warned her to avoid any emotional extremes, negative or positive.

"Did the woman have anything in her hands?" Julie asked.

"Yes. A knife," Lopez said anxiously. "With a black handle."

"And where was she going?"

"Into room 502."

After a few more questions that painted a clear picture that Mr. Lopez saw Tina marching off to kill her husband, it was my turn.

Lopez had refused to talk to Detective Smith, placing us at a definite disadvantage. It surprised me that Julie hadn't spent any time establishing how long Lopez had been on the fifth floor and where he was standing in relationship to Tina when he supposedly saw her go into Max's hotel room. I had to make a snap decision. Hammer away at him on these facts now, or save it for trial. If I ignored it now, Julie would assume we had missed it. Later, at trial, both he and Julie would be caught off guard when we brought it up. Even though I knew our case wasn't strong enough to cause Judge McKee to find a lack of probable cause, I decided this information was too important to leave until trial. First, though, I had to discredit Lopez as much as I could without divulging our suspicions that his whole story about seeing a woman with a knife was a big fat lie.

"Mr. Lopez, have you ever worn glasses?"

"No, Miss," he said proudly.

"And is your eyesight pretty good?"

"Yes, very good."

He smiled at me and I smiled back. He seemed to prefer my line of questioning to Julie's. That would soon change. "When's the last time you had an eye exam?"

"I don't remember."

"Was it in the last five years?"

"No."

"The last ten years?"

"No, I don't think so." He nervously looked to Julie for advice she couldn't give him.

"So it's been at least ten years since you've had your eyes examined?"

"Probably."

He finally figured out that I was trying to suggest that his eyes had failed him on the night of Max's murder and he resented me for it.

"Have you ever had your eyes examined, Mr. Lopez?"

"Sure. Yes." Lopez nervously bit his fingernail.

"And was it here in the United States?"

He looked worried now. "No. Back in Mexico."

"Now, going back to the night of Mr. Montgomery's murder.

How far away were you from the woman you believe you saw on the fifth floor?"

"About ten feet." He sounded increasingly unsure of himself.

"Can you estimate ten feet for me?"

"Objection, calls for speculation," Julie said without any real conviction.

The judge didn't even blink. "Overruled."

Lopez was again confused by the legal banter.

"Go ahead," I said, "you can answer the question."

"You want me to show you what is ten feet?" he asked.

"Yes," I said. "Measuring from where you're seated, show me how far away you think ten feet would be?"

"From here," he said, pointing to the rim of the witness box, "to the back of that table."

"Let the record reflect that Mr. Lopez has identified the distance from the outer edge of the witness box to the rear of the prosecutor's table," I said. The distance Lopez estimated was easily more than thirty feet, not ten. "Mr. Lopez, the woman you saw, how was her hair styled?"

He paused. "I don't remember."

"Do you remember what color shoes she was wearing?"

"No."

"What about earrings? Was she wearing any earrings?"

"No, I don't know." He seemed to shrink an extra inch with each "no" answer.

"Was she wearing a watch?"

"I don't know."

Lopez could see that Julie was perturbed. He was obviously concerned that his series of "no" answers might make the prosecutor mad enough to deport him.

"Exactly how long did you observe the woman?" I asked.

"Only a few seconds."

"How many?"

"Just a few, I don't know."

"More than ten?"

"I don't know."

"Less than ten?"

Julie was on her feet this time. "Objection, asked and answered, argumentative, calls for speculation. Mr. Lopez has stated that he doesn't remember how long he looked at Mrs. Montgomery in that hallway. No need to keep badgering him."

"Sustained. Let's move it along, counselor," Judge McKee warned.

Julie had just gotten in a pretty nice swipe, referring to Mrs. Montgomery's presence outside Max's hotel room as if it were fact. I hope she didn't pull that at trial.

"What were you doing on the fifth floor, Mr. Lopez?"

"I was delivering dinner to room 529."

"Was room 529 located at the same end of the hallway as room 502?"

He paused to revisit the floor plan in his head. I could have handed him a diagram of the floor, but he wasn't my witness and I wanted his memory to fail him. "No, 502 is on the other end."

"Did you see where the woman went?" I asked.

"She went down the hallway." He looked over at Julie. "Toward number 502."

That had to be another prosecution-fed response. "Did you actually see the woman go into room 502."

He froze. "No," he said softly, as if he had failed.

"Then where did she go?"

"I don't know," he admitted.

"So let me get this straight, you were headed for room 529, but you supposedly saw a woman at the opposite end of the hallway?"

"Uh, no, I—I, I just saw her walking by."

That was news to me. "She walked past you? I thought you said she was at the other end of the hallway, ten feet away?"

"Yes."

"Yes, what?"

"I saw her at the end of the hallway."

"But did she actually walk past you?"

"No, no," Lopez said, shaking his head, confused now. "She walked past me down to the end of the hallway."

"Hold on Mr. Lopez, I need you to be very clear. Did the woman walk past you or not?"

His shoulders drooped. "No, I don't think so."

"Was the woman's back to you?"

Out of the corner of my eye I could see Julie begin to rise from her seat, probably to accuse me of beating up on Lopez again. But then she sat back down.

"Probably."

"Probably? You're not sure whether the woman's back was to you or not?"

"Probably, yes."

"Is it yes, Mr. Lopez, or is it you're not sure?"

He glanced nervously at Julie. "Yes, I'm sure." He pointed at Tina. "It was that lady, I'm sure."

"That's not what I asked you, Mr. Lopez. What I'd like to know is whether the woman's back was facing you when you saw her on the fifth floor?"

"Yes, I saw her back."

I still didn't get as clear of a response as I'd wanted, but this would do for now. The testimony Lopez had just given would not play well for the prosecution before a jury. Juries didn't like shaky IDs. If Lopez only saw the woman from the rear, how could he be so sure it was Tina? Julie would no doubt try to better prepare him for trial, but if he tried to change his testimony, we'd pull out the prelim transcript and make an even bigger fool out of him.

"Mr. Lopez, what's the lighting like on the fifth floor?"

"Objection, vague and ambiguous."

Before the judge could respond, I retreated. "Your Honor, I'll rephrase my question."

"Mr. Lopez, were the lights on the fifth floor as bright as the ones in this courtroom?" I stopped and looked around the room.

Lopez followed my gaze. "Uh, no, darker."

Julie was about to spring up from her chair at any second.

I sauntered over to the defense table and picked up a photograph.

"I'd like to introduce a photograph which has been previously marked as Exhibit 15." I handed the document to Mr. Lopez.

"Do you recognize this photograph, Mr. Lopez?"

"Yes, it's the hotel. The fifth floor. I can see the room numbers. It's the hallway, where I saw the lady." He eyed Julie. "I mean, Mrs. Montgomery."

I turned and looked over my shoulder. *Was Julie sending him eye signals?* "Does that picture accurately reflect the lighting on the fifth floor the night Mr. Montgomery was killed?"

"Yes," he said, staring at the picture.

So far all I'd done was shore up the testimony Julie had elicited. I walked back to the table, and looked down at my witness outline, but my eyes did not focus on a single word. I needed some time to think. I was going to take one last shot. Lopez was such a shaky witness, maybe if I pressed him hard enough, he would give me the answer I needed.

"Mr. Lopez, the lighting in that hallway is not very bright and you were several feet away from the woman. Are you certain the woman you saw at the end of that hallway was my client?"

Lopez looked over at Tina as if he were reexamining her face. Then he glanced at Julie. "Yes," he said, nodding his head vigorously. "I am one hundred percent positive that is the lady. I know for sure because she turned around and looked back at me," he said, suddenly gaining confidence. "That's what made me remember her. She looked at me like she was about to do something bad."

It was my turn to freeze up. I wanted to ask him exactly what kind of look that might be, but I didn't want to make matters worse. *Damn.* Where should I go from here? My mind went blank. I felt like I was about to drown and my life preserver was just inches out of my reach. I stayed planted, trying to look composed, my hands held out in front of me, my fingers forming a teepee. When you get a bad answer, one you're not sure you can get the witness to retract, the best response is to move on to another topic. Act like it never happened. But a case of nerves had attacked my brain and I couldn't think of another question. All eyes were off Lopez and on me.

I turned to the judge. "Your Honor," I squeaked, "I have no further questions of this witness."

CHAPTER 36

The judge called a recess just before noon. David, Tina, and I headed for the courthouse cafeteria where we all ate turkey sandwiches on stale bread, pretty much in silence. There wasn't really much to say. Lopez had identified Tina walking down a hallway, knife in hand, with an evil-intentioned look on her face. If we weren't able to shake his identification at trial, Tina might as well pack up her toothbrush now. Fortunately, neither David nor Tina brought up that last zinger Lopez had zapped me with. I already felt bad enough.

When we returned to court after our lunch break, Julie called her next and final witness, Max Montgomery's longtime personal assistant. The prosecution planned to use her to paint a picture of Max's extracurricular activities, setting the scene for Tina's motive to kill.

Ernestine Frye was petite and polished, and looked like an older version of Tina. She'd been Max Montgomery's right hand for over twenty years, following him through three separate career moves.

She testified, quite reluctantly, about the many women who called Max's office for reasons that obviously had nothing to do with business. She reminded me of President Clinton's Betty Curry. She was fully aware of Max's wrongdoing, but it wasn't her job to play morality police.

After Julie completed her questioning, sufficiently painting Max as the louse that he was, my only goal was to show that Frye had no evidence that Tina knew about her husband's affairs. This would go over bigger with the jury, and would probably have no impact at all on Judge McKee, but I might as well get my practice in now.

"Mrs. Frye, you often helped Mrs. Montgomery with her charity work, didn't you?" I asked. It wasn't my plan to put her on the spot if I could help it. She didn't want to be here anymore than I wanted her to be.

"Yes, we worked together on several fundraisers." Her voice had an eloquent air about it, as if she had been taught the importance of enunciation even before she had learned to talk.

"Can you describe the type of things you helped her with?"

"Basically anything she needed. I would address envelopes, help with the food planning, scout out locations. Things of that nature."

"And you considered Tina a friend, didn't you?"

"Yes, I considered Mrs. Montgomery to be a friend," she said unconvincingly.

Of course, most people are on a first-name basis with their friends, I thought. I would have to ask her to refer to Tina by her first name at the trial.

"In fact, Mrs. Montgomery often dropped by the office to invite you to lunch, didn't she?"

"Yes, quite a few times." Mrs. Frye smiled nervously. She did not trust me.

"And around Christmastime, she would take you on shopping sprees at Macy's?"

"Yes," she nodded. "Yes she did."

"And Mrs. Montgomery also sent money to your granddaughter when she was attending college at Spelman, didn't she?"

"Yes."

I cleared my throat and continued, softening my voice. "And during all of this time, you knew Mr. Montgomery was cheating on his wife, correct?"

Mrs. Frye's eyes registered shock. Or was it embarrassment?

Before she could respond, Julie was on her feet. "Objection, asked and answered."

"Sustained," the judge said.

I had to get to the point. "Mrs. Frye, you never shared with Tina the fact that her husband was cheating on her, did you?"

She looked down at her hands. "No, I didn't. It wasn't my place."

"And Tina never asked you any questions about her husband's affairs, did she?"

"No."

"And for all you knew, she didn't know anything about them?"

"That was my assumption," Mrs. Frye said, anxious to throw Tina a bone. "Mr. Montgomery did his best to keep everything from her."

"Did you ever get any angry calls from women Mr. Montgomery was sleeping with?"

She looked down at her hands again. "Yes."

"How often?" I asked gingerly.

"I don't know," Mrs. Frye said softly.

"More than five times?"

"Yes," she said guardedly.

"More than ten times?"

"Yes."

"More than twenty times?"

"Probably."

She looked up at me, her eyes begging me to put an end to this inappropriate public display. I ignored her plea. I had a job to do. "Would you say any of these women sounded angry enough to kill him?"

This time Julie was irate. "Your Honor! Objection! Calls for speculation!"

"Sustained," the judge said, annoyed.

I kept moving. "Mrs. Frye, to your knowledge, did any of the women ever threaten Mr. Montgomery?"

She perked up again, sensing another opportunity to help Tina. "Yes."

"Tell me about those threats."

"Well," she began slowly, "when Mr. Montgomery tired of a woman, he simply stopped returning her calls. Some of them got very upset when I wouldn't put them through. They threatened to call his wife, to come down to his office. To do whatever they had to do to get him to talk to them."

"Did any of them threaten him with physical violence?"

"I can't remember any names, but I do remember a couple of women who did."

I made a mental note to have Detective Smith follow up on that information. "In your opinion, did those threats appear to be serious?"

Julie was on her feet again.

This time I didn't wait for the judge's ruling. "Your Honor, I'm asking for the witness to give me her opinion regarding whether the threats appeared—in her opinion—to be serious. That's perfectly allowable."

Judge McKee paused as if she weren't sure whether the question was appropriate or not.

"Overruled," she bellowed after a moment's pause. "Ms. Henderson, you may proceed, but I'm not impressed."

I nodded at Mrs. Frye, urging her to continue.

"Yes, some of them seemed quite serious. I told Mr. Montgomery that I wanted to report the calls to the police, but he wouldn't let me."

"Did you feel Mr. Montgomery's life was in danger?"

"Yes, I did." She definitely wanted to help Tina. I could see it in her eyes.

"Are you aware of Mrs. Montgomery ever threatening her husband?"

Her eyebrows arched in disdain. "Heavens no. Mrs. Montgomery was much too dignified to behave like that."

"I have no further questions."

Judge McKee turned to Julie. "Anything else, Ms. Killabrew?"

She hesitated, then stood up. "Just a few more questions," she said. "Mrs. Frye, you were assisting Mrs. Montgomery with the fundraiser the night her husband was killed, is that right?"

"Yes."

"And you worked alongside her for most of the night, didn't you?"

"Yes."

"But at some point during the evening, Mrs. Montgomery disappeared, isn't that right?"

"Objection," I said. "Beyond the scope of the cross."

The judge looked aggravated. "I'm going to allow some leeway here," she said. "You may continue, counselor."

Mrs. Frye squirmed in her seat. "I wouldn't say she disappeared. She just had some matters to attend to."

"Did you happen to ask anybody where she went?"

She paused. "Yes, I asked the vice chairperson if she'd talked to Mrs. Montgomery before she left."

"And what did the vice chairperson tell you Mrs. Montgomery said?"

The irritated look in David's eyes told me I should be objecting. He scribbled the word "hearsay" at the top of his legal pad.

I didn't know where Julie was headed, but I was out of my chair. "Objection, calls for hearsay."

The judge scowled at me, and Julie looked annoyed. David just turned away.

"Ms. Henderson," the judge said impatiently, "this is a preliminary hearing. Hearsay testimony is permissible at a prelim, though not at trial. When you go home tonight, I suggest you brush up on the rules of evidence."

I shrank back into my seat. *You little prick*. David was trying to screw me. I gave him a hateful look, but he refused to meet my gaze.

"You can answer the question, Mrs. Frye," the judge said.

"I'm sorry. I'm not sure I remember the question."

Julie walked closer to the witness box. "I'd be glad to repeat it," she said smiling. "When Mrs. Montgomery disappeared that night and you asked the vice chairperson if she'd talked to her, what did the vice chairperson tell you?"

Mrs. Frye looked apologetically at Tina and averted her eyes. "She told me that Mrs. Montgomery said she was going back to her room."

"Did you happen to go to Mrs. Montgomery's room to see if she was okay?"

"Yes."

"And did you find her there?"

"No."

"And how long was it before she eventually returned?"

"I'm not sure. An hour maybe."

After a short recess, the prosecution closed its case. I informed the court that the defense did not intend to call any witnesses. There was no reason to. We didn't have a single witness, except Tina, who could refute the prosecution's testimony. And we didn't want to educate the prosecution about our defense, what little there was.

On the way out of the courtroom, I pulled David off to the side.

"That little stunt you pulled in there wasn't funny."

"What're you talking about?" he said, feigning ignorance.

"I'm talking about your telling me to make that hearsay objection when you knew hearsay testimony was permissible at a prelim."

He stuck out his chest. "I don't know what you're talking about. I didn't tell you to do anything. I was just doodling. I had no idea you were taking cues from me. I thought you were the lead attorney."

You asshole!

"Anyway," he said, turning to leave, "I guess instead of brushing up on the rules of criminal procedure, you should've been reading the evidence code, huh?"

CHAPTER 37

Judge McKee promised to render a decision within the week. In the meantime, we needed to prepare Tina for the inevitable.

The day after the hearing, David, Neddy and I convened at Tina's house. I invited Neddy to tag along because I didn't expect our heart-to-heart to go well. During our ride home after the prelim, Tina seemed quite optimistic that Judge McKee would find no probable cause and allow her to replace her bulky ankle bracelet with a more attractive piece from her extensive jewelry collection. But I considered the testimony of Lopez and Frye pretty disastrous for the defense. In Tina's naïve layman's mind, since no one saw her stab Max to death, she should go free.

When we had all settled into the purple living room, Neddy mapped out the case as objectively as possible, trying to help Tina view the evidence from a legal perspective. Tina promptly went into hysterics, convinced that she would spend the rest of her life in prison.

"The prosecution won't have it this easy at trial," Neddy said, trying to calm her down. "They'll have to convince a jury, not a judge. And there're a few tricks we have up our sleeve. We feel we can truly discredit Oscar Lopez. Our detective found two witnesses who'll testify that Lopez told them he wasn't sure the woman he saw had a knife in her hand."

Tina looked alarmed, then angry. "Why wasn't that evidence used at the hearing?" she demanded.

We had purposely kept this information from Tina, fearing that she would insist on us using it at the prelim. David gave me an I-told-you-so smirk.

"Because it wouldn't have mattered," Neddy explained. "It's still likely that the judge will find probable cause even if our witnesses had testified. At trial, we can spring our witnesses on the prosecution and on Lopez. That single point may be enough to convince one juror to vote not guilty."

Neddy was doing a good job of explaining our strategy. Tina seemed reluctant to ever question her advice. And after a little more hand-holding from Neddy, by the time we left, Tina seemed prepared to face the inevitable.

There were no surprises when Judge McKee rendered her decision the following day.

We were all gathered in court, except for Neddy, who stayed at the office. Until the police dropped her as a suspect in Lawton's murder, she couldn't run the risk of having some reporter stick a microphone in her face.

The court session barely lasted ten minutes. Judge McKee took the bench and quickly went to work. "Based on the evidence, I find that the prosecution has demonstrated probable cause to proceed with the trial of Tina Montgomery on the charge of murder in the first degree."

Even though we'd advised Tina of this likelihood, she looked horrified and raised her hands to her face. "How can anybody think I killed my husband?" she cried out. "I loved Max."

I put my arms around her. A move intended to quiet more than comfort.

Judge McKee glanced over at us. I thought she was going to pick up her gavel and bang us into silence, but she proceeded over Tina's muffled cries. She assigned the case to Judge Clara Graciano for trial. Graciano was a young Italian fireball who relished cases that put her in the spotlight. I could hear the reporters behind us scribbling furiously on their legal pads.

"I have a couple of warnings for both sides," Judge McKee continued. "Ms. Killabrew, you've been spending a lot of time talking to the media. I want to remind you that your job is in the courtroom, not on the courthouse steps. I want Mrs. Montgomery to have a fair trial. And if you continue wasting your time getting your mug on the news, you may find yourself facing a gag order."

Then she turned to me. "Ms. Henderson. I understand you're a pretty fine lawyer from a pretty fine trial firm. But this is a criminal case, not a civil lawsuit. I suggest you spend some time reviewing the Evidence Code. The courtroom isn't the place for you to learn the basics of the hearsay rule."

Tina was still sobbing, while David seemed to be glowing inside.

"That's it. Court dismissed."

An hour after my most humiliating courtroom experience, O'Reilly ran into me at the elevator and followed me into my office. He closed the door and took a seat before I bothered to offer him one. I assumed Tina Montgomery had already made her distress call, firing me as her attorney.

He patiently waited while I discarded my purse and briefcase and flopped down behind my desk.

"I understand things didn't go too well before Judge McKee today," he said sympathetically.

"That's an understatement."

"What happened?"

"Why don't you tell me? I assume you're here because you already got the play-by-play from Tina Montgomery. Is she firing me?"

He leaned back and kneaded his fingers behind his neck. "No, she didn't call. I talked to David. He thought you were a little unsure of yourself during cross-examination and said you didn't know that hearsay was admissible at a prelim."

The tiny hairs on the back of my neck stood up. "That's not exactly true. And anyway, you knew when you assigned me to this case that I didn't know criminal law," I said.

"My mistake," O'Reilly said fumbling for words. He was not good at beating around the bush. "You really needed a break after the Hayes trial. I should've realized that. I'm going to talk to Mrs. Montgomery. It might be best to take you off the case."

His words filled me with a confused mix of emotions. On the one hand dumping this case and running home to my husband was exactly what I wanted to do. But I'd never been kicked off a case before and I didn't want to be kicked off this one. The *Times* had run a big article praising me and Neddy. Now Neddy was off the case because she was a murder suspect and I was about to be thrown off for incompetence. Would they have to write a retraction?

"You have to be kidding!" I said, with more emotion than I intended. "You can't make another change. How would that look? So what? I didn't know that hearsay evidence was admissible at a prelim. Now, all of a sudden, everybody's ready to charge me with malpractice? I know this case. I can do this. I'm a good attorney."

"I know you are. But I had no business taking you out of your element. I was too focused on the possible publicity you and Neddy could bring to the firm."

"And now that the publicity isn't so good, you're abandoning us?"

He did not like my characterization of his decision. He sat up and leaned forward. "I thought you were having difficulty with the idea of defending someone you thought might be guilty?"

"I'm over that. I really don't think it's a good idea to change attorneys on this case again," I insisted. "I have to think this stuff with Neddy will blow over soon. That's who I should be trying this case with. Not David."

O'Reilly's forehead wrinkled. "I didn't know you two had such a contentious relationship. That won't be good for the client."

"I'll do whatever I have to do to make sure Tina Montgomery is well represented. Even if it means getting along with David until Neddy's back. Just don't take me off this case. Besides, who else would handle it?"

"I was thinking about letting David fly solo."

"Tina won't go for that," I said quickly. "She'll take the case to another firm."

"Look, Vernetta—"

I cut him off. I did not want to be taken off this case. I had to hit O'Reilly where it hurt. "The next story in the *Times* about Max Montgomery's murder is going to take a crack at our firm and the revolving door of attorneys you've assigned to this case." When he wiped a hand across his face, I knew my words had registered. O'Reilly's foremost concern was always the firm. I decided to go for the jugular.

"If you make another change, the whole firm'll look incompetent. We'll never get another high-profile criminal case."

He paused and I allowed him to ponder my last point in silence. I could see he was imagining the possible headlines.

"Okay, okay," he said, standing up. "You're still on the case, but I don't want any more screwups."

CHAPTER 38

"Girlfriend, you look like you've aged ten years," Special said, staring up at me. "What's up with that?"

I called her from the office seconds after my conversation with O'Reilly and begged her to meet me for a drink at T.G.I. Friday's after work. When I arrived, she was already seated at our regular booth near the bar and was halfway through a Long Island iced tea. A Diet Coke was waiting for me.

As usual, Special looked spectacular. She was wearing a hot pink Lycra top and skintight stretch jeans with a gold chain dangling from her hips.

"I may look like I've aged ten years," I said, sliding into the seat across from her, "but it feels like twenty."

"I think it's definitely time for you to take a vacation."

"I could use one," I said. "I'm stressed out from the Montgomery case. I'm trying to help Neddy deal with her situation, and Jefferson has shut down completely."

"I can't help you with the first two, but I can help you with problem number three." Special shoved her Long Island iced tea to my side of the table. "First, take a sip of this. You drink too much Diet Coke."

I started to protest, but then took a sip to avoid a big battle. It tasted awful. I preferred fruity tasting drinks like piña coladas and strawberry daiquiris.

"You need to be there for your man," Special began. "Jefferson's not the kind of brother who can ask for help. He's silently crying out for it, but you've been too busy saving everybody except him."

"Special, I've been trying to help him, but he's closed up like a clam. Every night when I come home he's either nursing a glass of Hennessy or he's not there."

She pointed a pink porcelain fingernail at me. "Now see, that's the operative word—*night*. Perhaps you ought to think about trying to get home before the streetlights come on."

"What for? When I do come home, he never wants to talk."

"Damn," Special said shaking her head. "I'm amazed that all you supereducated women don't know jack about men. Even the ones you're married to. You need to spend a little less time in the courtroom and a little more time out on the street learning something about life. Men, brothers in particular, ain't trying to talk to nobody when they have a problem, especially not their women."

I was not in the mood for one of Special's lectures, but I knew it was too late. "Then what am I supposed to do, Miss I-Know-Everything-About-Everything?" I said.

"Correction," Special said with righteous indignation. "I don't know everything about everything. I just know the male species. And what I know about Jefferson is that you need to be there for him. Sit there and watch TV with him. Rub his shoulders. Give him a special treat, if you know what I mean. I bet you still go to bed wearing flannel every night. You need to pull out some of those negligees you got at your bridal shower and give that brother a lap dance every once in a while. Married women forget how to cater to a man."

"Special, I need some real advice. Not everything is about sex."

"You're missing my point. I'm not saying it's about sex. It's about making him feel like a man. That's more important now than ever since the doctor told the brother his johnson is shooting blanks."

I took a sip of my Diet Coke, which was watered down from the melted ice.

"And if I were you, I'd be a little worried about Jefferson not being at home when you get there in the evenings. You keep on working all hours of the day and night and that brother's going to find his way into some other babe's arms."

I erased that thought from my mind. "I'm not worried about that. Jefferson's not that kind of guy."

Special stretched her neck backward with the dexterity of a giraffe. "If I didn't know better, I'd swear you didn't grow up in the 'hood. There's no such thing as a brother who won't tip under the right circumstances. I agree that Jefferson's not the kind of dude who's going to be out there running five or six babes, but I wouldn't put it past him to go drown his sorrows by getting him a little somethin', somethin' on the side. Particularly when his woman's never available. When's the last time y'all had sex?"

"Since he found out he was sterile, he hasn't exactly wanted any."

"Yep. Your boy is definitely ripe for the picking by some of these L.A. hoochies who know a good man when they see one. You need to be careful. You want me to keep an eye on him?"

"Keep an eye on him?" I chuckled. "Exactly how would you propose to do that?"

"Girl, I can follow his ass. I'd be good at it, too. I had to follow this fool I was dating last year. I knew his ass was messing around. Caught him red-handed and wasn't shit he could say. Never even knew I was tracking his ass. If I could find the start-up cash, I'd open me up a private investigations firm specializing in tracking down cheating men," she said. "I already thought up the name. 'Bust-A-Brother.' "

I couldn't help laughing. "Special, I've got a serious problem and you're cracking jokes?"

"I'm not joking." She was actually offended by my lack of support for her proposed business venture. "My office would be right on Crenshaw Boulevard and MLK across from Wal-Mart. That's a high-traffic area so I know I'd get a lot of business."

"Well, thanks, but no thanks," I said. "If I need a private eye, I'll hire a real one. You're not even supposed to know about our little problem, remember? So please don't mention it to Jefferson. I just have to figure out how to make him stop feeling like he's defective or something."

"He'll come around," she said, reaching over and squeezing my hand. "But in the meantime, it's only natural for him to feel like less of a man. You know how much stock brothers put into their penises. Jefferson's a good dude, but he's going to need you to be patient with him. You don't have to coddle him, just be somewhere in the vicinity when he's ready to reach out for you."

As crazy as Special acted sometimes, what she said made sense.

"I just wish I could take some time off, but I can't," I said. "I'm praying Neddy doesn't end up being charged with her husband's murder. That means I'll effectively be handling the Montgomery case by myself because David is useless and I don't trust him as far as I can throw him."

"Girl, you don't have to be everybody's savior. You're doing the same thing you did when you worked at Brandon & Bass. Putting your job before your man." She stopped to wag a disapproving finger in my face. "You lucked out once. You may not be so lucky the second time around. Anyway, don't be putting your neck out for Neddy's behind. She probably killed that man."

"No, she didn't," I said.

Special's hands flew to her hips. "And just how do you know that?"

"Because I just do," I insisted. I tried to block out the angry words I heard Neddy shouting at her husband. *I'll kill you before I give you a dime.* I refused to believe she could be guilty of murder. Tina, yes. Neddy, no. Hell no.

"Girl, sometimes I wonder how you ever got a law degree." Special picked up a cube of ice from her drink and started crunching on it. "Is that what you're going to tell the judge? 'Neddy's innocent because I just know she's innocent.' I wouldn't blame her if she did kill that fool. Ain't no way in hell I'm paying a man alimony, particularly some sorry chump like that. Does she have an alibi?"

"Not really. She was home by herself. Didn't make any phone calls and can't point to anyone who can verify her whereabouts."

"Damn," Special said, turning up her glass. "It definitely don't look good for that sister."

CHAPTER 39

I spent the next few days preparing motions in limine, exhibit lists, witness lists, and all the other boring but important administrative paperwork required before trial. Neddy was available when I needed to bounce an idea off of her, but she was growing increasingly distant. My hopes that the police would find another suspect and take her off the Most Wanted List were fading fast.

As I was leaving the office late one night, it hit me that I should be doing something besides waiting on the police to clear Neddy's name. Since she was always bragging about what a great sleuth Detective Smith was, maybe he could help track down Lawton's killer.

I tried to set up a lunch meeting, but Detective Smith was conducting a stakeout for another client and couldn't see me until the following evening. We met at seven at the California Pizza Kitchen not far from the O'Reilly & Finney offices.

"Thanks for meeting with me," I said, once we were seated.

"No prob. Anything I can do to help Neddy, I'm in."

From the hopeful look on his face and his eagerness to help, I sensed that he might have an interest in Neddy that extended beyond her legal predicament.

"As you can imagine, the fact that the police actually consider Neddy to be a suspect in her husband's death is really getting to her," I began. "The firm took her off the Montgomery case because of it. I know Neddy didn't kill her husband and I need to find some evidence to prove it. Except I'm not an investigator. That's why I need your help. Where should I begin?"

Detective Smith pulled a small notepad from his shirt pocket. "We typically start with the evidence we find at the crime scene: fingerprints, footprints, blood, and so on. If that leads no place, then we focus on the people who had a motive for wanting the victim dead."

"Unfortunately, most of the evidence leads straight to Neddy," I said. "Her fingerprints, and probably her DNA, too, are all over the house because she lived there. And she was in a bitter divorce battle with Lawton, so there goes motive."

"Yeah, I hear he was trying to get alimony."

"You heard right," I said. "So how do I find out who did it, or how do I prove Neddy didn't?"

He stopped to think for a minute. "Where was she at the time he was murdered?"

I picked up my water glass. "At home, but there're no witnesses to confirm that."

"Did she make any telephone calls?"

"Nope."

Detective Smith scratched his ear. "What time did she leave the office that night?"

"I don't know, why?"

"It's really hard for people to accurately recall their whereabouts with respect to time," he explained. "I've seen it happen all the time at trial. People make guesses that are really way off. For example, what time did you get home three nights ago?" he asked.

I tried to remember. "I think I worked late. I'd say I probably got in around eleven."

"Probably or definitely?" he probed.

I tried, but I couldn't remember for sure. "I would say 11:15 would be a pretty good estimate."

"If your life's on the line, you need to know for sure. Could you swear that it was 11:15 when you walked through the door?"

I stopped to think again. "I remember turning off my computer around 10:30. It would take me about ten minutes to gather my stuff and take the elevator to my car and another twenty-five minutes to drive home. Yeah, I'd say it was sometime between 11:05 and 11:15."

"So now it's possibly as early as 11:05. Ten or fifteen minutes can make a big difference. Just ask O.J."

I nodded. "I see what you mean. So where do we start?"

"Does she live in a house or an apartment?"

"A condo. In Redondo Beach. Why?"

He asked for her address and scribbled it down. "Because even though she claims nobody saw her come home, that doesn't mean somebody didn't. It's good that she lives in a condo. It's very possible a neighbor saw her."

"So I should go knock on doors and ask people?"

"Not you, me."

"You're willing to do that?"

"Of course. Neddy and I go way back. Like you, I find it hard to believe that she could've killed the man."

We signaled our waiter and ordered lemonade, Sedona tortilla soup, and a couple servings of the sesame ginger chicken dumplings appetizer to share.

"I should also talk to the neighbors on the street where her husband was murdered," he said. "They may've seen something. And then I'll check my sources to see if I can find out what evidence the police have collected."

"What can I do while you knock on doors?"

"How about just being a good friend to Neddy. I'm sure she needs that right now."

"That's not a problem." His thoughtfulness amazed me.

"Hey," Detective Smith said, as if a light bulb had just flashed on in his head, "do you have to swipe a key card to get into your office building?"

"Not the entrance to the building. Just the parking garage and the floor we work on. Why?"

"I think those things are computerized. There should be a record showing what time Neddy left. In a fancy high-rise like yours, there might even be videotapes. That would confirm what time she left the office that night for sure. You should also get a record of when she logged off her computer."

I began to get excited. "This is great. I'll check with Building Security and our Information Technology department first thing in the morning. You have no idea how anxious I am to get the cops off Neddy's back."

He smiled and saluted. "I'm here to serve."

CHAPTER 40

I left my meeting with Detective Smith optimistic that we were going to find some evidence to clear Neddy. I hoped Jefferson was home. I wanted to share my good news and devote the rest of the evening to him.

When I opened the front door, the stench of alcohol slapped me in the face. Jefferson was sitting in the living room, still dressed in his work clothes. A floor lamp in the far corner of the room provided virtually no light. All the windows were closed and the air was muggy and suffocating. I was not happy to see him lounging on our beige Ethan Allen couch in his grimy work pants. His feet, still in his dirt-encrusted work boots, were propped up on the glass coffee table next to a bottle of Hennessy. He was holding an empty glass in his hand.

"The great lawyer has arrived," he said, raising his glass toward me in a makeshift toast. His words were slurred.

I'd never seen him this drunk before and I didn't know what to say or do. I felt totally inept at helping him deal with his pain. I knew that lighting into him about his drinking and abusing our furniture would be a mistake.

"How was work today?" I asked, unable to come up with anything better or safer.

"Just fine. What about you? How many murderesses did you save from the gas chamber today?" he said laughing.

I refused to take his sarcasm to heart. "Maybe one. Detective

Smith may be able to help me find some evidence that could clear Neddy."

"Aw, that's some really great news, baby. Congratulations." Though his words were slurred, I could still detect the contempt in them.

I pulled off my jacket and took a seat next to him on the couch. I reached for his right hand and slipped my fingers through his. I wanted to tell him that it was okay, that it didn't matter that he was sterile, but I kept hearing Special's voice ringing in my head, telling me that the best thing to do was just be there for him. So as hard as it was to do, I sat there beside him, saying nothing.

After a few minutes, he laid his head on my shoulder. He reeked of sweat and alcohol.

"This is a muthafucka, ain't it?" he said, jerking away from me and leaning forward to place his glass on the coffee table. He missed it by several inches. The glass fell to the carpeted floor and rolled away.

"Oops!" he laughed. "I guess I'm a little drunk, huh?"

A little drunk my ass.

"You know what I'm going to do tomorrow," he said. "I'm going to call up Belinda Caldwell and tell her about herself."

Now I was beginning to fear that he was getting delirious. "What are you talking about, Jefferson? Who's Belinda Caldwell?"

"She said I got her pregnant in the eleventh grade, but that couldn't have happened since . . ." He closed his eyes, then opened them again. "I gave her ass five hundred dollars for an abortion. I always thought she was lying 'cause she looked too happy when I saw her at school two days later. I'm calling her ass up and getting my money back."

I pulled him closer to me, but remained silent.

"This is really a muthafucka, ain't it?" he said again, scratching the two days of growth on his chin. "I guess I should've figured it out. I did a lot of unprotected fuckin' after high school, and I never once got a babe pregnant." He raised his hand and pretended to aim a gun at me. "Pow, pow," he laughed. "Oops, I missed. The great Jefferson Jerome Jones is shooting blanks."

I could still hear Special whispering instructions in my ear and it was the only reason I was not saying something useless, like everything would be fine.

"Man, man, man." A sharp whiff of alcohol closely followed each of his words. "This is so fucked up."

Jefferson pulled away from me, pressed his chin to his chest and stared down at his groin. "How could you betray me like this, man?" he said, roughly grabbing his groin. "This is pretty fucked up, you know that? As much pussy as I got for you? I got you some of the baddest babes in L.A. and this is how you treat me? I always took good care of you. Never let you get gonorrhea or syphilis or none of that other shit. And just because I banged you up one fuckin' little time, you go and do some shit like this to me. This is really fucked up, man. You know that? This is really fucked up."

Tears began to stream down his cheeks.

I slid into Jefferson's lap and wrapped my arms around his thick neck and pressed my cheek against his. The stubble along his jaw felt like sandpaper. He was holding onto me so tight I had to struggle to breathe. I felt his chest heave up and down and I knew that he was trying hard to keep his anguish inside. When his silent cries finally found a voice, his sobs escaped in strong, muffled surges.

I cried with him, the reality of our situation painfully clear. I would never give birth to a little boy who would be the spitting image of his father. And if Jefferson's views on adoption didn't change, we would never be parents—to any child. The same way Jefferson's sterility had rocked him, the thought of us never being parents was an unbearable possibility for me.

The lawyer in me continued to search my mind for words of comfort, though deep down, I knew that words would not help him. It took some time, but I eventually gave up. I don't know how long we sat there. But for some time we held onto each other, rocking and crying until we both drifted off to sleep.

CHAPTER 41

Jefferson and I spent a long weekend together, just kicking it at home. We watched a string of old movies and ordered out for pizza on Saturday and Chinese food on Sunday. I got to work early on Monday and had a fairly productive day. Close to six, while I was debating whether to call it a day, I looked up to find Neddy standing in the doorway of my office. The old, bitter Neddy, not the one I now considered my friend.

"I understand you've been playing detective," she said. Her voice had a vile undertone to it.

I knew she'd had it rough lately, so I decided not to take her nasty attitude personally. "Yes, I have," I said smiling.

I hadn't heard back from Building Security or the IT guy yet, so I didn't want to get her hopes up until I had an idea of exactly what the records would show. But since she'd apparently found out, I'd have to tell her something. "I talked to—"

"Detective Smith. Yeah, I know. Why don't you just mind your own business?"

"What?"

She walked closer to my desk and hovered over me, her eyes filled with rage. "I said why don't you mind your own damn business?"

I was dumbstruck. Why was she attacking me? "I was just trying to help you," I said, struggling to maintain my cool. "And I think I have."

"I don't need your help," she snarled.

I was ready to take the same spiteful tone, but, as with Jefferson, my gut told me to cool it. If I were in her shoes, I'd be a bad-tempered basket case, too. "Maybe you should sit down," I said.

She ignored my suggestion and remained standing.

"I'm going to do you a favor right now," I continued. "I'm going to assume that you're attacking me because you're stressed out from everything you've been going through. So I'm not going to take it personally, and—"

"I'm attacking you because you apparently think I killed Lawton," her voice cracked slightly. "I know you heard me that day I was on the phone with him, when I told him I'd kill him before I'd pay him alimony."

I started to deny that I had heard anything, but changed my mind. "Yeah, I heard you, but you're wrong. I don't think you killed your husband. Why're you so angry? I'm just trying to help."

"First, I find out that you've got Detective Smith talking to my neighbors, then you have the nerve to ask Building Security for my key card printout to see when I left the building."

I glanced at the open door, knowing I should go over and close it, but I didn't. We might be resorting to blows shortly and somebody would need to come in and break up the fight before we killed each other. "I asked for that printout so I could help show you couldn't have killed Lawton because of the time you left the office. I'm trying to help you, Neddy."

"Are you?"

I couldn't believe it. She was serious.

"David said you didn't like the fact that Tina and I were so close. He thinks you're jealous of me."

I was speechless. How could she possibility give credence to anything David had to say? I'd been working my ass off trying to save her behind and this was the thanks I got? I inhaled and tried to remember that she was not herself.

I stood up so I could gawk back at her on a more level basis. "Why don't you go someplace and calm down and come back and talk to me when you've had a chance to think about what you're saying."

She continued to glare at me. "I know exactly what I'm saying. According to David, you're happy to have the lead on the Montgomery case."

Every time she mentioned David's name I wanted to scream. I walked around to the front of my desk and stood inches from her. She took a single step back. "You're really trippin', now," I said, my voice low, but angry. "You're attacking the wrong person. Anything David says is a lie. I can't believe you're jumping all over me when all I've been trying to do is help you. Can't you see what David's trying to do? If he drives a wedge between us, he's the next logical person to try this case."

We locked eyes until she finally looked away. "I'm only trying to help you, Neddy," I said.

"Well, don't go doing me any favors. I can handle my own problems."

"Fine, then," I said.

The minute she stormed out, I headed for David's office. On my way, I brushed past a paralegal, nearly knocking her into the wall. "Sorry," I said without slowing down.

I barged into David's office and slammed the door shut behind me. "I don't appreciate you trying to undermine my relationship with Neddy," I said.

Starbucks mugs, hats, and other coffee-related souvenirs littered his office. There had to be at least four empty cups in the trash can next to his desk. He even had a poster-sized picture of the Starbucks founder hanging over a short bookcase. He was too weird. As much money as he spent on Starbucks coffee, I hoped he owned stock in the company.

"I don't know what you're talking about," he said, glancing up at me for a quick second, then turning back to the brief in front of him.

"I'm talking about you telling Neddy that I was jealous of her relationship with Tina Montgomery. Where'd you get that crap from?"

"Did I lie?"

I could feel a lump of fury forming in my throat. "I know what you're trying to do, David, and it's not going to work."

"I don't know what you're talking about."

"You're trying to ruin my relationship with Neddy so you can end up trying this case. But that'll happen over my dead body."

"Ummm," he said. "Is that what I'm trying to do?"

"We may have to work together, but we don't have to like each other. I'm sorry I overshadowed you on the Hayes case. But whatever jealousy you have, you need to just deal with it."

His laugh was much too loud. I knew that I'd hit a nerve and that knowledge pleased me. He leaned back in his chair and smiled up at me. "What reason would I have to be jealous of you?"

"I could list them for you, but it would take too much time. Just understand that I know what you're up to."

He looked at me through narrowed eyes. "Get out."

"Gladly."

CHAPTER 42

Nowadays, when O'Reilly entered my office, I could tell almost instantly from his body language whether the news was good or bad. From the slump of his shoulders and the way his eyes avoided mine, this news was bad, really bad.

It had been three days since my square-off with Neddy and I hoped O'Reilly hadn't gotten wind of our spat.

"We need to talk," he said, closing the door and taking a seat across from me.

"Okay," I said, eyeing him cautiously.

"I'm putting Neddy back on the Montgomery case."

Before my confrontation with her, I would have considered this good news. Right now, I wasn't so sure. "You're not concerned anymore about her being a suspect in her husband's death?"

"My sources at the D.A.'s office tell me that's no longer the case," he said. "And I think you deserve the credit for that."

"What do you mean?"

"Neddy was wrong about the time she told the police she left the office the night her husband was killed. Those reports you had Building Security dig up provided the alibi she needed. She drove out of the garage at 10:37 P.M. The security cameras even have her on tape. It would have taken her a good twenty-five minutes to make it to Leimert Park. Lawton was already dead before she'd even pulled out of the garage. And it appears he had a pretty big gambling problem. He owed money, a lot of it, to some very mean dudes. That's where the police are focusing their investigation now."

I was relieved at the news, though I wished it had come before my big blowup with Neddy. "Okay, judging by the look on your face, there must be some bad news along with the good," I said.

He looked away. "I'm taking you off the case." O'Reilly blurted this out as if he were bracing for a verbal barrage from me. "I think you need to regroup from the Hayes case. I've put a lot on your shoulders lately. You need a break."

"O'Reilly, I thought we already had this conversation."

"Well, we're having it again."

"So who'll be handling the case with Neddy?" I asked.

"David."

I briefly closed my eyes and looked away. "No," I said.

O'Reilly stared at me. "What did you say?"

"I said no."

"You don't exactly have a choice in the matter," he said sternly.

"I don't care. You're not taking me off the case. There's no reason to."

O'Reilly must've been as shocked as I was at my defiance. He wasn't sure what to say next. We'd always had a pretty cool relationship, but I had never seen him tolerate anyone talking to him the way I just did and I knew he didn't like it.

"You need a break," his tone was paternal. "You've been under a lot of pressure. You never got a chance to take a breather after that Hayes trial."

I was probably kissing partnership goodbye, but I didn't care. His decision had nothing to do with me needing a break. This was all about my handling of the prelim. "If you're putting Neddy back on the case, then why take me off? I don't even think Tina Montgomery likes David."

"Frankly after that lecture Judge McKee gave you, I don't think Tina's feeling too warm and fuzzy about you either."

"So did Tina initiate this?"

"No. I did," he said, asserting his authority. "Look, I had no business putting you on this case in the first place. I'd love to give you an opportunity to learn criminal law. But you were right. I was wrong to expect you to cut your teeth on a high-profile case like this."

I didn't respond.

"And David's a little concerned that you can't be objective. He thinks you believe Tina Montgomery is guilty and that may be clouding your judgment."

"David's a prick," I said.

"Good lawyers usually are." O'Reilly laughed.

I did not laugh along with him.

"What about all that great publicity you'll be missing out on?" I asked. " 'Two smart, attractive African-American women defending a rich, African-American socialite.' Weren't those your words?"

O'Reilly leaned back in the small chair and allowed it to teeter on its two back legs. "I think this firm's had quite enough publicity for a while." He rocked the chair forward and hopped up.

"Wait," I said, feeling totally hopeless. "I have a compromise." I stood up and walked up to him.

He raised a hand to stop me. "Vernetta, the decision's been made."

"Just hear me out." I softened my voice. Challenging him the way I had was probably a mistake. Why don't you let all three of us try the case?"

He paused. This was not something O'Reilly had considered.

"We don't usually staff three attorneys on a criminal case. We—"

"C'mon, O'Reilly," I said, pleading with him. "You started this whole thing. I didn't even want to be on the case to begin with. Now I'm all psyched up about it and you're tossing me aside. We can consider it a training experience for me. I won't bill any of my work on it and I'll still handle all my other cases, too."

"Exactly how do you propose to do that?"

"I have no idea, but I will. I doubt the trial will last more than a few weeks. Judge Graciano runs a tight ship."

He paused just long enough for me to know that he was going to grant my wish. "Okay, Vernetta," he warned. "You can stay on the case. But you better not make me regret this decision."

CHAPTER 43

I was wrong when I thought the verbal spanking from Judge McKee was the most embarrassing moment of my legal career. It wasn't.

Early the next morning, I was eating cinnamon French toast prepared by my husband, who was finally beginning to act like his old self again, when a headline on page two of the *L.A. Times'* California section made me gag. LEAD ATTORNEY ON MONTGOMERY DEFENSE TEAM ILL-EQUIPPED TO HANDLE CASE.

The article went on to describe my hearsay screwup during the preliminary hearing and to question why Tina Montgomery would hire an attorney with no criminal law experience. The only good thing about the article was that it ran *after* my conversation with O'Reilly. If he'd read it first, there was no way I'd still be on the case. Before I could decide whether to scream or cry, the telephone rang.

"I'm calling to say thanks," Neddy said, her voice tentative.

It's about friggin' time. "Thanks for what?"

"For saving my life," she said gently.

"I wouldn't exactly go that far."

"I would," she said, with clear regret. "I'm sorry I went off on you. I've really been on edge lately. I know David's a jerk. I should've known you were only trying to help. And thank God you did. I really am sorry."

I reached for a bottle of Mrs. Butterworth's and doused my French toast with more syrup. "No problem," I lied. It was going to take a minute for me to warm up to her again.

"You don't sound so good," she said.

"That's an understatement. I guess you haven't read the paper yet. Go get the *Times* and take a look at the front page of the California section."

She put the phone down. I heard footsteps, followed by the sound of turning newspaper pages. "Oh no!" she said, picking up the telephone. "What happened?"

"Well, let's just say I didn't exactly know that hearsay was A-OK during a preliminary hearing." Every time I thought of that stunt David pulled my forehead ached.

"I can't believe David didn't tell you that."

"Actually, he basically led me to believe that it wasn't admissible."

"What?" Neddy said. "What happened?" She still didn't see David as the asshole I knew him to be.

"I really don't feel like going into it now." I stuffed a piece of French toast into my mouth. "I'll tell you about it later. I don't know if you know it yet, but you're back on the Montgomery case. O'Reilly was going to take me off, but I fought the good fight and won. But the concession is David stays on, too."

"So there'll be three of us?"

"Not really. Two and a half. I'm the half."

"Well, I'm just glad you're still on the team," she said. "What time are you going into the office today?"

"I'm not. I'm taking a mental health day and treating myself to a day at the spa."

"You deserve it," Neddy said.

I cut a piece of French toast and stabbed it with my fork. "As the youngsters say, no doubt."

CHAPTER 44

I could always count on Special to be up for a day of playing hooky from work. We were standing in the lobby of the Burke Williams Day Spa in Santa Monica waiting to check in.

"You called in sick?" I chided Special. "Why didn't you just take a vacation day? If somebody catches you here, you could lose your job."

"Girl, they're charging us eighty-five dollars an hour for a massage. Ain't nobody I work with make enough money to be up in here."

"Okay," I warned her, "I'm an employment lawyer. Calling in sick when you're not constitutes good cause for termination."

"Not for me," she said. "I got so much stuff on my boss, the day I go, she's going to have to pack up her shit, too."

We both laughed.

A receptionist handed us locker keys and we walked down a long, softly lit hallway to the locker room. The scent of eucalyptus and sandalwood wrapped us in tranquility. I was long overdue for this treat. We undressed and slipped into plush blue robes and made our way to the Quiet Room.

We took neighboring seats in a row of comfy recliners separated by purple velvet curtains. Colorful scented candles provided just enough light. Since we were the only ones in the room, we ignored the "No Talking" sign.

"So how are you and Jefferson doing?" Special asked.

I yawned and stretched at the same time. "Better. Much better. We're even back to semiregular sex. I'm just trying to figure out how to broach the subject of adoption with him."

"Don't."

"Why not?"

Special was slow to respond. "Because he's not ready yet."

"And how would you know that?"

She began to sputter her words. "Uh—I—uh...because he told me."

I sat up in my chair and snatched back the curtain separating us. "And when did he tell you that?"

"A few days ago. I ran into him when I was out and we chatted a bit."

"Ran into him where?"

"Out." She pulled the curtain forward, separating us again.

I snatched it back. "Out where?"

She stalled for a few seconds. "Friday's," she said finally.

"You're lying. Jefferson hates Friday's. Why're you protecting him? Where was he?" I demanded.

"I can't tell you," she moaned. "I promised him I wouldn't."

"I don't care what you promised him. You're *my* best friend, not his. Where the hell was he?"

"I'll tell you, but only if you promise me you won't say anything to him about it. Swear?"

I held up my hand. "I swear," I said.

"I'm not playing," Special warned. "Jefferson's my homey. I want him to know that I won't go blabbing his business."

That was a joke. Special couldn't hold water if you handed it to her in a glass. "Okay, okay. Now tell me."

She winced. "I ran into him at a strip club."

"Is that all?" I leaned back in the recliner. "Girl, I thought you were going to tell me you found him with some woman."

Special looked at me with a flabbergasted expression. "You're not mad?"

"Mad? No. Which one was it? The Barbary Coast in Gardena?"

"Yeah," Special said slowly, still in shock.

"Girl, Jefferson's been going there for years. Sometimes he comes home from that club so damn horny we have the most incredible sex. I don't have a problem with him hanging out there."

"I can't believe this," Special said.

"I'm not as uptight as you think, huh?" I said, looking over at her. Special's eyes were as wide as the clock on the wall. "Jefferson has no idea that I know that's his little hangout. One of my friends told me her husband saw him there about a year ago. Hey, wait a minute," I said, sitting up again. "What were *you* doing there?"

"Just cooling out."

"Since when did you start cooling out at strip clubs?"

She looked as if she were trying to think up a quick lie, then suddenly threw up her hands. "Since I've been busy watching your back."

"Special, just how were you watching *my* back?"

"You told me Jefferson was drinking too much and staying out late. That's a deadly combination. So I decided to look after your interests and follow him. I told you I was thinking about starting my own private investigations firm. This was basically a practice run. Anyway, all he was doing was nursing a drink and kicking it. He wasn't even trying to get a lap dance."

"Special, you actually went to the Barbary Coast by yourself?"

"Yep. And you know I had to fight off quite a few brothers who had the nerve to be all up on me like I was some stripper."

"Special, you're crazy," I said. "Certifiably crazy."

She laughed. "Girl, I had a good time. The sisters in there ain't got nothing on you and me. Most of them weren't even that cute and I know I could wiggle my ass better than half of 'em. I couldn't believe how much money the brothers in there were kicking down. I bet some of them girls are making five, six hundred dollars a night in tips."

"Oh, so now you're thinking about being a stripper?"

"Maybe. That's some good money. It's a helluva lot more than I make now slaving eight hours a day."

"Wait," I said, still amazed at Special's antics. "Let's get back to Jefferson. What did you two talk about?"

"A whole lot of stuff. Me and brother-in-law had a nice, long heart-to-heart. He's lonely."

"Lonely?"

"Yeah. And he told me all about his little problem. He figured you'd already told me anyway." Special jumped up, grabbed an apple from a sofa table across the room, and sat back down. "Like I told you when you were working like a maniac at that other law firm, that brother's not going to be willing to play second fiddle to your career forever. He's just taken the kind of blow few men could handle, but he's handling it. You need to be there for him. Let him know you need him as much as he needs you. He told me that, too."

"Special, I can't just quit my job."

She bit into the apple and sat back down. "Ain't there some law firm out there where you can work nine to five?"

"Not that I'm aware of," I said.

"Then you're going to end up like all these other professional black women, well-educated, loaded, and manless. Jefferson needs a woman who needs him."

I could feel one of Special's lectures coming on. "I do need him," I said.

"When's the last time you told him that?"

I didn't respond because I couldn't remember if I had ever said those exact words to my husband. But certainly Jefferson had to know that I needed him.

Special hopped out of her chair and stood in front of me, noisily chewing her apple. "You and Jefferson are as different as night and day. That's why they say opposites attract. He's totally laid back. You're Ms. Independent. I'm not saying change who you are. He was apparently attracted to that. But plan some time in your day, or at least in your week, to make your man feel like a man."

"Aw, here we go. The world according to Special."

"Mock me if you want to," Special said, pointing her half-eaten apple at me. "But you know I know what I'm talking about. Men are really simple to please, especially black men. But women don't understand that. All you have to do to keep the average brother happy is make him a pot of spaghetti once a week, blow him three times a month and tell him he's The Man every now and then and he's basically good to go."

"Thanks for the advice," I said, turning my head. "Is that it? This is the Quiet Room, you know. Why don't you have a seat?"

"Nope, I ain't done yet." She tossed the apple core into the trash can, a good ten feet away, and actually made it. "Now, you know I've dated my share of married men. And it always baffled me that no matter how bad their marriages were, they weren't trying to file for divorce. Some of them hadn't had sex with their wives in years and their kids were grown and gone. A couple of them stayed put because they were scared their wives would take them to the cleaners, but for most of 'em, money wasn't the issue. Contrary to what we believe, I think most men want to honor their marriage vows and support their families, but it's hard when good-looking women are putting it in their faces every day and they have to come home to some evil bitch who's complaining because he left the toilet seat up. On top of that, she's gained fifty pounds and don't want to have sex no more."

Special was getting on my nerves. "You'd gain fifty pounds and lose interest in sex, too, if you had two or three kids to look after, a full-time job, all the household responsibilities and the weight of your entire extended family's problems on your back."

"That may very well be the case, but what's a forty-year-old man supposed to do? Give up sex just because his wife don't want to give him none? That's like handing a brother a Go-Get-Your-Pussy-Elsewhere pass."

"Special, for one thing, you've never been married, so I don't consider you to be an authority on the subject. And second, I don't understand why you're telling me this. Jefferson and I don't have that problem."

"Yeah, you say that now, but you're going to end up taking him for granted just like every other married woman I know." She stopped to stretch, bending over to touch her toes. "And I don't understand what's so hard about giving your man some nooky on a regular basis. It don't cost you nothing and it don't take that long. We're talking about, what? Twenty, thirty minutes tops out of your day. And despite all that Mandingo bullshit, it's probably more like five or ten minutes for brothers in our age range. Why is that so hard to do?"

I hoped the attendant called us for our massages soon because once Special got on her soapbox there was no stopping her. "I get your point," I said. "From now on, I'm going to skip lunch and run home and seduce my husband."

"You can be facetious if you want to," she said, finally sitting back down.

I took her silence as a good thing.

"How's that Montgomery case going?" she asked after a few short seconds.

I didn't want to talk about Tina Montgomery either, but in light of the topic we had just finished discussing, this one was definitely the more appealing of the two.

I leaned forward in my chair and scanned the room to make sure we were still alone. "Fine, for now, I guess. But I almost got myself thrown off the case."

"What for?"

"I guess you didn't see the paper this morning. I made this stupid objection at the preliminary hearing and there's an article about it in today's *Times*. I basically had to beg O'Reilly not to take me off the case."

Special flew out of her chair and was hovering over me. "What the hell is wrong with you? I know you like this law stuff, but you actually begged to stay on that case when you know how much Jefferson needs you right now?"

I hadn't really thought about it like that. From her vantage point, I guess my actions did seem pretty selfish. "Special, if I'd let them throw me off the case, I never would've been able to live down that stupid mistake. All anybody would've remembered about me is that article in the *Times* basically calling me incompetent. I have to stay on this case to prove to everybody that I'm not a bungling idiot just because I didn't know about some hearsay rule. There's no way I'm going to let that misstep screw up my partnership chances."

"You haven't heard a word I said," Special said, more serious now. "It's all about your job. What about your man?"

"My man is just fine."

"No he isn't! He needs you right now. You're taking it for granted that he's always going to accept playing second fiddle to your career. But that's a dangerous gamble, girlfriend."

I couldn't take her preaching at me anymore. "Why don't you just let *me* handle my marriage and my career?"

"Okay," she snorted, sitting down again. "And I'll try to be a good friend and not say I told you so when Jefferson gets fed up with being neglected."

She sulked to herself for a short while, but in no time started up again. "I feel so sorry for black men. They get the worst rap for the way they treat women, but we're really a big part of the problem."

"Whatever, Special. It's not like you haven't screwed over half the men in L.A."

"You're wrong," she said. "Not quite half. Maybe about a third. Anyway, I understand men and what it takes to make them happy. Most women don't."

"Please spare me another lecture," I pleaded.

"No," she insisted. "You need to hear this." She got up for the fourth time and started pacing around the room. "People are always dogging brothers out, claiming they don't take care of their families, that they can't keep a job, and that they run around. Assuming there's some truth to that, you have to look at the root cause. First, their mamas baby 'em to death so when we get 'em, it's basically too late because they're already ruined. But instead of building them up, all we do is tear them down. Black men take more crap from their women than any other group of men on the planet."

Special was walking back and forth in a straight line now, acting like she was delivering a sermon to a packed church. "It drives me nuts hearing how bad some of those heffas at my job talk about their men. One of them was complaining the other day because her husband bought her some freeway flowers. You know, them flowers you see them selling on the freeway off ramps that cost about ten bucks. She gave them back and told him she didn't want that 'cheap-ass shit.' Can you believe that? Can you imagine how he felt? He was just trying to do something nice. Now, when do you think that brother's going to buy her ass some flowers again? That's the very reason all our men are flocking to white women. A white girl would've been smiling like those ten-dollar flowers were a diamond necklace. And when they died, she would've pasted 'em in her damn scrapbook."

"Special, I don't know why you're telling me this," I said. "I don't treat Jefferson like that."

"Yes, you do," Special insisted. "Every time you run out the door to play savior to one of your clients, it's just like taking some freeway flowers and flinging them in his face."

I tried to take in the smell of the eucalyptus and ignore what Special was saying.

"I guess you don't have nothing to say to that, huh, counselor," Special taunted. "And you can get mad at me if you want to, but sometimes people need to hear the truth, even if it hurts."

"I'm not mad at you," I said halfheartedly. While I wasn't willing to concede that all of her pronouncements applied to me, some of what she was saying definitely hit home.

CHAPTER 45

The few months leading up to the Montgomery trial passed by in a flash. Neddy, David, and I spent nearly every waking hour together, plotting, planning, and strategizing.

We agreed that Neddy would do the opening statement and closing argument and most of the key witnesses, while David and I would divide up the rest. David wasn't all that happy about the arrangement since it basically made my role equal to his, but there was nothing he could do about it. Whenever there was a dispute over trial strategy, David and I deferred to Neddy's judgment and experience, letting her resolve any stalemates.

I arranged to meet Neddy for lunch the Saturday before the start of the trial at Aunt Kizzy's Back Porch, a soul food restaurant in Marina Del Rey that was usually packed with as many whites as blacks.

"You ready, girl?" I asked, meeting her outside the restaurant and giving her a hearty hug. Neddy was dressed in a burnt orange blouse and loose-fitting taupe slacks. She looked amazing. Her hair was texturized and her stylish cut—curly on top and faded along the sides and back—made her look much younger. She was even wearing a cute bronze lipstick. We walked inside and were seated right away.

"As ready as I'm going to be," she said. "What about you?"

"Scared, but ready to roll," I said.

"You don't have anything to be scared about." She reached over and squeezed my forearm.

"Oh, yes I do. If you make a misstep during trial, it'll be no big deal. But if I do, you can bet O'Reilly'll never let me live it down. It might even cost me partnership. Don't forget that I practically had to get down on my knees and beg the man to let me stay on the case."

"Don't sweat it. You've got backup."

A waitress interrupted us to take our orders. Every dish on the menu was named after a relative of the owner. I chose Uncle Wade's baked beef short ribs with collard greens and macaroni and cheese, and Neddy ordered Cousin Willie Mae's smothered pork chops with black-eyed peas and cabbage.

"When's the last time you talked to Tina?" I asked, grabbing a cornbread muffin from a basket on the table.

"This morning," Neddy said, shaking her head. "And she's getting more and more neurotic by the minute. Between dealing with her and Julie, I'm the one who should be ready to have a nervous breakdown. If I see Julie's face on TV one more time, I'm going to blow."

"I'm surprised the reporters haven't been trying to interview you."

"I've gotten a few calls, but you know how I hate trying my cases in the press. They love you one minute and slam you the next. There's not a reporter in this town I trust."

A waitress set Mason jars filled with lemonade on the table. "Well, do you have any last-minute advice for me, counselor?"

"Yep. Just do me one favor," she said, pausing to measure her next words. "Please try to get along with David."

I pouted. "Why aren't you asking him to try to get along with me?"

"I already have. If you guys behave like you've been acting for the past few weeks, the jury's definitely going to pick up on it and it could affect how they view our defense."

"Okay, okay," I said. "I'll try not to slug him in open court. You got your opening statement memorized?"

"Yeah, but I'm not sure I'm giving one. Sometimes it's best for the defense to waive opening statement until after the prosecution has closed its case."

I was surprised. The opening statement and closing argument were often the most dramatic part of the trial. It was a lawyer's chance to use emotion rather than fact to sway the jury. "Why would you do that?"

She had a troubled look on her face. "I just have a feeling we're going to get some surprises from Ms. Julie. If I make an opening statement saying I'm going to prove X, Y, and Z, and Julie throws me for a loop and I can't back up what I said in my opening, then I've lost my credibility with the jury."

"What's the downside to not giving an opening?"

She took a sip of water. "The main downside is that the jury'll probably assume we don't have a strong defense. And it's not that I'm not going to do an opening, I'm just going to wait until after the prosecution closes its case."

"That's a tough call," I said, glad that it wasn't mine to make.

She clasped her hands together and rested her elbows on the table. "My biggest concern is still this tightrope we're walking about Tina's knowledge of her husband's affairs. Like I said before, Julie can easily produce a parade of witnesses who can testify that Max was screwing women from coast to coast. But based on the names on her witness list right now, not a single person can verify that Tina actually knew about his infidelities. Without proving Tina's knowledge, the prosecution has no motive."

The three of us had spent hours arguing over this strategy. Both David and I thought it was dangerous, not to mention unethical, to skate around the issue of whether Tina knew about her husband's affairs. It was the one thing, the only thing, David and I were in complete agreement on.

"Well, you certainly know my view on tiptoeing around that issue," I said, knowing that I wasn't going to be able to convince Neddy to change her mind. "There's no way we can ethically introduce any testimony that Tina didn't know about her husband's affairs. It would be a blatant lie."

Neddy glanced over her shoulder, then to the left and right. The tables on both sides of us were empty. "We're not going to lie or do anything unethical," she said, lowering her voice to a whisper. "Assuming the prosecution fails to call any witnesses who can confirm Tina's knowledge of Max's affairs, all I'm going to do in my closing is point that out—that the prosecution failed to produce any evidence that Tina knew about her husband's extracurricular activities. I won't be saying Tina didn't know, only that the prosecution failed to prove that she did."

"That's what you call a lawful lie," I said smiling. "But there's still the possibility that Julie could produce some contrary evidence after she closes her case-in-chief. So it's still risky."

"This whole discussion may be a moot point." Neddy reached for her lemonade. "I'm sure Julie has some shockers for us. So we'll just have to play it by ear."

Our food arrived and we dug in.

"I can only imagine Julie's opening statement," I said, when we were almost done with our meal. " 'Ladies and gentlemen of the jury, I, the great Julie Killabrew, will prove to you beyond a shadow of a doubt that I am the most incredible lawyer who has ever lived.' "

Neddy grinned as I reached for another cornbread muffin. "I hear Julie's looking at this case as the springboard to her political career," I said.

Neddy arched an eyebrow in skepticism. "She has to win the case first."

"You still confident she won't?"

Neddy lowered her voice again and leaned over the table, bringing her head closer to mine. "There're a lot of variables, but I really don't think she'll be convicted. That assumes, however, that we luck up and get a good jury. All we need is just one person to go our way."

"But what about Oscar Lopez's testimony? Even if we call those other two employees who'll testify that Oscar was lying about the knife, he's still pretty sure the woman he saw was Tina."

She waved away my concern with a terse swipe of her hand. "That's the testimony that bothers me the least. Do you know how many cases I've had where eyewitnesses were flat-out wrong about what they saw? Lopez will be easy to discredit. I'm going to have a ball cross-examining him."

Neddy broke into a sheepish smile. "And don't you dare ask me again how I can do what I do. My focus is on the facts and the law, remember?" She stopped and toyed with her fork. "To be honest, sometimes I feel really confident that Tina's innocent, but other times, I look into her eyes and I see years of betrayal and enough smoldering anger for her to have actually done it. I know what I went through after only a few years with Lawton. I can't imagine enduring that kind of treatment for more than a quarter of a century."

I couldn't imagine it either, which was one reason my gut kept pointing toward Tina's guilt.

When we were done eating, the waitress retrieved our empty plates and took our dessert orders. I didn't bother to look at the menu. I already knew I wanted Miss Flossie's floating sweet potato pie. Neddy ordered Grandmother Zady's peach cobbler.

"So how're things going with you and Jefferson?" Neddy asked.

"Better, but he's still not willing to talk about his situation and I've been letting it go. But we really do need to talk."

Her eyes were sympathetic. "Girl, you know how brothers are about communication. When he's ready to talk, he will and not a minute before."

"You've definitely got that right. It's amazing that he was the one pushing for a family and now I'm the one who's hearing the call of motherhood. I've been really thinking seriously about adopting—soon."

"This is a big switch," she said, surprised.

"Yeah, I know."

"Well, girl, take it from me," she cautioned, "the law and motherhood aren't exactly the best mix. A baby's going to be even more demanding than a trial. And when you get overwhelmed, you can't run to some judge to ask for a continuance. Something has to give. You ready for that?"

"That's the strange part," I said, fidgeting with my napkin. "I think I definitely am."

CHAPTER 46

After having lunch with Neddy, I rushed home to surprise Jefferson with a home-cooked meal of meatloaf, garlic mashed potatoes, and black-eyed peas—all of his favorites. Once the trial started, we would barely see each other. Cooking this meal was going to help me alleviate some of my guilt pangs about abandoning my husband in his time of need.

When Jefferson walked in just after dark and saw the table set, he feigned a heart attack, Fred Sanford-style.

"Oh, Elizabeth, this is the big one! I'm coming to join you, honey!" He stumbled into the kitchen and reached out for a chair to break his fall.

I playfully socked him on the arm. "That's not funny. You act like I never cook."

"I ain't answering that question on the grounds that *you* might be incriminated," he said.

I gave him a big, sloppy kiss. "Go get out of them funky clothes and come back so I can pamper you like the king that you are."

It was absolutely hilarious watching him skip into the bedroom like a big goofy kid. I heard the shower running and in a flash he was back, still damp, with a towel draped around his waist.

He reached out for me and brought his lips to mine, kissing me so fervently that I wanted to cry out. It had been some time since we had really connected.

He reached out to unbutton my jeans, but I grabbed his hands in protest. "C'mon baby, we have to eat first."

"I am going to eat first," he said smiling.

He continued to undress me, then led me into the bedroom.

"You're awful frisky tonight," I said.

He just smiled and laid me down on the bed, then crawled in next to me. We were both laying on our sides, facing each other. "I'm crazy about you, you know that?" he said.

"Ditto," I replied. He smelled fresh and clean. I traced his chest muscles with my index finger. He pulled me on top of him and for a long time, we just held each other and it felt good.

"Jefferson, I just want you to know that it doesn't matter that—"

He cut me off. "I don't want to talk about that. I just want us to stay right here and kick it."

After a few minutes, he laid me on my back and positioned himself next to me. I felt his hand exploring my body, lightly touching me, slowly, deliberately, as if his fingers had eyes that were searching for some special place. He kissed the curve of my neck as his hand descended from my breasts, to my waist and beyond. A wave of excitement stimulated every nerve in my body.

His fingers were talking to me, telling me I was loved. He soon replaced his fingers with his tongue, retracing the exact same path his fingers had traveled. As I felt myself reach a point beyond my control, I pulled him to me and took him in. We thrashed about in a wild, yet coordinated series of fervent motions. It was as if Jefferson could feel the exact same fiery sensations I felt. As his pace quickened, my screams went from thunderous cries to faded whimpers. Seconds later, his groans had also faded and we held onto each other, twisted like a rope, still panting heavily from our encounter.

He lifted his weight from my body and kissed my forehead.

"Now that we've had dessert," he said smiling, "it's time to back up and have the main meal."

We quickly finished eating and climbed into bed to watch TV even though it was only 8:15. I lay across Jefferson's chest as we watched an episode of *The Sopranos* Jefferson had recorded on our new TiVo system. This was the most relaxed I'd felt in a long time. I hated all the drama I'd gone through in the last few weeks, and I was thankful for this brief lull before the storm. When the show ended, Jefferson started channel-hopping.

A news tease returned the tension to my body.

"*What is sure to be one of the most-watched trials in L.A. in years begins on Monday—the murder trial of Tina Montgomery, accused in the vicious stabbing death of her husband, Max Montgomery. Join us for the latest after this brief commercial break.*"

Jefferson entwined my fingers with his. "You ready to roll?"

"I guess so."

"You don't sound too confident."

"I guess I'm a little scared. A woman's life is on the line and I'm going to be partially responsible if she's found guilty."

"Not if she did it."

When the commercial ended, we listened as a reporter rehashed the details of Max Montgomery's murder and speculated about the evidence that would be presented at his wife's trial.

I picked up the remote and changed the channel. "That really pisses me off. They're basically trying the case on TV. No telling how many potential jurors were watching that story. That's why nobody in this city can get a fair trial."

"I have to ask you this question again," Jefferson said. "Do you think she did it?"

This time I didn't try to hedge. "I don't know."

"Ms. I-Have-An-Opinion-About-Everything still doesn't have one?"

"It's turning out to be a weird case. As Neddy put it, there're a lot of variables."

"All I know is, even if the brother was as big a ho as everybody's making him out to be," Jefferson said, "he didn't deserve to die like that."

"Some people feel he got what he deserved."

"Is that what you feel?" Jefferson asked.

"I don't know."

"You don't know?" He pulled away from me. "You're telling me it's cool to kill a brother just because he cheats on his woman?"

"It's not just the cheating, it's the overall betrayal," I said. "If she did kill him, I'm just saying part of me understands. It's like the battered women's syndrome. You take it for years and then suddenly you just snap. There should be a cheated-on woman's syndrome."

Jefferson looked genuinely shocked. "Nah, baby, you're wrong. What about all that women's lib crap y'all like to spout? Where's your self-respect? Why does a man cheating on you have to destroy you? If the brother couldn't keep it zipped up, she should've just took her shit and left." He hit the mute button.

"So if you walked in and caught me cheating, you're not getting enraged and strangling me? You're just leaving?" I asked.

Jefferson thought about my question for a moment. "I'm not saying I wouldn't want to resort to violence, but I don't think I would. I know how to keep my temper in check. Some people don't. I would definitely have to leave the vicinity—fast. But I don't know why we're talking about this because it would never happen. You'd never cheat on me."

The lofty assurance in Jefferson's voice bugged me. "You sound awful confident about that. In fact, you sound a little too confident."

"You wouldn't," he said. "You ain't got it in you."

"What does that mean?"

"You're not stupid and you're not greedy. As long as your needs are being taking care of, you're not about to stray."

He was right. But I still didn't like his staunch confidence about it. "What about you? Are you going to stray?"

"Highly unlikely."

"Highly unlikely? How about absolutely no way, José?"

"Girl, you know me. As long as you're taking care of business at home, then we're cool."

"So, if I stop taking care of business, that gives you the right to mess around?" I asked.

Jefferson chuckled. "You know what? I can see where this conversation is going. Let's just change the subject." He hit the volume button on the remote control, filling the room with sound again.

"I don't want to change the subject," I said, half joking, half serious. "Basically you're telling me you don't respect your marriage vows?"

He raised an eyebrow and laughed. "I'll never understand female logic. How in the hell did you take that giant-ass leap?"

"For better or worse. Remember? You just said, if it gets bad, you get to screw around."

Jefferson laughed louder. "That's not what I said. What I said was—never mind what I said. It doesn't matter. What I meant was, as long as our relationship is straight, you don't have to worry about me trippin'."

"You just said it again!" I said, socking him on the arm. "If our relationship gets rocky, you plan on cheating."

"You know what? We need to change the subject for real now because you're trippin'. I love you. And you know that. I'm not going nowhere. And I don't want to go anywhere. Let's talk about something else."

I grabbed a pillow and pouted.

"C'mon, baby, don't trip." He pulled the pillow from me and began tugging on my earlobes with his lips.

"Stop it," I said, laughing.

He climbed on top of me and tickled my stomach. I laughed wildly and summoned up all my strength, but couldn't get out from under him. He finally stopped tickling me, rolled over, and pulled me on top of him.

"This is fun," I said. "It's been a long time since we just hung out and acted crazy like this."

"And whose fault is that?"

"Objection, nonresponsive." I leaned in closer and kissed him. "Can I talk to you about something?" I asked.

"Aw, shit. Whenever you want to 'talk,' it usually ain't good. What's up now? If you tell me you're taking on another big case after this one's over, I'm filing for divorce. Tonight."

"I can't believe you said that." I socked him even harder this time. "And no, I don't have another case." I laid my head on his chest. "I want to talk about adoption."

I felt his chest muscles harden.

"You did hear me, right?" I asked.

"Yeah," he said curtly.

"And...?"

"And that's not something I want to talk about right now."

"Why not?"

"Because I just don't."

"Jefferson, we have to deal with this."

He stared at the TV screen and didn't say anything for a long time. I decided to wait him out.

"I don't want to raise anybody else's kids," he said finally. "And I definitely don't want to do it by myself." Jefferson sat up, resting his back against the leather headboard, and I joined him.

"What does that mean?"

"That means that the next case that comes up, you won't be here. You don't make time for me and I doubt you'll make time for a kid."

His words stung like a punch in the face. "Then I'm confused. What the hell did we just do?"

"You amaze the fuck out of me sometimes," he said, turning to face me. "You cook dinner once every six months and think you deserve a fuckin' award. Don't play me. Your career is first. Then me. I've been trying to deal with that. So if we adopt, is the kid coming before me or after me?"

The venom in his voice startled me. In my heart, I didn't feel that I'd put my career first, but if the measuring stick was time, I had to admit that lately Jefferson had come in a distant second.

"You're not second to my career. I just can't control my work schedule the way you can."

"Yes, you can," he charged. "I know lawyers who don't spend all day and night at the office."

"And I doubt any of them work at a firm with the reputation of O'Reilly & Finney. It comes with the territory."

He made an exasperated sucking sound. "There're other firms in L.A. Other good firms. And like I keep telling you, you don't need to make partner to validate yourself. You'd be a good lawyer whether you were working for the best firm in the city or the worst one. And anyway, I don't know why we're even discussing this. It would be the same thing no matter where you worked. You're a workaholic by nature."

I didn't want to argue about my work schedule because there was no way for me to resolve the issue short of quitting. Neddy wasn't even on partnership track and she worked hours just as long as mine. I wanted to get back to our conversation about adoption. The thought of never being a mother frightened me.

"So are you telling me you won't consider adoption because I work too much?"

He switched channels and the familiar melody of a McDonald's jingle filled the room. "That's one reason."

"And the others?"

He closed his eyes and looked away. "I just don't want to adopt, Vernetta, okay?"

"I didn't know you felt that way."

"I didn't know I did either."

I took the remote from his hand and hit the mute button again. "You'd really want us to live our lives never being parents?"

"You know that's not what I want. It's just how it is. Anyway, I don't understand the big switch. I had to basically threaten you to make that appointment with Dr. Bell. Now, all of a sudden, you're ready for motherhood."

"It doesn't have to be right away. But it bothers me that you don't even want to talk about adoption. This is a decision we should make together."

"That's a joke, right?" he said, his eyes boring into mine. "We don't make any other decisions together. Why should this one be any different?"

My eyes told him that he'd hurt my feelings, but he didn't make any effort to say or do anything about it.

"Let's just talk about this some other time." He hopped off the bed and grabbed his jeans from a nearby chair. "I'm going to the store to get some ice cream. You want anything?"

Yeah, a baby. "Yeah, check the refrigerator," I said instead. "I think we're low on milk."

CHAPTER 47

Bright and early on Monday morning, a long line of reporters, spectators, and courthouse gadflies lined up outside Judge Graciano's courtroom as if it were Caesar's Palace and they were waiting for admission to the heavyweight fight of the year. We were already seated at the defense table when the bailiff finally allowed the spectators to flood into the courtroom. We turned around to watch as they scurried for the best possible seats.

I looked over at Neddy, seated next to me. She showed absolutely no sign of fear. I, on the other hand, was a ball of nerves. Neddy was wearing a powder blue skirt suit with a gray blouse and black leather pumps. I'd changed three times before finally walking out of the door in a double-breasted, navy blue skirt suit that made my hips look too big. I wished I'd worn something else.

Tina, seated next to Neddy and flanked on the far side by David, was professionally dressed in a lavender Evan Picone dress with a wide belt. I smiled. I guess Tina's idea of dressing down was wearing something that cost less than five hundred bucks. I noticed age lines in her face that hadn't been there during our first meeting. Her makeup, as usual, was flawless. Her eyes were no longer puffy. I guess she wasn't crying herself to sleep anymore. David drummed his ingers on the table. He was probably experiencing caffeine with-awal. We'd been at the office since six that morning and he wasn't le to make a second Starbucks run.

A quiet commotion hit the room as Julie strolled in, obviously intent on making an entrance. I had to admit she looked good in black. She was wearing her trademark long-waisted jacket and a short skirt with a black and white pinstriped blouse. Her hair was pulled back into a conservative bun. Her lipstick was an enticing rose-colored shade that matched her nails. Her co-counsel, Sandy, trailed awkwardly behind her, struggling with a box of documents too heavy for one person to carry. I'd heard her only role would be to hand Julie exhibits and perform whatever gofer tasks Julie demanded.

Julie looked in our direction and politely nodded before taking a seat. A move intended solely for the benefit of onlookers.

When Judge Graciano finally took the bench, it was clear that she, too, had spent some extra time in front of the mirror that morning. She was a tiny woman whose smooth skin did not betray her fifty-plus years. Her hair had a fresh cut and the collar of her pink silk blouse peeked out of the top of her drab black robe, giving it a bit of life. Her only makeup mistake was having applied too much blush to her cheeks.

The judge rushed through the administrative matters and made it clear that she wasn't going to allow us to take forever to pick a jury. And she stuck to that vow. We had the jury seated in two and a half days.

Julie used all of her preemptory challenges carefully, excluding any potential juror, male or female, who'd had any kind of run-in with domestic violence. For Neddy, anyone who seemed to have an unusually strong religious conviction was stricken. The Bible said "thou shalt not kill" and didn't mention any exceptions for cheating husbands. We couldn't take a chance on someone interpreting that verse literally.

When *voir dire* ended, seven women and five men were seated. There were four whites, six Hispanics, and two blacks. Four of the Hispanics were men, and there was only one black female and one black male. The rest of the jurors were female. The alternates were all white women. Based on the jurors' responses to the *voir dire* questions, my nonscientific study pegged Juror No. 7, a black woman in her fifties, and Juror No. 9, a Hispanic woman close to forty, as our best bets for a hung jury. There was something about them, something I couldn't precisely pinpoint, that told me they had experienced the pain of betrayal. I only hoped their personal experiences gave them enough empathy to reject the circumstantial evidence against Tina.

Following the lunch break, Julie gave a brief opening statement that sounded like one of her press conferences. She began by discussing her theory of the case, methodically describing the evidence she planned to introduce during the trial. Evidence that she claimed would prove Tina Montgomery was a murderer. Neddy decided to waive opening statement, which didn't seem to faze the jurors. At least not as far as I could tell.

The first two days of testimony posed no surprises. The crime scene investigator and the coroner presented exactly the same testimony they had offered at the prelim, only longer. Neddy crossed the crime scene investigator and David took the coroner, both without incident. Ernestine Frye, Max's personal assistant, didn't lay any smoking guns on the table either. On cross, I cautiously honed in on the fact that Frye had no evidence that Tina Montgomery knew about her husband's many affairs. The jurors seemed to be paying close attention to the testimony and none of them had dozed off yet.

During an afternoon break on the second day of testimony we convened in a small conference room we would be using throughout the trial to discuss matters in private.

Neddy looked worried.

"You okay?" I asked.

"There's still nobody on the D.A.'s list of witnesses who can corroborate that Tina knew about her husband's affairs. Without that, the prosecution has no motive. This case is too important for Julie to let that point slide."

David pulled a chair out from the table and sat down. "Well, that can only mean Julie has a surprise witness for us."

"But how can she surprise us?" I asked. "We've seen her witness list. She can't just introduce a new witness midtrial."

"Technically," David said, "but there're ways to get around that. All she'll do is tell the judge she just discovered some vital witness she didn't know about. There's no way she's closing her case without showing that Tina knew about Max's infidelities."

Tina closed her eyes, but didn't speak.

Neddy turned to her. "I know we've asked you this before, but is there anyone who can testify that you knew about your husband's affairs?"

Tina looked off into the distance, as if she were mentally running through a list of friends and acquaintances. "I guess there could be somebody, but I can't think of a single person who'd voluntarily come forward. Unless . . ." Tina's voice trailed off and a look of dread covered her face.

"Unless what?" Neddy asked.

"Kinga," she said slowly. "I'm sure Kinga must've overheard some of the arguments between Max and me."

We all looked at each other. How had we forgotten about Kinga?

Neddy reached for a legal pad, and started jotting down some quick notes. "Did the police ever question her?"

"Yeah," Tina said, still worried. "Right after Max died, and also on that day when they searched the house. But I don't think they asked her all that much about my relationship with Max."

"Yeah, but they took you away in handcuffs," I reminded her. "They could've questioned her after you left."

"Kinga would've told me. We have a really good relationship. She was as upset about Max's death as I was."

"Is Kinga at your place now?" Neddy asked.

"Probably. She lives in the back house."

Neddy glanced at her watch and turned to me. "The judge is calling a recess around four. I need you to get over to Tina's place as soon as we break and find out if Kinga talked to the police or the prosecution. And if she did, find out everything she told them. We'll be back at the office waiting for you."

CHAPTER 48

It took me more than an hour to make it from downtown L.A. to Brentwood. I jogged up the walkway of Tina's house and leaned on the doorbell for what seemed like an eternity. I was about to give up and check the back house when I heard the muffled sound of footsteps. Even after I announced my name, Kinga stared at me through the peephole for several seconds before opening the door.

"Mrs. Montgomery isn't here," she said, as politely as before, but with much less of an accent. All traces of her East Indian ancestry were camouflaged by a pair of jeans, tennis shoes, and a short-sleeved, V-necked top that exposed ample breasts for a woman her size. Her shiny, thick black hair was now curled about her face. She looked like a hip, attractive college student. Not somebody's housekeeper.

"I'm here to talk to you," I said. I boldly stepped inside the foyer since Kinga gave no indication that she planned to invite me in. "Let's have a seat in the living room." This time, I led the way.

There was a look of uncertainty on Kinga's face as she sat down across from me in the purple room. "I don't think I should be talking to you without clearing it with Mrs. Montgomery first."

This time, I heard absolutely no trace of an accent. *What was that about?*

"Don't worry," I said, "Tina knows I'm here. I need to ask you a few questions that could help us with her case."

I pulled a yellow legal pad from my bag and settled into the purple couch. Kinga took the chair where I usually sat. During my prior visits, Tina had always sat alone on the couch. Now I understood why. It had a cushy, luxurious feel to it. Like it was stuffed with down feathers.

I explained to Kinga that I needed to ask her some questions about the Montgomerys' relationship that would be crucial to Tina's defense. She confirmed that the police and someone from the prosecutor's office had questioned her about the Montgomerys' marriage right after Max's death. Kinga said she told them both that she didn't know much since she spent most of her time in the back house. The police talked to her again on the day they searched the house, and had asked where Tina kept her shoes and clothes. They also wanted to know the location of every trash can, both inside and outside the house.

"Did you ever hear Mr. and Mrs. Montgomery arguing?" I asked.

She seemed surprised at the question. "No, not that I can remember."

When her eyes avoided mine I knew that she was lying. "Kinga, this is very important," I said, my voice stern, but gentle. "If you were called to testify, could you swear to that on the Bible?"

She averted her eyes again and didn't answer.

"It's okay if you did. Tina was the one who told us you might've overheard their fights. Can you tell me what they argued about?"

She rearranged herself in the chair, curling her feet underneath her body. "Max had other women," she said finally. Her statement sounded very casual, as if she personally accepted that as part of the male psyche. "Mrs. Montgomery didn't like it."

"How often did you hear them arguing about that subject?"

She looked up at the ceiling as if she were counting the fights in her mind. "Many times."

"Tell me about them. What did you hear?"

She looked away. "I can't remember anything specific."

"Just try," I urged.

She inhaled, then complied. "It was always the same. Mrs. Montgomery yelled at him and accused him of seeing other women and he just told her she was paranoid."

"So she was angry?"

Kinga nodded.

"How angry?"

"I don't know," she said tersely. "I don't have an anger meter."

Kinga's attitude was beginning to bother me. I noticed that her eyes nervously moved to my legal pad whenever I began taking notes. I stopped writing and placed my pen on the coffee table, hoping she would open up to me. "Do you think Tina was angry enough to kill her husband?"

Her eyes widened and her brow furrowed. "How would I know that?" Her words were noncommittal but her eyes said yes.

"When was the last time you heard them arguing?"

Kinga swallowed hard. "I heard Mrs. Montgomery on the phone screaming at Max, telling him she hated him. That he couldn't treat her like some whore and that he would get what he deserved."

Get what he deserved? I reached for my pen, then stopped. "When was that?" I asked.

"Early in the morning," Kinga said, pausing, "the day before Max was murdered."

This time I felt Kinga studying me, waiting for *my* reaction. My first thought was anger. This was something Tina should have told us. I couldn't remember if we had specifically asked her the last time she argued with her husband, but even if we hadn't, Tina should have volunteered that information. As I pondered this news and how this information might damage Tina's defense if Kinga were called as a witness, tears started to roll down Kinga's cheeks.

"Are you okay?" I asked.

She nodded.

Kinga had worked for the Montgomerys for five years. I hadn't even stopped to realize how close she might have been to Mr. Montgomery. His death was obviously painful for her, too. "I only have a few more questions," I said. "Is that okay? Maybe we should take a break?"

She limply waived her hand, instructing me to continue.

I pulled a tissue from my purse and handed it to her. She took it and dried her cheeks. She seemed embarrassed by her tears, but suddenly loosened up and began to share with me many intimate details of the Montgomerys' marriage. Details Tina had neglected to disclose.

"When they had dinner parties, he brought women he was sleeping with here to the house," she said with astonishment in her voice.

"Said they were business acquaintances, but they weren't. And Mrs. Montgomery knew. She had to know. A woman knows when her man is screwing around. She may not have admitted it to herself or to anybody else, but she knew."

I heard spite in Kinga's voice. Spite aimed at Tina, not Max. I was too stunned to say anything, so I didn't.

"Mrs. Montgomery spent all her time trying to be the perfect wife. But that wasn't what Max wanted or needed." It struck me as odd that she called Max by his first name, but not Tina. "She was plastic, phony," she continued, disparaging Tina. "All she cared about were her fundraisers and her elegant little dinner parties. I did all of the work and she got all of the credit. He didn't give a damn about that stuff, or her either." She smiled in a wicked kind of way that unnerved me. "And no matter how hard she tried, there was nothing she could do to make Max give a damn."

She curled up in an upright fetal position and hugged her knees to her chest. I waited for her to continue, but she began to cry again. Just a whimper at first, then her sobs intensified.

"Kinga, are you going to be okay?"

"She didn't deserve him," she bawled, pressing her face into her knees. She continued to speak, but her hiccup-filled sobs made it impossible for me to make out her words.

I pulled more tissues from my purse and handed them to her. "Maybe we should take a break," I said.

She lifted her head weakly. "No. I don't need a break. You asked me if she were angry enough to kill him. Yes. Yes, she was," Kinga sniveled. "And she did kill him. I know she did!"

"What? What are you saying? You think Tina killed Max?"

Her whole body nodded *yes*.

I didn't know what to say. "Why? Why do you think that, Kinga?"

"Because she hated him," Kinga continued to sob. "And she didn't want any other woman to have him."

She was so distraught now that I was praying she would retract her words once she calmed down.

"I loved that man so, so much," she said. "And he loved me, too."

I stared at her, the significance of what she was saying slowly registering. "Kinga, are you telling me you were seeing Max?"

"I wasn't *seeing* him," she said indignantly, as if that word cheapened their relationship. "He was my lover. I loved him and he loved me. I was supposed to be with him that night," she said, crying out again. "He was waiting for me in that hotel room."

CHAPTER 49

By the time I walked out of Tina's front door forty-five minutes later, my stomach was a ball of knots and I felt queasy. I started up my SUV and dialed Neddy on her cell phone.

"Where are you?" I asked.

"What do you mean 'where am I'? We're at the office, just where I'd said we'd be." She sounded irritated and exhausted. "So what did you find out?"

"Are Tina and David in the room with you?" My heart was beating as fast as the fluttering of a hummingbird's wings.

"Yeah. Why don't you call back on the office line and I can put you on the speaker—"

"No!" I shouted.

"Calm down," Neddy said. "What's going on?"

"I'll tell you in a minute." I was practically hyperventilating now. "What I want you to do right now is act like everything's fine and walk out into the hallway and close the door behind you."

"What?"

"Please, Neddy. Just trust me."

She told David and Tina to excuse her for a second. Then I heard the sound of the door closing.

"You're scaring me, girl," Neddy whispered. "What happened? Is the news from Kinga that bad?"

"It depends on how you look at it. She definitely heard the

Montgomerys going at it. Lots of times. But she lied to the police about it."

"So what's the problem?"

I was so wound up I didn't know which news to deliver first. "Tina and Max had a pretty nasty argument over the telephone the day before he was killed. And Tina was apparently furious enough, not to mention loud enough, for Kinga to hear every prophetic word of it. At least Tina's portion of the conversation. To hear Kinga tell it, Tina has quite a little temper."

"I can't believe Tina didn't tell us about that fight." I could hear the frustration in Neddy's voice. "Wait a minute, but if Kinga never told anybody about it, then we don't have anything to worry about, right?"

"Yeah. But wait until you hear this. Guess what little hot mama Max was waiting for in that hotel room the night he was killed?"

Neddy didn't say anything for a second. Then reality registered. "Kinga? Oh shit!"

"See why I wanted your ass out of that conference room?"

"Max was screwing her, too! What a lowlife!"

"You're telling me? Kinga had sent him an invitation, an anonymous one, inviting him to the hotel for an evening of—let's just call it romance."

"So Max showed up there not even knowing who he was going to meet?"

"You got it."

Neddy actually whistled this time. "Damn, he was a ho!"

I breathlessly recounted everything Kinga had told me. She had been sleeping with Max for about six months. Mostly in hotel rooms, but on occasion, when Tina was out, they had made love in the back house where Kinga lived.

"And to hear Kinga tell it," I said, "the man definitely had some stuff he needed to bottle up and put on the grocery store shelf. She got tired of waiting for him to set up their next little tryst. So she decided to surprise him."

I could almost see the astonishment on Neddy's face through the telephone. As I approached a yellow traffic light, I hit the gas and sped through the intersection. I reminded myself to concentrate on the road before I ended up in an accident.

"Kinga's little anonymous invitation told Max what hotel to go to, what time to be there, everything," I said. "Apparently, Max got off on stuff like that. Anyway, when she walked into his hotel suite all dolled up and ready to sex him up, she found his bloody body slumped in the tub. Instead of calling the police, which would've required her to explain what she was doing there, she hightailed it home and kept her mouth shut."

"Wait a minute," Neddy said, "didn't Kinga know Tina was holding her fundraiser at the Ritz?"

"Apparently not. For some reason, Tina didn't ask her to help out on this one. And by the way, Kinga definitely has no love lost for the boss lady. Actually, she despises the woman."

Neddy whistled again. "This is by far the most bizarre case I've ever handled."

I made what was definitely an unsafe lane change and hopped onto the 405 Freeway. I prayed that there were no police in the vicinity. "Ditto for me. So what're we going to do with this information?"

"We're not going to do a damn thing," Neddy said.

"Are you serious?" I said. "The fact that Kinga was seeing Max makes her a possible suspect. What if she's lying about finding him in that hotel room already dead? We don't know that she didn't kill him. She was deceitful enough to be screwing Tina's husband right under her nose...maybe she killed him. The way she sat there wailing over him, she was definitely crazy in love with the man."

"Then why would she kill him?" Neddy asked.

"Maybe she was pissed off about his other women or maybe he'd promised to leave Tina, then changed his mind. I don't know. But pointing the finger at Kinga could mean an acquittal for Tina."

I waited as Neddy pondered my theory. "You're jumping the gun," she said finally, but not convincingly. "We don't have anything solid enough to conclude that Kinga killed the man."

"Since when does it have to be solid?" I said. "And I disagree. How about the fact that she doesn't have an alibi? She supposedly went back to the Montgomery mansion after fleeing the hotel. But she couldn't give me the name of a single person who could verify that. And one more thing, guess what size shoe Kinga wears?"

"Don't tell me."

"Yep, a six."

I allowed Neddy a few seconds of silence to mull over this information. "If we run to the police with this stuff, it could backfire," she said. "Tina and Max had a terrible argument the day before his death and on top of that he was screwing the housekeeper. Those two pieces of evidence alone sound like additional nails in Tina's coffin if you ask me. Kinga will point the finger at Tina and Tina will point it back at Kinga. And since Tina's the one on trial right now, I'd say chances are, she'd lose the finger-pointing contest. So let's just lock this info away and pray that it doesn't come out at trial."

The traffic on the freeway had slowed to a crawl and I was getting antsy. "I don't know, Neddy. I think we need to think this through more carefully. You've been saying all along that you believe Tina's innocent. Based on what I just told you, Kinga could be her scapegoat."

"Sounds like now you're the one who thinks she's innocent," Neddy said.

"I don't know what to think," I said, looking at the bumper-to-bumper traffic ahead and wondering whether I should take the streets. "I'm confused as hell."

"This is too wild. Get back down here so we can talk. I need to hear the whole story one more time."

"I'm on my way," I said, "but you know how slow the 405 can be."

"Well, I'll be here no matter when you get here," she said. "In the meantime, I'm giving Tina a piece of my mind for not telling us about that big shouting match she had with Max," Neddy said. "Then I'm sending her home so we can talk."

"What about David?" I asked.

"What about him? He *is* part of the defense team."

"I know, but I really think we should keep this information between the two of us until we figure out what we're going to do with it."

Neddy gave my suggestion some thought. "Okay," she said, exasperated. "I'll send both of them home."

CHAPTER 50

Neddy and I stayed at the office until one o'clock the next morning, wrestling with all the possible consequences of Kinga's revelations. In the end, we agreed that the information could do Tina more harm than good. If Kinga became a suspect, she would no doubt tell the police about Tina and Max's last argument, giving Tina a clear motive for murder. The fact remained that Tina was the one allegedly seen outside Max's hotel room with a knife in her hand, not Kinga.

Early that next morning, when I walked into the O'Reilly & Finney conference room where David, Tina, and Neddy were waiting, Tina was the first to speak.

"What exactly did Kinga say to you yesterday?" she asked anxiously.

After I'd hung up with Neddy last night, she had given David and Tina a brief summary of Kinga's revelations. Leaving out, of course, Kinga's affair with Max. So why was Tina asking me to recount what Kinga had said?

"You must've really scared her," Tina continued. "She left me a note last night telling me she had a family emergency and had to rush back to New York. Her mother's been sick for quite some time, but I can't help wondering if that was really the reason she left."

Neddy and I shared a knowing glance.

"Well," I said, joining them at a long conference table covered with boxes and documents, "like Neddy told you last night, she definitely heard a lot of the squabbles between you and Max about his affairs."

Tina hung her head and massaged the back of her neck. "I'm just thankful that Kinga's on my side," Tina said.

"What do you mean?" I asked.

"She probably left town so she couldn't be subpoenaed. Now she won't have to testify about the way Max and I argued all the time. I really owe her."

Neddy's eyes flashed me strict instructions not to touch that fairy tale. Not that I had planned to.

Tina rubbed her eyes and turned to Neddy. "I was thinking about the things you said last night. I know you don't believe it, but I guess I just blocked out the last fight I had with Max. Anyway, we weren't arguing about his affairs. Well, at least not directly."

"Then exactly what *were* you arguing about?" I asked.

"He'd promised to escort me to the Crystal Stairs fundraiser. I'd been planning the event all year. I was the chairperson. He'd said he would go and then called me up claiming he'd been called away on business. I was pretty upset."

"Wait a minute," David said, "why would he meet some woman at the same hotel where he knew you were having that fundraiser?"

"I never had a chance to tell him where the event was being held. Max never would've shown up there knowing I could possibly run into him. He wasn't that much of a louse."

Neddy looked at me. *Oh yes the hell he was,* her eyes said.

True to form, the lack of sound made Tina uncomfortable. "Yes, I was angry with Max about standing me up," Tina said, eager to explain herself. "But not angry enough to kill him."

"If Kinga's called to testify, we're fried," David said dejectedly.

"No," Tina said sharply, "*we're* not fried, *I'm* fried."

"Hold on," Neddy said, standing up. When her brain got going, she liked to pace. She had to step around boxes, but she found a nice pathway on the far side of the room. "Based on everything we know at the moment, Julie doesn't know anything about your final argument with Max. And there's no reason for us to believe she'll find out."

"But Julie's called almost everybody on her witness list," I said. "There's no way she's going to close the prosecution's case without putting on some evidence that points to a motive."

"Maybe she doesn't have any," Neddy said smiling. "I thought it was weird that she never expressly stated that Tina knew Max was screwing around in her opening statement or at the prelim. She talked about Max's philandering, but she never once said Tina knew about it."

Neddy rummaged through one of the boxes on the table and pulled out a legal pad filled with her handwritten trial notes. "I wrote down Julie's opening statement almost word for word," Neddy said, flipping through the pages. "There's nothing in here."

"Julie's not that sloppy," I insisted. "She wants to win this case. She's been in the media constantly. We're underestimating her. She's got a big surprise in store for us. And anyway, it may not be that big of a stretch for the jury to infer that Tina knew."

David suddenly sat up in his chair and turned to Tina. "When you and your husband were arguing that morning, it was on the telephone, right?"

"Yes," Tina said.

"How did he respond?"

Tina looked confused. "What do you mean 'how did he respond'?"

David impatiently drummed two fingers on the table. "Did he raise his voice? Did he scream back at you?"

"Yes," Tina said. "Max was as much of a hothead as I was. We were both yelling at each other."

"And you also said he was basically up front with the women he dated. That they knew he was married, but chose to see him anyway."

"Yes . . ." Tina said, not making the connection. I didn't know where David was headed either.

"During that conversation, did you accuse him of being with a woman?"

"Well...yes."

"And did he deny it?"

"Of course."

David stood up and turned to Neddy. "I bet I know who Julie's going to surprise us with." He had a horrified look on his face. "There're still a couple of secretaries from Max's firm on Julie's witness list who haven't testified yet. What if Max was with one of them when he made that call to Tina?"

Tina's mouth gaped open.

"If someone was with him, I'd bet good money that Julie knows who she is. And I'd bet double-to-nothing that Julie's going to call her to testify about the angry screaming match she overheard Max having on the phone with Tina the day before he was murdered."

CHAPTER 51

As we neared the end of the first week of testimony, we were no longer holding our collective breath, waiting for some classy vixen to stroll into the courtroom and recount Max and Tina's final shouting match. Maybe David's theory was wrong. I no longer had my fingers crossed for good luck, but I kept my legs tightly crisscrossed just in case.

We were feeling even more confident following the morning break on Thursday, when Julie advised the judge that she planned to close the prosecution's case the following day. Most of that morning had been taken up with housekeeping matters and the testimony of Carla Winston, a secretary from Montgomery's firm who proudly testified that she had slept with Max for several months. We were on pins and needles for the bulk of her direct exam, but if she knew anything about Max and Tina's big blowup, she wasn't telling. The closest Julie got to establishing Tina's knowledge of her husband's affairs was the secretary's claim that Tina once saw her and Max at lunch together, which Tina told us was a lie.

On cross, it didn't take Neddy long to attack the secretary's character and render her testimony useless.

"Please forgive me, Ms. Winston, but I can't remember if the prosecution covered this with you. You did know Mr. Montgomery had a wife when you started sleeping with him, correct?"

"Yes," she said through tightened lips.

"And you actually knew Mr. Montgomery's wife, didn't you?"

Neddy was purposely repeating the word "wife" to morally distin-
guish Tina's relationship with Max from that of the secretary's.

"I knew her, but it wasn't like we were friends or anything like
that." Winston seemed anxious to show that she did have some scru-
ples. She was a good-looking, thirty-something brunette with obviously fake breasts on full display through her sheer, low-cut blouse.
Max was certainly consistent about that physical trait, I thought.

During Julie's direct examination, Winston had gloriously lapped
up her fifteen minutes of fame. Now she looked like she wanted to
crawl under a table.

"You did volunteer to help Mr. Montgomery's wife with a charity
auction a couple years ago, didn't you?"

"Yes. But only because Max asked me to. The firm encourages us
to get involved in charitable activities."

"And you even had lunch with Mr. Montgomery's wife to plan
that fundraiser, correct?"

She gently tugged on the sleeve of her blouse, which produced a
more expansive view of her bosom. "Yes, but other people from the
firm helped out, too."

"And Mr. Montgomery's wife bought you a Christmas present a
few months after that fundraiser, didn't she?"

Winston shuffled nervously, unhappy that Neddy was making her
out to be a back-stabbing tramp. "The Christmas present was actually from both of them."

"But Mr. Montgomery's wife personally delivered it to you at
your desk and thanked you for helping her with the fundraiser,
right?"

"Yes," she said meekly.

"And you never bothered to tell Mr. Montgomery's wife that you
were sleeping with her husband, did you?"

"No, of course not."

Neddy moved closer to the witness box. "And, to your knowledge, no one else told Mr. Montgomery's wife that you were sleeping
with her husband either, correct?"

"I guess not."

"And do you think Mr. Montgomery's wife would've bought you
a Christmas present and personally delivered it to you if she'd known
you'd been screwing her husband?"

Julie jumped out of her chair. "Objection. Calls for speculation. Argumentative. Badgering the witness. Irrelevant!"

"Okay, okay," Judge Graciano said. "Sustained. You know better, counselor."

Neddy was already on the way back to her seat. "I'm sorry, Your Honor. I have no further questions."

I enjoyed the scornful looks the jurors were shooting toward the witness box as Winston sulked out of the courtroom.

At the end of the day, Neddy, Tina, David, and I convened in our courthouse meeting room, feeling the possible taste of victory. So far, things looked fairly good. Oscar Lopez, the waiter at the Ritz-Carlton, had crumbled under a tough cross-examination by Neddy. On direct he testified that he had seen Tina in the hallway outside room 502, but after Neddy finished bouncing him around like a ping-pong ball, he wasn't sure he had even been on the fifth floor. He also admitted telling more than a couple of his coworkers that he wasn't exactly sure Tina was carrying a knife. And by the time he stepped down from the witness stand, he was no longer certain whether the woman he saw was wearing a long dress or a short one. Neddy's cross-examination definitely scored major points with the jury.

So far, Julie's case was totally circumstantial. Other than Tina being at the hotel for a very good reason and her size-six feet, there was no other evidence linking her to Max's murder.

Neddy glanced at her watch. It was close to five. Just as we were trying to decide whether to head back to the office or call it a day, we heard a knock at the door.

"Come in," Neddy said.

Sandy, Julie's voiceless sidekick, entered the room. "We just got word that our investigator located someone we've been trying to track down for several weeks. He'll be our final witness. Here's a motion to amend our witness list."

She placed a document on the table and turned to leave.

Neddy scanned the motion and handed it to David. "Wait a minute!" Neddy shouted, standing up. "This last-minute ambush stuff is so typical of Julie. And she doesn't even have the balls to come in here and tell us herself. I'll be opposing your motion. You had just as much time as we did to identify your witnesses. This unfair surprise is prejudicial to my client."

"Tell it to the judge," Sandy said, and left.

David was still reading the document. "Who's Garrett Bryson?" He had not bothered to look up at Tina. If he had, he would have noticed that her silky brown skin had turned a frightening ash white.

Neddy glared at Tina. "Well, who is he?"

Tina's shoulders noticeably sagged as we all waited for her to respond. "He's someone I used to be involved with," she said finally.

Neddy had a hand on her hip. "And why does the prosecution want to call him as a witness?"

"He'll be able to testify that I knew about Max's affairs."

"Aw Christ!" David said, obviously seeing Tina's acquittal as well as his book deal evaporate.

"Tell me what he knows," Neddy said, grabbing a legal pad and sitting back down.

I thought Tina was going to cry, but she didn't. "He knows that I was unhappy in my marriage."

"How long were you seeing him?"

"About a year. But that was almost three years ago."

"Is he married?"

"No."

"We're going to oppose the prosecution's motion," Neddy said, "but I doubt we'll prevail. If the witness has some relevant information, there's no way the judge is going to exclude it." She briefly closed her eyes and pinched the bridge of her nose. "We need you to tell us everything you can about your relationship with this guy."

For the next hour, Tina took a grilling from her own attorneys. We asked for times, dates, and places. We also asked if there'd been any other men in her life. Tina assured us Bryson was the only one.

She described Bryson as one of Max's male groupies—men who wanted his power and wealth but had no practical means to attain it for themselves. Hanging onto Max's coattail was the closest they would ever get to his millions. Most times, Tina and Bryson met at his condo in Carson. Bryson claimed to be a real estate developer, but a flashy business card with his picture on it was the only sign Tina ever saw of that. He clearly envied Max and sleeping with his wife was a way to soothe his jealousy.

"Did you love him?" Neddy asked.

Tina laughed sarcastically. "No, not really. But sleeping with Garrett was my way of getting back at Max. Garrett was also good—very good—at making me feel like a million bucks. In and out of bed."

She didn't seem at all embarrassed about discussing her own sexuality.

"Wait a minute, this might not be such a bad thing," David said looking at Neddy. "If she were seeing another man, maybe she didn't care what her husband was doing. We can argue that she went out and had her own affair. That she wasn't some angry, scorned woman with a motive to kill."

Neddy wasn't impressed with David's theory. She grimaced and looked sternly at Tina. "When we first met with you, we asked you to be completely honest with us. And you weren't. First you neglected to tell us about that argument you had with Max the day before he died. Now this." Neddy had been fuming ever since Sandy walked out of the room. I realized now that she was angrier at Tina than at the prosecution.

"We can't do our best work when you're not honest with us," she continued. "Surprises like this could really hurt your case. What if I'd made an opening statement claiming there was no evidence that you knew about your husband's affairs? That would've killed my credibility, and instead of viewing you as a sympathetic, cheated-on wife, the jury would've viewed both of us as liars." Neddy bit down on her lip. "Is there anything else we need to know about this Garrett Bryson?"

"Yes." Tina dropped her head so low it almost touched the table. "I told Garrett I wanted to kill Max for cheating on me."

CHAPTER 52

When we returned to court the next morning, Julie was decked out for victory. Her beige tailored suit was complemented by a girly, light pink blouse with ruffles at the neck and wrists. Her hair was in a youthful ponytail now, accented with pearl barrettes that matched a larger pearl lapel pin. She was wearing a sweet-smelling perfume, probably musk oil. Whatever it was, she had used too much of it.

The morning started with Neddy and Julie squaring off over what we viewed as the prosecution's last-minute sabotage attempt.

"I understand that we have a motion to address before bringing the jury in," Judge Graciano said, staring down at us from her perch.

"Yes, Your Honor," Neddy began. "The defense opposes the prosecution's motion to amend its witness list. Ms. Killabrew failed to notify us of this witness in a timely manner. This unfair surprise will be extremely prejudicial to my client as we've had no time to prepare for the cross-examination of Mr. Bryson."

The judge turned to Julie. "This *is* quite late, Ms. Killabrew," she said. "Are you telling me you just discovered this gentleman's existence?"

This was the first time I saw panic on Julie's face. So she was human. "No, Your Honor, we knew of Mr. Bryson's existence and the fact that he might have relevant information, but we did not know his whereabouts. Frankly, Your Honor, I think he was trying to dodge our subpoena, and he managed to do so for quite some time. But his testimony is very important. It goes directly to the defendant's motive."

The judge paused to mull over the predicament.

Julie was probably lying but we had no way of proving it. This was a premeditated tactic to end her case with a bang. Testimony from a surprise witness at the end of her case was Julie's *modus operandi*.

Judge Graciano usually didn't need a lot of time to make a decision. She also liked to err in favor of the defendant. It looked as if she were leaning toward excluding Bryson's testimony.

Julie must have realized this. "Your Honor," she said sweetly, "I have a suggestion that might remedy this problem. Even though the defense team had all last night to prepare for the cross of Mr. Bryson, I wouldn't object to taking a recess to give them more time to gear up for his examination."

I knew Neddy was saying a silent prayer. We needed the judge to exclude Bryson's testimony. A recess wouldn't do us any good. Tina had already told us everything we needed to know about Mr. Gigolo. We'd been up all night working on his cross.

The judge finally made her decision. "I'm going to allow Mr. Bryson to testify," she said warily. She turned to Neddy. "Would the defense team like to take a recess to prepare for the cross?"

"Just a second, Your Honor," Neddy said, hurrying over to huddle with David and me. "What do you think," she whispered, "should we take the time?"

"The jury's already getting antsy," I said. "Let's just get this over with."

"I agree," David said.

Tina looked as if she wanted a voice in the matter, but Neddy didn't ask for her opinion.

Neddy turned back to Judge Graciano. "No, Your Honor, we won't need a break. Let's just proceed."

After the bailiff herded the jury into its wooden box and allowed the spectators back in, Julie took the floor.

"The People call Garrett James Bryson," she said commandingly.

When Garrett Bryson strutted into the courtroom, a loud, sustained murmur swept through the place like a tornado. Julie had leaked the identity of the prosecution's surprise witness to the media right after delivering the motion to us, so everyone in the room was hyped to hear what he had to say. Bryson was an attractive man, tall and lanky, with smooth chocolate skin. His cool stride, expensive pinstriped suit, and monogrammed cuff links gave him a snobbish air. I was a good five feet away from the center aisle, but I could smell the strong, lemony scent of his cologne when he passed us on the way to the witness box.

Julie's direct examination of Bryson was both titillating and damaging. She quickly had Bryson recount his yearlong sexual liaison with Tina, which had ended abruptly. Bryson claimed he had simply tired of her. Julie then moved on to the testimony she needed to seal her case—Tina's motive for murder.

"Mr. Bryson, did the defendant ever talk to you about her husband?"

"Yes, very often," he answered, quite full of himself.

"Did she tell you she loved her husband?"

"Yes, very much."

"If she loved her husband, why was she having an affair with you?"

Neddy was on her feet. "Objection, calls for speculation."

Julie gingerly raised her hand before the judge could rule on the objection.

"I'll rephrase the question, Your Honor," she said. "Mr. Bryson, did the defendant ever tell you why she decided to have an affair with you?"

"Yes." Bryson smiled. He crossed his legs like he was lounging on his living room sofa. "Well, there were two reasons. First and foremost, I'm a pretty charming guy," he chuckled, but he was the only one in the room who seemed amused. "And second, she was with me because her husband was cheating on her and she wanted to get back at him."

"That didn't bother you?" Julie asked, in feigned surprise.

"No, not really," he said. "I had my needs, she had hers. It was all about sex."

I saw Juror No. 7, the African-American woman, fold her arms. She definitely wasn't feeling Mr. Bryson.

"Did you ever witness the defendant express any hatred toward her husband?" Julie was now walking closer to the jury box, grandstanding.

"Yeah, she told me—"

"Objection," Neddy said hurriedly. There was nothing inappropriate about the question. I assumed Neddy was just trying to wreck Julie's rhythm.

The judge shot Neddy a chiding look.

"Your Honor, the witness was asked if he ever 'witnessed' my client express any hatred toward her husband," Neddy said defensively. "Recounting what she told him is not 'witnessing' anything."

"Overruled," the judge said. "I think the witness can recount what he witnessed as well as what the defendant might've told him, counselor."

"Thank you, Your Honor," Julie said. She was certainly smiling a lot today. "Go ahead, Mr. Bryson, tell me about the hatred the defendant expressed toward her husband."

Bryson went into a detailed discussion of how Tina would call him after a screaming match with Max and tell him how much she despised her husband. Other times, when she suspected that he was out fooling around, she would come running to Bryson and he would comfort her, mostly with sex.

"Mr. Bryson, why do you think the defendant stayed with her husband?"

"Because she—"

"Objection, irrelevant, calls for speculation," Neddy said with confidence this time.

"Sustained," the judge said.

"I'll rephrase, counselor," Julie said, eyeing Neddy. "Mr. Bryson, did the defendant ever tell you why she didn't leave her husband?"

"Yeah," Bryson began. He answered every question as if he were reading from a script. "She wasn't about to give up the millions, the fabulous house, and the prestige she got from being Mrs. Max Montgomery. She grew up in North Philly with next to nothing. And now, for the first time in her life, she was somebody. But it was all a farce. Everybody in town knew Max had more women than Wilt Chamberlain."

A couple of the jurors frowned in disgust, including Juror No. 7, who was quickly becoming my favorite. I only hoped they were feeling sorry for Tina.

"One last question, Mr. Bryson," Julie said, walking back toward the prosecution table. "Did the defendant ever express any interest in harming her husband?"

Neddy stirred as if she wanted to object, but restrained herself since there was no valid objection she could make.

"Yeah, all the time." Bryson paused for dramatic effect, knowing his next words would be played and replayed on every newscast in L.A. "She said she wanted him to die and she wanted to be the one to kill him."

The jurors responded with a collective gasp. Neddy slid her note pad my way, scribbled *we're screwed!* on it, then scratched out the words before Tina could see them.

Julie walked over to the prosecution table and opened a file, acting as if she were searching for something. Silence hung heavy in the courtroom with all eyes focused on her. I knew exactly what she was doing. She didn't have another question. She was allowing Bryson's final words to linger in the minds of the jurors.

"I have no more questions, Your Honor," she said finally, glancing over at Neddy. "Your witness."

The judge turned to Neddy. "Counselor, you may inquire now."

Neddy posed her first question from her seat. "Mr. Bryson, how would you describe your current relationship with Mrs. Montgomery?" There was a twinge of suspicion in her tone.

"I'd say we were friends," he bragged. "We don't really see each other anymore, but there're no hard feelings between us."

Neddy slowly rose from her seat and walked toward the witness box. "Really? You weren't upset about her not agreeing to loan you fifty thousand dollars?"

The prosecution obviously hadn't prepared him for that question. For a few seconds, he lost his cool demeanor. "No, I wasn't," he said, finally.

"You didn't hang up the phone on her the fifth time she told you she wouldn't loan you fifty thousand dollars?"

He knew that the longer he delayed answering the question, the more he would look like a liar. But his brain apparently wasn't fast enough to come up with a credible lie. He pretended to pick a piece of lint from his pants leg. "I don't remember."

"How many women have you dated this year, Mr. Bryson?"

"Objection, irrelevant," Julie said.

Neddy turned to the judge. "Your Honor, may we approach?"

I could not hear what was being said as Neddy and Julie spoke in whispers to the judge, but I knew that Neddy was probably explaining that she needed to establish that Bryson had a history of dating rich women and using them for their money. This would go directly to his credibility. In her closing argument, Neddy planned to ask the jury to disregard Bryson's testimony as the false accusations of a spurned gigolo.

When Neddy and Julie left their huddle with the judge, the sour look on Julie's face told me that Neddy had prevailed.

"Please answer the question, Mr. Bryson," the judge ordered.

He gave Judge Graciano a surly look, then turned to Neddy. "I'm sorry, what was your question?"

"My question was, how many women have you dated this year?"

He again paused way too long and he knew it. "I'm not sure."

"Would twenty be about right?" Neddy goaded.

"Perhaps. There's a shortage of good brothers out there," he said jokingly, turning to the jury for a laugh. None of them gave him one.

"And how many of them did you borrow money from?"

"None," he said proudly.

Neddy walked over to the defense table and picked up a file and appeared to be reading from it. "Mr. Bryson, didn't you borrow money from Mrs. Alma Dawson?"

His face registered panic. "Well, uh, yes."

"Ten thousand dollars, correct?"

"Yeah," he said, barely moving his lips.

"And Mrs. Lucille Jenerette. How much did you borrow from her?"

His upper lip began to twitch. "I don't remember."

"Does five thousand dollars sound about right?"

"I don't know. I don't exactly recall." He was sitting straight up in the chair now.

"And what about Mrs.—" Neddy paused. It looked as if she were reviewing a very long list. She moved her finger up and down the page, silently mouthing names. But there were no other names. The two women she had already mentioned were the only ones Tina had found out about after her affair with Bryson ended.

Neddy looked up and said, "Before I go on, we need to backtrack for a moment, Mr. Bryson. When I asked you a few seconds ago how many women you borrowed money from, you said none. That was a lie, wasn't it?"

"No, it wasn't," he snapped. "I just didn't remember."

"Well, let's test your memory with this next question. How many of the women did you pay back?"

He shifted in his seat. "I don't know. Some of them were gifts, not loans."

"Would it be correct to say that you didn't pay any of them back?"

That twitch had now moved from his upper lip to his left eye. "Maybe."

"You make your living by romancing rich, lonely, married women, don't you, Mr. Bryson?"

He chuckled and tilted his head sideways. It was easy to see how he wooed women. "No, counselor, that's not how I make my living. I make my living in real estate."

"Really," Neddy said. "How many real estate deals have you closed this year?"

He fidgeted with the button on his shirt, but Neddy did not wait for his answer. "Would zero be correct?"

His lips tightened. "I'm not exactly sure."

"You'd still be seeing Mrs. Montgomery if she'd loaned you that fifty thousand dollars you wanted, wouldn't you?"

"Probably not," he spat back. "I don't date murderers."

Neddy lost it. "Objection, Your Honor!" she shouted, waving her hand in the air. "Move to strike. Mr. Bryson's defamatory statement was highly inappropriate!"

"Mr. Bryson," the judge said sternly. "I'm not having that in my courtroom. Nobody here's been convicted of anything." She turned toward the jury box. "The jury is directed to disregard Mr. Bryson's last statement."

Julie clasped her hands and smiled. The damage had been done.

CHAPTER 53

The fact that it was Friday and we didn't have to return to court the following morning was the best thing that could be said about today's session. After Bryson's testimony, we definitely needed a couple of days to regroup.

As soon as the bailiff announced "court's in recess," Detective Smith rushed Tina past the army of reporters who shoved microphones in her face on a daily basis. David, looking beat from the long hours, said he was off to meet some friends for a drink. We all agreed to reconvene Saturday afternoon for another strategy session. By the time the courtroom had cleared out, Neddy and I were the only ones left in the empty hallway.

We made our way to the underground parking structure behind the courthouse. Neddy was unusually silent. I wanted to console her, but decided that now was not the time. She loaded a box of documents into the trunk of her car, which was parked just a few feet from mine, and motioned me over.

"We need to talk," she whispered, "but not here."

"What's going on?"

"I'll tell you tonight. Can you meet me at Harold and Belle's at eight?"

I went home and was relieved to find that Jefferson wasn't there. I couldn't face another guilt trip over the disappearing act I'd been pulling since the start of the trial. I took a hot bath and left for the restaurant.

When I arrived, Neddy was nursing a drink at the bar.

"You look refreshed," I said.

"Looks can be deceiving," she replied.

"You're not still bummed out about today, are you?"

"Shouldn't I be?"

"No, you shouldn't." I climbed onto the stool next to her. "It's not your fault that Tina lied to us."

"I know," she said, exhaling. "But it's not really what happened in court today that's got me down. I need to share something with you. But let's wait until we get seated."

It seemed to take forever before the hostess led us to a table. Neddy turned down the first table offered to us because it wasn't secluded enough. I could hardly contain myself, I was so anxious to hear what she had to tell me. Fifteen minutes later a small table for two near an emergency door at the back of the restaurant became available.

"Okay, what's going on?" I asked, after we had received our menus. "You've really got me worried."

"You won't believe it," she said, pulling a folder from her purse and handing it to me. "Take a look at this."

I opened the folder and pulled out a three-page document. "What's this?"

"It's a report I asked Detective Smith to prepare after Kinga told us about Tina's shouting match with Max. I figured since Tina had failed to mention that, she'd also probably neglected to tell us a few other things. And I was right."

The first page summarized Tina's relationship with Bryson. "Were there any other men besides Bryson?"

"Yep. Two of them. Just keep reading," she said.

"Detective Smith is incredible," I said, as I skimmed the report. "How'd he pull this together so fast?"

"I have no idea. But he's definitely good at what he does."

After finishing the first page, I didn't spot anything significant about Bryson that we didn't already know. I skipped ahead to page two. Ken Harris was a lover from Tina's past who had resurfaced after her marriage. Their relationship lasted only a few months.

"What's that saying?" I asked, as I continued to read. "What happens in the dark will eventually come to the light? Tina should've just left Max. As much money as he made, she'd have been set for life. There was no reason for her to stay with him and put up with his crap."

"Easy for us to say. We weren't wearing her shoes," Neddy said. "But I think Bryson was right. It was all about the prestige of being Mrs. Max Montgomery. That's why she got so angry when he couldn't make that fundraising dinner with her. The only thing she wanted was to have him on her arm that night and he refused."

"This is some interesting stuff," I said, "but I don't see how it makes things any worse than they already are. With a husband like Max, I think she had a right to get her needs met any way she pleased."

"You haven't gotten to the third man she was seeing," Neddy said with a deadpan look on her face.

I turned to the last page, then spotted a name that caused a chill to run through my body. "Please tell me the name listed here is not who I think it is?"

Neddy stared at me, then reached for her water glass.

"Tina was seeing Lawton? *Your* Lawton?" I said.

"You got it."

I quickly read the four-paragraph summary and looked up at Neddy.

The expression on her face confirmed that we were on the same page. "Do you think Tina may've had something to do with Lawton's murder?" I asked, not sure I wanted to hear her answer.

"I don't know," Neddy said. "Anything's possible."

We both sat there staring at each other until the waiter showed up and took our orders.

"Wait a minute," I said, after the waiter walked away. "I thought you said the police think Lawton was killed over a gambling debt?"

"That's only a theory."

"But Tina was already a suspect in her husband's murder when Lawton was killed. There's no way she'd be bold enough to run out and kill somebody when she was already under the microscope for one murder."

Neddy's lips turned into a menacing smile. "It would be the perfect cover, wouldn't it? How many proper, upstanding citizens do you know who go out and kill while they're already a possible suspect in one murder? Nobody would've ever suspected her."

"Who else knows about this?"

Neddy breathed deeply. "Just Detective Smith."

"Do you think Julie has looked into Tina's background?" I asked.

"I don't think so. The investigators at the D.A.'s office talk a lot, at least the lousy ones do. And Detective Smith hasn't heard a thing from any of his contacts. Anyway, it would go against the prosecution's theory. They're trying to prove Tina killed Max Montgomery because he was a womanizer. Julie doesn't want any evidence that Tina was out there getting her own freak on. The only reason she called Bryson to testify was to prove that Tina talked about killing Max for cheating on her. Besides, Bryson was the prosecution's last witness. Julie's closed her case-in-chief, remember?"

"I can't believe this," I said. "Assuming she is responsible for Lawton's death, what do you think was the motive?"

"Unlike Max, Lawton always lied to his women. If she were seeing him, I guarantee you he didn't tell her he was married. With everything she was going through with Max, finding out that her new lover was cheating on her, too, had to be a major blow."

"Maybe she found out and just snapped."

Neddy toyed with her cloth napkin. "Lawton was killed the day *after* I told you and Tina about my nasty fight with him at his lawyer's office. If she did kill him, that's not snapping, that's premeditated murder."

I didn't know what to say. "Are you going to confront Tina with this information?" I asked.

Neddy unfolded her napkin, then refolded it again. "I don't know," she said.

I slid the report back into the folder. "First the stuff about Kinga, now this. Do we have a legal obligation to report this to the police?"

"Nope," she said shaking her head. "In fact, I contacted the anonymous ethics hotline at the State Bar just to make sure. We'd only have an obligation to go to the police if we had evidence that Tina was about to commit a crime. The fact that in the course of our defense we discover information that leads us to believe she may've committed a different crime is protected by the attorney–client privilege."

I propped my elbow on the table and massaged my temples with my thumb and forefinger. "Sometimes what we do sucks," I said.

"No lie there," Neddy replied.

Our waiter set a big bowl of gumbo in front of Neddy and a plate of crab scampi on my side of the table. Neddy began enjoying her food. I was too sick to my stomach to eat.

"How do you feel?" I asked. "Are you still okay defending Tina?"

Neddy looked down at the table for a minute. "Yeah, of course," she said, dishing her spoon into the gumbo. She paused again, then looked me dead in the eye. "If Tina did kill Lawton, she basically did me a favor."

CHAPTER 54

Since our adoption talk or, I should say, our non-talk, things had been pretty strained between Jefferson and me. Our lack of time together only added to the distance between us. On most nights, by the time I arrived home, Jefferson was already asleep, and on most mornings, he was up and out of the door before I rolled over and noticed that he was gone.

The day after my dinner with Neddy, it was close to midnight when I stuck my key in the door. We'd spent that entire Saturday prepping for the opening of the defense's case-in-chief on Monday. I walked into the den and dumped my briefcase and purse on the dining room table. I clicked on the light and browsed through the mail. Both the gas and electric bills were in pink envelopes, which meant they were final notices. It was my job to pay the bills from our joint account. I'd never hear the end of it if they shut off our utilities for nonpayment. I stuck the bills in the side pocket of my purse. I would have to find some time to pay them online.

Although I was positively bushed, my brain was too wired to let me sleep. I headed into the kitchen to make some hot chocolate, but halfway there I backtracked and decided to take off my clothes and slip into one of Jefferson's T-shirts first.

When I tiptoed into the bedroom, I was surprised that Jefferson wasn't sprawled across the bed. I peeked into our spare bedroom, which doubled as an office. He wasn't there either. I went back to the living room, peered out of the front picture window and noticed that his truck was not parked in the driveway or in front of the house. I was so tired I hadn't even noticed when I drove up. It wasn't in the garage either.

It was after midnight. *Where the hell was he?*

I picked up the phone to call him on his cell. When I heard his voice mail come on, I hung up. Maybe he was mad about my being out so late. He was probably staying out on purpose to make a point. I definitely had to make this up to him once the trial was over. Maybe we'd take a vacation. He'd been talking about going back to Montego Bay, where we'd spent our honeymoon.

I headed back toward the kitchen and decided to make coffee rather than hot chocolate. I needed the caffeine to help me stay up until Jefferson got home. I just hoped he wasn't somewhere getting pissy drunk. The thought of him out on the highway as much as he'd been drinking lately scared me to death. But I refused to start imagining the worst.

When I stepped up to the cabinet to grab the coffee, I noticed a pink Post-it note stuck to the door. It bore Jefferson's awful handwriting. I felt a sense of dread even before I read it.

I removed the note and purposely sat down at the kitchen table before looking at it. The message was short and succinct:

> *V—Decided I needed some space, so I'm moving out for a while. I doubt you'll even notice I'm gone. J.*

Without thinking about it, I balled up the note and threw it across the room. It bounced off the wall and fell into the trash can. I sat there for a long time, feeling like somebody had kicked me in the stomach.

I marched back into the bedroom, without my coffee, and climbed into bed. My huge, empty, king-size bed. Since marrying Jefferson, I had never slept in it alone. Not even one night. It didn't feel right. I couldn't stay there. I got up and walked into the den and turned on the TV.

I couldn't believe Jefferson had moved out. Things hadn't been *that* bad between us. Yes, I was preoccupied with Tina Montgomery's trial, but things weren't so awful that he had to leave without even telling me.

I picked up the phone to call Special, but I could hear her words echoing in my head. Special would no doubt read me the riot act. She had been nagging me for weeks to spend more time with my husband. I didn't want to hear that refrain again so I dropped the receiver back into the cradle.

Neddy would have been far more sympathetic, but she had her own troubles to deal with right now. A dead husband and the task of defending the woman who may've killed him. I didn't have the heart to wake her up in the middle of the night.

As I sat there staring at the TV screen, it took far longer than I would have expected for the pools of water to finally form in my eyes.

He didn't miss a beat. "Then it's on you."

The waitress, a hefty black woman with zigzag cornrows, walked up at exactly the wrong moment. "May I take your order?"

"I ain't hungry," Jefferson growled, not even bothering to look up at her.

"I'll have a Diet Coke and a Boca burger with cheddar cheese, well-done, and a small salad, ranch dressing on the side. And he'll have the turkey club, no tomatoes. Lemonade, extra sweet."

Sensing the tension between us, the waitress scribbled down our order and hurriedly walked off.

"What you just did is exactly what I mean," Jefferson said. "It's all about you."

"What? Because I ordered a sandwich for you? I only did it because I know you're probably hungry. The only reason you said you weren't is because you're in a funk."

"No, you ordered for me despite my telling you I wasn't hungry because everything has to be your way."

"Excuse me for caring whether you eat or not."

He just stared at me.

Out of force of habit, I glanced at my watch again.

"Sure you don't have to go save somebody from the electric chair or something?"

"Your sarcasm isn't helping anything, Jefferson. I need you to talk to me." I reached out to take his hands, but he pulled them away.

"I've been trying to talk to you for weeks, but you haven't been listening."

"Okay, I'm ready to listen now."

He filled his cheeks with air and blew out a long, slow breath. "Baby, I just need some time," he said, his voice so gentle it scared me. "This ain't the way I imagined my marriage would be."

My heart began to pump fear. "Jefferson, I—"

This time, he reached out and took my hands in his, and it felt good. "I love you," he said, smiling for the first time. "And I know you love me. But your career seems to be the most important thing in your life right now. You ought to see how you light up when you're talking about one of your cases. I just don't move you that way. I wish like hell that I did. But I don't."

He squeezed my hands tighter. "And it finally hit me the other day

CHAPTER 55

By nine o'clock the next morning, I had called Jefferson three times and he had yet to call back. I was about to call him again when the phone rang. After firmly rejecting my suggestion to come home so we could talk, he agreed to join me for a late lunch.

I was the first to arrive at the Denny's off Wilshire Boulevard near a construction site where Jefferson was doing some electrical work. I couldn't remember the last time he had worked on a Sunday. The fact that he was working today was a signal to me that he was trying to stay busy to keep his mind off of what was going on between us.

The restaurant was nearly empty. This was not exactly where I would have preferred to talk, but Jefferson said he couldn't stay away from the work site for long.

I saw him walk in before he spotted me. As he made his way over to the booth, his face was stern and sullen. His body, strong and taut. He was wearing his typical work garb: jeans and a white T-shirt. I was dressed in a gray terry-cloth jogging suit.

I glanced at my watch as he approached.

"We on the clock?" he said, as he slid into the booth. "What? You have to run back downtown to save some criminal?"

I decided to ignore the comment. There was no way I was going to start a fight with him, even though I felt just as much anger as heartache. "We have all the time you need," I said.

"I don't need any time. You called this meeting. What's up?" His face said he'd rather be someplace else.

"So this is the way we solve our problems? By walking out on each other?"

One side of his lip formed a lopsided smile. "This is a good start," he said. "At least you're finally willing to recognize that there even *is* a fuckin' problem."

"What's going on Jefferson? This isn't like us."

"I'm just tired of it."

"Of what?"

"Everything," he said, his voice full of contempt. "I'm tired of taking a backseat to your career. I'm tired of being there when you need me but you never being there when I need you. I'm tired of sitting home at night by myself. I see less of you now than when we were dating. Why'd we even get married?"

What he had just said made me mad. He knew how things were when I was in trial. My schedule was nothing new. He was changing the rules. "So you're telling me you want out? You want a divorce?"

He took a good long while to respond. "Always the lawyer," he said. "Cut directly to the chase."

I was thankful that he'd sidestepped my question. I would not ask it again. "So, where are you staying?" I asked. Maybe it would be best to warm up with some small talk.

The look on his face told me he didn't want to say, and that pissed me off even more.

"I'm only asking so I'll know where to reach you if anything happens."

He turned to look out the window. "You've got my cell number."

He must've sensed I was ready to blow so he relented. "I'm kicking it at the duplex in Gardena," he said curtly. "The one on Yukon Street."

With who? It hit me that maybe another woman had something to do with his departure. He had said that as long as his needs were being taken care of it was "highly unlikely" that he would ever mess around. I guess I hadn't been meeting his needs lately. "I thought both units were rented," I said.

"Nah. The tenant in unit B moved out last month."

"You didn't tell me that."

"You're never home long enough for us to have a conversation. There's a whole lot of stuff I haven't told you."

This wasn't working out the way I wanted it to. "Jefferson, if I

haven't been around when you've needed me, it's because I didn't know you needed me. Every time I try to talk to you, you shut down."

"That's because you're always jamming me up about adopting. I told you, I ain't with that. I find it funny that motherhood is so important to you all of a sudden. Maybe you need to find a brother whose dick is functional."

You think I don't want to be with you because you're sterile? "C'mon Jefferson, what're you talking about? This is nuts. I don't want to be with anybody else. I want to be with you. I love you. Baby or no baby."

His shoulders relaxed a bit, letting me know he needed to hear those words.

"Jefferson, you have to tell me what I need to do. You're saying you need me, but you don't exactly act very needy."

"I don't have to act needy to want my woman around," he said heatedly. "Why the fuck you think I married you? We live in the same house and I never see you."

"If my being around is the issue, then I can fix that."

He reared his head back. "How many times have you told me that in the past year?"

I sighed and looked away, probably because I knew he was right. I'd been promising to slow down for months. The lawyer who cried wolf. Except that I wasn't wolfing this time.

"No, I'm serious." He cocked his head to the side. "Do you know how many times?" He gave me a few seconds to answer and when he saw that I wasn't going to, he answered for me. "Too many times to count."

I was beginning to feel defensive. This wasn't all about m "You act like you didn't know I was a lawyer when you marri me. I don't work any harder now than I did before we were m ried."

"That's my point," he said, raising his hand in the air for em sis. "We're married now. Something has to give."

"You asking me to quit my job?"

"No. I'm asking you to have a normal life and not to spend waking hour down at that damn firm."

"And if I can't do that right this second?" I was backing against the wall only because that was exactly what he wa to me.

when I was sitting home at eleven o'clock all by myself again that you may not be capable of giving me what I need."

He released my hands and took a sip of water. "And you need to understand that maybe I can't accept what little you can give me."

I tried to breathe but I couldn't. Fear had taken my breath away.

CHAPTER 56

Less than an hour later, I was standing outside Special's apartment, bawling like a newborn baby.

"Just stop crying and tell me what happened." Special wrapped her arm around my shoulder and pulled me inside. She had an alarmed look on her face and I could tell that if I didn't stop crying and tell her what was wrong, she was going to start crying, too. She led me over to her leopard print couch and hugged me as I continued to sob.

"What's wrong? Stop crying and tell me what's wrong."

"Jefferson left me," I wailed.

"What?" She pulled away so she could see my face.

"He said I don't make enough time for him," I sobbed. "And I know you're going to say, I told you so."

"No, I'm not," she said, pulling me to her again. "You can't help it, you've got an A-type personality."

"Thanks a lot," I sniveled.

"Girl, please. That man ain't going nowhere. He loves your dirty draws." She stood up and took me by the hand. "C'mon in the kitchen with me. I'm going to fix us a drink and then tell you what you need to do to get your man back."

I followed Special into the kitchen and watched her make strawberry daiquiris in her Proctor-Silex blender. "That's enough, Special," I protested when she began to douse the blender with enough rum to ensure that I wouldn't make it home without a DUI.

"Girl, hush. What you need right now is a nice, strong buzz."

"Drink this," she said, shoving a cocktail glass in my face and joining me at the kitchen table. My head was beginning to spin though I had yet to take a sip. I could never sit in Special's kitchen for more than a few seconds. The bright orange and yellow striped walls always made my head hurt.

"Okay, you know the man loves you, right?"

"Yeah, I guess so," I said, holding the glass, but not drinking from it. "I mean, I thought he did."

"And ain't no other babe up in the mix as far as you know, right?"

"I don't know."

"Girl, you know that brother ain't steppin' out on you. And you know he's definitely been feeling a lot of pain after finding out his ding-dong don't work like it should."

"But I thought he was back to his old self."

"Um, um, um," she said, shaking her head from left to right. "You book-smart women continue to amaze me with all the things you don't know. If you found out that you didn't have any eggs and couldn't get pregnant—ever—would you be okay in a few weeks? Hell no. He may look like he's doing fine, but he's not. Jefferson's hurting and he needs you."

"I can't just quit my job and stay home and babysit him."

"You don't have to quit your job, but you need to stop trying to be superlawyer and devote some time to your man. I couldn't believe it when you told me they were going to take you off that Montgomery case, but you begged them not to. You've been down there day and night trying to help save that rich bitch when you know she killed her husband. You're going to help her ass go free and when the trial's over, she's going to find herself another rich man to take care of her prissy little behind and you're going to be sitting up here with me every night. You need to start making time for Jefferson—right now."

"It's too late," I said, wiping my runny nose with my sleeve. "He said he doesn't think I can give him what he needs."

She took a big swig from her drink. "Can you?"

"Yeah."

"But do you want to?"

"Of course I do." I took a swallow of my drink and nearly choked. "Special, this stuff is too strong."

"You're such a lightweight," she complained. "Back to Mr. J. Are you sure you can give him what he needs? Because it seems to me you get off on trying them cases more than you do on that big handsome buck you're married to."

"I love Jefferson. You know that."

"Then start acting like it."

"How? It's probably too late."

"Girl, it ain't never too late if you got what it takes. I know men better than any woman you know, right?"

"I guess so, Special."

"You guess so? Oh, hell nah." She pushed her chair back from the table. "You better give me my props."

I smiled weakly. "You're the bomb, Special. Especially when it comes to men."

"Okay, then." She got up and walked over to the kitchen counter. "The brother said he wants some space, so we're going to give it to him. First, don't call him. The more you go whining and sniveling around his ass, the more he'll be turned off. That brother was attracted to you because of your strength and now he's pushing you away because of it. You just need to learn how to balance your business side and your feminine side. A brother needs both."

I started to whimper again.

"Girl, stop all that crying." She was leaning against the kitchen counter, facing me. "I already told you, that man ain't going nowhere. All he's trying to do is teach you a lesson."

"And what lesson would that be?"

"Duh?" she said, as if I should know the answer to my own question. "To stop taking his ass for granted."

"Well, call him and tell him I've learned my lesson and he can come back home now," I said, pouting.

"Don't worry, homey," Special said. She walked over and squeezed my shoulder. "Things happen for a reason. This is going to end up being both a lesson and blessin'. Mark my words. That Negro says he wants some space, so we're going to give him some. Then, we're going to reel his ass back home real nice and slow."

CHAPTER 57

Coping with the pain of what I hoped was my temporarily broken marriage was harder than I'd ever imagined it could be. Every time the phone rang I prayed it was Jefferson. Most of the time it was Special, calling every five minutes to check up on me. I finally had to tell her to stop it because my nerves couldn't take it.

When I walked back into the courtroom Monday morning, I vowed to put my personal problems out of my mind and pour one hundred percent of my energy into being the third chair on the Montgomery defense team. Not that I hadn't already been doing that.

So far, even with Bryson's testimony, the case was still a close call. At least that's what all the TV pundits were saying. Neddy's cross-examination had effectively discredited Bryson's testimony. One local radio station even conducted a poll asking listeners to call in with their thoughts on Bryson's credibility. The final results placed him neck and neck with the mother of the boy who sued Michael Jackson. I hoped the jury felt the same way.

Neddy's opening statement was short and sweet. By introducing Bryson's testimony, Julie had demonstrated that Tina had a motive to kill her husband, so Neddy hammered away at the only thing left in Tina's favor—the fact that the prosecution's case was totally circumstantial.

Neddy's style was quite different from mine. She preferred to stand a good distance away from the jury box, never invading the jury's personal space.

"Good morning, ladies and gentlemen of the jury," she began. "As you already know, I'm Neddy McClain, and I'm one of the attorneys representing Mrs. Tina Montgomery." She turned and glanced warmly in Tina's direction. "You've heard a great deal of evidence from the prosecution. Some of it seemingly pretty damaging to my client. But I use the word *seemingly*, because in a trial, the evidence isn't always as it appears."

"You're now about to hear our side of the story, which will differ significantly from the prosecution's version. And as you listen to our case, there are some things I want you to remember and take particular note of."

Neddy painstakingly ran down a long list of missing evidence, the most significant being DNA that might link Tina to her husband's murder.

"You have to remember that Mr. Montgomery was viciously stabbed, over and over and over again. Yet, there's not a shred of physical evidence—a drop of blood, a hair fiber, or even a footprint—linking my client to her husband's murder. The standard of proof here is reasonable doubt. You have to believe—*beyond a reasonable doubt*—that my client killed her husband after twenty-seven years of marriage. Is it really reasonable to believe that she killed him right in the middle of a ritzy fundraising dinner she organized in a hotel full of her friends and colleagues? You be the judge."

She went through several other implausible facts, skillfully making eye contact with each member of the jury. "I ask that you listen to our evidence with the same open mind that you used to consider the prosecution's evidence. If you do, you'll know beyond a reasonable doubt, ladies and gentlemen, that Mrs. Tina Montgomery is innocent of the crime for which she has been charged."

I surveyed the jury. In addition to Juror No. 7, three of the white women also seemed to have vibed with Neddy's appeal. I couldn't make a call as to the rest of them.

During the first two days of the defense's case, Neddy presented a parade of witnesses who'd helped Tina with the fundraiser. All of them testified that they didn't notice anything out of the ordinary about Tina the night Max was killed. A hotel worker who helped Tina carry some leftover programs out to her car after the event was over cast serious doubt that Tina could have killed her husband and returned to her fundraising duties as if nothing were wrong.

The night before our third day of testimony, David, Neddy, and I camped out at the office poring over the daily transcripts, searching for any holes in the testimony that we needed to fill. We had already put on the bulk of our case during our cross-examination of the prosecution's witnesses, meaning that most of the information we wanted the jury to hear had already been elicited. It didn't make sense to recall the same witnesses to rehash the same events. That could bore the jurors, or worse, piss them off.

The only witnesses we had left were another four or five character references we planned to call to testify that Tina was an upstanding member of the community who could never hurt a fly. There was not a single witness, on either side—other than Garrett Bryson, whose motives were suspect—who testified that they had ever seen Tina angry or upset. She was always the epitome of graciousness. We wanted to leave the jury with the impression that Tina was simply too sweet to commit murder.

It was close to midnight and the O'Reilly & Finney conference room smelled of stale pizza and cold coffee. The table was littered with soda cans, balled up napkins, and half-used legal pads.

"What're you staring at so intensely over there?" Neddy said to David. She rubbed her eyes and yawned.

"I don't believe it!" David said.

"You don't believe what?" Neddy stood up to stretch, showing no real interest in David's outburst.

"I think we missed something—something big." David was bending over a document, holding it just inches from his nose.

Neddy and I walked over to David's end of the table and peered over his shoulder. He was reading the autopsy report.

"Look at this," he said excitedly, taking a yellow marker and highlighting several words.

We both silently read over David's shoulder.

"Look at the amount of blood in the intracranial region," he said.

"We already know how he died, David," Neddy said disappointedly, flopping down into the seat next to him.

"No," he said, "I think the coroner may have missed something."

"So," I said, wanting him to stop all the theatrics and get to the point, "exactly what did he miss and why do we care?"

"What if Max didn't die from the stab wounds?" He looked earnestly at both of us.

"And what if O.J. kidnapped the Lindbergh baby?" I said. "Maybe you should make a Starbucks run. I think you might be suffering from caffeine withdrawal."

I pulled out a chair on the other side of the table, and sat down across from the two of them.

"No, I'm serious." He looked at Neddy and then at me. "What if Max Montgomery didn't die from his stab wounds?" He stood up and began walking around the room. He was smiling now and his eyes were as bright as the yellow highlighter he was twirling between his fingers.

David was getting on my nerves with his dramatics. "If Max Montgomery wasn't stabbed to death, then how did he die?" I asked.

David lowered his voice to a whisper as if he were scared someone might overhear us. "What if he died from an aneurysm?"

I smirked and folded my arms. "And what if the President is going to nominate you for the next vacancy on the U.S. Supreme Court?"

David's eyes begged for understanding. "You don't get it," he said. "Based on what I just read in that autopsy report, it's possible that the man had an aneurysm. You don't get an aneurysm from stab wounds."

"And how would you know that?" I asked.

"I know that because my father's a neurologist and my mother's a medical transcriber and they're both hypochondriacs. While you guys grew up watching *Brady Bunch* reruns, the three of us were discussing blood vessels, tissue samples, and neurological functions. My parents thought that if I ate, drank, and slept medicine, I'd grow up to be some famous surgeon. Instead, it totally turned me off to medicine. They still haven't forgiven me for going to law school."

"You probably couldn't have gotten into a decent medical school anyway," I said.

"Wanna bet?"

"Children, children, please behave," Neddy chided. She had an engrossed look on her face. "Go on, David."

I couldn't believe she was actually buying David's bizarre theory.

"Like I said," David continued, "according to the autopsy, there was a lot of blood in Max's head. That shouldn't happen from a stab wound. But a ruptured aneurysm could be one explanation for it. And it looks like the coroner missed this."

"So you're saying you think Max had an aneurysm that ruptured?" Neddy asked.

He nodded. "That's exactly what I'm saying."

"But that doesn't mean he wasn't stabbed to death," I said.

"Maybe it does," David said. "If the aneurysm happened first, then even though he was stabbed, he wasn't *stabbed to death*."

Neddy and I gazed at each other with baffled expressions.

David ignored the cynical expression on my face. "Most people who suffer from aneurysms have a family history of the condition. What if Max did?"

"Wait a minute," I said. "You actually want us to go into court tomorrow and argue that Max was already dead from a ruptured aneurysm when he was attacked in that hotel room?"

David looked me in the eyes, his face deadly serious. "You got a better theory?"

CHAPTER 58

David and Neddy headed off to court the next morning, while I stayed at the office and scoured the Internet, reading everything I could find about aneurysms. While there was some risk that the jury would wonder about my whereabouts, our need to explore David's theory far outweighed any harm that might result from the curiosity about my absence. David confirmed his hypothesis with a phone call to his father, who agreed that a ruptured aneurysm was indeed a possible explanation for the excessive blood in Max's cranium. His father also confirmed that this was something the coroner could have easily missed.

As I continued my research, the more I read, the more I found myself believing that it was actually possible that this aneurysm theory might have some validity. Neddy planned to stretch out what little testimony we had left to give Detective Smith and me time to dig up some information about Max's medical history. Unfortunately, Tina knew little about her husband's medical history. She directed us to the three doctors she knew of. The first two were too busy to take my call. I decided to make a personal trip to the office of the third, whom Tina believed was the most recent doctor Max had visited.

By 9:30 that morning I was parked outside the office building of Dr. Davon Davis, waiting for his office to open. I sat in the car and reread the information I'd printed out from the Internet. It frightened me that you could be otherwise healthy but suddenly drop dead from an ailment you didn't even know you had. After reading one website where aneurysm survivors shared their experiences, I promised to get myself an MRI as soon as the trial was over.

When I walked into Dr. Davis's office, the first thing that struck me was that it looked like a hotel lobby—a glitzy hotel lobby. Dr. Davis definitely wasn't part of some low-cost HMO that accepted ten dollar co-pays.

The artwork on the walls was probably purchased at a gallery on Melrose. The muted orange, mustard, and beige walls made me want to fold up in a yoga pose. I couldn't quite place the smell that seemed to be shooting from the air vents. It could've been jasmine. The place resembled a plastic surgeon's office, not a neurologist's. The two middle-aged white women waiting to see the doctor didn't look the least bit sick.

After identifying myself as a lawyer and telling the receptionist that I had an urgent, private matter to discuss with the doctor, she told me Dr. Davis would try to squeeze me in between his patients. I was hoping to gather the information I needed and then meet Neddy and David back at the courthouse in time for the lunch recess.

After about twenty minutes, I got up and approached the receptionist, a straw-thin blonde, for the second time. Her tight, low-cut blouse revealed a pair of massive breasts that were almost resting on the desk. They had to be full of silicone.

"Any idea when Dr. Davis might be able to see me?" I asked again, trying not to stare at her big boobs. The thought of having breasts that large made my back hurt.

"I've told him you're here," she said, sweetly, not an ounce of attitude in her voice. "It might help if you could give me a little more information about why you need to talk to him."

I paused. I didn't want word leaking out about our new theory. In my experience, secretaries and receptionists were the single most reliable transmitters of gossip. I couldn't have Ms. Blond Betty Boop on the phone after my departure calling up the local TV news station with a scoop. We wanted to make sure our theory, if true, hit Julie like a neutron bomb. But I had to get Dr. Davis to talk to me first.

"Well," I said, lowering my voice, "as I told you before, this is a really confidential matter. I represent the wife of Max Montgomery, who was a patient of Dr. Davis. I need to talk with him about Mr. Montgomery's medical history. Mr. Montgomery's wife is on trial for his murder and we think the doctor may have some information that could be helpful to her defense."

The flash of recognition in her eyes told me that she'd had more than a receptionist–patient relationship with Mr. Max. *Damn!* The dude had really made the rounds.

"Well, patient information is confidential," she said, still as polite as a Wal-Mart greeter. She could definitely teach the grumpy receptionist at my doctor's office a thing or two about customer service.

"This is a matter of life and death," I said, wondering if her hauntingly green eyes were also phony. "I'll only need just a few minutes of Dr. Davis's time. I believe the doctor may be able to help save Mr. Montgomery's wife from being wrongly convicted."

The receptionist stood up and dashed through the private door behind her.

It was only another five minutes or so before she showed me into the doctor's office. His personal digs were just as lavish and trendy as the rest of his office. The colors here were soft blues and greens. Definitely the handiwork of an interior decorator.

When Dr. Davis held out his hand to greet me, all I could do was stare. His white coat was crisply starched and he had a clean-cut, boyish face. His body was lean but muscular. I suddenly felt out of place in this palace full of beautiful people. Everything about him was perfect. Perfect caramel-colored skin, perfectly trimmed mustache, perfectly buffed fingernails. Definitely gay.

"Ms. Henderson, how can I help you?" he said, flashing a set of bright whites whose glossy shine told me they had been under the laser. I had not expected the deep baritone in his voice.

"Dr. Davis, I represent Tina Montgomery." I pulled out my business card and handed it to him. "You're probably aware that she's on trial for the murder of her husband, Max Montgomery. He was one of your patients."

He nodded.

"I don't think she killed her husband," I said, realizing for the first time, that if Max had indeed suffered an aneurysm, then my statement was actually true. "And you can help us prove that."

"How so?" he asked.

"First, what I'm about to tell you is highly confidential and I need your agreement to keep it that way. It's very important that you don't share our conversation with anyone, even your staff."

He nodded again.

"We believe Mr. Montgomery may have experienced a ruptured aneurysm just seconds before he was stabbed," I said, carefully watching his reaction.

He arched a single brow. "So is your theory that the aneurysm killed him, not the stabbing?"

"Exactly."

"So, you're not saying that Mrs. Montgomery didn't try to stab her husband to death, only that the aneurysm beat her to it?"

He was definitely quick. "No, not at all. We're saying that Mrs. Montgomery didn't stab him *and* that whoever did was stabbing a man who was already dead."

He scratched the back of his head. "So exactly what is it you need from me? I have a very busy practice. I don't have time to be hauled into court." Even when he frowned, he looked good.

I sidestepped his concern. If he had the information I was hoping he did, he would definitely have to testify. We'd have Detective Smith serve him with a subpoena, leaving him no choice. "What we need," I said, "is to find out whether Mr. Montgomery had any risk factors for aneurysms."

"You understand that that's confidential patient information," he said.

"Yes, I do. But his wife's on trial for his murder. The autopsy report shows that there was an excessive amount of blood in his cranium at the time he died. We understand that could be an indication that he had a ruptured aneurysm." I took the autopsy report from my briefcase and handed it to him, then watched as he began to read it.

"But our theory alone is not enough," I continued. "If Mr. Montgomery had been diagnosed with an aneurysm or had a family history of aneurysms, that information, coupled with the autopsy report, might be enough to convince the jury that the aneurysm is what killed him. And that would win Mrs. Montgomery an acquittal."

He looked up from the report and seemed to be mulling over what I'd just said. But I could already tell from his body language that he was going to help us.

"Mr. Montgomery had been having excruciating migraines for several months," he said. "About four weeks before he died an MRI confirmed that he had a brain aneurysm."

Dr. Davis abruptly stopped. A look of regret covered his face. "I scheduled surgery. Twice. But Mr. Montgomery put it off both times. Claimed he had business matters he couldn't postpone even though he knew failing to have the surgery could kill him."

What he had just said got me so excited I had to force myself to remain seated. I wanted to snatch the phone from his desk and call Neddy.

He turned to look out of the window to his right, probably wondering if he should have tried harder to get Max into surgery.

"So your theory that Mr. Montgomery died from a ruptured aneurysm isn't just possible, Ms. Henderson," Dr. Davis said, turning back to face me. "It's quite probable."

CHAPTER 59

The first thing you learn as a practicing attorney is that more often than not, the success of a particular defense strategy often has very little to do with the actual facts of the case and a whole lot to do with luck. Tina wasn't just lucky, she'd hit the Super Lotto Plus.

The next day, Julie didn't even blink when Neddy called Dr. Raymond Riddick to the stand.

It was routine in any case that involves medical evidence for the attorneys on both sides to include a medical expert among their list of witnesses, even if they have no intention of ever calling the expert to testify. Our chosen medical expert was Dr. Riddick, a former emergency room physician who had testified in dozens of cases involving stab wounds. Now here's where the luck comes in. Dr. Riddick was also a board-certified neurologist, which meant he knew a great deal about brain aneurysms.

"Dr. Riddick, what is your practice area?"

"I'm a neurologist, which means I specialize in the diagnosis and treatment of nervous system disorders, including diseases of the brain, spinal cord, nerves, and muscles." Dr. Riddick resembled Tom Hanks with a slightly larger nose.

"Can you tell the jury how long you've—"

Julie was on her feet, waving a copy of the doctor's curriculum vitae we had produced. "The prosecution will stipulate that Dr. Riddick is qualified to testify as an expert and that he's board-certified in neurology, even though I have no idea why that's relevant."

Judge Graciano did not like Julie's added commentary and the judge's scolding glare told Julie and everybody else in the courtroom that it was inappropriate.

"Your Honor," Neddy said, "I have a right to cover the witness's educational background for the jury. After all, he is testifying as an expert."

"You're right, counselor," the judge said. "But let's see if we can speed things up a little."

Neddy ran through the rest of Dr. Riddick's medical background, which included a couple of degrees from Harvard and a residency at Johns Hopkins. He currently worked in the trauma center at Cedar-Sinai in Los Angeles.

"Dr. Riddick, I'd like to show you Exhibit 12, the autopsy report. Have you seen this document before?"

"Yes, I have."

"Please turn to page three and read the third line down for me."

"Cause of death: multiple stab wounds."

"Now can you read farther down the page, the fourth paragraph, where the report refers to intracranial bleeding. Please explain what that means."

Dr. Riddick took a few seconds to review the report. "It means that the coroner found bleeding in the cranium. From the amount of blood noted here, I'd say it was pretty excessive."

"Is it normal to find that much blood in the cranium following a stabbing in a lower part of the body?"

"No. There's no connection between the two."

"Then what could cause the bleeding found in Mr. Montgomery's head?"

Dr. Riddick turned to face the jury. He testified often and had a confident, authoritative communication style. "Probably two of the most common sources would be trauma to the head or a ruptured aneurysm."

Julie leaned over and whispered something to Sandy. I saw nothing but confusion on her face.

"Is there anything in the report that indicates Mr. Montgomery suffered trauma to his head?"

Dr. Riddick scanned the autopsy report again. "No. There was a slight bruise on the right side of his head. But there's nothing here that would indicate that Mr. Montgomery suffered the kind of head trauma that would cause this much bleeding."

"Dr. Riddick, can you please explain to the jury, in layman's terms, exactly what an aneurysm is?"

"Objection, irrelevant," Julie shouted.

"Counselor," the judge said to Neddy, "I would have to agree. Can you tell me where you're going with this?"

"Your Honor, I need just a little leeway here. You'll see shortly that Dr. Riddick's testimony is quite relevant."

The judge grimaced. "Okay, but just don't take all day getting there."

Neddy returned to her witness. "Dr. Riddick, you were about to tell the jury what an aneurysm is."

"Sure. There are two kinds of arteries in the human body—blood vessels and veins," he said. "The human brain contains a dense network of arteries that are normally sturdy enough to last a lifetime. But if there's a weak spot in an artery and blood presses against it, it begins to bulge. This bulge, if it occurs in an artery in the brain, is called a subarachnoid hemorrhage or brain aneurysm. If it ruptures, it's usually fatal."

"Would someone even be aware that they had an aneurysm?" Neddy asked.

Dr. Riddick turned to face the jury again. "No. About five percent of the general population have aneurysms, but most don't know it because they're asymptomatic. As long as the wall of the artery remains intact, an aneurysm is a silent tragedy waiting to happen. Often, there are no symptoms."

"What causes an aneurysm?"

"Several factors could be the source—high blood pressure, a head injury, a brain infection. Most aneurysms, however, result from a developmental abnormality. Those who suffer from them are genetically predisposed."

Neddy walked back over to the defense table and prepared to move in for the kill. "Based on your review of the information in the autopsy report, in your expert medical opinion, is it possible that Max Montgomery suffered a ruptured aneurysm the night he was stabbed?"

Julie shot up out of her chair. "Objection! Calls for speculation!

Irrelevant!" Her fists were clinched and she was yelling at the top of her lungs. "This is complete speculation, Your Honor!"

Loud murmurings whipped back and forth across the courtroom. Everybody in the room, including Judge Graciano, seemed riveted by Dr. Riddick's testimony.

"Counsel, please approach the bench!" the judge said, almost as rattled as Julie.

As the three of them huddled near the bench, I knew Julie was arguing that this line of questioning was totally speculative. But Neddy could counter that by asserting that a medical expert has the right to give his personal opinion regarding the cause of death and that the defense had evidence to support Dr. Riddick's theory.

When I saw Julie's shoulders sink, I knew that Judge Graciano was going to allow Dr. Riddick's testimony.

Neddy walked back up to the witness box and faced the doctor. "Dr. Riddick, I'll ask the question again. Based on your review of the autopsy report, in your medical opinion, is it possible that Max Montgomery suffered a ruptured aneurysm?"

"Yes, it is."

Julie was gripping the edge of the table, poised for her next objection.

"And what is that conclusion based on?" Neddy asked.

"The excessive amount of blood in the intracranial region as stated here on page three of the autopsy report." He pointed at the document.

"And if Mr. Montgomery did suffer a ruptured aneurysm, in your medical opinion, could it have happened after he was already dead from the stab wounds?"

"No, because—"

"Objection!" Julie almost fell to the ground trying to get out of her chair. "There is no valid basis for this speculative testimony!"

Once again, murmuring from the captivated audience filled the courtroom. The judge seemed increasingly concerned about the line of questioning as well.

Neddy had a confident look on her face. "Your Honor, Dr. Riddick is a Harvard-trained medical expert who's testifying as to his personal medical opinion. Ms. Killabrew will have an opportunity to cross-examine him."

Judge Graciano rubbed her forehead. "I agree," she said, though it sounded like she didn't. "Overruled."

Every pair of eyes in the room focused on Dr. Riddick.

"Now, Dr. Riddick," Neddy continued, "you were about to explain why you don't believe the aneurysm could have ruptured *after* Mr. Montgomery was already dead."

He turned to face the jury again. "You need a buildup of blood pressing against the wall of an artery to cause an aneurysm to rupture. If Mr. Montgomery had been killed by the stab wounds, his heart would've stopped pumping. That would've immediately stopped the buildup of blood in the brain, relieving the pressure on the aneurysm, preventing it from rupturing."

"So what you're telling us, Dr. Riddick, is that assuming Mr. Montgomery had an aneurysm and that the aneurysm ruptured, it wouldn't have ruptured if he had already suffered a fatal stab wound."

"Yes. That's exactly right."

Julie was out of her chair again, but the judge waved her back down before she could even open her mouth.

A couple of reporters eased out of their seats and dashed for the door, no doubt wanting to be the first on the air to report this new theory of Max's cause of death. Neddy had done an excellent job of setting up Dr. Davis's testimony. When we called him to testify about Max's personal medical history, even the judge would be convinced that it was the aneurysm, not the stab wounds, that killed him.

Neddy borrowed a page from Julie's playbook and pretended to look through a folder on the defense table. She wasn't searching for anything in particular. What she was doing was giving the jury time to mull over Dr. Riddick's dramatic testimony.

"One last question, Dr. Riddick," she said, turning back to face him. "In your expert medical opinion, would it be correct to say that whoever stabbed Max Montgomery in that bathtub was very likely attacking a dead man?"

"Yes," he said, nodding his head up and down. "That would be quite correct."

CHAPTER 60

During the afternoon recess, Neddy slapped a motion to amend our witness list on the corner of the prosecution table. When Julie read it, her face turned bright red.

"What's this?" she said politely, though her flaming cheeks belied her calm demeanor. She was probably still smarting from her lousy cross-examination of Dr. Riddick. Every angle she'd used to attack his testimony had failed.

"It's exactly what the caption says it is," Neddy replied.

I was standing near the defense table. Most of the spectators were out in the hallway and Tina and David were next door in the meeting room.

The document quivered in Julie's hand. "So is this tit for tat? I amend my witness list, so you amend yours?"

"No, I don't play those kind of games." Neddy smiled. "I amended my witness list because I have a valid witness to call whose existence I didn't know about earlier. As it states in the motion, Dr. Davis was Max Montgomery's personal physician. His testimony is key to our defense. We only discovered a couple days ago that he had relevant information."

"Then maybe you should've advised me of that a couple of days ago," she sulked.

"And maybe you should've shown me the same courtesy before you paraded Garrett Bryson in here."

Julie smiled arrogantly. "Well, I'm opposing the motion," she said.

"Tell me something I don't know."

Just then, the judge climbed onto the bench and asked the bailiff to hold off on bringing the jury back in. I ran next door to get David and Tina.

"I understand there's a motion we need to discuss before bringing the jury in," the judge began.

"Yes," Julie said, before Neddy could speak. "I'd like to oppose the defense's motion to introduce a new witness. This constitutes unfair surprise as well as cumulative testimony."

"Counselor, do you have an offer of proof as to the doctor's testimony?" Judge Graciano asked, as she skimmed the motion.

"Dr. Davis will testify regarding Mr. Montgomery's personal medical history, which directly relates to our theory that he suffered an aneurysm."

"Why wasn't this witness identified earlier?" she asked.

"Because we learned this information less than forty-eight hours ago, after discovering that the coroner had listed the wrong cause of death on the autopsy report. Then we had to track down Mr. Montgomery's personal physician."

"Introducing a witness this late in the trial could be extremely prejudicial," the judge said. "Is this your last witness?"

"Yes, Your Honor." Neddy was trying hard to keep her cool. It sounded as if the judge were about to tell her she couldn't call Dr. Davis. We had gained a lot of ground with Dr. Riddick's testimony. But we needed Dr. Davis to seal things for us.

Julie went mute. Like most smart lawyers, she knew how to keep her mouth shut when things appeared to be going her way. I was surprised that she didn't try to argue that Dr. Davis's testimony would violate the doctor–patient privilege. Both Neddy and Julie looked as if they had stopped breathing. I hoped that the judge made a decision before one of them passed out.

"I'm granting your motion," the judge said suddenly. She waved her hand toward the court reporter. "Let's put this on the record. I want defense counsel's reasoning for coming forward so late in the trial clearly spelled out in the record."

"Your Honor—" Julie began, alarmed at the judge's decision.

"Save it. I've made my decision."

Julie forged on anyway. "Your Honor, I'd like to request that we break for a couple of days to allow the prosecution to prepare for the cross-examination of this witness."

We didn't want a break in the case. One juror was already dozing off for a good part of the day. We needed Dr. Davis's testimony to closely follow Dr. Riddick's. That would clearly hammer home that it was highly likely that Max Montgomery was already dead when he was attacked in his hotel suite.

"Your Honor," Neddy said, as respectfully as possible, "we're fine with giving the prosecution a break to prepare for Dr. Davis's cross, but we'd like to request that you do so after the defense completes its direct examination of Dr. Davis. The doctor has a very busy practice. He's made plans to testify tomorrow morning and has cleared his surgery calendar. I've already provided Mr. Montgomery's medical records to Ms. Killabrew. The defense strongly urges the court not to unduly prejudice the defendant by disrupting the flow of the trial. The jury's already suffering from cabin fever."

The judge was quiet for a while, then raked her fingers through her hair. "You're right, counselor. The jury's anxious to get this trial over with and so am I." She glanced at her watch. "It's close to four now. Let's break for the day. After Dr. Davis testifies tomorrow morning, if the prosecution needs time to prepare for its cross, I'll give the prosecution half a day. But we need to move this trial along."

CHAPTER 61

By my estimation, next to Dr. Riddick, Dr. Davis would be the most important witness to take the stand during the entire trial. When the bailiff called his name the following morning, the entire courtroom seemed to be on pins and needles.

Dr. Davis strolled down the center aisle like a movie star walking the red carpet. He had traded his white coat for a navy blue gabardine suit straight off the pages of *GQ*. He had not been happy when Detective Smith served him with a subpoena, but I'd managed to calm him down after explaining how critical his testimony was to Tina's defense, and by promising that he would not have to hang around the courthouse waiting to be called to the stand.

Neddy quickly covered Dr. Davis's educational background, which was quite impressive. Princeton undergrad, UCLA Medical School. He was board-certified in both neurology and plastic surgery. Now everything made sense. I'd later learned that Dr. Davis's office had two separate entrances—one for his neurology patients, and one for his plastic surgery candidates. Tummy tucks and breast enhancements were his specialties. Neddy wisely glossed over that aspect of his practice.

"Was Mr. Montgomery a patient of yours?" she asked.

"Yes, he was. I treated him for the last few months."

Julie slowly rose from her chair. Someone must have fussed at her for losing it during Dr. Riddick's testimony because she was the complete picture of composure. "I object, Your Honor. Dr. Davis cannot disclose information about Mr. Montgomery's medical condition. Doing so would violate the doctor–patient privilege."

I surmised that Julie had purposely avoided raising that objection earlier with the judge, keeping her last trump card close to the breast in hopes of derailing our aneurysm theory.

"Your Honor, Ms. Killabrew could've raised this issue at the time the court heard our motion. Since she failed to do so, she's waived that right. In any event, if Ms. Killabrew had done her research she would know that since Mr. Montgomery is deceased, his wife can waive the doctor–patient privilege, and she chooses to do so. I refer the court to California Evidence Code Section 993."

Judge Graciano was clearly annoyed with Julie. The judge had already made it clear that she intended to allow Dr. Davis's testimony. "Overruled," she said.

Julie self-deflated and sat back down.

Neddy turned back to her witness. "Dr. Davis, can you tell us the reason Mr. Montgomery came to see you?"

"He was experiencing some very severe migraines. He'd gone to several doctors and no one could help."

"Were you able to determine what was causing his migraines?"

"Yes, I was." Dr. Davis was being a perfect witness, allowing Neddy to lead him through his testimony, just as we had asked him to do.

"Please tell the jury what you discovered."

"I ordered an MRI and determined that Mr. Montgomery had a brain aneurysm."

"Was this the result of an injury?" Neddy asked, knowing that it wasn't.

"No, we traced Mr. Montgomery's aneurysm to a genetic abnormality. He had a grandfather on his maternal side and a paternal uncle who died of aneurysms. It's very rare to have a history of aneurysms on both sides of the family."

"How did you treat Mr. Montgomery for his condition?"

Dr. Davis briefly lowered his eyes and grimaced. "I wasn't able to."

"What do you mean?"

"I recommended surgery, but Mr. Montgomery kept putting it off. We scheduled the surgery two different times. Frankly, I think he was afraid. The surgery would've taken weeks of recovery. He also had some concerns about the scarring that would've remained after we made the incisions on his skull."

"Did you advise Mr. Montgomery of the risk of delaying the surgery?"

"Absolutely. But he considered himself pretty invincible," Dr. Davis said sadly. "His business was very important to him and he was reluctant to take the time off. I think he felt that because he'd lived with the condition as long as he had, a few more weeks couldn't hurt."

For the first time during the trial, Tina started to cry. I reached over and patted her hand.

"Can you tell the jury what you told Mr. Montgomery about his condition?" Neddy asked.

"I told him that without surgery his migraines would get worse and if the aneurysm ruptured, he could die. Instantly."

"Dr. Davis, what were the odds that this would eventually happen?"

The doctor looked down at his hands, his face telegraphing his regret. "What were the odds?" he said, repeating Neddy's question. "There were no odds. If Mr. Montgomery didn't get surgery to alleviate the pressure, the aneurysm was going to rupture and unless some miracle occurred, he would die."

Neddy picked up a document from the defense table. "Did you review the autopsy report?"

"Yes, I did."

"Is there anything in the report that would indicate that Mr. Montgomery's aneurysm had indeed ruptured?"

"Yes, the excessive amount of blood in the intracranial region as noted on page three. That's typically what you find in the case of a ruptured aneurysm."

Julie was gripping the edge of the table again. It was killing her to see her case evaporate into nothing before her eyes.

"When you say 'intracranial region,' you mean the brain, correct?"

"I'm sorry, yes," he said, flashing his dazzling Dentyne smile.

"In your medical opinion, would it have been possible for the aneurysm to have ruptured if Mr. Montgomery had already been dead from the stab wounds?"

Dr. Davis shook his handsome head. "No. If he'd already been dead, there wouldn't have been enough pressure for the aneurysm to have ruptured because of the reduced blood flow to the brain that follows death."

Neddy walked slowly back to her seat. "Your witness, counselor."

Julie rose from her seat, but her feet seemed glued to the floor. She'd told the judge earlier that she would not need any additional prep time after all. I wondered if she now regretted that decision.

"Mr. Davis—excuse me—Dr. Davis, were you aware of Mr. Montgomery's educational background?" Julie's tone was intentionally condescending.

"I know he had an M.B.A. from Wharton, because we talked about it once."

"So you would agree that Mr. Montgomery was pretty well educated, right?"

I looked at Neddy, who stared back at me. Neither one of us had any idea where Julie was headed.

"I would say so," Dr. Davis said, as confused as we were about Julie's line of questioning.

"And you claim you told him that without surgery he would die?"

"I don't claim that. That's actually what I did." He seemed insulted that she was calling him a liar. Julie was purposely trying to ruffle his feathers and Dr. Davis didn't like it. I prayed that he didn't do anything to hurt his credibility with the jury.

"You really expect us to believe that a man as smart and successful as Mr. Montgomery would ignore your advice to have a surgery that would've saved his life? Exactly when did you supposedly deliver this news to him?"

He straightened up in his seat. This time, he didn't let her question get to him. "About three weeks before he died," he said calmly.

"Can you tell me the date?"

"I could if I had his medical records in front of me. I'm sure I made a notation in the file."

Julie had a copy of Mr. Montgomery's medical records, but there was no way she was going to hand the file to him. She stared skeptically at Dr. Davis, who politely stared back. She walked over to the prosecution table and opened a folder, then closed it.

"So, Dr. Davis, exactly how many of your patients have died because you failed to ensure they got the care they needed?"

"Objection!" Neddy said loudly. "Irrelevant, argumentative, badgering the witness."

"I agree," the judge said. "Sustained."

Julie proceeded, seemingly unfazed by the judge's ruling. "You never actually examined Mr. Montgomery's brain, did you?"

"Yes, I did."

Julie immediately realized her mistake. "Excuse me," she said. "What I meant was, you never examined his brain after he died."

"No, I did not."

"So, you really don't know for sure whether his aneurysm ruptured or not, do you?"

"No, but based on the autopsy—"

Julie jumped in and cut his answer short. "That was a yes or no question, Dr. Davis, and you answered it. Thank you." She lingered near the far corner of the jury box. "Doctor, the autopsy report doesn't specifically state that Mr. Montgomery experienced a ruptured aneurysm, does it?"

"No, but—"

"You've answered the question," she said, raising her hand to silence him.

Neddy went nuts every time Julie refused to let Dr. Davis complete his answer. I did, too. We'd have a chance to rehabilitate him on redirect, but it would be better if he were allowed to complete his statements now.

Julie walked up so close to the witness box, I thought she was going to climb in. "You actually expect the jury to believe that the coroner was careless enough to overlook the fact that Mr. Montgomery had a ruptured aneurysm." Her voice dripped with sarcasm.

"It wouldn't be the first time," Dr. Davis said coolly. "The court system is full of cases of incompetence by the coroner. It happens more than it should."

Of course, Julie knew that. That was the reason she wasn't recalling the coroner to rebut Dr. Riddick's testimony. The word we heard was that the medical experts the prosecution retained to examine our theory actually agreed with it.

Julie headed back to the prosecution table and took a sip of water, then abruptly turned around to face the doctor.

"Dr. Davis, isn't it possible that Mr. Montgomery experienced a ruptured aneurysm and suffered a fatal stab wound at exactly the same moment?"

Dr. Davis stopped to think about her question. Every muscle in my body tensed.

"Yes," he said, pursing his lips. "It's possible."

She raised a finger in the air. "So you can't really say with one hundred percent certainty that Mr. Montgomery died from a ruptured aneurysm and not the stab wounds, can you?"

"With one hundred percent certainty? No. But between the two—"

Julie raised her hand again, refusing to let him finish. "That's fine, Dr. Davis. You've answered the question."

This time, Neddy pounced out of her chair. "Objection! Counsel has repeatedly refused to allow Dr. Davis to finish his answers, Your Honor. The witness should be allowed to fully complete his response."

The judge turned to the doctor. "Dr. Davis, were you finished responding to that last question?"

"No, I wasn't," he said. This time, the doctor shifted in his seat and directed his comments directly to the jury. "What I was going to say was, while it's possible that the aneurysm and a fatal stab wound could've happened at the exact same moment, it's highly unlikely that Mr. Montgomery suffered a fatal stab wound first and *then* suffered the rupture of his aneurysm. If he had already died from the stabbing, there wouldn't have been enough pressure in the brain to cause the aneurysm to burst. So assuming it ruptured, and based on the amount of bleeding noted in the autopsy report, it almost certainly did, the ruptured aneurysm is more than likely what killed him, not the stab wounds."

Julie sneered at Dr. Davis. She opened her mouth to speak, then dropped her hands to her sides and marched back to the prosecution table. The look of defeat on her face seemed etched in stone. "I have no further questions of this witness."

CHAPTER 62

The next morning, and all weekend long, the TV and radio news reports echoed the same theme spread across page one of the *L.A. Times*: DRAMATIC TESTIMONY TURNS TIDE IN MONTGOMERY MURDER CASE.

I was feeling great about the trial, but lousy about my personal life. It had been a long, tough week without Jefferson. As I pulled into the parking lot behind the Criminal Courts building on Monday morning, I grabbed my briefcase and was about to jump out of my Land Cruiser when my cell phone rang.

I flipped it open and saw Jefferson's cell number appear. My heart stopped. We hadn't spoken since our disastrous lunch the weekend before. It had been hard not calling him, but I'd received strict instructions from Special that doing so would be a mistake and I was sticking to the plan—for now.

I pressed the talk button. "Hi, Jefferson," I said, even before he had a chance to greet me.

"How're you?" he asked.

"I'm okay," I lied. "And you?"

"I'm hanging in there," he said, coughing. "I see from the newspapers that you guys are kickin' butt at trial."

I wondered if he had a cold. He never took care of himself when he got sick. I gathered from the muffled sound of the radio in the background that he was in his truck. "Yeah, it's going pretty well," I said.

"Well, congratulations." There was no sarcasm in his voice, but no overwhelming sincerity either.

"Thank you."

I didn't know what to say next. I wondered if he felt as awkward as I did. *How in the hell did we get to this?*

"Well, I—I uh, I didn't really want anything, in particular," he said. "I just thought about calling you because I saw the newspaper story."

Jefferson, please come home! "Well, uh, okay. Thanks for calling."

It took every ounce of strength I could muster to hang up the phone. I sat there for a few minutes wondering if I should have told him exactly how much I missed him. No. He was the one who walked out on me and I wanted him to come back home without my having to beg him to. I composed myself, then raced upstairs to meet Neddy and David before the start of today's court session.

The prosecution was unable to regroup after Neddy's double-doctor whammy. Julie's cross-examination of Dr. Davis did nothing to disprove our theory that Max was already dead when he was attacked in his hotel room bathtub. Even if the jury bought Julie's attempt to show that the ruptured aneurysm and a fatal stab wound could have happened at precisely the same moment, that would still raise an issue of reasonable doubt as to the cause of death. We rested our case after calling one additional character witness. The prosecution had no rebuttal witnesses, so the judge scheduled jury instructions for the following morning and closing arguments for the day after.

The night before our closing, I was sitting on the carpeted floor of Neddy's office, listening to her rehearse, and it wasn't going well. She stood in front of me, pretending to address the jury. But she couldn't seem to remember what she wanted to say and there was no real emotion in her voice. As I looked up at her, this was the first time I'd noticed the wear and tear the trial had taken on her. We had all been working eighteen-to-twenty hour days, but as the lead attorney, Neddy had taken the brunt of it. Her raccoon eyes were flanked by a mass of fuzzy, lifeless half-curls, her stylish haircut all but gone. The way her slacks hung off of her hips made me wonder how much weight she had lost.

"Damn," she said, tossing the white index card onto her desk. "I keep forgetting the next transition point." Neddy liked to memorize her entire argument, but had written down the points she planned to cover in outline form on the card, just in case she forgot something.

"Let's just take a break," I suggested.

She plopped down behind her desk just as the telephone rang.

Neddy picked it up on the second ring. The strange look on her face made me nervous.

"Vernetta's here with me," she said into the telephone. "I'm going to put you on speakerphone."

It was Sandy, Julie's little mouthpiece. She wasted time with a few pleasantries before getting to her point. This was only the second time I'd heard Sandy speak. Julie hadn't allowed her to examine a single witness.

"Ready for closing arguments?" she asked.

"That's the only reason we're still here plugging away," Neddy said.

"How's your client doing?"

"She's hanging in there," Neddy said cautiously. "And how's your co-counsel?"

"She's fine."

Neddy flashed me a bewildered look. This could not be good news. The last time Sandy made contact, it was to spring a witness on us. What the hell could the prosecution pull on us at this late date?

Neddy waited, her silence indicating that the next words would have to be Sandy's.

"Let me get to the point," Sandy said finally. "We think the jury could go either way. Is your client interested in taking a deal?"

Neddy grabbed a legal tablet, quickly scribbled on it, and held it up for me to read. *We got 'em!*

"I'm listening," Neddy said, smiling.

"We're offering manslaughter, two to five."

Neddy chuckled softly. "I'll talk to my client and get back to you," she said. "But I'm a little curious. What evidence suddenly takes us from murder to manslaughter?"

"Well . . ." Sandy stumbled a bit. "If our theory is correct and your client stabbed her husband because she was enraged at finding him in that hotel room waiting for another woman, heat of passion provides a mitigating factor."

"Okay . . ." Neddy said, not convinced.

"This is a great offer," Sandy continued. "Mrs. Montgomery probably wouldn't serve more than a couple of years."

"Yeah," Neddy said, "but for a crime she didn't commit."

"Well, we'll need to know your answer right away," Sandy pushed.

"Like I said, I'll get back to you after I talk to my client," Neddy repeated. "But I can tell you now, I doubt she'll accept your offer."

Sandy apologized for the intrusion then hung up.

Neddy hit a button, cutting off the speakerphone. "They're running scared! That bitch Julie was too arrogant to make the call herself. Manslaughter? No way."

I had a different take. It was still my belief that Tina had stabbed her husband, aneurysm aside. I wasn't ready to dismiss the prosecution's offer out of hand. "What if the verdict goes against us?"

"It won't," she said. "Of course, we have an obligation to present the offer to Tina, but you know she won't take it."

"Should we be encouraging her to?"

"No," Neddy said. "I really think the jury buys our theory that Max died of an aneurysm."

"But we can't be certain of that."

Neddy stood up and leaned against the wall behind her desk. "Julie did an excellent job of helping us show what an asshole Max Montgomery was. Tina didn't come out as untainted as I would've liked, but she's still a victim here, too. The jury needs someone to feel sorry for. And I'm banking on them empathizing with Tina, not Max. With that and our aneurysm theory, there's enough reasonable doubt for the entire jury to vote not guilty."

I wasn't so sure, but Neddy was the one who had years of experience defending criminals, not me. "Okay," I said, deferring to her judgment. "Let's get back to the closing."

Neddy yawned loudly. "I'm so tired. I just hope I can make it through tomorrow."

"You will," I said. "Let's pick up from your summary of Bryson's testimony."

Neddy walked back in front of the desk to face our imaginary jury. She studied the index card for a few seconds, then laid it down on the desk. She started to open her mouth, then stopped.

"What is it?" I said.

"I have an idea," she said, her eyes brightening. "And I hope you're with me on it." She smiled in a way that told me I might have a slight issue with whatever she was about to say.

"I want you to give the closing argument tomorrow."

"What! Why? No." I was suddenly on my feet, facing her. "I think you'll do fine."

"Yeah, but you'll do better," she said. "I heard nothing but praise about your opening and closing in the Hayes trial. I really want you to do it. I'm *so* tired." She sat down on the edge of the desk.

"It'll seem weird if I do the closing. You did the opening and David and I only examined a few of the witnesses. The jury identifies with you as the lead counsel."

"Exactly. And now they'll get to hear from another African-American woman who's going to bat for her client. It might seem weird if David did the closing, but not you. I think some jurors root for attorneys who look like you and me because they don't see us in the courtroom all that often. We're the underdog. People like rooting for the underdog."

"What's that got to do with me giving the closing? You got quite a bit of melanin in your skin, too, you know."

Neddy laughed. "Yes, I know that. But I think the jury resonates with you. I noticed that whenever you questioned a witness. And it's not like you don't know the case. You've practically memorized my closing already. All you need to do is add a few of your own touches and you're done."

A wave of excitement washed over me. Part of me would kill to do the closing argument in a case of this magnitude. But another part didn't want my summation to be linked to the verdict in a case I felt so conflicted about—guilty, innocent, or hung.

"And besides," Neddy continued, "being able to say you delivered the closing argument in a case this big won't exactly look bad on your resumé. After we recess tomorrow, your closing argument will be replayed on every TV station in town. Everybody knows you're already a shoo-in for partnership. This'll cinch it."

I thought about everything Neddy was saying. I also thought about the fact that she was giving me an incredible opportunity. "Thank you," I said softly.

She winked. "Not at all."

"No, really. I know you're tired. But you're not *that* tired. I really appreciate what you're doing." I reached out and hugged her.

"Okay, okay," she said, hugging me back. "You don't have to get all mushy on me." We both sat down at a table across from her desk.

"Let me ask you something," I said, taking the index card she was handing to me. "Why'd you decide to get off partnership track?"

"I like practicing law, but I hate the business side of it. All the administrative and political bull that comes along with being a partner would drive me nuts. First, you only get to eat what you kill. If you don't have enough of your own clients, you'll eventually be asked to leave the firm. Then, no matter how many clients you have, there's still tremendous pressure to bring in more. So if you're not a rainmaker, you won't last long. Then there's the competitiveness. You think you and David don't get along? That's nothing compared to the jealousy between some of our esteemed partners. You'll never see Joseph Porter at one of O'Reilly's little dinner parties because they despise each other."

I had already heard that rumor.

"And no matter how well the firm does, it's never enough. The higher they climb, the higher they want to climb. Last year, the firm had a record year financially. This year's goal is to beat that number by ten percent. Next year'll be the same thing. Which means you have to bill more hours or find bigger and richer clients. It never ends. You better be damn sure you really want to join that dysfunctional little cult."

I hadn't thought about any of the things Neddy was telling me. I'd only focused on the achievement of making partner. If it happened, I would be the first black woman to be anointed with that title in the firm's history.

"Thanks for the advice," I said. "You've really been a good friend, Neddy. Win or lose, I'm glad O'Reilly assigned us to this case."

"Win or lose?" Neddy exclaimed. "Girl, we're not losing! I can't wait until you stand up to deliver your closing tomorrow morning. Julie'll be so surprised she'll probably gag."

I grinned. "Now, *that* I'd like to see."

CHAPTER 63

When I walked into the crowded courtroom the next day, I felt nervous, but not in an anxious or tense way. Unlike my experience the first day of the prelim, I didn't want to throw up. I wanted to dance a jig around the courtroom.

Neddy and I had stayed at the office until almost one. I'd always had a knack for quickly memorizing things, so committing the closing to memory went pretty fast. We then spent the rest of the night working on technique. Our styles were quite different so we traded pointers. Neddy gave me feedback on my pacing, eye contact, physical stance, and facial expressions. Even though I'd only had four hours of sleep, I felt energized.

Tina seemed fine with the idea of my delivering the closing, but only after Neddy lobbied for the switch. David, surprisingly, didn't seem put out about it either.

Julie was already seated in the courtroom when we arrived. For the past couple of days, she had been playing hide-and-seek with the media. The courtroom was the one place where they couldn't hurl questions at her. She was no longer a smug picture of contentment. She looked sleep-deprived and she wasn't dressed in one of her snappiest outfits. The dark brown suit she wore seemed too big around the shoulders. Her light blue blouse, like her face, had little of its original color left. Her chipped nail polish told me she was up too late rehearsing her closing to deal with minor cosmetic matters.

Neddy walked over to Julie before she could sit down. "My client isn't interested in your offer."

"Fine," Julie barked back.

Judge Graciano wasted no time getting things rolling. "Ms. Killabrew, you may proceed with your closing," she said, almost the minute she took the bench.

Julie rose tentatively, walked about five feet from the jury box, and faced the panel. "Good morning, ladies and gentlemen," she began. "I'll be the first to admit that there've been quite a few surprises in this trial. But I don't want you to be swayed by surprises or by clever trial tactics or by the kind of emotional stuff you see on those legal dramas on TV. This isn't *Law & Order* or *The Practice*. In real life, you must look at the facts. If you do that in this case, the only option you have is to return a guilty verdict."

Julie quickly reviewed the "facts," a word she hammered away at repeatedly as she went through the testimony of each of the prosecution's witnesses. "It's a fact that Tina Montgomery was married to a man who, for twenty-seven years, did nothing but betray her. That's a fact the defense didn't even bother to dispute," Julie said, turning to look Neddy's way for effect.

"It's also a fact that Mrs. Montgomery wanted her husband dead. She'd said as much to her lover, Garrett Bryson, on more than one occasion. I suspect the defense will ask you to disregard his testimony. They want you to believe he wanted revenge because Mrs. Montgomery supposedly refused to loan him money. But those aren't the facts, ladies and gentlemen. As he testified, Mr. Bryson didn't come forward willingly to give his testimony. If he'd had an ax to grind, he would've run to the police with his story. But he didn't do that. He still considered the defendant his friend. He didn't want to testify, but the law compelled him to. There is no valid reason for you not to believe Mr. Bryson's testimony that the defendant wanted her husband dead."

Julie walked over to the prosecution table and picked up an enlarged photograph of the lobby of the Ritz-Carlton showing people milling about in evening wear. She held it out in front of her for the jury to see. "It's also a fact that Mrs. Montgomery was at the Ritz-Carlton hosting some fancy fundraiser on the night her husband was killed. And we know that Mr. Oscar Lopez, a room service waiter, saw her headed toward her husband's hotel room." She put down the photograph and picked up the murder weapon. "Just like they're going to try to discredit Mr. Bryson's testimony, the defense also wants you to believe that Mr. Lopez didn't really see what, in fact, he saw—the defendant, steak knife in hand, marching down that hallway. Don't fall for the defense's deception."

She placed the knife on the prosecution table and walked over to the jury box. "Try as they might, there's a lot of testimony in this case, testimony that the defense did not, and could not, refute. Testimony that they would like you to ignore." Julie took her time, staring earnestly at each member of the panel, taking them step by step through the evidence.

"A member of Mrs. Montgomery's fundraising committee testified that during the middle of the event, the defendant disappeared for upwards of an hour at about the same time Mr. Lopez saw her in that hallway. What was Mrs. Montgomery doing all that time? Based on the evidence, she was maliciously stabbing her husband to death because she was finally fed up with his constant betrayal. Ladies and gentlemen, the facts of this case make it clear that Mrs. Montgomery had motive, as well as opportunity, to commit this heinous crime."

It was another ten minutes before Julie moved on to attack the testimony of the two doctors. "The defense is quite aware of the damaging evidence introduced by the prosecution," she continued. "That's why they came up with their last-minute theory about an aneurysm. How convenient. 'Mr. Montgomery was already dead, so let my client walk,' is basically what they're saying to you. Don't buy it. Why? Because their defense is nothing but a sham. Dr. Riddick is a paid medical expert and for that reason, his testimony is suspect. As for Dr. Davis, I can't dispute Mr. Montgomery's medical history, but what the defense is trying to sell you is just too convenient, too coincidental. Don't you think it's a little strange that Dr. Davis would diagnose Mr. Montgomery with something as serious as an aneurysm, then do nothing when he refused to have lifesaving surgery? Didn't he have an obligation to at least alert the man's wife?"

Julie pursed her lips and feigned indignation. "Since the defense couldn't refute the facts of this case, what did they do?" She paused, then snapped her fingers. "They dreamed up a ruse to draw your attention away from the facts, away from the evidence. I wonder what TV show they got their aneurysm theory from. *ER? CSI,* perhaps?"

I saw Juror No. 7 roll her eyes. She didn't appreciate the personal dig at us.

"Don't let the defense get away with this sham," Julie said, lowering her voice almost to a whisper. "And don't let Tina Montgomery get away with murder."

Nobody moved, including me, as Julie made her way back to her seat. With the exception of Juror No. 7, I couldn't tell one way or the other how well Julie's closing had resonated with the panel.

The judge called a fifteen-minute recess.

"You ready?" Neddy asked, after the judge left the bench.

I inhaled. "Yep. What did you think of Julie's closing?"

"Decent," Neddy said. "But she was bouncing all over the place. She didn't have a clear theme. And it was a mistake to attack our aneurysm theory the way she did. The standard of proof is reasonable doubt. And the medical evidence we produced presents a whole lot of it."

"I think I'm going to stray a bit from the closing we rehearsed," I told Neddy.

"What? Why?" She looked worried.

"I want to play off Julie's closing," I said.

Neddy paused. "Are you sure? You memorized your closing perfectly last night."

"I think I am," I said, feeling a burst of confidence.

Neddy gave me a warm smile. "Okay, girl, do your thing."

The fifteen-minute recess felt more like fifteen seconds to me.

"Is the defense ready?" the judge asked, directing her question to Neddy. "Yes," I said, standing. There was a silent rumbling in the courtroom as I took the floor. Julie leaned over and whispered something to Sandy.

As I approached the jury box, I reminded myself to speak slowly and deliberately as Neddy had advised, and to make eye contact with each individual member of the jury at some point during my closing.

"Ladies and gentlemen of the jury," I began, "Ms. Killabrew was right. This case has been full of surprises. And I have to say, no one was more surprised than I was to find evidence that an aneurysm, and not stab wounds, had killed Mr. Montgomery."

"Objection, Your Honor!" Julie shot up so far out of her seat, she almost hit the ceiling. "Counsel is not permitted to make unsupported personal statements. Her closing must stick to the evidence."

My ad-lib wasn't starting out too well. I couldn't even remember what I'd just said. I could see alarm in Neddy's face. I refused to even look at Tina. For a second, I thought I saw O'Reilly sitting in the back row. When I looked again, he wasn't there. Was I so nervous now that I was hallucinating?

It was somewhat taboo to make an objection during a closing argument and anyway, I was sure I'd heard Julie mention her own opinion during her closing. She had taken me out of my groove. I had to relax and get back on track. I cracked my knuckles and turned to Judge Graciano before she could rule on Julie's objection.

"I'm sorry, Your Honor, Ms. Killabrew is correct. My opinion doesn't count. It's the evidence that matters. It won't happen again." I said a quick prayer and returned to my closing. "Ms. Killabrew wants you to look at the facts," I said. "Well, so do I. But I want you to focus on the *undisputed* facts."

"Undisputed fact number one," I said, holding up my index finger, "there's no evidence linking Mrs. Montgomery to the scene of the crime. No blood, no hair, no fibers...nothing. Based on that alone, there's reasonable doubt."

I held up two fingers now. "Undisputed fact number two, the prosecution's so-called eyewitness, Oscar Lopez—to put it simply—is not credible. He testified that he saw Tina Montgomery carrying a knife, then admitted to two of his coworkers that he really wasn't sure he saw her with a knife after all. And considering how dim the lighting was in that hotel hallway, it's understandable that he was confused about what he saw. Mr. Lopez told you himself that he didn't remember whether the woman he saw was wearing earrings or not, how her hair was styled, or whether her dress was long or short. That's not surprising when you consider that Mr. Lopez hasn't had his eyes examined in over ten years. Again, there's reasonable doubt."

I felt light on my feet as I walked from one end of the jury box to the other. I looked at Juror No. 7. Her eyes told me she was definitely rooting for me. I was straying quite a bit from the closing argument I'd rehearsed with Neddy, but Juror No. 7 let me know that my ad-lib was going over big, at least with her.

"Undisputed fact number three." I held up three fingers now. "Garrett Bryson, who claimed Mrs. Montgomery wanted her husband dead, was nothing more than a spurned gigolo. And for that reason, he's not credible either. My client refused to loan him fifty thousand dollars. Simply put, revenge fueled his testimony."

I continued in the same vein, reinforcing each and every fact in our favor and attacking the facts against us, methodically taking each one and logically explaining why it provided a basis for reasonable doubt.

"Finally," I said, "there's the cause of death." I marched over to the defense table and picked up the autopsy report. I was hitting my stride now. I felt like I was in total control of the courtroom. I'd had great closing arguments before, but this one felt very different. I had just stepped up to the plate, gripped the bat, and was about to whack a home run straight across center field.

"There's no dispute that Mr. Montgomery had an excessive amount of blood in his cranium. It's right here in the autopsy report," I said, holding the document in one hand, pointing to it with the other. "We didn't make that up. The prosecution could've brought the coroner back to explain to you why he missed this. But she didn't. Why? Maybe it would have been too embarrassing for him to have to admit his big mistake.

"You also heard two doctors, Dr. Riddick and Dr. Davis, tell you that intracranial bleeding was evidence of a ruptured aneurysm. And just weeks before his death, Dr. Davis had advised Mr. Montgomery that he had a brain aneurysm that could kill him instantly if he did not have surgery. But, as you heard Dr. Davis testify, Mr. Montgomery ignored that advice.

"Both Dr. Riddick and Dr. Davis testified that, in their trained medical opinions, it was highly unlikely that Mr. Montgomery suffered an aneurysm *after* he was stabbed. If he'd been stabbed to death, there wouldn't have been enough pressure in the brain to cause Mr. Montgomery's aneurysm to rupture. There's nothing 'convenient' or 'coincidental' about their testimony. Mr. Montgomery was already dead when he was stabbed in that bathtub. The aneurysm killed him. Not the stab wounds and not his loving wife, who stayed by his side for nearly three decades despite some very trying circumstances."

I looked over at Neddy, who smiled at me. "Those are the *undisputed facts*, ladies and gentlemen." I turned and nodded in Julie's direction. "The prosecution and the defense are in complete agreement on one thing. When you retire to the jury room to begin your deliberations, we both want you to look solely at the facts. If you do that, you can only come to one conclusion...that Tina Montgomery is innocent of the charge of murder."

I walked back to the defense table and took my seat. Everybody's eyes were on me. The jury, the judge, the spectators, and even the prosecution seemed to be frozen in place. I'd definitely given it my best shot. I wasn't totally sure how well my closing had gone until Tina, who'd barely said two words to me since the trial began, gently squeezed my forearm and whispered, "Thank you. You were incredible!"

CHAPTER 64

Neddy, Detective Smith, and I escaped to a tiny Chinese restaurant not far from the courthouse. The court clerk had given us a pager that would buzz us when the jury had reached a verdict, had a question, or needed some testimony read back. David stayed at the courthouse with Tina, who was convinced that it would be a short deliberation and didn't want to leave. I wasn't so sure.

We were shown to a small table covered in a worn, checkered tablecloth. Detective Smith pulled out Neddy's chair and waited for her to sit, then realized he had neglected to extend the same courtesy to me. He belatedly reached over to do so, but I was already seated.

"So if it's a hung jury, which jurors do we have to thank?" Detective Smith asked, as he poured tea into a tiny cup for Neddy, then for me.

"Juror No. 7, for sure," Neddy and I said in unison with tired chuckles.

Detective Smith wrinkled his brow in surprise.

"You think so?"

"Hell, yes," Neddy said. "That sister is definitely identifying with Tina. She's probably had a man or two step out on her."

"And based on the attitude on her face," I said, "I'd bet she's banged a few of 'em upside the head in her day." We all laughed.

"I don't see it." Detective Smith rested his hands on the table. "My money's on Juror No. 8. She frowned every time Julie opened her mouth." Juror No. 8 was a fortyish white woman.

"Maybe," Neddy said. "But did you see Juror No. 7's face every time somebody talked about Max's endless supply of women? She would roll her eyes and her lips would turn down in the corners in a little snit. I think she definitely thought Max deserved what he got."

Nobody laughed this time.

"I just hope they don't come back with a guilty verdict." Neddy opened her menu, then closed it. "Tina'll never make it in prison."

"Prison?" Detective Smith said. "I thought the prosecution filed this as a special-circumstances case. We need to be worried about the death penalty, don't we?"

"That was just a bluff," Neddy replied. "Julie never mentioned it again after the arraignment."

We ordered and talked for a while longer, exchanging our views on various aspects of the trial. When a waitress set dishes of shrimp fried rice, *kung pao* chicken, egg rolls, and beef with broccoli on the table in front of us, we all reached for a sample of each and ate in silence. In minutes we sat staring at empty plates.

"Guess we were pretty hungry, huh?" Detective Smith said, looking stuffed, which was hard to do for a man his size.

Neddy and I smiled at each other. It wouldn't have been polite to point out to Detective Smith that he had gobbled down three-fourths of the food.

"Well, if Tina is acquitted," he said, "she owes her freedom to you two." He squeezed Neddy's forearm and grinned. "You've both done a helluva job."

Neddy raised her hands, palms outward. "Hold on," she said. "She has David to thank. He was the one who scrutinized that autopsy report, which led to the discovery of Max's aneurysm."

"Don't sell yourself short," Detective Smith insisted. "Even if you guys hadn't discovered that evidence, the jury was already leaning your way."

I felt compelled to join in. "Neddy, Tina owes you a lot, too," I said. "You tried the case under some pretty difficult circumstances and you never doubted her innocence. I don't know if I could've held up the way you did with everything you've been going through."

I didn't realize the irony of my words until they were already out. I had been carrying a pretty heavy burden myself. During the day, when the trial consumed my every thought, my marital woes remained somewhere in the distance, outside of my peripheral vision.

But the minute I stepped through my front door, they came crashing back into focus. For a second, my thoughts lingered on Jefferson and I wondered what he was doing. *Was he with another woman?* I tried to shake that frightening thought from my mind.

"No matter how it goes," I said, squeezing Neddy's shoulder, "it's been an incredible experience for me. I've definitely learned a lot from watching you these last few weeks."

"Hey, hold up," Neddy said, forming a time-out signal with her hands. "You guys are going into overkill now."

"Well, win or lose," Detective Smith said, "Tina Montgomery couldn't have had a better defense team." He covered Neddy's hand with his and she actually blushed.

We chatted some more about our perceptions of some of the jurors while we waited for the check. Detective Smith stood up and headed for the men's room, giving me a chance to talk to Neddy alone. I'd been noticing the sparks flying back and forth between the two of them and I was anxious to find out whether my instincts were right.

"Is there something going on between you and the detective?" I asked.

"What? What makes you say that?" The glow on her face contradicted her words.

"Because the man is all over you. Every chance he gets, he reaches across the table to touch you. And he talks about you like you were God's gift to the law."

Neddy smiled again. "You're exaggerating. He complimented you, too."

"Yeah, but his eyes didn't light up when he talked about me. And he didn't pull out my chair when we sat down at the table like he did yours. Now I understand why we got all those investigation reports so quickly. He was trying to score points with you."

"You're imagining things. Detective Smith has been totally professional. And after all I've been through, a man is the last thing on my mind right now."

"Yeah, okay," I said skeptically. "I bet as soon as this trial is over, he's going to be on you like white on rice."

"No way," she said, but something in her eyes told me she wasn't as opposed to that scenario as she was professing to be.

"How's Jefferson?" she asked.

I briefly closed my eyes. "I wish I knew."

Neddy's head involuntarily jerked backward. "What do you mean you wish you knew?"

"I didn't tell you, but Jefferson moved out." I picked up the glass of water in front of me and took a quick sip.

"Moved out!" Neddy exclaimed. "When? I can't believe you didn't tell me." She was practically out of her seat. "What happened?"

"I don't know. I came home one night and he was gone." Tears began to well up in my eyes. "I knew he was upset about the trial taking up so much of my time, but I didn't know he was *that* upset."

"I can't believe this! When did he leave?"

"It's been over a week."

Neddy reached out and hugged me. Her embrace was a big comfort. "I can't believe you've been dealing with that on top of the demands of this trial."

"I can't believe it either. I miss him so much." I dabbed at the corner of my eyes with my napkin.

"Hang in there, girl," Neddy said encouragingly. "From what I've heard, it sounds like you've got yourself a good man. He'll come to his senses."

"Well, I'm just giving him his space and hoping he does."

Detective Smith rushed up to us, snatched some money from his wallet and tossed it on the table. "The pager just went off," he said. "Let's go."

When we got back to the courtroom, it was empty except for Julie and Sandy, the court clerk, and the bailiff. Tina and David walked in a few seconds later. They had been across the street at a sandwich shop.

Julie seemed to be purposely ignoring us. I made eye contact with Sandy but there was absolutely nothing to read in her bland brown eyes.

The jury had been deliberating for just over two hours. I didn't know if that was a good sign or a bad one. Had they reached a verdict already? Maybe they wanted a portion of the transcript reread.

After a few minutes, the clerk escorted us into the judge's private chambers.

The judge straightened the papers on her desk while we all scrambled for seats. The bailiff had to bring in an extra chair. Tina, Neddy, and I took the couch, while David, Sandy, and Julie sat in chairs, forming a semicircle around the judge's desk.

The tiny room resembled a high school counselor's office. It had rusty, metal-lined windows that opened with a crank, a couple of neglected house plants, and an entire wall of bookshelves containing casebooks nobody opened anymore because the same information was more easily accessible online.

My heart was racing. I could only imagine how Tina felt.

"The jury has indicated that they're deadlocked," the judge said.

Tina's body wilted with relief. Neddy looked over at me, her eyes flashing victory. We would have preferred an acquittal, but we'd take our win any way we could get it.

Julie could barely contain herself. "Your Honor, the jury hasn't even deliberated for a full day yet. They're probably just anxious to go home. I would strongly urge you to instruct them to continue with their deliberations to see if they can reach a verdict."

Judge Graciano frowned at her. "If you had let me finish, you would've learned that that is exactly what I intend to do. I'd never dismiss a jury in a case of this magnitude after such a brief deliberation. I just wanted to give you all advance notice of my decision."

The judge leaned back in her chair. "The jury's been consumed with this case for quite some time and they probably just need a break. I'm calling a recess for the day and having them resume their deliberations tomorrow morning at nine."

CHAPTER 65

I decided to take a couple of much-deserved days off while we awaited the jury's verdict. The downtime was long overdue, but it allowed my every thought to linger on my husband. It felt like I had a big hole in my heart. I missed Jefferson desperately.

I was trying as hard as I could to follow Special's advice. Jefferson wanted space and I was giving it to him. But the house was like a mausoleum without him.

When we were first married, we would occasionally play hooky from work and lie in bed and watch cartoons. I turned on the Cartoon Network, which had our favorite lineup, but for some reason, Scooby Doo wasn't as funny without Jefferson's play-by-play.

To keep myself from calling Jefferson, I dialed Special's office.

"Hey, want to go see a movie after you get off from work?"

She was munching on something crunchy. "Since when do you have time to see a movie on a weekday?"

"Since we closed yesterday and the jury's deliberating."

"Sorry, homey. Have to go get my wig done when I get off and you know Shawnta's going to have me up in there half the night," Special said. "So what you think? Is homegirl going to get off?"

"Hope so," I said. "And stop saying 'get off.' It makes it sound like she's getting away with something."

"You know that heffa killed her husband."

"I'm going to ignore that comment because you're my friend."

We gossiped about the trial for a few minutes, then I turned to the real reason for my call. "Special, I really think it's time for me to call Jefferson and ask him to come home."

"Don't do it," she warned. "That would definitely be a mistake. It hasn't even been that long yet."

"Yes, it has. It'll be two weeks on Saturday. This is nuts."

"He ain't called you at all?"

"He called me a few days ago, but only to tell me he read about the Montgomery trial in the newspaper."

"Girl, you ain't reading between the lines," Special said. "That brother didn't call to talk about that case. He called to talk to you and the case was the only way he could do it and still keep his balls."

"Yeah, but we're still exactly where we were when he left. I'm going to call him and ask him if he wants to see a movie."

"No!" Special ordered. "Let the brother stew a little bit longer. He's got to really miss your ass. Just give it one more week."

One more week? There was no way I could hold out that long.

I hung up and called Neddy's house, but she didn't answer. She had decided to take a few days off, too. I decided not to leave a message. I hoped she was out with Detective Smith having a good time.

I stayed in bed until one o'clock and then went to 24-Hour Fitness to work out. On the way home, I rented a couple of DVDs and spent a lonely evening watching two of my favorite movies, *Splendor in the Grass* with Warren Beatty and Natalie Wood, and *Friday* with Ice Cube and Chris Tucker. A sad love story to bring me down and a hilarious comedy to take me back up. I ate a whole bag of Pepperidge Farm Chocolate Chunk cookies and half a container of Haagen-Dazs Chocolate Chocolate Chip ice cream. If Jefferson stayed away too long my hips were going to be as wide as our living room couch.

From force of habit, I woke up around six the next morning and vowed not to spend another day moping around. I decided to devote the morning to some of the tasks I'd neglected around the house. First on the list was going through my closet and getting rid of all the old clothes I never wore. Jefferson constantly complained about my overstuffed closet and the fact that I didn't wear half of the clothes I owned. Luckily, we had separate closets. I began stuffing worn-looking blouses and pants that no longer fit into a large, plastic garbage bag that I planned to drop off at Goodwill. When the bag was full, I decided to store it in Jefferson's closet, which wasn't nearly as packed as mine.

The second I clicked on the light, the empty space in front of me almost brought me to my knees. I rarely had a reason to enter Jefferson's closet and the last time I had, just after he'd moved out, only a few items were missing. But he'd apparently been back within the last few days because only a few items remained: a couple pair of pants that were too tight in the waist, and a bright green shirt, which I knew he hated. He'd taken everything else.

I walked out of the closet, ran over to the dresser we shared, and checked his drawers. They were empty. All of them. I sat down on the side of the bed as tears began to roll down my cheeks. He'd taken all of his clothes because he wasn't coming back. Special was wrong. Jefferson wasn't trying to teach me a lesson. He'd never been one to play games. That was what I liked about him from the start. He always put his cards on the table. There was no way I was going to reel him back home.

Without thinking about it, I picked up the telephone and dialed Jefferson's cell phone. He answered groggily, which surprised me. He should've been at work.

"Good morning," I said.

"What time is it?" He sounded annoyed at being disturbed.

"After nine," I said.

I was disappointed that he didn't sound glad to hear from me. "I just wanted to talk," I said.

"About what?"

"About us."

He didn't say anything at first. "Uh, my head's not on straight right now. I was out pretty late last night. How 'bout if we do this some other time?"

The rejection hit me hard. "No problem," I said, quickly hanging up the phone.

This time, I was too shocked to cry. *Out pretty late last night.* It was a weeknight. Had he already moved on that fast? Jealousy filled my head with visions of some sleek young body lying in bed next to him. That was probably the only reason he couldn't talk.

This was crazy. We loved each other. There was no reason Jefferson shouldn't be lying in bed next to me. The truth was, he was devastated about being sterile and blaming everything on my career.

I tried to get angry at him, but there was too much fear in my heart for any fury to take hold. I wanted my husband back. But short of begging him to come home, I had absolutely no idea how to get him there.

CHAPTER 66

After a few days off, I was anxious to get back to work. It was simply too lonely at home. This was the jury's fourth day of deliberation and we were beginning to worry. I had just dropped by Neddy's office to chat when the court clerk called, notifying us that the jury had reached a verdict. The judge wanted everybody back in the courtroom by ten o'clock. Neddy, David, and I piled into Neddy's BMW. Detective Smith agreed to pick up Tina.

Once both sides had arrived, Judge Graciano wasted no time calling things to order. A heavy tension filled the air as the jurors filed back into the jury box. As a group, they seemed anxious to get to their seats. None of them made eye contact with anyone, not even each other. Juror No. 7 had her lips formed into a severe frown. The same position they'd been in during most of Garrett Bryson's testimony. I didn't know whether that was a bad sign for us or the prosecution.

The judge asked both sides to rise. I nervously shot up out of my chair, which made a loud screeching sound. It would have tumbled to the ground if I hadn't grabbed it in time. I felt everyone staring in my direction.

"Jury foreman, have you reached a verdict?" Judge Graciano asked.

"Yes we have."

Juror No. 11, the only African-American male on the panel, turned out to be the jury foreperson. I definitely wouldn't have pre-

dicted that, and in my mind, it didn't bode well for Tina. We watched
as he passed a sheet of paper to the court clerk, who passed it to Judge
Graciano. She briefly read it and handed it back to the court clerk,
who passed it back to the foreman. The eyes of the entire courtroom
tracked the path of the paper holding Tina Montgomery's fate as it
floated from one hand to another to another.

I was wearing a new pair of extra-pointy-toed pumps and my feet
hurt. I gingerly shifted my body weight, trying not to attract more
unwanted attention. I was on the end, closest to the prosecution table,
next to Neddy. Our arms touched, but we were mentally oblivious to
the physical contact. Tina was flanked on one side by Neddy and on
the other by David. I looked over and saw that Julie's posture had
lost its former haughtiness but her head was still held high, her chin
jutted slightly outward, signaling a contrived confidence. A newcomer
to the room might have assumed that Julie was the one on trial.
Sandy was completely obscured from my view by Julie's leggy frame.

"In the matter of The People versus Tina Montgomery," the jury
foreman began, "we find the defendant, Tina Montgomery...not
guilty of the charge of murder in the first degree."

A combination of cheers, groans, and claps swept across the
courtroom. Tina's head snapped backward, as if she were looking up
to God, then fell low to her chest and she began to sob. David and
Neddy simultaneously embraced her. Without even thinking about
it, I reached over and grabbed her hand, taking it into mine and
squeezing it hard.

A rush of pent-up emotions impaled my body. I wanted to cry,
too, but the tears did not fall. This ordeal was finally over and we
had accomplished the task we'd been paid to perform. But what had
I accomplished? Another feather in my professional cap. One that
would surely lead to partnership and a coveted place among a list of
very select attorneys. Would it be worth it?

After the celebration that was sure to follow the verdict, I would
have to face the reality that my husband would not be coming home
tonight or, very possibly, any other night. And despite what the jury
had just declared, I still had my doubts about Tina's innocence.
While I believed that Max Montgomery had actually suffered a ruptured aneurysm the night of his death, I was still convinced that it
was Tina who had fanatically attacked him in that bathtub with the
intent to kill. His ruptured aneurysm made her innocent in the eyes

of the law, but not in God's eyes. My nagging fears about Tina's role in the death of Neddy's husband only made my conscience ache more.

"We won," I finally heard Neddy mumble ever so softly. "We actually won." The astonishment that saturated her words told me her reservations about Tina's innocence had run much deeper than Neddy had been willing to reveal.

Neddy was still protectively holding onto Tina, whose body shook in tearful surges, strong enough to have hurled her to the ground had Neddy and David not been propping her up. *Had Neddy forgotten that the woman in her arms might have killed her husband?*

I wasn't sure how long the judge had let our jubilation go on. A couple of reporters created a ruckus dashing out of the courtroom, causing Judge Graciano to finally pick up her gavel and demand order. There were still a few important administrative matters to attend to before we could all leave.

I glanced over at the prosecution table. Julie was consumed with organizing papers into a folder on the table in front of her. She occasionally glanced hatefully in the direction of the jury. When she finally looked my way, I could see anger in her eyes. All of a sudden she stopped and turned toward the bench, "Your Honor, may we please have the jury polled?"

I could swear I heard Judge Graciano curse under her breath. "If you would like, counselor," she said, her tone indicating that she thought it was a useless request. Both sides had the right to have each member of the jury state out loud how he or she had voted. Perhaps it was Julie's hope that her evil gaze could intimidate one or two of them into reversing their decisions. That would mean a mistrial, and the prosecution would get a second shot at trying to prove Tina's guilt. But I had never known any jury polling to produce such a result.

One by one, each member of the jury responded to the question, "Do you find Tina Montgomery guilty or not guilty of the charge of murder in the first degree?" By the time we'd heard the twelfth "not guilty," Juror No. 7 was glancing toward our table with a humongous smile on her face. The others, too, seemed to be wearing a look that said they were proud to have performed their civic duty.

"If there's nothing else, I'd like to dismiss the jury," Judge Graciano said.

"We have nothing further," Neddy said.

"Ms. Killabrew?" the judge asked.

"Thank you, Your Honor, nothing further," Julie said in a weak, defeated voice.

After the judge explained what an important role jurors play in an organized society and thanked them for their service to their community, the jury panel quickly cleared out of the courtroom while the spectators' section emptied more slowly.

"Just get me out of here," Tina finally said, her voice hoarse from sobbing. "Get me the hell out of here."

CHAPTER 67

After talking to the press and celebrating at Tina's house, Neddy and I decided to treat ourselves to a late lunch at the Houston's restaurant near Tina's house.

We were slowly coming down from the high of our victory and reality was setting in with a stone-hard edge. At least it was for me. There were still lots of questions that needed to be answered. But we had to accept the fact that we might never know for sure whether Tina had stabbed Max in that hotel room. That, I could accept. What I couldn't swallow was not knowing whether Tina was responsible for Lawton's murder.

"I know you don't want to hear this," I began, as we sipped strawberry margaritas from gigantic cocktail glasses, "but we need to talk to Tina about Lawton. Don't you want to know if she had anything to do with his murder?"

"Not really," Neddy said, reaching for a piece of sourdough bread and slapping it with butter. "We need to just let it go. We don't have any evidence of her involvement. All we have is a hunch. If we did a casting call for everybody who wanted Lawton dead, we'd need the Staples Center to hold the crowd." She took a bite of bread and kept talking. "And even if Tina told us she did kill him, the attorney–client privilege prevents us from doing anything about it. So why bother finding out?"

"Okay, fine," I said. "But the woman was screwing your husband and never mentioned it to you. After we found out about Bryson, we asked her if there was anybody else and she lied to us. We need to confront her about that."

"She was probably too embarrassed," Neddy said. "And we aren't exactly squeaky clean here. We had obligations to her that we breached, too."

I frowned. "Like what?"

"Tina obviously didn't know Kinga was sleeping with Max, or she would've fired her a long time ago. We kept that information from her and I'm not sure it was the right thing to do—ethically or legally."

There's no way I wanted to broach that subject with Tina. Kinga had wisely quit her job and skipped town. That sleeping dog needed to keep slumbering, and I told Neddy as much. But I still felt there were things we needed to discuss with Tina. "I still can't believe you don't want to know whether she killed your husband," I said.

Neddy rolled her eyes. She looked more exhausted than I felt and that was hard to do. "I'd like my entire life with Lawton to remain buried. Discussing this with Tina will dredge up a whole new crop of emotions that I'm not sure I can handle. If Tina did kill Lawton, it's not going to change anything."

"Okay, then," I said, "I'd like to know if she was the one who stabbed her husband in that hotel room."

Neddy shook her head. "We have no right to ask her that."

"I don't care. I want to know."

"Well I don't. And even if she did it, she's not going to be stupid enough to admit it to us."

It took another round of margaritas and considerable prodding, about twenty minutes' worth, before Neddy finally agreed that Tina owed us some answers. We finished our meal and headed back to Tina's house.

When we rang her doorbell, Tina answered the door looking refreshed and smelling of rose-scented soap, holding her gaudy wine goblet. The sleeveless, cinnamon-colored pants suit she was wearing glowed against her skin. She could have walked right out of a Revlon ad. Tina embraced us so enthusiastically you never would have known we had just left her place an hour or so ago.

She was so happy and relieved about her acquittal that she didn't notice that our mood had changed dramatically since our earlier visit. She assumed we had returned to continue the celebration. She led us back into her purple living room, practically floating in a pair of beige ballerina slippers.

"What would the two finest attorneys in L.A. like to drink?" she asked merrily.

"Nothing for right now," Neddy said, taking a seat. I joined her in an adjacent chair.

"There's something we need to talk to you about," Neddy began. "You're not obligated to answer, but we hope that you do. Everything you tell us is protected by the attorney–client privilege."

Tina's smile disappeared. She set her goblet on the coffee table, then immediately reached for it again, confirming for me that her drinking was the security blanket I'd always assumed that it was.

Neddy looked first at me, no doubt for encouragement, then went on to tell Tina about Detective Smith's report and how it had detailed her affair with Garrett Bryson. When Neddy noted that the report had also listed the names of two other lovers, Tina's eyes fell to the floor. She raised the goblet to her lips and took a long sip.

"The fact that you were seeing Lawton and never mentioned it to us made us wonder if the reason you didn't was because you had something to do with his death." Neddy spoke as gingerly as possible. "And I'd like to know if that's the case."

I examined Neddy's face. I could still see vestiges of the agonizing years of her own abusive marriage. I also saw something that told me she wanted to hear Tina's answer to her question as much as I did.

Tina didn't speak for a long while. "Wow," she said, "this is quite a surprise. I thought you were going to ask me if I killed my husband."

She went silent again, this time for much longer. Neddy and I anxiously waited her out.

"First, let me tell you why I stabbed my husband in that hotel room," Tina said, placing her wine goblet on the coffee table. She looked earnestly at Neddy. "Then I'll answer your question about Lawton."

CHAPTER 68

Neddy and I listened for close to an hour as Tina recounted the intimate and distressingly sad details of her life with Max Montgomery and Lawton Joseph Brown. The only two men she had ever loved.

From the moment she began her story, anguish crept into her eyes and assumed her voice, forcing her to speak when her lips seemed unwilling or unable to form the proper words. After a minute or so into her monologue, Tina never allowed her eyes to settle on Neddy's face or mine. It was as if she were making a confession before some invisible television camera positioned across the room. She constantly wrung her hands and I could hear a soft patter as her right foot nervously tapped the shiny maple floor. Tears would sporadically roll down her cheeks, then dry up to make room for a fresh stream.

Tina started her tale with a different version of the facts she had fed us during our first meeting. Though her voice cracked at times, she did not speak in a tone that solicited sympathy. Her intent was to explain, not justify, her actions.

Tina admitted now that she wasn't exactly sure when Max's philandering had begun. She doubted that it had started after their marriage, as she had told us before. She assumed Max saw other women during their whirlwind year of dating, but she was simply too contented with her new life to notice. She'd landed a gorgeous, incredible man whose very presence in a room, even when he was only in his twenties, radiated charisma and power. It didn't make sense to go searching for a dark cloud when her ordinary, lackluster existence had been presented with a silver lining so bright it sparkled like a diamond.

But in no time, the naive young wife came to realize that she was not the only woman in her charming husband's life. In the beginning, Tina would angrily confront Max with her suspicions. At that point, she'd had nothing more than suspicions to go on as Max, particularly in the early days, had been very discreet with his affairs. His assertions that her suspicions stemmed from her own childhood insecurities, not any infidelity on his part, had actually seemed plausible to her. Max would convincingly deny her accusations, pamper her with gifts, and bestow upon her what she cherished most—his time. But weeks and sometimes only days later, his focus was back on business and other women.

By their fifth or sixth year of marriage, Tina had grown tired of tracking his whereabouts. She had also tired of his broken promises. But not so tired that she had ever contemplated leaving. At some point, she convinced herself that she had a worthy role to play in Max's life and slowly morphed into the kind of wife she convinced herself that he needed. She worked hard at being the elegant hostess and developed into an admirable role model for other young wives in the local philanthropic community.

In the eyes of onlookers, she was a smart, beautiful, vibrant woman, even as the gray hairs and age lines made uninvited appearances. But in private, she was a pathetic, lonely little woman whose self-esteem was being slowly eroded by her husband's growing neglect.

While she prayed things would change, the older Max got, the sloppier he became. Though she tried, she could not ignore the late-night ringing of his cell phone, the smell of perfumes she didn't wear, and her inability to contact him for hours at a time. Over time, she had been forced to shy away from friendships with other women because she feared that her acquaintances, and none of them had been any more than that, would become the target of Max's insatiable lust. She had never been particularly close to her family, so that left her no one to turn to. Predictably, she eventually sought companionship outside of her marriage.

There had been four other men in her life, she told us now, not three. None of them of any real significance except for Lawton. The first affair happened in her eleventh year of marriage. The brief reunion with Ken Harris, a lover from her college days, was a failed attempt to recapture something from a past she usually kept hidden. The second affair, the one missing from Detective Smith's report, was a meaningless fling with Martin Young, a longtime colleague of Max. Had she chosen to stay on that path, there could have been many, many more, as Max's business associates were both plentiful and willing. But except for Martin and Garrett Bryson, she had rebuffed their advances. It greatly surprised her that Max had become enraged when she revealed during an angry confrontation that she had slept with Martin. His double standard aside, she interpreted Max's heated show of emotion as a sign that he still loved her.

But soon an awkward distance began to develop between them. As amazing as it sounded, he treated her as if *she* had betrayed *him*. They continued to share occasional intimate moments, but Max was becoming more and more aloof and uncaring.

In time, they argued more than they got along, usually about his being away so much and Tina's suspicions about him sleeping around. Even though she knew it was a lie, he continued to insist that she was just paranoid. Tina began occupying her time with philanthropic activities, and the more visible she became in the community, the more Max made the rounds.

That night at the Ritz-Carlton, simply by chance, Tina had spotted Max standing at the registration desk. At first, seeing him had filled her heart with excitement. She immediately assumed that he'd shown up to surprise her. But then she noticed that he wasn't wearing his tux. She also remembered that she'd never told him where the fundraiser was being held.

Tina stopped to take a sip from her wine goblet, then realized that it was empty. This was the first time Kinga was not around to instantly refill it.

Neddy and I remained engrossed by her story, both of us perched on the edge of our seats. For me, it was like watching a movie. My mind had a clear picture of every scene.

Seeing Max in the hotel lobby and knowing that he was probably there to meet another woman had filled Tina with a rage so intense it temporarily immobilized her. As he walked off toward the elevators, she returned to the ballroom, resumed her seat at the head table, and tried to finish her bland chicken dinner. Minutes later, buoyed by anger and her second glass of brandy, she decided she had to confront him. To catch him in the act, once and for all. He would not be able to accuse her of paranoia this time. When she marched out of the ballroom, confrontation—not murder—was her only goal.

Gaining access to Max's suite had been easy. The month before the fundraiser, she had been practically living at the hotel and made friends with two of the desk clerks as well as one of the bellmen. That night, she simply told the desk clerk that she had forgotten her room number which, of course, wasn't written on the plastic key card. Two Montgomerys appeared on the computer screen that held the list of registered hotel guests. "Was it 420 or 502?" the clerk had asked. Since she was in room 420, the other room had to be Max's. It was as easy as that.

I was captivated by her story and had a dozen questions rolling around in my head. I couldn't help myself and blurted one out. "But how'd you get into his room?"

She smiled as if that were no big deal either. Earlier in the day, the hotel manager had instructed one of the bellmen to give her access to the freight elevator so that she could transport items into the ballroom. After the fourth trip, the bellman got tired of the interruptions and handed her the pass key, making her promise not to tell anyone about his flagrant violation of hotel policy. The pass key opened every room in the hotel.

As she made her way to Max's room, her heart was beating so furiously she could hardly breathe. When the elevator doors opened onto the fifth floor, her feet refused to move and the doors began to close. Just before they did, she pressed the fifth floor button a second time and stepped off the elevator. As she entered the hallway, she noticed a used room service tray on the floor outside one of the rooms. A steak knife sitting on a plate of half-eaten food practically called out to her, she said. She scooped it up, grasping the handle with a soiled dinner napkin.

"So, Oscar Lopez did see you in that hallway with a knife in your hand," I said.

"Probably," she replied.

I looked over at Neddy to see how she was taking all of this. I couldn't tell a thing from her expression. It was as blank as a sheet of paper.

Instead of knocking on the door to Max's room, she let herself in using the pass key, being careful to use the napkin to turn the door handle. Murder was not on her mind when she entered the room, she told us again. She had planned to surprise Max and his whore, threaten them with the knife, and tell him she was going to divorce him and take him for everything he owned.

When she stepped inside the room, she found no one there. She remained just inside the door, examining every inch of the suite. One of Max's suits hanging over the back of a chair was the first thing that caught her eye. When she noticed the red teddy lying across the bed, her rage intensified.

A noise from the bathroom startled her and she assumed that Max and his mistress were in there together, naked. She tightened her grip on the knife and gathered her courage. She had not been paranoid all these years—she'd been a fool. As she tiptoed to the doorway of the bathroom, she braced herself for the sight of Max and his mistress in the act.

But there was no woman in the bathroom with Max. He sat alone in the tub, surrounded by candles, submerged in a pool of rose petals, a bottle of Dom Pérignon sitting on the floor. The bathroom looked like a scene from some romance movie. He was obviously waiting for his little slut to arrive.

"Why, Max?" she said to him in a teary whisper. "Why wasn't I enough?"

He looked in her direction, but there was confusion, not shock on his face.

As we listened, tears began to fill Tina's eyes, making the image of her standing in that bathroom doorway so real that I was right there with her.

Max's failure to respond only enraged her more. "So, I'm the one who's paranoid!" she screamed. Still no response. As she took a step closer to him, he seemed to be in a drunken stupor.

"I don't deserve to be treated like this!" she cried. "And you're not going to treat me like this anymore!"

Tina said she did not stop to think. She felt like she was caught up in a trance and someone else controlled the movements of her body. She darted over to the tub and began furiously jabbing at Max with the steak knife. He did not fight back or attempt to escape her blows. She stabbed and stabbed until her arm tired. When the fury of it all had completely exhausted her, she wiped the handle clean with the dinner napkin, dropped the knife to the marble floor, and fled from the room.

After taking only a couple of steps into the hallway, Tina realized that her shoes were tracking blood. She slipped them off and tucked them underneath her arm. Her chest covered in blood, she dashed for the stairwell and rushed to her own room, one floor down, terrified of running into another hotel guest. She made it safely there without being spotted and immediately shed her clothes. She wrapped her dress, stockings, underwear, and the dinner napkin inside a plastic bag and hid them at the bottom of her suitcase. After cleaning her shoes, she slipped into another black dress, one almost identical to the one she was wearing. Luckily, she had brought it along because she hadn't been able to decide which one to wear. She then headed back to the ballroom and resumed her role.

Her absence from the dinner had only lasted about forty minutes, not an hour as one of the witnesses testified. She made sure to slip the pass key underneath some papers on the bellman's desk without being noticed. Later that night, Tina mentioned to the bellman that she had returned the key earlier in the evening, hoping that he had not gotten around to looking for it yet. She was afraid that her access to the pass key would come out during the trial. The bellman, who had worked at the hotel for years, probably never came forward with that information because he feared losing his job.

Tina stopped and finally looked over at us, signaling the end of her tale.

"So, Max really was in the midst of the aneurysm when you stabbed him?" I asked.

"Probably. I think that's why he never answered me."

"Then you didn't kill him," I said encouragingly. "The aneurysm did." My own words surprised me.

"No," Tina whimpered, as more tears rolled down her cheeks. "I killed him. I can't blame his death on the aneurysm. If the aneurysm hadn't happened, the stab wounds would've killed him. The jury let me hide behind the aneurysm, but I'm not going to allow myself to do that. This is something I'll have to live with for the rest of my life. I know it sounds crazy, but I loved him *so* much."

Neddy got up and moved over to the couch next to Tina and wrapped her arms around her. I went to the kitchen to fetch a bottle of wine and returned to refill Tina's goblet.

She took a sip, then looked at Neddy. "I'm so sorry about Lawton," she sobbed. "Yes, I was seeing him, but I swear I had no idea you were his wife."

Neddy was crying now, too. As they hugged and rocked each other, my own eyes began to moisten.

Tina finally pulled away from Neddy and, without our prompting, began explaining how Lawton had come into her life. Their chance meeting happened at the Barnes & Noble bookstore not far from her home, about six months before Max's death. He stood behind her in line, struck up a conversation about the copy of the Walter Mosley novel she was buying, and invited her to continue their conversation over coffee at the Starbucks across the street. After exhausting the subject of their literary interests, they turned to their own lives. That first bookstore chat lasted two hours and was soon followed by regular coffee house encounters, all premised on their mutual love of literature.

Lawton told her from the start that he was trapped in a bad marriage and that leaving his wife would have meant leaving his two kids. Something he could not—would not—do. Tina was willing to accept his situation because she had no desire to give up her own lavish lifestyle. Being with Lawton made her predicament with Max bearable. He was the first man in years who seemed to enjoy just being with her. Sex came later, after she had fallen in love with him. And when they finally made love, Lawton treated her like delicate china, loving her in a way that Max had not, as if they had some spiritual connection to each other's soul.

I glanced at Neddy. She was holding Tina's hand now. Her eyes locked on Tina's face. I still could not tell how or what she was feeling. There was no way I could have listened to another woman describe being with Jefferson.

The day that Neddy had recounted her vicious divorce battle and her plans to take a leave of absence from the firm, Tina realized that *her* Lawton Joseph Brown was the same man who had destroyed Neddy's life. That meant that Lawton's professions of love to her, like his promises to Neddy, had been nothing but lies. Not only had he cruelly and intentionally deceived her, he was also about to cause her to lose the attorney who could help her go free.

When Neddy and I left her house that evening, Tina spent the rest of that night and much of the following day in tears. When she couldn't cry anymore, she decided she had to confront Lawton. She called him on the telephone and told him she knew about how he had treated Neddy. Lawton did not try to explain or offer an apology. Whatever tales Neddy had told her, Lawton said, were all lies. He then reminded Tina that she was a married woman herself, and that they were both cheating on their spouses, so she had no right to act so sanctimonious. In the end, he laughed at her for being so gullible and hung up.

She sat there, stunned, refusing to believe he could be so callous. He had hurt her deeply, more deeply than Max had with his affairs, and she wanted him to know that. She called back, but he didn't answer. Though Lawton had never invited her to his home—they had always rendezvoused at expensive hotels, places she had paid for—she knew exactly where he lived. Still reeling from his harsh words hours earlier, she pulled up outside his house, Neddy's house, just before midnight. She sat behind the wheel for nearly thirty minutes before gaining the courage to walk up to the door.

When she finally did, she was surprised to find the door cracked. Pushing it open, she stepped inside and called out Lawton's name. When he didn't answer, she stopped, afraid that she would catch him with another woman. She could smell the odor of marijuana and thought about turning around, but instead headed down a narrow hallway and into a small living room, which was empty. Farther back, along the same hallway, she spotted the kitchen, which opened into a spacious den. She was about to turn around and head upstairs when she spotted a trail of blood near a sliding glass door about five feet from where she was standing. She took a few more steps, then froze. When she saw Lawton's body sprawled in an open area behind a long couch, she let out a gasp.

She rushed over, squatted down, and pressed her hand to his neck, hoping to feel his pulse. But there was none. His chest was covered with blood and she could see that he had been shot several times. A gun lay next to his head. She looked down at her hand and the blood, Lawton's blood, brought back visions of Max in the hotel room bathtub—and fear gripped her. She stood up and wiped her hand on her blouse. She was about to be charged with Max's murder. Her presence in the house of another murdered man, one who had also cheated on her, could not be explained away. She had to get out.

She checked to make sure that she had not stepped in any of the blood and snatched a paper towel from a metal dispenser on her way out of the kitchen. When she reached the front door, she wiped her prints from the spot where she had pushed the door open, then calmly walked to her car and drove home.

"I couldn't call the police," she cried to Neddy. "They would've tried to pin his murder on me. But I wouldn't have let them charge you with murder. I would've come forward. I swear."

Both Tina and Neddy were sobbing uncontrollably now. Tears were streaming down my own face and I wasn't sure why. Either I was caught up in the emotion of everything I had just heard or the pain I felt over the absence of my own husband had overwhelmed me. I think it was probably both.

EPILOGUE

"Hey, everybody, it's time," an unfamiliar male voice yelled from the back of the packed twentieth floor conference room. "They just did a tease. It's the next story after the commercial break."

Once again, David and I, and this time Neddy, too, occupied center stage at a legendary O'Reilly & Finney victory celebration. It was more than twenty-four hours after the verdict and it had been a day of nonstop congratulations. David and Neddy were brimming with pride. I wanted to run for the nearest emergency exit.

A rapt silence fell over the room as everyone focused on the sixty-inch plasma TV hanging on the north wall. We all listened intently to the reporter's dramatic recap of the Montgomery trial. My stomach turned when the scene switched to Neddy, David, and me flanking Tina on the front steps of the Criminal Courts building.

"The jury in this case did exactly what they were supposed to do," Neddy said, speaking into a sea of microphones. "They listened to the evidence and rendered a decision based on that evidence. And relying on the facts alone, the jury found our client innocent. The prosecution, meantime, wants to complain about legal maneuvering. The truth is, justice prevailed in that courtroom today."

When the report ended, the entire room applauded.

O'Reilly was smiling from ear to ear, no doubt already counting the new criminal cases that would come pouring through the door because of Tina's acquittal.

He walked over and stood near the television, diverting all eyes in his direction.

"I want to congratulate Neddy, Vernetta, and David for the finest piece of criminal trial work I've seen since Johnnie Cochran told the jury, 'If the glove doesn't fit, you must acquit.'" The room vibrated with laughter.

"Trial work is not just about the facts," he continued. "It's about how you spin them and how deep you dig for the truth. Unfortunately, in this country justice is not always about right or wrong. It's about who has the best legal defense. And without a doubt our team here out-lawyered the prosecution by leaps and bounds."

O'Reilly raised his glass in the air. "Now let's party!" he shouted.

As our colleagues encircled us to extend more congratulations, I eased away and pretended to be surveying the selection of food on a table near the window. I turned back to watch as David and Neddy gracefully accepted their kudos. Neddy acknowledged me from across the room with a weak shrug.

"Too much celebration for you?" O'Reilly asked, walking up behind me.

"You might say that," I replied.

"Well, I just want you to know I'm glad you convinced me to let you remain on the case. I hear you gave a helluva closing argument. And you may not believe it, but that glowing review came from your nemesis, David."

That was surely a surprise. I owed David a compliment as well. "Without David's analysis of that autopsy report," I said, "Tina would probably be behind bars right now. So he did a pretty fantastic job himself."

"You might want to tell him that," O'Reilly suggested.

"I will," I said. And I planned to.

O'Reilly looked at me with pride. "You know this trial puts you on the A-list of criminal defense attorneys, don't you?"

"No way," I said, holding up both hands. "Criminal law is not for me. It takes too much out of you. Right about now, I'd love a nice, simple sexual harassment case."

"You're kidding me, right?" O'Reilly's face turned grim.

I shook my head and picked up a shrimp. "No, I'm not kidding at all. I don't think I have what it takes to do criminal work."

O'Reilly grabbed me by the shoulders and peered down at me.

"You just need some time to recuperate. Right now, you're like a pregnant woman who's just delivered. The pain is too new. But in a week, all you'll remember is the good part. Like the amazing result you guys achieved for Tina Montgomery."

His mention of pregnancy seemed to jar my entire body. I thought about Jefferson and a heavy lump formed in my throat. I swallowed hard and choked back a tear.

O'Reilly gave me a fatherly pat on the back and headed over to Neddy and David. Within seconds, Detective Smith filled the space that O'Reilly had just vacated. "Shouldn't you be over there getting a few pats on the back, too?"

"I'll pass," I said, trying but failing to muster up a smile.

I was still stunned by Tina's disturbing revelations. Although I empathized with the betrayal she'd experienced, that didn't change the fact that she had brutally stabbed her husband and that I had helped get her off. I felt sick inside. The thought of having to spend another night without my husband made me feel even worse.

I had dedicated nearly every waking hour to Tina's trial for the past few weeks. And what did I have to show for it? Some wonderful media attention, a great chance at making partner, and increased visibility in the legal community. But so what? I'd always assumed I could have it all. The great career, a loving husband, brilliant children. But as I looked around the conference room, there wasn't a single attorney there, to my knowledge, who had achieved that utopia. Most were either divorced or married to their jobs. Why did I expect my life to be any different?

I packed a plate with strawberries, cheese cubes, and rye crackers and made my way back to my office. I set the plate on the corner of my desk and began piling documents from the Montgomery case into storage boxes. I only wished I could erase all memory of Tina's trial from my mind as easily as I could clear the documents from my desk.

About ten minutes later, Neddy barged through the door.

"How dare you run out on our victory celebration?" she said smiling. She was certainly handling all of this a lot better than I was.

"I'm sorry," I said. "I'm just not in much of a mood for celebrating."

Her smile slowly dissipated. "Are you okay?" she asked, closing the door.

I sat down behind my desk, while Neddy took a seat across from me. "I guess I'm just drained."

"Vernetta, you have to forget about everything Tina told us yesterday."

I gave her a hard look. "How can I? How can you?"

"Easy. It's just something we have to do. We did exactly what Tina Montgomery paid us to do," she insisted. "We gave her our best and because of that the jury found her innocent."

"Correction," I said, "the jury found her not guilty. That's not the same as being innocent. And we know for a fact that she's not."

Neddy inhaled sharply. "Max suffered an aneurysm. You do believe that, don't you?"

"Yeah, I believe it," I said, "but that's nothing but a technicality. She was trying to kill the man and she would've if that aneurysm hadn't beat her to it."

"Maybe not. If he hadn't suffered the aneurysm, he probably would've been able to overpower her and take the knife from her."

I shrugged. "What about Lawton? Don't you care that his killer is still out there?"

"Not really," she said softly. "Lawton was probably killed by someone he owed money to or some other woman whose life he ruined. It doesn't much matter to me whether the police catch his killer or not." Neddy hesitated, her face suddenly solemn. "I know this might sound like a cruel thing to say, but things happen for a reason. Maybe Lawton got what he deserved. Max, too."

I understood the agony Lawton had brought into Neddy's life, but her words still shocked me. She saw my eyes widen, but she didn't back down.

"Lawton lived his life intentionally hurting people," she said adamantly. "You can't live like that without facing repercussions for your actions—sooner or later."

I didn't know what to say. If this was the kind of detachment it took to be a criminal attorney, I was definitely in the wrong line of work.

"So, let's just stop all this sadness." Neddy stood up. "Guess where I'm going tomorrow morning?" she nearly chirped.

I tried to smile. "Sorry, Neddy, I'm not in the mood for any guessing games."

"Up to Santa Barbara for a long relaxing weekend," she said, ignoring my melancholy mood. "And guess who's joining me?"

I could see genuine happiness in her face. "Don't tell me," I said, growing more excited for her by the second. "Detective Smith?"

A big grin lit up her face.

I got up to embrace her. "So, I was right," I teased. "He does have the hots for you. He seems like such a nice guy. I'm so happy for you."

"Thanks," she said, beaming like a woman in love.

There was a knock on the door and to my surprise, Special walked in.

"Girrrrl," she said, both hands planted on her hips, "I had to bring my ass down here to congratulate you in person! Y'all just pulled off the acquittal of the century!"

Neddy and I both laughed.

"This is my best friend, Special," I said, introducing the two of them.

Special was wearing a sleeveless lavender sundress and an awestruck expression on her face. "When I get in trouble, I'm calling y'all. I never would've believed anybody could've gotten that woman off in a million years. Y'all are the bomb!"

"Thanks," Neddy said, inching toward the doorway. "Well, I'll leave you two alone. And Vernetta," she said, before closing the door, "please cheer up."

I slumped back into my chair, but Special remained standing. "Cheer up? After what y'all just pulled off, you should be ready to party. Why're you looking so down and out?"

"Because I feel like crap," I sighed. "Special, I really miss Jefferson." My eyes started to moisten.

She walked over and squeezed my shoulder. "I know you do, girlfriend. That's why I'm here. Don't get mad at me," she said, taking a cautious step backward, "but I have a guy I want you to meet."

I rolled my eyes at her so hard they should've bounced out of my head. "What? Are you nuts? I don't—"

She held up a hand cutting me off. "Just hear me out."

"I don't need to hear you out because you're nuts," I growled. "I'm still a married woman. The only thing I'm doing tonight is crawling into my big empty bed in my big empty house."

"C'mon," she begged. "He's a really nice guy and he knows

you're separated. He's just looking for somebody to hang out with. I don't mean to make you more depressed than you already are, but you did say Jefferson took all the clothes out of his closet, right? It doesn't sound like he's planning on coming home any time soon. So ain't no need for you to be sitting home crying in your soup."

Her prediction of Jefferson's unlikely homecoming was not something I wanted to hear. But I was too mad to even speak.

"As a matter of fact," Special said, walking toward the door, "the person I want you to meet is right outside."

My mouth fell open and I shot out of my chair. "No way! I can't believe you're trying to fix me up!"

She waved me back into the chair. "Just go out with us for one drink. Then you can go home."

"No!" I shouted. "There's no way I'm going out tonight. And definitely not with some man you dragged in from who knows where. You've lost your damn mind!"

"Calm down, girlfriend, calm down," she said. "I'm just trying to help take your mind off Jefferson."

"Well, you're doing a lousy job. I'm not doing it!"

"Fine then." She grabbed the doorknob. "If you won't go out with the man, the least you could do is meet him."

Before the expletives in my head could reach my lips, Special had opened the door and poked her head into the hallway. "C'mon in," she said.

I was ready to wring Special's neck. "You and your friend can just—"

When I saw Jefferson standing in the doorway, my heart skipped at least six beats. He was wearing a big goofy smile and his eyes told me he was just as happy to see me as I was to see him.

"How you doing?" he said, sounding uncharacteristically shy.

My smile was twice the size of his. "Now that you're here, I'm great," I said, trying not to cry. "How about you?"

"About the same as you, I guess."

Special put her hands on her hips and grinned sheepishly. "Guess you like my friend after all, huh?" She pointed a long, manicured finger at both of us. "I'm leaving now, but y'all are going to stay your asses in here until you make up. And that's an order." She walked out, then stuck her head back inside to give me a wink.

"Have a seat," I said to Jefferson after Special left.

EVERY REASONABLE DOUBT   347

He sat down in one of the chairs in front of my desk. I perched myself on the edge of the desk directly in front of him. I wanted to reach out and touch him, but something held me back. We just stared at each other, grinning.

"Congratulations on your verdict," he said.

"Thank you."

I was tired of playing games. I wanted him to know exactly how I felt. "I really miss you," I said.

"I miss you, too."

"Then why don't you come back home?"

His whole body seemed to relax. "Okay."

"So, it's as easy as that?" I asked.

He chuckled softly. "No, I don't think it's going to be easy at all." I could tell he was nervous. "I think we've got a lot of stuff to work out."

"Maybe we should think about getting some professional help," I said.

"Aw, man," Jefferson said, scrunching up his face. "I'll give it a shot," he said, "but I ain't telling my business to no white boy. If we gotta go to counseling, you have to find a brother. A down brother. And not some soft Poindexter-type dude."

I smiled. "Deal," I said.

He began looking around my office. "You know," he said, lowering his voice, "I understand how important this stuff is to you. If I was a big-time lawyer and had a slammin' office like this, I'd probably get off on it just like you do. But I need to feel like I'm important to you, too."

I could feel his anxiety. "You are important to me," I said.

He folded his arms and tugged on his bottom lip with his teeth. "You say that, but you never really show it." He sounded like a timid little boy.

"What do you need me to do?" I asked, looking him straight in the eyes.

"Nothing special. Just be there for me sometimes."

"I promise you I will."

He chuckled. "Girl, your track record ain't too good when it comes to keeping promises."

"I know that," I said earnestly. "But this time I'm ready to show

you I'm serious." I stood up. "As a matter of fact, I can start showing you right now."

The corners of his lips turned upward, stretching a smile across
his face. I plopped into his lap and gave him a big, wet kiss. He
cupped my face with both hands and kissed me with such intensity I
thought my lips would melt into his. I was so happy it hurt. It was
some time before we took a break to breathe.

"By the way," he said, leaning back so he could see my eyes, "I
overheard that little discussion you were having with Special before I
walked in. Made me feel kinda nice to know you weren't trying to
kick a brother to the curb and rush off into the arms of some other
dude the first chance you got."

"Never," I said. "These are the only arms I want around me."

I buried my head in the space between his head and shoulders and
we just held each other for a long, long time, saying nothing.

"I guess I owe you an apology," Jefferson said after a while.

I pulled back to look at him. "For what?"

"For trippin' so hard about—" He stopped as if he couldn't say
the words. "You tried to help, but I pushed you away. I just had to
come to terms with everything in my own way. And in my own
time."

"I understand," I said. I nuzzled my nose against his and we
kissed again.

"Uh… Hey, baby," he said, grinning big as I peppered his face
with kisses. "What if somebody comes looking for you? Sitting here
all hugged up like this ain't exactly appropriate."

I smiled and pulled him closer, although there was no space left
between us. "You've got it all wrong," I said, my voice cracking with
emotion. "Holding you like this is the most appropriate thing I could
ever do."